Returning

THE SPOTTED DOG SERIES

CHRISTINA SOL

For Lucy & Jackson
You two are my greatest blessings

CONTENTS

CHAPTER ONE

"Carmen, my dear, you *must* meet my neighbor's nephew."

It was official. Carmen Cunningham was in hell. Matchmaking hell.

She was done with relationships. All of them. After her last marriage had imploded, she'd dated here and there, but there hadn't been any sparks. Then after what had happened in Brazil . . . well, it was safe to say she was done.

Never. Again.

Casual dating? Nope.

Boyfriend-girlfriend? No.

Friends with benefits? Nuh-uh.

One-night stands? Nope—well, fine . . . maybe.

But actual *relationship* relationships? Nope. Done. Over.

Yes, she'd said those exact words countless times before. But this time, she meant them.

". . . he's newly divorced and quite the catch, my dear. He's the perfect mix of old money and new." Mrs. Weatherby's lips pursed as if her champagne had suddenly gone bad. "His children are truly the devil's spawn, but they'll be with his ex-wife, so no matter."

Lovely.

Carmen's smile didn't slip as she gave the woman a noncommittal murmur. She was pretty damn proud of herself. Her eyes hadn't rolled once—not *once*—this entire freaking evening. Granted, the evening had barely started, but she'd already had the same conversation four other times with four other women. She'd even been introduced to three of the *catches* in question. All three times, she'd nodded politely, made the expected small talk, and excused herself.

"At your age, Carmen dear, you really can't be too picky."

Of course. Because *picky* was a bad thing. Holy hell.

Inhale. Smile. Nod. Exhale.

Polite mask firmly in place, she listened to Mrs. Weatherby with half an ear. The whole time, she fought the desire to kick off her five-inch stilettos and flee the crowded Four Seasons ballroom. Because of *that* comment. Right there. That one little sentence uttered in passive-aggressive delight. *That* was why she hadn't wanted to come home.

The ballroom's sparkling New Year's decor was elegant and understated—classy but not too pretentious. The band's melodic jazz notes were a soothing backdrop to the clamor of voices and popping champagne bottles. Everything was beautiful. Still, Carmen had to suppress the urge to wrinkle her nose because the clash of perfumes and colognes— florals, citruses, and musk—nauseated her. Or maybe it was just the current discussion.

Most of the time, Carmen could steer conversations about her non-existent love life toward things that mattered. Her work at Clean Water Campaign. Politics. Sports. Music. Hell, anything besides the supposed salacious details of her personal life. That was off-limits. She never discussed her personal life. Ever. Fool me once and all that . . .

It didn't mean that people didn't gossip about her, because holy shit, did they ever. Especially now that she'd returned home. But generally, no one dared to gossip about her to her face. Mrs. Weatherby and her cronies—all long-time friends of her mother's—were the exception.

They didn't see Carmen as a badass, accomplished woman who led a small but extremely influential international nonprofit organization. A woman who had two master's degrees under her belt and spoke five different languages fluently. Well . . . *fluently* was a bit of a stretch. She could speak three fluently and get by in the other two, but whatever. No, the cronies saw her as a single, forty-year-old woman with three failed marriages who only needed to meet the right man. And, of course, they had *just* the man in mind.

Carmen had *chosen* to come home. Willingly. She had to remember that.

She continued to nod at the appropriate moments while Mrs. Weatherby droned on and on about her neighbor's nephew. For the life of her, Carmen couldn't think of one single thing to say to shift this crappy conversation to something else, *anything* else. She was off her game tonight, dammit, and she wanted to kick herself.

She was always so calm, cool, and unflappable. But the moment she'd stepped into this glittery ballroom, she'd been sucker punched in the gut. Who was the first person she'd seen?

Brian freaking McAllister. Ex-husband Number Three. Not-so-affectionately dubbed "McAsshole" by her younger brother, Parker.

Instead of throwing her shoulders back and meeting the prick head-on, she'd done the unthinkable. She'd turned in the opposite direction and let the cronies envelop her.

Now here she was, stomach churning. At least she'd come impeccably attired in her favorite little black dress—a simple, sleeveless, high-neck-high-back Givenchy number with a two-inches-from-inappropriate slit up her right thigh—that always gave her an extra boost of confidence. Something she desperately needed tonight.

Discreetly glancing around the ballroom, she searched for an excuse to escape.

"You aren't getting any younger, Carmen," Mrs. Weatherby said in a conspiratorial whisper, like they were old girlfriends. Then the woman glanced at Carmen's stomach with zero subtlety. "You may not look it, dear, with your amazing Filipino skin and all, but your eggs are most definitely old. Please tell me you've at least frozen them already."

The corners of Carmen's lips pinched. Her perfect fake smile faltered the tiniest bit, and her chest squeezed uncomfortably tight. Wow. The woman wasn't pulling any of her damn punches tonight. "Well, Mrs. Weatherby—"

"Prudence, dear." The older woman tsk-tsked. "We mustn't be so formal anymore. After all, you're no longer a child."

"Of course," Carmen soothed, though her own nerves were strung tight. "Well, Prudence, it's a good thing there is technology and many other options for women of my advanced years." She nodded to an imaginary person across the room, then air-kissed the other woman. "If you'll excuse me, I need to check in with my family. We'll catch up more at our table."

Stepping away from Mrs. Weatherby, she forced the tension out of her shoulders and took a steadying breath. She nodded to various acquaintances and colleagues and wove through the crowd to her family's set of tables at the far side of the ballroom. She loosened her grip on her wineglass. God forbid it shattered in her old, arthritic hands. Holy shit.

Forty-one was just around the corner, and the conversations at these damn fundraising galas still hadn't changed.

She'd known most of the people in this grand, opulent room the majority of her professional life, if not her entire life. After all, Seattle's nonprofit community was a tight-knit group. One that her family had been part of for decades.

Clean Water Campaign had been founded by her grandparents in the 1950s to provide clean water solutions to remote Pacific Northwest communities. Her parents had then expanded the organization in the 1970s to bring clean drinking water to villages in the developing world. As the company's President of Development and Operations, one would think people would have better things to talk to her about than her aging reproductive system, dating status, and wrinkles. But no.

Did her little brother, Parker—one year her junior—have to deal with conversations about having babies and keeping a trim, perky figure like a twenty-two-year-old? Of course not.

Barely an hour into the evening, it dawned on her that returning home had been a colossal miscalculation. Well, not *dawned* exactly. The potential ramifications of her mistake had been circling the edges of her mind since her arrival, like a fluttering butterfly. One that she refused to let land.

She'd fled Seattle three years earlier under the guise of work. At the time, she'd just been promoted to her current position at CWC. It was technically an office job, but she'd convinced everyone that instead of sitting behind a desk, it would be more beneficial for their nonprofit if she visited each and every international site they operated. It was an excuse everyone believed. Why wouldn't they? Carmen was dedicated to her work. Everyone knew that. What everyone didn't know was that she'd actually left to avoid—

Nope. She internally cringed. *Not going there, dammit.*

For nearly three years, she'd hopped from site to site, meeting local community leaders and politicians. Not once had she returned to Seattle. Using technology and the occasional international meet up, she'd kept in touch with her family. Beyond that, she'd embraced the nomadic lifestyle and planned on continuing down that path for the rest of her life.

But that old saying about best-laid plans was a cliché for a reason.

Three months ago, Carmen had returned to Seattle. She'd managed to throw herself into work, and everyone believed she'd come back for the organization's benefit. And she had. Technically, anyway.

With her workaholic tendencies, she'd also managed to avoid almost all social gatherings. Until now.

She faltered mid-step as she saw a familiar face coming toward her from the right. On her next breath, she pivoted, turning left. Instead of heading toward her family's tables, she zeroed in on the bar. Glancing down at her nearly empty wineglass, she ground her molars together. Yeah, she definitely needed something stronger if she was going to get cornered by McAsshole.

Last month, she'd run into her most recent ex-husband at a local coffee shop and made the mistake of stopping to talk. No, correction—she hadn't spoken. She'd listened to the abject bullshit that had spewed from his mouth. Then she'd avoided that particular coffee shop ever since.

They'd been divorced for a little over three years, and now the jackass wanted to get back together. Not because he missed her. Not because he loved her. But because he wanted to form an alliance. *An alliance*. His exact words. Like this was freaking *Survivor*. What a crock of shit.

She'd walked away before he could list out the bullet points—because she had no doubt in her mind that he'd created a list of reasons why a renewed alliance between them was a win. Just like he'd made a list of her shortcomings and ways she'd "needed to improve" during their ill-fated marriage.

One thousand percent not a win.

Earlier this week, Brian had left three painfully long voice messages on her office line saying they "needed to talk" to "reconnect" and "rekindle." All three times, she'd deleted the damn voicemails, then hit the treadmill for some punishingly hard runs to work off her anger and frustration. Not only at him, but at herself as well.

Now, watching him make his way toward her, she recognized that determined look in his weaselly eyes. She braced herself. God knew it was never good when your ex-husband wanted to talk to you at a public event. Ever.

Setting her now-empty wineglass on the bar top, she quickly scanned the liquor bottle display. "Macallan 18, please. Neat," she said when the bartender placed a monogrammed cocktail napkin before her.

"It was always so surprising you liked scotch." The mere sound of Brian's voice sent a chill running down her spine. And not the good kind of chill. "You're so petite that I always expected you to be a more docile drinker. Something more feminine, like a cosmo or lemon drop."

It took everything she had to keep her expression neutral. "Hmm, why is that exactly, Brian?" She knew *exactly* why but wanted to hear it out of the dipshit's mouth. And she knew he was dumb enough to say it out loud.

"You just look so innocent and docile and . . . sweet, like a little China doll. Or, in your case, a little Filipino doll." He chuckled to himself, and her fists clenched.

If she could punch him in the face, she would.

You're at a work gala, Carmen. You cannot *cause a scene.*

"Because truly, Carm, you're more like an exotic and docile little schoolgirl than a tough, burly scotch drinker. More meek and . . ."

Good God. If he said *docile* one more time, she was going to knee him in the balls. Causing a scene be damned. Shit, she might knee him in the nuts anyway.

Why the hell had she married this man in the first place? It hadn't been because of his great conversation skills. He obviously had none. It hadn't been because he'd supported her. God knew he'd never done that. And it hadn't been because he had a magical dick. Frankly, the sex had been okay at best. She couldn't fathom what she'd been thinking.

No, she took that back.

Carmen knew precisely why she'd fallen for him. Back then, he'd been better at the bullshit. Back then, he'd pretended to care, to love her for her. Pretended that she mattered.

And she'd bought it all. Proverbial hook, line, and sinker.

God, she'd been an idiot.

She'd laughed off the warnings and concerns from her family and friends, even though some had flat-out said Brian was only with her for her connections and money. She'd dismissed everyone, convinced Brian was right—they were all just jealous of their love.

But the joke had been on her. And like the first two, her third marriage had ended in divorce. Her first union had been fiery and emotional; the second, cold and distant. The last one?

Mortifying. Beyond embarrassing. Humiliating. And whatever other pathetic adjective she could tack on.

Now she was older and somewhat wiser. No more relationships. Or *alliances*.

"Carmen, we made a great team—"

"We actually didn't," she scoffed, her amiable demeanor slipping.

He continued as if she hadn't spoken, and she didn't

bother hiding her grimace. Some things never changed. "Just think, together, we could take over Clean Water Campaign. I could lead the board and, with your support and under my fresh new leadership, implement groundbreaking changes . . ."

Me, me, me, me, me. Again, some things never changed.

Carmen had no illusions that Brian cared one bit about CWC's mission to bring change and help communities. No. Brian was allergic to actual work. He just wanted a seat on their board of directors, which consisted of most of her family members and several equally wealthy and prominent Seattle business leaders. The combined net worth of CWC's board was ridiculous. Like, they-could-buy-small-countries ridiculous. Brian had always thought that if he were on the board, that excess wealth would rub off on him. Like some sort of magical osmosis.

"Brian, all I'm hearing is how this alliance will benefit *you.*" Not that she wanted anything to do with his stupid alliance. "I'm already on CWC's board, *and* I'm the president. The only two people higher up than me are my parents. You and I are never happening again. So, you're wasting your goddammed breath."

She turned from the bar but was jerked to a halt, her scotch spilling on her fingers as it sloshed over the rim of the glass. Brian's hand circled her bicep and clamped down. Hard. She gasped.

"Jesus, Carm," he hissed, yanking her closer. From the outside, she knew they looked like two friends huddled together for a private conversation. His grip tightened, and the first stirrings of panic began to overtake her initial anger. "Why are you being so fucking difficult? For once, why won't you just listen—"

"Sweetheart, there you are," a deep voice rumbled behind her.

Brian's grip on her arm immediately released, and he took a full step back.

The familiar scent of a spicy aftershave washed over Carmen, momentarily calming her erratic heart and dousing the panic and anger. A pair of firm yet soft lips brushed over her forehead, and a large hand settled at the small of her back.

"Excuse us," the man said, sending a withering glare to Brian, who'd paled at those two little dismissive words.

Carmen didn't spare Brian another glance. As she allowed herself to be steered away, she pasted the fake smile back on her face and clutched her companion's strong, muscular arm like it was a lifeline. Hell, it was. Still, she refused to admit that her heart was beating an unsteady rhythm, that her breath was shaky, that her asshole of an ex-husband had rattled her.

Shit. It was going to be a long damn night.

CHAPTER TWO

J ake Alvarez hated these kinds of events. Black tie. The fanciest ballroom in one of Seattle's most lavish hotels. Small talk with people he didn't have much in common with. Yet every year, without fail, he donned his tux, sucked it up, and came to this particular gala. Because one of the beneficiaries of this fundraiser was Clean Water Campaign. Not only did his mobile gaming company share an office floor with them, but the nonprofit had been founded by the family of one of his best friends.

John and Margaret Cunningham, the current heads of that family, were truly wonderful people and like second parents to him. Hell, he probably spent more time with them than his own parents. John and Maggie had treated him like family from the moment their son, Parker, had dragged him to a Sunday dinner during their freshman year of college. So, Jake really couldn't complain too much. Still, he hated these damn events.

It didn't matter that he'd spent the last fifteen or so years as a member of the multimillionaire tax bracket. It didn't matter that he'd created one of the most downloaded video game apps in the history of, well . . . apps. It didn't matter that his tuxedo was custom made by one of the top fashion designers in the world.

The truth was that he still didn't feel as though he belonged in this room. A room that he freely admitted was filled with some of his favorite people in the world. Many of them had more money than God, but at the same time, were genuinely kind and generous humans. Still. He felt like an impostor.

Unlike his best friends, Blake Sullivan and Parker Cunningham, Jake hadn't grown up wealthy or even surrounded by wealth. His family had been solidly middle class. And looking back, he now understood they had struggled for many years to achieve even that due to staggering amounts of financial debt. Because of him.

When anyone looked at Jake today, they saw a man who stood six feet, four inches tall and clocked in at two hundred and forty-five pounds of solid muscle. His buddies often joked he looked like he was The Rock's slightly less bulky little brother. And they weren't wrong. No one would ever guess that he'd been a scrawny, fragile kid who'd had three open-heart surgeries before he'd turned ten.

Usually, Jake was better at faking it. Better at pretending he knew what he was doing and acting like he belonged in any room. Most times, he actually believed his ruse—hell, was downright cocky about it. But the text messages he'd received earlier this evening had thrown him into a broody and nostalgic mood . . . none of which was good.

But enough of that, dammit. Squaring his shoulders on an exhale, he glanced around the bustling room, spotted his table—one of Clean Water Campaign's family tables—and started toward it.

After greeting the Cunningham parents, he slapped Parker and Blake on their backs. Though he worked in the same building as his two best friends, with the holidays just wrapping up, he'd barely seen them.

The three of them co-owned The Spotted Dog Irish Pub, located in Seattle's Queen Anne neighborhood. Blake owned the building that housed their pub and managed the day-to-day operations with Parker. Jake remained a silent partner, though he handled all the marketing and social media on the side. His primary focus was Alvarez Technologies, which was located on the building's second floor, along with CWC. Blake's private residence took up the building's entire third floor.

All of it—the bar, the building, Alvarez Technologies— had been made possible by a file compression program that he and Blake had created and sold to Microsoft in their final year of college. The deal had netted them a ridiculous amount of money. *Thirty million* ridiculous. But never one to sit idle, Jake had founded his mobile gaming company after graduation. Its success was more than he'd ever dreamed. A few months earlier, his game, Square Peg, had earned the honor of being the second most downloaded mobile game in history.

History.

Freaking blew his damn mind every time he thought about it.

Since the last launch, he'd been working nonstop to brainstorm ways to make the game even bigger and better. The cycle of needing to outdo the latest and greatest release was exhausting. But Square Peg was his baby. And he was up for the challenge.

"It's nice to see you come up for air, stranger," Parker said. "How are things in Square Peg-land? Is my avatar still the most popular?"

"Please don't feed this asshole's ego," Blake groaned, playfully shoving an elbow into his cousin's side.

Jake chuckled. In the latest update to Square Peg, he'd created a new world featuring an Old West-ified saloon that was, naturally, called The Spotted Dog. The fixed characters in the saloon were based on all the employees of their real-life Irish pub. For some crazy-ass reason unbeknownst to anyone, they'd gotten the most positive comments on the saloon's cook, who was based on Parker. Jake had made the mistake of mentioning it to his friend. They'd all yet to hear the end of it.

Jake wouldn't admit it out loud, but his team was thinking of making the cook's accessories and skin available for purchase in their next update. As Blake had pointed out, there was no need to feed Parker's ego. Their job as friends was to give each other shit.

"Bro," Parker began, his smile so mischievous that Jake couldn't help but brace himself for what was about to spew from his friend's mouth. It was either going to be full of shit or brilliant. "Maybe in the next update, you can do a more in-depth kitchen thing where the players can get clues and shit from me."

Jake barked out a laugh. Damn, brilliant it was. He slapped his friend on the back. "Let's meet next week, and I'll pick your brain."

"Shit," Blake grumbled with a roll of his eyes. "What the hell did I say about feeding this dipshit's ego?"

"It's not ego, dumbass," Parker said with a laugh. "It's *genius*. In fact . . ."

His friend trailed off, and a split second later, Parker's jovial mood was anything but. His lips pursed into an angry, thin line, and a flush crept over his face as his attention fixed on something across the room. As the seconds ticked by, the vein in his friend's head became more prominent.

Jake's brow furrowed with concern. Parker was one of the most laid-back people he'd ever met, but holy shit, the guy looked like he was about to murder someone. Jake's concern morphed to worry as Parker abruptly stood, almost knocking over his chair.

"Park, what the fuck?" Blake asked, rising as well. He slammed a hand on his cousin's chest to still him.

Jake scanned the opposite side of the room, and his gut turned when his gaze landed on a couple by the bar. Parker's sister, Carmen, and her dipshit of an ex-husband. Fuck.

"McAsshole," Jake muttered. There was a whole world of disgust wrapped in that one name, and he was immediately met by whispered curses from Blake and Parker.

McAsshole. Parker had given the nickname to the piece of shit before Carmen had even married him. From the moment Jake had met the bastard, the nickname had stuck. Hell, he wasn't even sure what the fucker's real name was.

Jake had no clue what the hell Carmen had seen in the guy. McAsshole had always treated her like shit, and when she'd called her brother all those years ago to say she was getting a divorce, they'd celebrated. McAsshole had been a horrible excuse of a human being when Carmen had been married to him, and Jake doubted the fucker had gotten any better in the years since.

Before Parker could take a step toward his sister, Jake slapped a hand down on his buddy's shoulder. "I got her, man. Take a breather because your mom's gonna kill you if you make a scene."

He waited until Parker met his gaze. Anger swirled over his friend's face.

"I got her," Jake repeated, squeezing Parker's shoulder.

There was nothing but truth behind those three words. Even though he and Carmen had known each other for a long time, in a way, their one-on-one friendship was fairly new. Regardless, he had her back.

After a moment, his friend released a breath, then lifted

his chin slightly. "I hate that motherfucker," Parker muttered as he sat back down.

"I think we can all agree on that one," Jake replied. Before he turned from the table, he caught Blake's stare. He received another chin lift, which he returned with one of his own. The silent message was received. Blake had his cousin's back.

Making his way over to the bar, Jake's steps faltered when Carmen awkwardly jerked forward.

What. The. Fuck?

Carmen was many things, but awkward was *not* one of them. Ever. His eyes narrowed as he hurried across the room. He couldn't see what had caused Carmen to lurch forward and spill her drink, but between that bastard and the bar, half her body was hidden.

Holy fuck. Had that asshole grabbed her?

"Sweetheart, there you are," Jake said, sliding up behind her. He took a second to calm himself before leaning down and brushing his lips over her forehead, his gaze never leaving the fucker in front of him. If he could have figured out a way to knock into McAsshole and level him without upsetting the crowd, he would have. Not the most mature move, but fuck, he hated this prick.

Straightening to his full height, Jake placed a possessive hand on Carmen's lower back and stared the asshole down. Because of his size, he knew he looked like an intimidating fucker on most days. But when he actually tried to look mean? Good luck.

"Excuse us," Jake bit out, putting as much disgust, disdain, and venom into those two words as he could. And from the way McAsshole blanched? Mission accomplished.

"Holy crap," Carmen said on an exhale as he steered them away from the bar.

He bit back a frown. At first glance, Carm looked like her usual poised self. However, he'd begun to recognize her expressions over the last few months. And while the pretty, practiced, and polite smile remained on her lips, he could see the worry in her eyes. The tension in the slight clenching of her jaw. The tight set of her slim shoulders.

He plucked the drink out of her hand and deposited it on the tray of a passing server. Instead of walking her back to their table, he led Carmen in the opposite direction, away from her family and onto the dance floor, joining the other dozen or so couples. He pulled her close, and while her smile never slipped, her body tensed further.

They swayed silently for a few beats before he leaned his head down closer to hers. "You okay, Carm?"

She exhaled and sank into his chest, her slight frame dwarfed by his much-larger body. Though she wore sky-high stilettos, her head barely reached his shoulders. She was so formidable, he often forgot how tiny she was. "He wants to get back together."

Jake's brows rose, and it took a moment to find his voice. Well then. He wasn't sure what he'd expected her to say, but it hadn't been that. "Is that something you want?"

Carmen had always been driven and a bit of a workaholic, but after she'd initially separated from McAsshole and moved in with Parker, she'd taken her workaholic tendencies to a whole new level. Considering Jake was also obsessed with his work, that said a lot. Then a couple months later, once her divorce and all the details had been finalized, she'd hightailed it out of there. For over three years, she'd traveled, barely ever coming back to the States, never once stepping foot in Seattle.

Then three months ago, with no warning, she'd moved back to town and turned her traveling position with CWC into a desk job. The transition had been seamless. Or maybe that was just Carmen. She had the ability to make everything look easy. But it made him wonder. If she could manage all the company's international locations remotely from Seattle, why had she insisted on being boots on the ground in the first place? Did she just not want to be in Seattle? Did she need a break? And if so, what had caused her abrupt return? Because, frankly, he'd been shocked—hell, *everyone* had been shocked—when she'd returned home.

Over the top of her head, Jake saw Carmen's dickweed of an ex-husband circling. He drew her closer, pulling her slim body flush against him. For being so petite, she did fit into his arms perfectly.

She looked up at him, one expertly shaped brow lifting in question.

Without taking his eyes off her, he nodded toward her ex. "McAsshole," he muttered, then chuckled when she bit back a smile. He hadn't a clue how the woman could make a tiny bite to her lower lip look classy. "I still don't get why you married that fucker in the first place. Say the word, and I'll take care of him."

"Take care of him?" Her brow arched even higher, and she gave up the fight. Something that was part smile and part smirk played on her wine-red lips. One of her hands squeezed his bicep. "Your jacked-up muscles are lovely and all, my friend, but last I checked, you're in game creation and Irish pub ownership. Not a wannabe mob boss."

"Fine," he conceded with an exaggerated grimace, "but it sounded tough, right?"

Her dark brown eyes rolled. "Yeah. So tough. I'm sure you can give him a swirly, then stuff him in a locker or something."

His mind flashed to middle school, to being the scrawny kid on the receiving end of the swirlies and locker stuffings. At the hands of little pricks like McAsshole.

Huh. Carm's suggestion had appeal . . .

"Holy shit, Alvarez, I was kidding," she said, humor and astonishment lacing her words.

"That's a crying shame, sweetheart," he murmured. It bugged him that McAsshole was sniffing around her. Based on the last few minutes, the man was still just as much of a dick now as he'd been during their marriage.

"Seriously, though." He leaned slightly away, enough to tilt her chin up with his finger. He slowed their dance steps and waited until she met his gaze. "If he gives you any trouble, you let me know. I won't 'take care of him,' but I can be an intimidating motherfucker if I need to be. If he messes with you? Makes you even the tiniest bit uncomfortable? Then I'll step in. Hell, I *need* to step in. Plus, you know that Blake and Parker will be more than happy to join the intimidation party. And my brother? While he isn't quite as big as me"—he flexed his arms, and she chuckled, as he'd intended—"my brother *does* legally carry a gun."

"I know." She squeezed his bicep again, a soft smile on her lips, and she let out a weary sigh. "I promise to call in the Brute Squad if I need to. It's just so freaking tiring having to deal with his bullshit again, you know?"

He studied her. Yes, she *was* tired. He could see it now—the fatigue hidden in her eyes.

His phone buzzed in his pocket.

"Wow," she murmured, shooting him a smoldering grin. "Is that your phone going off in your pocket, or are you just happy to see me?"

"Sorry," he chuckled. "I thought I shut it off. Not that I'm not happy to see you, of course." He lifted his chin toward their table. "But the glare your brother is sending me would kill any *extra* happiness there was."

"Good freaking God," she groaned, snuggling even closer. "Parker is ridiculous. However, it is funny how easy it is to rile up that poor boy."

Jake slid his hand a tiny bit lower on her back, splaying his fingers wide, possessively, but also reading her cues to make sure he didn't cross any lines. "As you know," he said, smirking when she met his gaze, her dark brown eyes twinkling with mischief, "I have no issues fucking with the guy."

She laughed, and her face lit up.

Damn, she's pretty.

Shit. The errant thought had his insides stilling.

No. It was fine.

He wasn't blind, after all; objectively, Carm was a beautiful woman. Always had been. Even when he'd been a freshman to her sophomore. And she'd always been way cooler than him.

But still. Looking down into her smiling eyes, feeling her slim body shake with laughter against his, Jake wasn't quite sure what the hell he was doing.

He probably shouldn't be talking sexual innuendos and getting touchy with his best friend's older sister. And besides, it was *Carmen*.

They'd known each other for what felt like forever. And now they were friends in their own right, having recently broken out of being friends who only hung out in a group. Getting to know her better, one-on-one, had taught him it took a lot to get those brown eyes of hers to sparkle and dance with genuine humor.

Ever since she'd returned, it seemed as though she'd been under tremendous amounts of stress. Sure, from the outside, she looked like her usual poised self. But as they'd grown closer, he'd seen the fatigue and tension that lay below her flawless facade.

Carm hadn't shared why she'd returned to Seattle with him, and he hadn't pushed. He figured she'd share if and when she was ready. In the meantime, he did everything he could to be a friend, whether that meant providing her an ear and a shoulder or supplying her with some levity to get her to laugh.

The more she loosened up, the more she laughed, the more he wanted to be around her. Because, frankly, Carmen was one of the coolest women he knew, and while she was extremely private, to the few she actually let in, she always gave as good as she got.

And she was hot.

Crazy hot.

It was just a fact. He wasn't a creeper trying to get in his friend's pants.

Flirting with Carm was fun. Harmless. It was kind of what they did. And lately, they'd been taking turns rescuing each other in these types of situations, acting as each other's backup.

A few weeks ago, in late November, they'd been in Las Vegas at the same time. She'd been the keynote speaker at some fancy symposium, and he'd been promoting Square Peg at a geek conference. He'd joined Carmen at her symposium's cocktail party to act as her man candy, staying by her side as the creepy men had lurked and leered.

The month prior to that, at his launch party for the latest Square Peg update, the predatory, man-eating vultures had been circling, so Carmen had hung on his arm, acting as if they were together.

Parker had just about had a heart attack when he'd thought Jake was messing around with his sister. Obviously, they weren't together, but they both had fun messing with Parker. They'd gotten touchy, but it hadn't crossed any lines. If anything, it had been safe. They trusted each other and had a lot in common.

The fact was that the other guys he'd usually hang out with—Blake, Parker, and his brother—now spent most of their free time with their significant others. As they should.

So, when he and Carmen had downtime, they gravitated toward each other. Whether that had started due to the sheer proximity of working on the same floor or their long-standing friendship, he hadn't a clue. All he knew was the woman was quickly becoming one of his closest friends.

Yes, he didn't touch his other female friends quite like he did Carmen—because either they were dating his best friends or they were his employees, and that would just be fucking weird—and he knew she wasn't usually very demonstrative either. But whatever.

Holding the woman in his arms wasn't a hardship. And if pulling her a little closer had that vein in Parker's neck throbbing, so be it.

Was it completely juvenile of him and Carmen to egg Parker on? Absolutely.

Did either of them care? Not one bit.

Jake spun her around and lowered his head to whisper in her ear. "Is Parker still sending me death glares?"

She glanced at her brother. Her lips twitched, then pursed. "Mmm . . . I don't know if I'd call them death *glares* per se, but more like death what-the-fucks."

He laughed, and his pocket buzzed with another text notification.

"Uh, should I be taking this personally, Alvarez?" The laughter in her voice let him know she was teasing. "If you have somewhere else you need to be, I will recuse you from 'save my ass' duty tonight."

He smiled and made a production of checking out her ass. "Nah." He pulled her close again. "I'm good. Just . . . drama."

"You? Drama?" Her dark brows lifted almost to her hairline, and he winced.

"I know, right?" It was no secret he was firmly anti-drama. God knew that was all he'd grown up immersed in, so now he did everything he could to steer clear. He had enough craziness at work; the last thing he needed was drama in his personal life.

"Is there anything I can do to help?"

He ignored the warmth that spread through him at her words and grinned down at the woman in his arms instead. Carm really was the best.

His pocket buzzed again, and an idea began to percolate. "You know, now that you mention it—"

"May I cut in?"

Carmen tensed in his arms, her face pinched with displeasure at the nasal voice. His jaw locked, and his grip firmed around her waist. No one put that wary look in her eyes. No one.

"Excuse me, but I said, may I cut in?"

Damn, that voice grated.

Jake wanted to kick himself for not paying attention, for not noticing that McAsshole was approaching. While he longed to put his fist through the dumbass's mouth, he couldn't. Well, *wouldn't*. There'd be no mob boss reenactments tonight. Looked like it was intimidating motherfucker time. Turning Carmen away from her ex, Jake gave the man his most menacing glare. "No."

For a split second, McAsshole went still. Then the fucker had the balls to step toward her, his hand outstretched.

Moving faster than he'd realized he could, Jake snagged the asshole's wrist, a wave of anger chilling his blood. "Touch her, and I break this."

McAsshole froze, swallowing hard.

Making sure to keep his body between Carmen and the little prick, Jake pulled the other man's wrist, yanking him closer. "Now fuck off," he said quietly, not breaking eye contact. "Before I make you," he added, dropping McAsshole's wrist.

If Carmen could slap herself upside the head, she would. Since when did she let Brian get to her, dammit?

Once her ex had scurried away, she let out a breath and allowed Jake to pull her back into his arms. A quick glance around the dance floor had her spine straightening. Sly glances and hushed whispers surrounded them. They'd created a bit of a scene.

Her chin lifted ever so slightly, and she made deliberate eye contact with those dancing around her, silently daring them to say something. They didn't.

Satisfied that the gossip was momentarily quelled, she turned her attention back to Jake and eliminated what little space there was between them. "Sorry about that," she murmured. While her body relaxed and settled against him, he remained tense, and she hated that her drama had caused that for her friend. He'd rescued her for the *second* time tonight from, arguably, the biggest mistake she'd made in her life.

She ran a hand over Jake's shoulder, hoping it would relax him a little and provide him some kind of reassurance. They were going on twenty-plus years of knowing each other, so she knew he avoided drama and kept things around him as mellow as he could.

Granted, many of those twenty years had gone by without seeing each other. But they'd always had an easy friendship, the kind where they didn't have to see each other all the time . . . or even talk regularly. And when they did reconnect, they simply picked up right where they'd left off. As someone who'd had countless friends come and go due to hectic traveling and schedules, not to mention the aftermath of post-divorce side-picking, she truly appreciated friends like Jake.

Now that she was back in Seattle, their easy friendship had deepened. But the last thing she wanted was to dump her pathetic, drama-filled personal life onto him. The fact that she even had a pathetic, drama-filled personal life had her itching to buy a plane ticket out of here. But running had never gotten her anywhere, had it?

"What's his deal?" Jake asked, bringing her back from her musings. "You said he wanted to get back together with you?"

She frowned as her earlier conversation with Brian replayed in her head. "Yeah, you could say that."

"Why?" It took everything she had to not cringe at the amount of disgust he managed to put into that one little word. "McAsshole sniffing around again because of your connections and trust fund?"

She flinched, and her body went rigid. "Ouch," she murmured, pulling away from the warmth of his chest. Both her stomach and gaze dropped to the floor.

Why, indeed? *Obviously,* it had to be for her money and connections, for the so-called *alliance* she could provide. From Jake's look of complete revulsion, great friend or not, apparently that was all she was good for.

"Christ, Carm," he groaned, his grip around her waist tightening, pulling her close again. "You know I didn't mean it like that. That fucker would be the luckiest asshole alive if he got you back. He's a tool. Period. What's his motive? That's the real question."

The mere thought that Brian would want her back because—oh, crazy talk—he actually loved her and missed her was apparently unimaginable to her friend. But Jake wasn't wrong. After all, her ex *was* a tool.

She knew she was being overly sensitive. Still. It stung. Though it shouldn't, dammit. After three divorces, she should know this by now. She needed to get her shit straight, for fuck's sake.

She was Carmen freaking Cunningham, the toughest, most badass bitch in the room.

She internally frowned.

Okay, fine. Maybe not *toughest* or *most badass*, per se. More like *kick-ass* and *most poised*. Yeah. Either way, she needed to act like it.

Taking a breath in, she straightened her shoulders. "Brian wants to get back together to, and I quote, 'form a mutually beneficial alliance.'"

Jake's jaw dropped. "Seriously?"

She pursed her lips. It was either that or snarl. Since they were at a gala, having one of the co-hosts snarling on the dance floor would be frowned upon. "You know how fast gossip spreads in this circle, right?"

Jake nodded with a roll of his eyes. "It's like middle school, except with obscenely wealthy adults with too much money and time on their hands."

"Exactly. When I came back to Seattle after being gone for the last few years, rumors started rumbling that my folks were going to retire. Since I'm president, the next logical step up for me would be my dad's role of CEO, which would mean that my current position would be opening up."

"That dumb fuck thinks if you got back together, then what? Your folks would just give him the open position? They didn't even do that, didn't give him *any* kind of position when you were married. Why the hell does he think that would change now?"

That was the million-dollar question. One Carmen didn't have an answer to. "Maybe he thinks it'll be different this time around since he actually has nonprofit experience now and—"

"Good evening, ladies and gentlemen," the emcee interrupted as the musicians switched to a softer background melody. "Please return to your tables. Our dinner program will begin momentarily."

Carmen eyed their table. Her brother and cousin had their heads together, glaring openly at them. "Don't look now, but Parker and Blake look like they're plotting something." She squeezed Jake's bicep again, unsure if she was trying to give or receive comfort this time. "You ready for this?"

"Bring it, woman." Jake shot her a grin that had her both chuckling and wincing. Two things she hadn't realized you could do at the same time, but there it was. "Carm, darlin', you *know* I love fucking with those two. Let's do this."

CHAPTER THREE

Jake glanced around the elegantly set table. A low vase of pristine white flowers, a scattering of tea lights in sparkling glass votives, and five open bottles of wine served as the table's centerpiece. While he generally avoided these types of events at all costs, he always made an exception for this one. At least the food at this gala was always fucking extraordinary. Hands down some of the best food in all of Seattle.

This wasn't your typical dry-as-dust conference banquet chicken slathered in a questionable and unrecognizable gelatinous sauce. God knows he'd had plenty of that over the years. No. His entrée was a dry-aged, prime bone-in ribeye with scallions and a miso demi-glace accompanied by a Yukon gold and Okinawan sweet potato puree.

Yeah. Exactly.

Carmen's entrée? A wood-grilled king salmon and sea scallop combo with a side of vegetables in a black garlic puree. Fuck yeah.

How the Four Seasons' kitchen had made both entrées

phenomenal—he'd snuck a couple bites of Carmen's—for two hundred-plus attendees was beyond him.

Unfortunately, the exquisite food didn't prevent his two best friends from shooting him what-the-fuck glares from across the table. It also didn't prevent Jake from shooting them a fuck-off glare back. They were all mature like that. Closing in on forty or not.

As CWC had co-sponsored the gala, Carmen was their official table host, with Parker and Blake acting as co-hosts. Carmen was the only one who technically worked for CWC, but all three sat on the organization's board.

Usually, the two Cunningham tables of eight were filled with their family and close friends. However, with both Parker and Blake's significant others unable to attend, along with a couple other family absences, they'd had to reshuffle the seating configurations.

At their table, rounding out their foursome, were two older couples from John and Maggie Cunningham's circle: the Weatherbys and the Shins. Both couples not only headed up their own nonprofit organizations, but they were also substantial donors to CWC. Which meant he, Blake, and Park had to be on their best behavior.

Mrs. Weatherby, who he was lucky to see only once a year at this event, was seated on the other side of Carmen. As the wine flowed and their magnificent dinners were consumed, the older woman continued to drone on and on about potential candidates for—Jake's lip curled in disgust—Carmen's Husband Number Four. Mrs. Weatherby used a tone that implied an intimacy between the two, but it rang hollow due to the sheer volume of the woman's voice.

The whole damn table nearly cringed at her rundown of who the latest eligible, wealthy bachelors in Seattle were. Hell, he *did* cringe when the woman wagged a heavily jeweled finger his way as an example of said eligible, wealthy

Seattle bachelor. Sure, Carmen could maintain a conversation about that kind of surface, frivolous, who's-who thing, but holy shit, lady. A little tact?

With each new name Mrs. Weatherby—or rather, "it's Prudence, darling, but do feel free to call me Pru, you handsome young man"—threw out, Jake saw the mask Carmen wore harden. The normal composure and soft humor in her dark brown eyes were gone entirely. In their place was a flat, cold gaze.

Carm was never rude, never gave the impression she was anything but enthralled with Pru's conversational subject. But Jake knew her. And he never wanted to be on the receiving end of that ultra-polite, ultra-calm, ultra-fake expression.

As the waitstaff cleared the dinner dishes and rounded the tables with coffee, tea, and hard liquor service—because nothing said fancy silent auction gala like copious amounts of booze—Pru prattled on.

"Carmen, dear, it really is such a small world. As you all know . . ." The woman added a dramatic pause to address the entire table. Because of course she did. "Our nonprofit organization works closely with CWC's efforts in South America, particularly Brazil. CWC works on clean water, and we work on establishing mobile clinics that can service remote areas." She turned her attention back to Carmen. "The point is we just hired a new position. A director of operations, if you will, to oversee and facilitate all our multinational interests, and he'll be based right here out of our Seattle office."

"Congratulations, Pru," Carmen replied, and Jake had to bite back a laugh. His friend had one hell of a poker face. "That's such a smart move. Having someone stateside to coordinate is so helpful. I've found it gives all the locations a bit of consistency. When I handled our operations overseas, being immersed in all the different global locations was a benefit, as I witnessed firsthand all the intricacies of each locale. At the same time, now that I'm well-versed in how each area works, it is an added challenge that is frankly unnecessary."

Damn. Jake leaned back in his chair, a grin growing across his face. She was smooth. Carmen had given the unbearable woman a compliment, followed by the tiniest been-there-done-that dig. Carmen was so good at this small talk bullshit; he truly needed to take lessons from her. She could do a whole master class on it and make a killing.

"Well, we're all hopeful it will work out," Pru said. "Then imagine my surprise when I found out our new director is actually an old friend of yours, dear."

"Oh?" No one else would have noticed how Carmen's brows lifted the tiniest bit on that one syllable. But he did.

"Yes. He had such wonderful things to say about you. He said the two of you worked closely together at multiple international locations over the years. Vincent Kapler?"

As Pru spoke, his friend grew still. Unnaturally still. This wasn't her polite-calm-fake expression. This was something else entirely. Something he couldn't quite put his finger on, but something he didn't like. At all. The back of Jake's neck tingled.

"Vincent was hoping to make it this evening but, unfortunately, had a scheduling conflict he couldn't avoid."

"That's a shame," Carmen said after a moment's pause. "Yes, he and I worked together numerous times over the last couple of years."

"He speaks very fondly of you, dear," Pru said, her voice an annoying singsong, as if Carm was some damn teenager looking for a prom date.

She gave a noncommittal hum. "As I said, Pru, he and I have worked together numerous times. He's very dedicated and well-connected in many international circles. I'm sure he'll be a wonderful asset to your organization."

"Vincent's quite handsome as well. Wouldn't you agree, dear? He's single too." Pru's eyes sparkled with matchmaking mischief, and it took everything in Jake's power to not tell the lady to cut the shit. "I mentioned to him that you recently relocated back to Seattle as well, and that you're single to boot. Perhaps we should all have dinner soon?"

"Prudence," Jake cut in. "Sorry, I hate to interrupt . . ." He didn't. Not one bit.

He moved his hand to the nape of Carmen's neck, and for a split second, she tensed. He gave her a soft squeeze, and the tightness in her shoulders eased. He rose, then leaned down toward her. He lowered his voice but kept it loud enough for the table to hear. "They're playing our song, gorgeous. Let's dance."

Not hesitating for one second, Carmen stood. "Of course, Jake."

Taking her hand in his, he intertwined their fingers, and she followed him onto the dance floor. Pulling her into his arms, he led her in a slow sway.

"Our song, huh?" The corners of her lips tipped up. "And what song is this exactly?"

He took a moment to listen to the sultry, jazzy tune, then shook his head. "No clue."

"Works for me." She chuckled. "Thanks for the save. Again. That makes three tonight, right?"

He shrugged. "I'm not keeping track." He truly wasn't. Because he knew she'd do the same for him. Though, thank God, he didn't have to suffer through anyone like Pru. In all honesty, he couldn't figure out who was more annoying: McAsshole or sweet ole Pru.

"I swear, my folks stuck Mrs. Weatherby at my table because they can't stand the woman either. How an organization that does such amazing work can have *that* woman as its matriarch is beyond me."

They swayed together for a few quiet moments before Jake spoke. "So, Vincent Kapler? Not as amazing as Pru makes out?"

"No, he is. It's just . . ." She cringed. "Was I that obvious?"

"Not at all. I just know you, Carm. What's his story?"

Her eyes narrowed, as if she were choosing her words with great care. "He's a good worker. I wasn't lying when I said he'd be an asset to their organization. But . . ."

He waited as her gaze moved around the room. When she didn't continue, he squeezed her waist. "Buuut?"

"Well, one could argue that it wasn't the wisest move on my part, but—"

Carmen suddenly tensed in his arms. Her tan complexion went ghostly white, and her focus locked on something across the room. His heart stuttered in surprise. What the hell?

He was about to turn to see what had caught her attention when her gaze shot to his, shock and panic swirling in her giant, dark brown eyes.

"Kiss me, Jake. Now."

CHAPTER FOUR

"Kiss me, Jake. Now."

Her friend didn't hesitate. A half second after she uttered the desperate command—her heart beating an erratic and frantic rhythm in her chest—he gently tipped her chin up with one finger and brought his lips to hers.

A tiny sigh escaped—from her or him, she wasn't quite sure—and she felt his lips curl up against hers in the smallest of smiles. She didn't care that they were in the middle of a crowded dance floor. That they were surrounded by colleagues and donors. That she had countless family members milling around. She needed this gorgeous, muscular behemoth of a man kissing her. Right. Freaking. Now.

Just when she thought he would pull away, his lips met hers again, soft and gentle. The hint of Jake's tongue had her belly fluttering as he nipped at the corners of her mouth. Her entire body relaxed into his of its own volition.

Breaking away slightly, he nuzzled the side of her face, his mouth close to her ear.

"You okay, sweetheart?" he murmured, laying a tiny kiss

on the top of her ear before meeting her gaze. His dark brown eyes, which had gone almost black, swirled with something she couldn't interpret. Something new and fiery. Something that squashed the trepidation and panic that, moments earlier, had threatened to overwhelm her. The soft warmth growing in her stomach calmed her and settled her fraying nerves.

Words escaped her.

She blinked. Twice. Damn. She hadn't expected that.

What *that* exactly was, she didn't know.

All she knew was that as far as kisses went, Jake's had been both sweet and stirring. And surprising.

Was she okay? Letting out a shaky breath, she did a quick internal inventory. Jake and his magic mouth had calmed the desperate panic that had clawed at her and eased the erratic beating of her heart. So, yeah. She was okay. Now.

While a part of her wanted to snuggle deeper into Jake's arms—God, what would this night be without him?—she knew she couldn't hide. She had to focus. Giving the surrounding area a quick and hopefully subtle scan, she let out a breath. Alongside the sly glances from her fellow dance floor occupants were nosy smirks and knowing grins. All that, she could deal with. No problem.

Because Vincent was nowhere to be seen.

"Yeah, I think so. Thank you yet again for the save, Mr. Alvarez."

Still tucking Carmen against him, he kissed her temple. From the outside, she knew they looked like she wanted them to—a couple enthralled with each other. "Care to explain what made you all pale and sweaty-palmed, sweetheart?"

Her nose wrinkled. Apparently, *enthralled* was not the word Jake would use. She tried to remove said sweaty hand from his grip, but he held firm.

"What's going on, Carm?"

She remained silent for a moment, desperately trying to arrange her thoughts. "You know how Pru said Vincent had a prior engagement?" She paused, unable to find the right words. Couldn't find a way to explain her complicated, irrational emotions without sounding paranoid. And ungrateful.

She let out a breath. This was Jake, dammit. She could be honest with him. He wouldn't judge.

Right?

"Go on," he prodded.

Goosebumps erupted over her flesh, and she tried to suppress a shudder. And failed. Praying Jake hadn't felt the tremor, she dropped her voice to a whisper. "I saw him here just now."

Jake ran his hands over her bare, suddenly chilled arms, and his brow furrowed. "Why this reaction, sweetheart?"

She hesitated. It wasn't that Vincent wasn't a nice guy. He was. If anything, she owed him. Hell, she owed him so damn much. If it hadn't been for Vincent . . .

Her mind screeched to a halt, and her heart knocked hard in her chest.

No. Just no.

She'd worked so hard to keep her mind from drifting back to that time. To what had happened. To that absolute nightmare. She couldn't go there. Not in her mind, not out loud, and most definitely not here in the middle of the freaking dance floor.

When Prudence had mentioned his name earlier, it had taken everything in her to not outwardly react, to not flinch at the mere mention of his name. And she hated herself for having those thoughts.

Vincent was a nice man, a good man. She wasn't being fair to him. She knew this, yet her heart had nearly stopped when Prudence had mentioned that he was now based out of their Seattle office. An office that was less than a mile from hers.

Then Carmen had spotted him on the far side of the ballroom. A ballroom he wasn't supposed to be in. Tall and handsome, with hair that wasn't quite blond and not quite brown, dressed in an immaculate tux. Their gazes had caught, and his face had lit up with a smile, his hazel eyes—eyes that knew too much—bright and happy as he'd made his way toward her. With her next breath, everything had come rushing back. Like a tidal wave of horror. Her chest had squeezed painfully hard. And she'd panicked.

"Carm?"

Her gaze refocused on the man before her, and uneasiness knotted her stomach. She needed some sort of explanation. Because after her mini panic attack and Jake's save, she owed her friend something. But her history with Vincent was so damn complicated. So, she settled on an excuse that was a half-truth. One that, prior to her world exploding, would have been the complete truth. Regardless, it would have to suffice.

"Back when I was in Bolivia, Vincent and I dated for a few months. We weren't super serious or anything, but we were exclusive. I ended things when I didn't want to pursue anything further. We remained friendly, which was good, since we ended up working with each other so much later."

"But?" he prodded, his brow crinkling.

She hesitated, the exact words she was looking for remained just out of her grasp. "Like I said, we stayed friendly, but after we stopped seeing each other romantically, he was . . . persistent." He'd never technically asked her out again. It was just a feeling. She could be totally off-base, but it felt as if he wanted to get back together and was biding his time until she was ready to give him another chance.

"Bolivia was a few years ago, right?"

"Two," she confirmed. "We were at the same project for about six months before I ended things and moved on. Then Vincent showed up at my next location in Venezuela. Then at two locations in the Philippines and again on this last stint in Brazil."

"Now he's here in Seattle," Jake finished for her. His lips pursed, and his brown eyes turned flinty.

She nodded, the first seeds of guilt taking root. Her nonprofit world was indeed a small bubble, and it wasn't uncommon to run into all the same people. Still. How often Vincent had popped up over the last two years made her uncomfortable.

Just like that, the guilt bloomed, souring her stomach. Nausea threatened.

Selfish.

She truly owed Vincent so much. Yet here she was. Ungrateful. Playing games to avoid him.

"I'm not being fair to him. Vincent really is a nice guy," she said, her voice unsteady. "He helped me out of a jam a few months ago when we were in Brazil." More like he saved her from a horrific nightmare. Now, the man reminded her of a time she desperately wanted to forget, to wipe from her memory. And *that* wasn't fair to him.

"It's just over the past year or so, he's been relentless about us hanging out and spending time together as friends . . ."

The man's tenacity had annoyed her, had made her uneasy. But if not for his persistence . . . she didn't want to imagine what would have happened.

Vincent didn't deserve her avoidance. He sure as hell didn't deserve the nausea that rose at the mention of his name. Because it wasn't his fault. At all.

It was hers. All hers.

She couldn't separate what had happened in Brazil from

Vincent. And that was so damn unfair to him. Because he'd saved her.

"Sorry, Jake." She dropped her head to his chest and let out a sigh. "I'm not explaining myself well. I'm sorry."

"You have nothing to apologize for, Carm." He brushed his lips over the top of her head and, for a moment, simply held her. "This guy makes you uncomfortable?"

Whether it was Vincent's fault or not, the answer was the same. "Yes. But it's not his—"

"Nope," Jake interrupted. "You feel how you feel and that's all that matters, sweetheart." He pulled slightly away and lifted her chin with his finger. The intensity in his gaze had her insides stilling, making her want to look away. His brown eyes narrowed the tiniest bit, as if he dared her to do just that.

She didn't. *Couldn't.*

"Whatever the reason, Carm, whatever it is that's making you feel guilty—because sweetheart, you obviously are—whatever's having you make excuses for this guy, that doesn't matter. He makes you uncomfortable. Period. And that's not okay." His lips pressed to her forehead before he tucked her back against his chest. "I've got you."

She didn't want to think about how Jake's simple words, his simple gestures, brought her so much comfort and eased the tension in her shoulders. All the same, she was thankful for them. Just as she was thankful for her sky-high stilettos, which were propping her up the five extra inches necessary to allow his chin to rest atop her head. It was . . . cozy. Yes, she prided herself on being tough and independent. But she needed a little bit of cozy right now.

"I have a proposal for you," he said after a moment, then remained silent.

Carmen couldn't help the grin that spread over her lips as she gazed up at the man. She loved watching his mind work.

With his magic lips pursed and his eyes unfocused, he looked as if he were solving a complex problem in his head or working out what she wasn't saying out loud.

Then his dark brown eyes met hers. Gone was the distracted haziness. Now they sparkled with mischief. "Let me be your boyfriend, and I'll get this guy off your back . . ."

Carmen's brows hit her hairline. "Excuse me?"

"And you can be my girlfriend for a few events and dinners and . . . things I have coming up."

She blinked. Twice. Again.

What? She must have misheard. Boyfriend? Girlfriend?

Jake chuckled, dropping his lips to her forehead again. "Pretend, Carm. Just pretend boyfriend and girlfriend. Kind of like what we're doing now, but for a couple months or so."

Her heart tripped hard in her chest.

Pretend.

Of course.

She studied him as she mulled over his proposition. If the past few minutes were any indication, having Jake near steadied her, particularly with the entire Vincent situation. Not to mention having Jake as her fake boyfriend would be a big ole fuck off to her ex. Huh.

Jake's proposal had merit. But her brow furrowed. "Do you think people would believe us? As an actual couple?"

Through the delicate crepe fabric of her dress, the heat of his fingers traced slowly down her spine. She couldn't suppress her shiver. This time, the goosebumps erupting over her skin had nothing to do with Vincent. Or Brazil.

"Uh, yeah," he murmured. The corner of his lips tipped up in a smirk that was somehow both adorable and sexy.

Whoa.

Not sexy.

Cute. His smirk was adorable and *cute*.

Jake glanced over her shoulder. "Actually, if the glares

your brother and Blake are shooting me are any indication, I'd make that a *hell yeah.*"

As he turned her, she stole a glance toward their table. Sure enough, Parker and Blake were staring at them—their expressions flittering somewhere between *What the fuck?* and *My eyes! Holy shit, my eyes!* She couldn't decide if the idiot duo's looks were amusing or insulting.

Before she could choose, Jake cleared his throat. "I know this probably isn't the time or place to discuss this, but . . ." Jake trailed off, his attention focused over her shoulder. The hand that had settled on her low back immediately stopped tracing circles. He placed deliberate space between their bodies, and a flush stole over his face. "Holy shit, Carm, I'm pretty sure your mom is trying to kill me with her eyeballs."

She chuckled and peeked over her shoulder. Then cringed. Yup. Mom's glare was in full force. Forty years old or not, when her mom gave her *the look*, Carmen complied. These past moments with Jake had made her forget she was supposed to be networking, making sure CWC's supporters and donors received one-on-one face time and remained happy. Usually, it wasn't a hardship. She truly appreciated their generosity with both their time and funds. However, that was the last thing she wanted to do tonight. But when duty called, she always answered. Always. "If it's any consolation, I'm pretty sure I'll be my mom's first casualty of the evening."

"Nah, it'll be Blake," Jake said with a snort. "Raven isn't here to keep him in line, so he'll do something stupid first."

"True." She couldn't help but grin, thinking of her whipped cousin and his spitfire of a fiancée. "What are you doing tomorrow?"

"Working. You?"

"Same." Her grin grew. Of course they were both working on a Sunday. As she looked up at him, she swore she could feel her mom's gaze boring a hole into the back of her head. A quick glance over her shoulder confirmed that, yes, her mom's blue eyes had indeed transformed into lasers. Carmen rushed on, "Crap. Mom's Super Scary Glare has made an appearance. I have to go be social, but meet up tomorrow after work?"

"Yeah." He chuckled, looping her arm with his as they made their way off the dance floor. "Come over when you're done with work, and I'll make dinner. I'll even make those empanadas you like."

Her footsteps came to an abrupt halt. "The chicken and potato ones?" He nodded, and she groaned, her mouth watering at the thought of those savory, delicious little treats. "That's not fair, Mr. Alvarez. You know those are my favorite."

"What can I say?" His smile was the epitome of charm. "I'll try to sweeten my proposal any way I can."

Proposal. Her stomach twisted at the word. How the hell was this any different from the *alliance* Brian had suggested?

No. Stop.

For one, she liked Jake. She respected him and knew he wouldn't purposely fuck her over. Second, it was *Jake*. That made it different . . .

Right?

Before she could formulate a third argument in her head, Jake was in front of her, hovering with one hand squeezing her hip, the other gently cradling her face. She should've felt smothered by him, uncomfortable as he crowded her personal space. The way he looked at her, as if he could read her thoughts, should have had her taking a giant step back.

She waited for the wariness to slither over her as it always did when someone got too close. But it didn't. And she refused to think too hard as to why.

"I can see the wheels turning in your pretty head. I know

you have to go do your hostess thing, but just think about it, okay? No pressure. I swear."

Right. Easier said than done.

She nodded anyway and let out a steadying breath, relaxing her shoulders. "Find me before you take off?"

"You got it, sweetheart." He pressed another kiss to her forehead, then tucked her hand back into the crook of his arm and led her to her family's tables.

CHAPTER FIVE

A throat cleared, and Jake glanced up from his computer monitors. It took two blinks before his eyes focused on the man standing in his office doorway. Another two blinks had his stomach dropping.

Parker.

Shit.

Jake straightened in his chair and grimaced at the kinks firing across his lower back. "Hey, man. What's up?"

His friend simply stared at him. Nerves pooled and churned in his gut.

Glancing at the time, Jake was shocked that it was almost three in the afternoon. When he'd arrived at his office at the crack of dawn, his focus had been crap. The first couple of hours had been an absolute struggle to concentrate on the updates he'd wanted to deploy. His mind had been a constant loop of three things: Carmen. That sexy-as-fuck dress. And her soft-as-sin lips.

And how she'd fit so damn perfectly against him.

Fine.

Four things.

Basically, the very *last* things he should've had on a loop in his brain.

After his fourth cup of coffee, he'd finally fallen into a groove, but he'd missed lunch. Again. So, it wasn't nerves that had his stomach in knots. It was just hunger.

Yeah. That's what it was.

His phone buzzed with a text, and he'd never been so thankful for a distraction. Glancing at the message, every already-tense muscle in his body tensed even further. Fuck.

Lara: Hey! So great chatting over the last few days. Can't wait to catch up more next weekend. I'll make reservations for us at John Howie Steak in Bellevue. Let me know if that works on your end.

Fine.

It was a combination of hunger, the pissed-off man in his office, and the drama of all that was Lara.

Holy hell.

The text on his phone's screen brought that familiar happiness he always got from his exchanges with Lara. But it also brought that tinge of dread. Also familiar. Because spending time with Lara and her douche of a husband was a special kind of hell.

He couldn't think about any of that right now. Because if the glare his friend was shooting at him was any indication, he had much bigger problems to worry about.

"Seriously?" Parker grumbled as he settled into the leather guest chair on the opposite side of Jake's desk.

His knotted stomach let out a loud growl. Now that his brain wasn't distracted by endless screens of code, the first tingling of hunger-induced annoyance began to swirl. And he sure as hell had no right to be annoyed at Parker. None at all. After the show he and Carmen had put on the night before, he deserved all the shit he was certain was about to fly his way.

Yanking open a couple desk drawers, he found a protein bar. This brand tasted like shit, but he didn't care; he just needed to keep the hanger at bay. He ripped open the wrapper and took a giant bite. Sighing as he chewed around what was basically cardboard—how the hell something could be both chalky and sticky at the same time, he hadn't a clue—Jake leaned back in his chair and returned his focus to his friend. "Sorry. You were gonna say?"

Parker shook his head, disgust etched on every inch of his face. "It's insulting that you eat that shit. You know there's a full kitchen one floor down, right? A kitchen that, need I remind you, as part owner of said kitchen, you have full access to."

"Lost track of time," he replied with a roll of his eyes. The Spotted Dog's chef took food seriously. Jake, on the other hand? Not so much.

Downing the last chalky and sticky bite, Jake crumpled the wrapper and tossed it into the trash, the sharp hanger pangs momentarily quelled.

A few seconds of awkward silence ticked by.

"So?" Parker asked, his brows arched with either exasperation or annoyance. Most likely a bit of both.

Jake fought a wince. He was fairly certain he knew why Park was sitting across from him but didn't want to presume. Didn't want to open that can of proverbial worms if he didn't have to. He'd only managed to dodge Parker and Blake's questions at last night's gala because both men, like Carmen, had been on host duty. Thank freaking God.

He glanced at the clock on his computer again. He was surprised it had taken Parker this long to hunt him down.

Knowing it was a chickenshit move, Jake remained silent. Chickenshit or not, he was one hundred percent fine with it.

"You going to tell me what's going on with you and my sister?"

Fuck no. Not if he could help it. "What did Carmen say?"

Parker's eyes narrowed. "Seeing as she left the house before Kate and I woke up, I haven't had the chance to ask her. Besides, Jake, I'm asking *you* what's going on."

Shit.

He and Carmen had exchanged a handful of texts throughout the day, but it had been their usual banter. Witty observations followed by questionably appropriate responses and memes. They were planning on meeting at his place later for dinner. Obviously, they had a lot to discuss. But Parker didn't need to know that. And just as obviously, his plan of meeting up with Carm later wasn't doing him one damn bit of good now, with Parker currently shooting eye-daggers at him. A trait his friend had apparently inherited from his mother.

There was no way in hell Jake would discuss what was going on with Carmen before he talked to the woman herself. However, he'd been staring at his computer monitors for the past four hours straight, reviewing the newest updates from his programmers, and his brain was fucking fried. There was no way he had enough brain cells left to come up with a convincing backstory on the fly. And yes, a *backstory* was better than a *lie*. So, he went with the truth as close as he could.

"Look, man, I don't know what to tell you. Since Carm moved back, she and I have been hanging out a lot, especially over the last month or so." All true.

"And . . ."

Jake shrugged. "And we like hanging out." Again, all true.

"Duuude," Parker said, so much exasperation in that one drawn-out word. It would have been funny if he weren't on the receiving end of it. "You freaking kissed my sister —*repeatedly*—last night. With tongue." His friend shuddered.

Yet again, everything Parker said was all true. Though

repeatedly was a bit of a stretch. He'd kissed Carm on the lips once. *Once.* If you counted all the other times his lips had found her forehead, cheek, top of her head, that little spot right next to her lips . . . then, yeah, he supposed Parker's use of *repeatedly* was somewhat accurate.

"Christ, Jake, are we seriously just going to ignore that shit?"

"Yeah, I did kiss her. And no, I'm not ignoring that." *But I sure as fuck would like to ignore* you, *dammit.*

Jake didn't know what to say. Words were failing him. He didn't know if it was the lack of food, his fried brain, the texts from Lara—which always stirred up a bunch of shit—or the recollection of how damn soft Carmen's skin was. But whatever it was? He was fucked.

Parker's eyes rolled. His friend opened his mouth to, no doubt, give him more shit, but Jake rushed on. "Look, I don't know what you want me to say. Carm and I have been hanging out a lot, and yes, we like each other. We kissed last night, and it wasn't the first time."

Christ. Why the hell had he said that? If he could bitch-slap himself, he would. Though technically it was true. He'd kissed Carmen before. But not like *that.* The other kisses had been on the cheek. Forehead. Crown of her head. Even an accidental peck on the lips when he'd gone left and she'd assumed he'd go right.

That kiss on the dance floor?

Yes, it had been born out of panic, out of a need for a friend to rescue a friend. And it had been just that. For about two seconds. Then it had become a kiss unlike any of the others they'd shared before.

It had been lingering. Sweet. Then something else. Something . . . hot. With the *tiniest* bit of tongue.

His dick twitched.

Holy shit.

He needed to rein everything back in. Stat.

Parker's brows rose, and Jake scrambled to remember what the hell he'd just said. And came up blank. Carmen and her lips. Those were the only images remaining in his mind. Shifting in his seat, he mentally recited some of his original Square Peg code to get his brain off Carmen and back into his current situation. This was, hands down, the very last conversation he wanted to have with his friend.

"Park, this . . . thing with me and Carm is all new. And no offense, but I don't feel all that comfortable talking to you about any of it before she and I figure it out."

"She's my *sister*, Jake."

"Believe me, man, I know that." And there it was. Parker hadn't said it in so many words, but it was still there.

An old hurt bloomed and burned deep in Jake's chest. A hurt he thought he'd put behind him decades ago. Obviously, he hadn't. This man was one of his best fucking friends. Parker didn't think he was good enough for his sister? Well, hell, Jake *knew* he wasn't good enough for Carmen. No one was. But to have Park come straight out and basically say it? To see that *no way in hell* look in his friend's eyes? Damn.

He let out a sigh that was part frustration and part disappointment. This conversation needed to be over. Now. "Aside from her being your sister, Carmen's an adult. You know I respect her completely, so don't make this weird, man."

"Me?" Parker scoffed. "*You're* the one making it weird."

Despite the awkwardness of the moment, Jake couldn't help but chuckle. "Nice comeback, asshole."

"Look, man," Parker grumbled, running a hand roughly through his hair. "You're one of my best friends, and this isn't one of those *stay away from my sister* things. Well, not really. I mean, it kinda is, but . . . fuck." His hands went back in his hair as he paused, as if trying to find the right words. "This is fucking weird, okay? The bottom line is you're one of the best guys I know. But it's still fucking weird."

Just like that, the old hurt in Jake eased a little.

Damn. Was all the Lara drama of the last few days fucking with his head? Was he being overly sensitive?

Christ.

Overly sensitive? What the hell was wrong with him? If he could kick his own sappy, sorry ass, he would.

Stirred up shit? There you go. Thanks, Lara.

His phone buzzed again, and he bit back a curse. Without looking at the display, he silenced it, then turned it face-down. The last forty-eight hours had been filled with so much bullshit—unfortunately, all of his own making.

"Jake, I don't know what it is, but there's something off with my sister. Ever since she came back to Seattle. I mean, you guys are close—" Parker winced the wince of an uncomfortable younger brother. "Rephrase. You've known her forever, so you've sensed it, right?"

Parker now had his complete attention. Because Jake *had* noticed. He nodded.

For as long as he could remember, Carmen had always been tough as nails, always uber-confident, always put together. But Parker was right. There was something just a little bit . . . off. A slight hesitation in her actions, her movements, her responses. For a woman who'd always been deliberate and so damn sure of, well, everything, it was different. Noticeable. To him and Parker, anyway. And after last night with Carmen's former coworker and her piece of shit ex-husband, Jake was on full alert.

"My sister would kick me in the balls if she ever heard me say this, but she's like those strawberry candies that every grandma had in their purses when we were growing up. You know, the ones where the wrapper looked like an actual strawberry?"

Jake's face scrunched in confusion, and he scoffed. What the fuck? "Uh, yeah, dickhead, she sure as shit would kick your ass. *Nobody* liked that nasty candy."

Parker's eyes rolled, his hand waving away Jake's words. "What I meant is that my sister's hard on the outside with just a tiny bit of sweet. But on the inside? Completely gooey and cloyingly sweet."

"Christ, Park." He shook his head. "You need to work on your analogies, buddy. Because the insides of those candies were shit." Parker opened his mouth to reply, but Jake cut him off with a slash of his hand through the air. "Absolute *shit*. But I get what you're saying. She's tenderhearted."

"She is."

His thoughts drifted to the evening before and part of the reason why they were in this predicament in the first place. "And her heart's taken a beating over the last few years." Parker nodded, a look of helplessness crossing his face. "First and foremost, Carmen's my friend. Whatever does or doesn't happen with us . . . well, truly, it isn't any of your business." Parker's mouth opened, so he rushed on. "But she means a lot to me." Over the last few months, they'd moved from being friendly to her becoming one of his closest friends.

Parker's chin lifted. "Thank you, man. That means a lot."

"You're welcome," Jake replied as he rose, nodding to the door. "Now, what do you say you show me what I can steal from the fridge downstairs? And I'm totally telling her you compared her to that shit-tastic candy."

CHAPTER SIX

Carmen stood before the condo's massive concrete, metal, and glass door. She pressed the buzzer, and shadows moved behind the textured glass. Seconds later, it swung open in a soundless whoosh. She bit her bottom lip. Hard. But it was no use. There was no way in hell she could prevent the laughter from escaping.

The look on Jake's face could only be described as abject relief. While it didn't exactly explain his panicked voicemail message begging her to come over earlier—no exaggeration, he'd literally said, 'I'm begging you, Carm, please come over as soon as you can!"—it piqued her curiosity about what was going on in his head. Who knew the man was so dramatic?

"Holy shit," he said on a loud exhale. "Thank you so much for getting here so fast."

Taking her jacket and purse, he turned and hung them on an ornate metal coat stand that, when she looked closer, appeared to be a welded bike frame with gears and chains as the various hooks. "Wow. Nice coat stand. I've never seen anything like it."

He led her through the entryway into his great room,

mumbling something about it being new and his brother and blowtorches. Used to Jake's ramblings, she didn't bother trying to comprehend what he was saying. Instead, she came to a halt and focused on the view.

She'd visited Jake's home numerous times. And each time, without fail, her breath caught at the view from his magnificent floor-to-ceiling windows. But today was the first time she'd witnessed a sunset. And it was freaking glorious.

As the sun began its descent behind the Olympic Mountains, the sky was colored with cotton candy pinks and purples. The waters of Puget Sound sparkled, interrupted only by the silhouette of a tiny ferry chugging along. A pang of envy tickled her soul.

Jake's phone rang, and he excused himself with a quick apology and more mumbling.

Wandering around, she saw that his place was more than just a spectacular view in an equally spectacular downtown Seattle high-rise penthouse unit. He'd managed to give the modern, open-concept condo a warm, inviting feel. Yes, she was pretty sure he'd hired an interior designer and decorator, but his personal touches were what made the enormous space cozy.

He had some standard and high-end sports memorabilia from the Seahawks, Mariners, and UW Huskies. But it was the surprisingly personal items mixed in that eased the bachelor pad feel. Interspersed on the shelves between souvenirs and trinkets were framed photos of his family and friends.

One showed Jake, Parker, and Blake at The Spotted Dog's grand opening party. The men stood with their arms slung over each other's shoulders and made a handsome trio. The joy and excitement on their faces warmed her heart. There was another photo of him and Matt, flanking their petite mother at what looked like some sort of promotion ceremony for his brother. This photo captured the seriousness

Jake tended to present to his family, but his obvious pride for his twin couldn't be missed.

Her favorite photo sat next to what she knew was one of Jake's most treasured possessions—a football signed by the entire 2014 Super Bowl-winning Seahawks team. A group shot from the latest Square Peg launch party a few months earlier. It captured both crews from The Spotted Dog and Alvarez Tech yukking it up. In the middle was Jake, with her tucked snuggly under his arm, his head thrown back, and his handsome face caught mid-laugh.

Relaxed and carefree.

It was an expression she didn't see much on him, a feeling she knew he didn't allow himself too often. Sure, he was always gregarious, and when he came out to play, he was the life of the party, but the times he truly relaxed were rare. And he seldom let his guard down. But at the center of the two oddball families he'd helped create, this photo captured one of those magical moments.

Glancing over the decor on his shelves, it surprised her again that her friend—a Type A workaholic like her—was a fan of dust collectors. As someone who'd lived out of two suitcases for roughly three years, she knew souvenirs took up precious space. While she loved the idea of little keep-sakes, she'd never allowed herself to buy them. From a practical standpoint, space had been limited. But tchotchkes also represented something else . . . something more cozy, more permanent . . . something she hadn't wanted at the time.

Now, living in her brother's guest room, space was still limited, but she almost regretted not picking up any along her travels. While the room she occupied was well decorated and styled, it was as sterile as a hotel room. And part of her now itched to have a place to put down those dust-collecting roots.

She'd been back for three months, and everything she had

could still fit in those two suitcases. Yes, she had a small storage unit that held personal items from her pre-traveling years. But considering she hadn't looked through or thought of any of those items in the last few years, did she even need them? Did they even matter anymore? So, the trinkets she spied here and there on Jake's shelves were . . . homey.

Finding a place of her own was on her to-do list. However, there were about nine thousand other items on that particular list as well.

When she'd separated from Brian, before taking off to travel the world for CWC, she'd moved in with Parker, and it had been perfectly fine. Sure, they'd occasionally bickered like any brother and sister, but they'd gotten along as roommates.

This time was different, though. Now, his fiancée, Kate, also lived with him.

Shortly after Carmen had moved in, Kate had been involved in a horrific attack, and nearly three months later, after endless weeks of recovery, Kate was finally getting back to normal.

While Carmen truly adored Kate and thought the woman was perfect for her brother, holy shit, talk about being a third wheel.

If she walked into the kitchen to see them making out like teenagers one more time, she was going to lose it. As it was, she walked loudly whenever she knew the two lovebirds were home. Just in case.

Maybe finding a place to live needed to move up a few spots on her to-do list. Glancing around Jake's spacious great room with its incredible view glittering in the background, she sighed. She could get used to something like this.

"Sorry about that," Jake said, making a beeline for the wine fridge. "No rest for the weary, right?"

Settling onto a high stool at his kitchen island, Carmen

nodded as he held up a bottle of cabernet sauvignon from The Walls Vineyards, one of her favorites in Walla Walla.

"Thank you." She picked up the glass he placed in front of her. After doing the obligatory swirl and sip, she paused to savor the cabernet's blackberry and spicy oak flavors, then nodded toward his phone on the counter. "Everything okay in Alvarez Tech-land?"

"The Spotted Dog, actually," he replied, pouring himself a glass. "I'm working on getting a feature on the Food Network for an Irish Pub special they're putting together for this coming March."

"Nice." No rest for the weary, indeed. "So, are you going to explain the mini panic attack you left on my voicemail earlier?"

Jake took a gulp—a rather large gulp—of his wine and nodded. "First, I have to apologize. I didn't pick up the ingredients for chicken empanadas."

Though her stomach was disappointed, she bit back a grin. "Because of your panic attack?"

The corner of his lips kicked up. "Yeah, I suppose you could say that. How about this instead . . ." From a drawer, he produced two menus, a very pleased-with-himself *ta-da!* expression on his face. "Serious Pie or Wild Ginger?"

Taking the menus from him, her lips pursed. Chef Tom Douglas's Serious Pie was always amazing. Every one of their pizzas was exquisite, from their potato pizza to their soppressata and leek to their clam and pancetta. And Wild Ginger? Basically, a Pacific Northwest institution of Asian fusion perfection.

"Let's go with Wild Ginger." She took a moment to review the menu she'd missed on her travels. "Definitely the seven-flavor beef and the Sichuan green beans. What else?"

As he slid in between her and the stool next to her to peek at the menu, the scent of his familiar bergamot and cedar aftershave tickled her nose, and the final bits of tension she'd carried from last night's gala eased.

"How about the duck, Mongolian noodles, and the green papaya salad so we can say we're healthy?"

She chuckled at the playful grin he shot her. "Perfect. Add an order of potstickers and rice too."

"White or brown?" he asked as he pulled up the restaurant's info on his phone.

She couldn't help the sound of disgust that escaped. With a raised brow, he paused mid-dial. Her eyes rolled. "White rice, Jake. Always. Brown rice is nasty and a waste of calories."

"It's supposed to be healthier for you."

"Yeah, because people don't actually eat that shit since it's so disgusting."

A teasing smile lit his face as he placed his phone down and turned, leaning on the island, facing her fully. "I didn't realize you were so passionate about this, Ms. Cunningham."

"Well, Mr. Alvarez, I'll have you know that there are a handful of things I'm passionate about. And not eating crappy food is one of them." She grinned at him over her wine, and for a heartbeat, their gazes locked.

Something passed between them. She didn't know what. But it was something that made her very, *very* aware of the man before her. His broad chest, the muscles that popped on his strong forearms, his flirty smirk. Warmth inched down her spine, and goosebumps rose on her arms. Refusing to look away, she bit her teeth down on her lower lip and nodded toward the menu without breaking his gaze. "You gonna stare at me all night, Mr. Alvarez, or feed me?"

Heat flashed in his brown eyes, and the warmth sliding down her spine exploded low in her belly. Inappropriate images flashed in her mind of him staring at her while he fed her—

Holy shit! What the hell are you thinking?

They both jerked as Jake's phone dinged. Heat raced over her face.

Clearing his throat, he eased himself onto the stool next to her, putting some space between them. He glanced at his phone. "Apparently, the gods have spoken, and feeding you it is."

Another image flickered in her mind. Her. On her knees. In front of him and—

Oh my God. Down, girl!

She peeked at his phone and saw texts from her brother and Blake. And just like that—bucket of ice water over her head. "Not gods, more like Tweedledee and Tweedledum."

He winked as he placed the phone to his ear. "I'm going to tell them you said that, sweetheart."

Once their order had been placed and she'd managed to tuck all errant and inappropriate thoughts of the man away, she topped off their wineglasses. "I know we got a little sidetracked there, but would you care to explain your little panicked voicemail from earlier?"

Jake grimaced. "Parker."

She waited for more. And was met with silence.

Okaaay.

"Annnd?" she prodded, drawing out that one word while waving her hand in a circular motion.

"He stopped by my office this afternoon and wanted to know what was going on with me and you."

Damn. She'd been afraid of that. She'd managed to dodge both Parker and Kate since last night's gala. But she knew her brother could be persistent. Especially when he was nosy. And if it concerned her? He was *always* nosy. "What did you say?"

"I evaded as much as I could." He shrugged as he took a

sip of his wine. "I basically said it was all new, and that I wanted to talk to you about it before him."

She nodded in approval and clinked her glass against his. "Nice deflection, Mr. Alvarez."

"Why, thank you, Ms. Cunningham." His playful smirk tipped into a frown. "However, I'm not sure he fully believed me."

After taking her own sip of wine, she pulled out her phone and showed him her missed call list. Six calls from Parker in the last hour. "I'd have to agree with you on that." She nodded at her phone. "There's double the number of texts from him too, but I haven't opened any of them so they won't show up as read on his end. I'm not gonna lie—the little red notification dot is driving me nuts."

He grinned at her. "You know you can change that, right?"

"What?"

He nodded to her phone. "You can turn off the read receipts so people don't know you've read the messages. They'll just show as delivered. Then you won't have that red dot staring at you and telling you you're a slacker," he said with a wink.

"Really?" Her brow furrowed. She was a tech-savvy person. At least, she'd thought she was. But apparently, she'd missed this basic tech function somewhere along the way.

"Yup," he said, popping the *P*. He held out his hand, fingers wiggling.

Placing her phone in his hand, she studied the man as he did whatever it was that turned off the read receipts.

Jake. Her friend.

She could trust him.

Right?

This proposal between them could work. God knew she'd hashed it over and over in her mind. Short of doing a formal cost-benefit analysis, she'd studied all the pros and cons.

She was solid in all things business. She knew this about herself. Hell, it was something she took immense pride in.

But romantic relationships? Not so much. After all, her track record spoke for itself.

However, this . . . thing . . . with Jake was, in a way, a business deal.

He wasn't proposing an actual romantic relationship. No. He was proposing a solution. Sure, they'd technically be engaging in a relationship, but it wasn't a *relationship* relationship.

She fought an internal wince. *Hey, high school.*

Jake's proposal was a mutually beneficial solution. They got along. Enjoyed each other's company. They already spent most of their free time together, anyway. So, what was the harm?

She recalled the twenty-plus text messages from Brian she'd deleted earlier today. What better way to get her idiot ex—and all her mom's matchmaking cronies—off her back than to be in a "relationship" with one of Seattle's most eligible bachelors?

Decision made, Carmen took a fortifying gulp of her wine and met her friend's gaze. A friend who, just a few short minutes ago, she'd had entirely inappropriate thoughts about.

Shit. She could use a scotch right about now. "So, Mr. Alvarez, are we actually going to do this?"

"You still want to?" he countered.

Her phone dinged with an incoming text. Jake turned the screen toward her, showing Brian's name on the display.

"Now, *that*"—she gestured with her glass of wine at her phone—"is what you call 'the gods have spoken.'"

Placing her wineglass down, she took her phone back and set it on the counter. Then she held out her hand for a shake. "Yes. Let's do this, Jake."

CHAPTER SEVEN

Shaking Carmen's outstretched hand, a surge of relief coursed through Jake that was so powerful it damn near left him lightheaded. Who knew this tiny slip of a power-house woman would be his savior? Hopefully, with her help, he could dig out of the stupid self-made clusterfuck he'd dropped himself into.

Their whole proposal was tricky, no doubt. He and Carm were friends. Great friends. That should have made all of it easier, but it didn't. Not really. Because there was also that bit of attraction. Definitely on his end . . . and if he was reading the last few minutes right, on hers as well. And *that* had the potential to complicate things.

Then there was Parker. And Blake. And their slew of nosy-ass friends.

He wouldn't fuck it up. He refused to. They'd figure this out, and it would be a perfect solution to both their issues.

Jake needed to look at it from a practical and detailed standpoint. He knew Carm well enough to know that she required the same. Everything needed to be spelled out, needed to be clear. They needed to be on the same page.

Rising from the island, he nodded toward the couch. She rose and followed. Making a detour to the bar, he retrieved a bottle of Macallan and lifted his brows in question.

"Yes, please," she replied, gratitude tinging those two words. She settled at the end of the leather sofa, her back to the armrest, her legs stretched out over the center cushion.

He took a moment to appreciate the picture she made. Her gray, silky-looking button-down blouse was tucked into slim-fitting black slacks. A thin black belt cinched her waist, and a pair of lethally high black heels completed her outfit. Her hair cascaded down her back in a shiny sheet of black, her makeup was minimal and flawless, and diamond studs twinkled from her earlobes.

Glancing down at his worn, faded jeans and Henley, he chuckled. Carmen was the epitome of sophisticated and completely put together. Even on a Sunday.

Handing her a lowball of scotch, he settled at the opposite end of the couch, sitting at an angle so he could face her. Then he shot her his most charming grin. Yes, he was taking this seriously and would go through things logically and point by point, but he sure as hell was still going to flirt with the woman in the process.

It's what they did. So how could he not?

"Shall we hash this out, Ms. Cunningham?" The corners of her lips twitched as she nodded. "Objective?"

She took a drink of her scotch, then her lips pursed in thought. "Continue to do what we've been doing. Pose as each other's significant others."

Her phone dinged with another incoming text. She glanced at it, and annoyance flashed on her face. He raised a brow, and she turned her phone's display toward him.

McAsshole's name lit up her home screen. Again.

Just like that, the ease he'd felt disappeared.

Jake wasn't a violent man. In general, people would describe him as happy. Gregarious. Sociable. But the way that shithead had treated Carmen last night? He wanted to put his fist through that fucker's face.

"How about this, Carm? Instead of continuing what we've been doing, I suggest we kick it up a notch. That way, there's no question we're together." He nodded to her phone. "I'll get that jackass to back off. And that work guy from the gala?"

"Vincent?" she asked, her voice steady. Too steady, too practiced, too polite.

He stilled at her reaction. It had only been a flash. The smallest of flinches. But he'd seen it. And added Vincent to the shit list right next to McAsshole.

He nodded, but remained silent. He hated that fake pitch in her voice.

Carmen cleared her throat. Then studied the glass in her hand like it was her job. "Well, aside from seeing him last night, he hasn't reached out to me, personally or professionally."

His eyes narrowed. *Yet.* That was the word he knew she was leaving out. He didn't know what was going on with this guy, but it was something. He planned to do everything in his power to protect her from whatever it was.

"Pru's organization is hosting a dinner in a couple weeks that I know both Vincent and Brian will be at," she continued, then shot him a teasing smile that was at odds with her tight shoulders. "I could benefit from having some big, muscular man candy with me if you're interested?"

"That works for me," he replied, nudging her foot with his knee. If she wanted to lighten the mood, he didn't have a problem with that. He sure as hell didn't want to think about either of those assholes, and he was sure she felt twice as strongly as he did.

"Aside from that dinner, there are three other evening events this month as well. A couple networking events and another thing with Pru's group. Do you want me to send you calendar invites to those, and you can let me know if they work for your schedule?"

"Yeah, that'd be great." He couldn't help but smile. Sure, this proposed relationship was going to be tricky, but they were so damn efficient together. It was fantastic. *That* was why it would work. "What do you have in mind for duration?"

———

Carmen glanced at the calendar on her phone. It was five weeks until Valentine's Day. Also known as her parents' wedding anniversary. It was their forty-fifth, and they were going big.

The mere thought of a giant family party had her stomach turning. It would be like the gala, but worse. Because since it was all family and friends, no one had to worry about appearances. She loved her crazy family—she truly did—but there was a reason she'd avoided the large, loud, two-steps-shy-of-chaos family gatherings for years. Even before her third divorce. But maybe having Jake with her would make it less . . . well, less "oh, you're single again?" Less "let me introduce you to—" Less freaking painful.

Her brows furrowed as she scrolled through her calendar and its countless meetings, engagements, and events. "There's a big fundraising event at the end of next month with the Seattle Opera," she murmured. "How about after that? The end of February?"

"That works," Jake replied, his attention on his own calendar. "But how about . . ."

Her interest piqued at his hesitancy. And the slight flush that stole across his cheekbones. Well, well, well. What was this?

"How about?" she prodded. When his flush deepened, her stomach did a flip. She didn't know whether to laugh or sigh a dreamy sigh.

Shit.

Laugh. Yeah. *No* dreamy sighs, dammit.

"Would you mind going through March? The week after Blake and Raven's wedding, I . . . um, I have a family reunion scheduled." He peeked up at her, and she gave up. Laughter bubbled out. The man gave some seriously good puppy dog eyes. So what if she sighed a little on the inside? After all, she wasn't blind. The man was ridiculously good-looking.

"Holy crap, Jake, does anyone say no to the puppy dog eyes?"

"Is it working?"

"Like you have to ask." She chuckled, pulling up the Notes app on her phone. "We can extend to after your family reunion. Is it local?"

"No, it's a week-long thing. Down in Mexico. Cancún, to be exact. That's a plus, right?"

"An excuse to escape the shitty Seattle March weather to go to Mexico?" Her grin grew. "Yeah. Not a problem, my friend."

She looked down at the list she'd started and cross-checked her calendar. "Okay, duration is roughly three months, give or take, but of course, we can adjust as necessary," she said, reading from her list. "What else?"

"How about pet names?" he asked with a smirky grin.

God, he was cute. "Well," she began, pausing to clear her throat. *Focus, Carmen.* "You do call me *sweetheart* already. So . . ."

"That's because you are a sweetheart, sweetheart."

Her brow arched. Hard. "Bullshit." She snorted.

"What?" He laughed. "You are sweet."

Right.

"Uh, I'm pretty sure you may be the only person on this planet who thinks that." Smart. Capable. A little bit scary? Yeah. But sweet? Hell, no. "What about you? What do you want me to call you?"

"What names have you used before?"

"Like with my exes?"

He nodded, amusement playing on his handsome face.

Pursing her lips, her mind drifted over her past marriages.

And came up blank. Nope. No pet names there. She'd simply used their first names, and they'd used hers. Huh. "I suppose I'm not really much of a pet name or nickname kind of person."

"Well, how about you test some out, and we'll see what sticks?"

"Okay, honey." A couple seconds of silence ticked by, then her nose scrunched.

He laughed and shook his head. "That one didn't feel right, did it?"

"No." She chuckled. "Not at all."

"Well, we're still early in our relationship, so there's still time to figure one out for me." He winked and reached for his glass.

"Fair enough. Now, what about PDA?"

Jake choked on his drink. Placing his glass down on the coffee table, he coughed for a few more seconds before resting his elbows on his knees and glancing over at her. His grin was somewhere between incredulous and smirky.

Her stomach flipped. Forget good-looking—the guy was flat-out hot.

"A little warning would be nice, sweetheart."

"Sorry." She flashed an innocent smile. She wasn't sorry. Not at all. Flirting with the man was fun.

Butterflies took flight in her stomach, shocking her; after everything that had happened in Brazil, she'd thought that part of her had died. So, while the stirring, heady feeling was probably not a good idea right now, she welcomed it. She just needed to exercise caution and remember what this arrangement was. She trusted Jake. Everything would be fine. "So, PDA?"

He was quiet for a moment as he stared at her. His laughter had turned to something more assessing, as if he were working out some complicated equation or code in his head. It took everything she had to hold his gaze, to not squirm under his scrutiny.

At long last, he broke the silence. "Carm, the very last thing I want to do is overstep with you. Our friendship matters—hell, *you* matter. How about I follow your lead?"

An unfamiliar feeling spread through her and had her stomach knotting. But in a good way, a way that she'd forgotten was possible. While she couldn't describe it, what-ever it was eased that tight ball of tension within her.

This proposal made her nervous—more than she'd ever admit out loud—but they'd be okay. Because it was Jake. And he was so damn sweet.

When was the last time a man, just a friend or not, had considered her feelings? "I don't want to overstep with you, either."

A sly grin grew on his handsome face. One she was sure melted the panties off any and all females. Probably some men too. The way her pulse had sped to double time? Without question, she wasn't immune. "Darlin', trust me when I say you *cannot* overstep with me."

"Oh, *darlin'* . . ." she teased. "Is that a challenge?"

His dark brown eyes heated, and goosebumps rose over her arms. "By all means, sweetheart, have at it," his deep voice rumbled. He leaned against the couch cushions, arm slung along the back, his grin turning into a smile that could only be described as naughty. "I'm up for it if you are."

Heat pooled low in her belly. *Careful there. You are so not ready for this.* He flashed her that smoldering grin, and she promptly told her inner voice to shut it. This was Jake. She could flirt with him. It's what they did. Besides, she hadn't been this relaxed in forever.

"Well then," she said, flashing him her own flirty smile, "challenge accepted."

His mouth opened, but before he could say anything, his phone dinged. After glancing down at the message, he tossed his phone onto the couch cushion.

"Food's here," he said, rising. "We'll table this discussion for later. But Carm?" He shot her a grin that promised nothing but trouble. "We *will* get back to it . . . and it'll be much more in-depth."

Once his back was to her, she let out the breath she hadn't realized she'd been holding and fanned herself with her hand. She couldn't help it. Because, holy shit, the man was lethal.

As Jake returned to the great room carrying more takeout bags than two people could possibly eat, he nodded toward the kitchen. She took a fortifying drink of her scotch and stood, following him.

Hanging out with Jake? Easy.

Flirting with the man? No problem.

Occasional PDA when she decided? Not a hardship. At all.

For three months? She took another drink, and the smooth liquor did nothing to soothe the fluttering in her belly. Yeah. She could keep her emotions in check.

Correction.

She *would* keep her emotions in check. After all, this was a mutually agreeable arrangement. But not in the gross ex-husband kind of way. Because Jake? She genuinely thought he was a great guy.

What could go wrong?

CHAPTER EIGHT

"Long day?" the dark-haired bartender asked Carmen, placing a double of Macallan onto the cardboard coaster in front of her.

She couldn't help the sigh that escaped. The work week had started as one giant clusterfuck. A typhoon was bearing down on the Philippines, right where two of their CWC teams were on site. It was nowhere near typhoon season, and to say everyone was scrambling was an understatement. The one benefit of the logistical nightmare was she'd been too busy to give Brian's countless texts and voicemails a second thought. From six in the morning to eleven at night, her ass had been planted at her desk.

And then today . . . she couldn't suppress the shudder that racked her body. Today had sucked.

So yeah. Long day. Long week—even though it was only freaking Tuesday. Long month. Long goddamn year.

"You have no idea, Raven," she replied, taking a sip of her favorite scotch, relishing the burn as the liquid slid down her throat.

Her day had started well before sunrise and by midmorning, had been a relative success. They'd not only managed to secure transportation to move their teams to a safer location, but they'd been able to secure the in-progress construction so, fingers crossed, the water filtration systems they were installing would survive Mother Nature's wrath.

Her relief at having her teams secure for the moment had been short-lived as the barrage of messages from Brian apologizing for his behavior at the gala had sent her mood plummeting. After his first text early that morning, she'd blocked his number and used the few hours of blessed silence to focus on her teams.

Then he'd somehow figured out she'd blocked him. How? She had no clue. But the endless messages had started back up. Only now, they were coming in from different phone numbers.

It was annoying.

And creepy.

However, all that had been nothing compared to the revulsion of her lunch excursion.

"How's the wedding planning coming along?" Carmen asked, needing anything to take her mind off what had happened earlier that day.

"Nice deflection." Raven chuckled. "But it's going well. Between Kate and Blake's mom, everything's basically done."

"If I can help at all, just let me know. Logistics are kind of my thing."

Raven added another splash of scotch into her glass and gave her a knowing look. "You know, Carmen, if you ever want to word vomit, I'm here to listen. No judging, and I swear I'm like a steel trap."

Her brow arched. Raven was engaged to her cousin. Steel trap wasn't exactly believable. The less her sweet yet nosy-as-hell cousin knew about the drama of her life, the better.

"I see what you're thinking, but trust me. I've been a

bartender a long time. Discretion is part of the job description, no matter who I'm banging."

Carmen laughed, nearly choking on her scotch. "*Banging,* huh?"

"Banging, gonna marry in a few weeks, whatever," Raven said with a wink. "But seriously, if you say something should be kept between us, I promise it will be."

"I appreciate that and . . ." A too-familiar brunette sat on the barstool next to her. Carmen could feel the other woman's eyes boring into her skull, but she couldn't bring herself to look.

"Hey, Carm," Kate said, worry coloring those two words. "I'm so sor—"

"Nope," Carmen interrupted, draining half her glass. "You know I adore you, Kate, but I can't even freaking look at you right now."

Raven's jaw dropped. "What the fuck, Carmen? Not cool."

While she admired Raven's loyalty to Kate, there was no way in hell she was apologizing. Not for her words or her curt tone. With a shake of her head, she downed the remainder of her drink, slamming the empty glass onto the bar top.

She should have seen the signs, dammit. Situational awareness was something she'd been consciously working on.

She'd run home at lunch to retrieve the wallet she'd accidentally left behind—something she *never* did. But she'd been distracted by the chaos of the typhoon evacuation this morning.

She'd been distracted again as she'd hustled into the kitchen from the garage, focused on the emails and texts from her ex-husband bombarding her phone. Then, when she'd entered the living room and tripped over a pair of yoga pants, it had been too late. Now her eyes, ears, and brain were all bleeding.

Carmen tapped her empty glass, indicating her need for a refill. The woman on the opposite side of the bar simply crossed her arms over her chest, her face masked in annoyance.

Fuck. That.

"Uh-uh. You know what's not cool, Raven? Seeing your brother buck-ass naked on the couch with this chick"—she jerked her head toward Kate—"also buck-ass naked and riding him like she's a goddamn rodeo queen."

Raven's jaw dropped for the second time in mere minutes, and the woman's gaze ping-ponged between her and Kate. "Holy shit, Kate. I don't even think *I* can look at you right now, either." Raven spun around, grabbed the bottle of Macallan, and filled Carmen's glass nearly full. The woman's mouth opened, then closed. Then opened again. "Just to clarify, are we talking cowgirl where she exposed her lily-white ass to you? Or reverse where you got the whole damn show?"

Carmen's stomach lurched as the memory burned in her brain. She took a large, large swallow of scotch. "Unfortunately, I now know her tits are perky and real, and she's fully waxed."

"Oh my God." Kate's mortified groan had Raven's laughter filling the pub. "Holy crap, Carmen. I swear, Park swore you were at work."

"I was at work." She could see, in theory, how Raven found this humorous. She would have laughed as well if it had been *anyone* besides her brother and Kate. "And I really, really, *really* should have stayed at work."

"I am so sorry," Kate murmured, her face buried in her hands as a still-belly-laughing Raven wiped tears from her face.

Carmen hadn't been lying. She absolutely adored Kate. She really did.

But no. Just no.

"Damn, Raven, I can hear you laughing all the way in the kit—" Her brother's words died on his lips as he rounded the bar. A scarlet flush spread over his stupid face. A face that was looking anywhere but at her. "Uh, hey, Car—"

"Oh, hell no, little brother. You need to turn your ass right around and march back into the kitchen. I can barely look this one in the eye"—she tipped her head toward Kate, who she technically had yet to make eye contact with—"and I sure as *hell* can't look at you right now." Vomit rose in her throat as the words her brother had been saying to his fiancée mid-fuck ricocheted in her mind.

One thing a sister should never, *ever* need to know? That her brother was a dirty talker. A *filthy* talker. So, so, *so* disgusting.

As Parker backed away, hands up in surrender, his face still red, Carmen turned to Raven. "I need to move."

Raven placed a shot glass in front of her. She didn't think twice, didn't even question what it was, and tossed it back, hissing as the tequila tore a fiery path down her throat.

"I'd offer you our guest room," Raven said, clearing away the shot glass and replacing it with a glass of ice water. "However, seeing as Blake's your cousin and all, and truly has zero inhibitions—especially in comparison to who I *thought* were Mr. and Mrs. Prude over here!" She winked at Kate, whose face still held a grimace and was a bright, bright shade of pink. "I'm not sure our guest room situation would be any better for you."

Good. God.

Her poor brain didn't need any images or sounds of Blake in *any* stage of undress with the firecracker in front of her. "Raven, I'm in total agreement with you there."

"Oh my God, Carmen. Seriously, I'm so sorry you had to see that," Kate repeated, giving her a quick side hug.

"Same, Kate. Same." Shaking her head, she chuckled and patted her friend's arm. After all, what the hell else was she supposed to do?

"Before I run out to dig a big hole and bury myself in it," Kate said, getting down from her barstool, "please excuse me while I go kill Parker first."

"See ya, cowgirl," Raven called out with a laugh. At both Carmen and Kate's pained groans, Raven caught her eye. "Too soon?"

Grabbing the soda gun, Raven refilled Carmen's water and nodded toward something behind her, her perfectly arched eyebrows wagging in an overexaggerated manner. "What about moving in with ole hunk-fest over there?"

Turning, Carmen froze as Jake walked in. He'd obviously just come from the gym. Clad in dark gray sweatpants, a white fitted T-shirt that left *nothing* to the imagination, and an unzipped black hoodie, the man looked positively delicious. Shit.

Swinging back around to face Raven, she schooled her features and laughed. She hoped like hell it was her polite work-event laugh. But considering she'd just consumed *way* too much alcohol in a *very* short period of time, and the fact that heat—which had nothing to do with liquor—was pooling low in her belly, she was pretty sure what came out was more of a strangled-cat laugh.

Double shit.

"Moving in with Jake?" Yup, there was a definite squeaky quality to her words. She sipped her water in hopes it would ease her suddenly parched throat. It didn't. "That's jumping the gun a bit, wouldn't you say?"

"What's jumping the gun?" Jake asked, kissing her temple.

He let out a tired sigh as he settled onto the barstool Kate had just vacated.

Dammit. The man had taken less than five seconds to turn her brain into mush. Because his chest? Ridiculous. She was pretty sure she could even see the cut of his abs through his fitted T-shirt. And that little, nonchalant kiss to her forehead? Holy freaking hell.

"Carmen needs a new place to live," Raven said, tossing a cardboard coaster down in front of him, her indigo eyes dancing as they darted back and forth between them.

With her elbows propped onto the bar top, Carmen dropped her head into her hands. *Holy shit, kill me now.*

"Come again?" he asked.

Carmen could hear his brow scrunching in confusion. How? She hadn't a clue. But she knew with certainty that he'd have that little wrinkle between his eyebrows if she looked.

She sat up and glanced over at Jake. Yup. There it was.

"Exactly!" Raven laughed, placing a beer before him. "Ole Carmen here has seen too much of Kate and Parker *coming* and needs to move ASAP." The woman snickered at her own stupid pun and pointed a finger at Carmen. Her friend's face was flushed with satisfaction. "See what I did there?"

Shaking her head, Carmen couldn't help but chuckle along with her cousin's fiancée. This one was a pistol, and Blake had his hands full for sure. And she couldn't be happier for her cousin. Because, as they said, Raven was one of the good ones.

Stealing a glance at Jake—who still had that cute wrinkle right between his dark brows—she tried to find the words. And shuddered. "I left my wallet at the house this morning, so at lunchtime, I went home to get it. And . . . " Her stomach rolled. Ugh, she couldn't get the words out. Barf.

"And she walked in on Parker and Kate," Raven continued for her, "going at it on the couch like—how did you say it again? Oh yeah, like Kate was a fucking rodeo queen." Her brows gave another exaggerated wag. "Get it? A *fucking* rodeo queen?"

Jake simply stared, shifting his gaze between her and Raven. He blinked twice. Then burst into laughter.

CHAPTER NINE

Carmen set the handset down on her office phone and leaned back in her chair. Relief and exhaustion warred within her. Although it was still pre-dawn over there, she'd finally connected with one of her teams in the Philippines, and it seemed as if everyone had made it through the typhoon relatively unscathed. Now it was a waiting game to see how bad the flooding would get. However, they had communication with their people, and that's what mattered.

Her growling stomach told her she'd missed lunch. Again. Checking her calendar, she groaned in gratitude when she saw her late afternoon meeting had been canceled.

Maybe she'd run down to the pub and sneak some food. Her brother owed her, after all. Like any good big sister, she planned on lording the traumatizing events of yesterday over his damn head for the rest of their lives. Which meant free food for life. Even as gross as Parker was to her right now, there was no question the guy could cook.

"Knock, knock."

The sudden intrusion made her jump. With her hand to her heart, her gaze swung to the door. Then she let out a breath, sinking back into her cushioned chair. "Holy shit, Jake. Heart attack."

"Sorry, sweetheart." He stepped into her office, that playful grin on his face as he held up a paper bag. "I come bearing gifts, so hopefully you'll forgive me."

She gestured to the chair opposite her desk and eyed the bag. Because it was safer than eyeing the man.

Gone was the drool-worthy workout wear. In its place was Business Jake wear: dark jeans and an untucked button-down shirt with the sleeves rolled to the elbows. Equally drool-worthy, seeing as the man sported some serious arm porn and—

Dammit! Focus. On. The. Bag.

She recognized the bright yellow logo—a juice bar and vegan café a few blocks down. She tried to hold back the nose scrunch. She really did. But if the chuckle that left Jake's mouth was any indication, she'd failed.

"My forgiveness will depend on what's in the bag."

Settling into her visitor's chair, he kept the bag on his lap. "Well, I know you love their carrot-apple-banana smoothie," he said, reaching into the bag. His hand emerged with a to-go cup of the bright orange concoction, which he placed on her desk.

"Not bad, darling. Not bad." The corners of her lips ticked up, and she shook her head. "Nope. *Darling* doesn't work."

His brow arched. "I call you darlin' sometimes."

"Well, darling and darlin' are different. Besides, it sounds better coming from you than me." She winked and nodded to the bag when he laughed. "What else do you have in there?"

As much as she loved the smoothie, she was *starving*. With the stress of . . . well, everything . . . she needed something heartier. Something with substance. Something . . . less vegan.

"I came by at noon to see if you wanted to get some

lunch." Her brows rose in surprise. "But Elise," he continued, referring to CWC's office manager, "said you were going to be tied up in nonstop calls. She also let me know that your three-thirty canceled. And I figured you wouldn't have had time to get lunch, so . . ." He gently shook the bag.

Warmth bloomed in her belly. Damn. He really was the sweetest guy.

Clearing her throat, she gave him a get-on-with-it gesture. He pulled out a fruit bowl and placed it next to the smoothie. A fruit bowl.

Yes, that was disappointment replacing the warmth in her belly.

"Don't worry, sweetheart, I've got ya." Jake chuckled, and she fought a wince. Her poker face was off today. And she didn't want to think too hard about why.

It wasn't the man in front of her.

Nope.

It was the stress.

Yeah. That was it.

"The fruit bowl is for me," he continued as he pulled out a brown takeout box and placed it in front of her. "This bad boy is for you."

Her stomach let out another growl as she opened the box flaps. Eyeing the contents, her mouth watered. "Holy shit, Jake," she murmured. "I think I love you."

"Hell yeah," he said with a laugh. "Definitely means I'm forgiven for the earlier heart attack."

"Uh, buffalo chicken wrap with blue cheese crumbles and avocado—"

"*Extra* avocado."

With her hands full of the spicy and savory wrap, she smiled. "One thousand percent forgiven, my friend."

He mimicked wiping his forehead. "Well, the wrap was to feed you because I can't have you wasting away. But I'm not gonna lie—the rest of the stuff in this bag is to bribe you. Think it'll work?"

Swallowing a bite of the tangy chicken, her eyes rolled. "Again, it depends on what's in the bag."

He pulled out a small bakery box, and she moaned when he lifted the lid. It was the cookie trifecta: snickerdoodle, chocolate chip, and oatmeal raisin.

"Sold. But I get to take any leftover cookies home."

"By all means," he replied.

A couple heartbeats later, her eyes narrowed. Was that a flush staining the man's face?

Wiping her hands on a napkin, she took a sip of her smoothie and leaned back in her chair. "What's with the blush, Jake?"

His flush deepened, and she was mesmerized. He raked a hand over his face, then shot her the puppy dog eyes. She couldn't have held back her chuckle even if she'd tried. "Oh, this is gonna be a good one."

"Are you free for dinner Saturday night?"

"Oh no, mister," she teased. "There's gotta be more to it than that."

"Yeaaah," he drawled. "You know that expression—*paint yourself into a corner?*"

She nodded, and when he pointed to himself with a sheepish smile, her grin grew. "I'm intrigued, Mr. Alvarez. Truly, truly intrigued."

<hr>

The edges of Carmen's lips ticked up, but she didn't laugh in his face. Thank God for small miracles.

"Well," Jake began, "instead of *paint yourself into a corner,* this is more like *totally fuck yourself over.*"

Carmen's dark brown eyes danced with humor. She took

another sip of her smoothie, then snagged a cookie and gestured with her sugary treat. "Please. Do continue."

Shit. His mind raced to find the right words, to somehow make this sound less pathetic.

Nothing. Nada.

Fuck.

"So, I have an old college friend coming into town this weekend and . . ." Yup. There was no way to make this sound less pathetic. Fuck it. "I mentioned that I was seeing someone."

Carm's body froze; her only movement was the arching of her right brow. "Are you?"

"You know I'm not." He didn't think it was possible, but her brow arched even higher. Heat raced over his face.

He was a goddamn idiot. He could add countless dollars to his bank accounts and muscles to his body, but deep down, he was still that fucking awkward kid. The loser who never quite measured up. Who never, *ever* got the girl. Fuck. May as well come clean. Get the ridicule out of the way. "I wanted to save face, to not let on that I haven't seriously dated anyone since her."

Carmen's eyes widened with obvious surprise, but she quickly schooled her features. "Why would that matter? It's not like you've been a monk."

He grimaced. It was true. He hadn't. But he also hadn't indulged in random women or relationships as much as Carmen or *anyone* thought. "Because it's been well over a decade—hell, closer to two—since Lara and I were together."

"Wait." Carmen held up a hand as her brows furrowed in thought. "You're talking about *Lara* Lara? Like your girlfriend from college?"

If his chair could swallow him whole—immediately—he'd be eternally grateful. He waited a heartbeat, then sighed in disappointment when both he and the chair were still there. "Yup."

She stared at him, and he tried his best not to squirm. "Are you still hung up on her?"

Carmen's question had him jerking back in shock. Shock he quickly tried to play off with a laugh. "I wouldn't say that." He honestly wouldn't.

But he also wouldn't *not* say that.

Did that even make sense? Shit.

The unfortunate fact was that Lara was the one he compared all the women he dated to. Another unfortunate fact? Thus far, all the women he'd dated had lacked in comparison.

Carmen smiled as she sipped her smoothie. "You lie for shit. You know that, right?" His face must have registered the shock he felt, because Carmen's grin turned into a laugh. "You may have your colleagues and minions fooled, buddy, but you can't fool me." She snagged another cookie and waved it between them. "We spend a lot of time together, you and I, and I know your tells. There's more. Spill."

Damn.

With a resigned sigh, he reached for an oatmeal raisin cookie. Carmen smacked his hand away and gave him a stern shake of her head.

He chuckled. How could he not? It didn't matter that his carefully crafted persona was about to be blown to hell; the woman in front of him was too damn cute.

His hand hovered over a snickerdoodle and, eyes locked on hers, his brows rose in question.

The smirk she shot him as she nodded eased some of the discomfort stirring inside him. Why? He hadn't a clue. But he stuffed the delectable cookie in his mouth and prayed it gave him a few more seconds to think of what the hell to say.

"When I was texting with Lara over the last week or so, I

may have agreed to meet up with her and her douche husband for dinner this weekend."

Heat flooded his face again. For real, if the damn floor would just dissolve and suck him through it, it'd be appreciated.

"And?" she prodded.

His eyes went to the ceiling, and he prayed she wouldn't look deeper into what he was about to say. So. Fucking. Embarrassing. "And I said I'd bring my girlfriend. I may have also mentioned that my girlfriend's name is Carmen, and that I had to check with her first." He brought his gaze back to her and gave her his best puppy dog eyes.

"Oh, babe, of course you did." She grinned, then stilled, as if some kind of realization was dawning. Damn. "Sooo, just so I'm clear, this me-being-your-girlfriend thing was all before we actually agreed to me becoming your girlfriend last Sunday, right?"

Of course she'd put two and two together. He'd been an idiot to think she wouldn't. "Yeah," he admitted with a wince. "I hope that's okay? And that you're free for dinner this Saturday?"

Her teeth sank into her lower lip as if she were fighting a smile, and she glanced at her computer. After a couple clicks of her mouse, she nodded. "Dinner on Saturday works. And for the record, I like *babe*. You?"

A weight lifted from his chest.

He let out a breath and nodded, a smile begging to cross his lips, but he held it back. "I would definitely not be opposed to you calling me *babe*." Not one damn bit.

She took an oatmeal raisin cookie from the box and placed it on the napkin in front of her, then closed the lid and spun in her chair, placing the box on the bookcase behind her. He could have sworn he heard her chuckle, but couldn't be sure.

When she spun back around, the grin she'd sported had grown. Yup, she'd been biting back a laugh. "The cookies are all mine now. So, what have you told Lara about me?"

"Not much," he murmured, trying to gather his thoughts.

Thinking back to his texts with Lara over the last couple of weeks, he frowned.

They'd dated seriously in college but had broken up right before he'd graduated. Then, shortly after, he'd irrevocably fucked things up. He'd thrown himself into his work as a result—first with Alvarez Technologies and then later with The Spotted Dog.

A handful of years after they'd split, Lara had gotten married. He'd received an invitation and had politely declined. Instead of attending the blessed affair, he'd gotten blackout drunk.

Over the years, they'd reconnected via social media, and while their friendship wasn't what it had been, they'd kept in casual contact. Then roughly two years ago, she'd reached out, and they'd started talking again, beyond mere social media messages and comments.

It had been awkward—hell, it was *still* awkward—but he owed it to her. Her husband, whom he'd met, was a complete tool, but she seemed happy, and that's what mattered.

"What exactly does 'not much' entail?" Carmen asked, pulling him back from his thoughts.

"Just that we've been dating since you got back into town a few months ago."

Carmen's eyes widened in surprise, but the humor in her gaze lessened his embarrassment. "A few *months*? Got it."

He didn't know why he'd said that to Lara.

No. He did.

They'd been talking on the phone, and for the first time, she'd asked him point-blank if he was seeing anyone. He'd frozen. There was no way in hell he could tell her the truth:

that every woman he'd dated since her had paled in comparison. He couldn't—no, *wouldn't*—be that pathetic.

He'd panicked. And he'd said yes, *of course* he was seeing someone.

When Lara had giggled and pressed for details, the first face that had popped into his mind had been Carmen's. He recalled how his panic had lessened as he'd told Lara about her. What she looked like, how brilliant and accomplished she was.

"Hold on," Lara had interrupted. "Do you mean Carmen *Cunningham*? As in Parker's older sister?"

For the second time during that conversation, Jake had frozen. How the hell had he forgotten that Lara knew who Carmen was? They'd all gone to UW at the same time. While Carmen had been a year ahead of Jake and two ahead of Lara, because Parker was one of his best friends, Lara had known who Carmen was—though he didn't think they'd ever hung out.

"Uh, yeah." He'd cleared his throat, ignoring the ominous feeling of his lie about to crash down around him. "Carmen Cunningham, Parker's sister."

Lara had giggled again—he couldn't recall her giggling quite so much before—then exclaimed, "I can't wait to catch up! I've heard so much about her, but we never got to know each other."

Jake shifted in his chair and refocused on the present. "Lara actually knows you—well, knew *about* you through Parker. But you were a senior and about to graduate by the time she and I were seriously dating."

"Okay," Carmen murmured, a thoughtful look on her face, as if she were taking everything he'd said—and hadn't said—and filing it away. "At dinner, how do you want to play this?"

His forehead scrunched. He had no idea what the hell he

was doing. He was just so damn thankful Carmen hadn't told him to fuck off for being a presumptuous asshole. So, he did the only thing he could. He shrugged.

Carmen smiled, her face filling with a reassuring warmth that was two shades shy of pity. He fought a cringe when she continued, her voice holding the tone of one speaking to a very young—and not very bright—child. "Seeing as our relationship has been going on for a few months now . . ."

"Thank you, Carm," he interrupted, taking in the woman before him. Her right brow arched in question. "For not only agreeing to come to dinner, but for not making me feel like a complete dumbass."

The pity smile on her face melted away and was replaced by one that was genuine. And stunning. "You're fine, Jake. You'd do the same for me." She broke the last bits of the cookie in front of her in two. "Now, we can play it like we're still casually dating, or super serious and in sappy, crazy love, or somewhere in between."

The idea of playing a sappy man who was crazy in love with Carmen held quite a bit of appeal. It would probably be a bit much for dinner with Lara and her douche husband, though. "How about somewhere in between, but leaning toward serious?"

"That works," she said with a nod, placing the final bite of her cookie in her mouth.

"Does seven work—" His thoughts came to a halt as her tongue darted out to catch a crumb, and his eyes locked on the motion. The tip of her pink tongue traced the corner of her mouth. Then, just like that, it was gone. He startled, realizing he'd stopped talking.

Shit. His gaze snapped to hers and held. Something flashed in her dark brown eyes. Something hot. Something sexy. Something that had him remembering how soft her lips were, how the tip of her tongue had felt against his . . .

A rapid knock at the door broke their eye contact.

"Sorry to interrupt," Elise said.

Carmen's gaze swung to CWC's office manager, and Jake shifted in his seat and tried to stealthily adjust himself. Christ. What the hell was wrong with him? Not the time or the place. It was like he was a damn high schooler.

"These just arrived for you," Elise continued.

At Carmen's frown, he turned to the woman in the doorway. Elise held an enormous bouquet of pink and purple flowers, a sheepish and apologetic look coloring her face.

Glancing back at Carmen, he saw her frown had been replaced by pursed lips that even a blind person would recognize as pissed off. Granted, pissed looked mighty fine on the woman, but that wasn't the point.

"Did you check the card?" Carmen asked, her voice laced with disgust. The other woman nodded.

"If you want, I'm heading over to my parents' place for dinner tonight and can give them to my mom."

Carmen's shoulders relaxed a fraction. "If you don't mind, Elise, I'd really appreciate that."

He frowned. What the hell was he missing?

"It's not a problem, Carm. I'm taking off in about ten minutes, so I'll lock up on my way out, okay?"

"Thanks again, Elise."

"Of course." She turned and smiled at him. "See you later, Jake."

He nodded to Elise. When she cleared the door, he focused his attention back on Carmen. Her hands were clenched in tight fists, and she sat ramrod straight. "What's going on, sweetheart?"

With a grumble, she slouched back into her chair. "My fucking ex-husband . . ."

That dickhead was still bothering her? "And?"

"He's sent flowers each day this week, and like"—she

motioned to the empty doorway—"I've given them all away. He's been calling and texting nonstop. I even blocked his number yesterday, but now he calls from different lines. It's annoying."

His blood chilled. Annoying? That sounded more like a fucking stalker. "Have you seen him?"

She shook her head. "It's been so busy the last few days. I'm basically here, at home, or in my car. Well, technically, it's Parker's car." She paused for a breath, and worry churned in his gut. Then she rushed on. "I've been gone so long, and I haven't had the chance to pick up a new one. Since Park has two cars and he's a good brother, he didn't put up a fight when I swiped the keys to his Audi." She cleared her throat, then waved a hand in the air. "Anyway, Saturday at seven?"

Holy shit, what was going on? Carmen was deflecting. And rambling. The first, she was a master of. The second? Highly unusual. The woman tended to be concise and to the point. Her word vomit could only mean that McAsshole's excessive attention bothered her more than she'd admit.

He'd give her this deflection. But he'd sure as hell be talking to both Parker and Blake—and his SPD brother— about keeping their eyes open for McAsshole . . .

CHAPTER TEN

Carmen shot up in bed, her heart racing, her hair plastered against her sweat-soaked skin. Four heartbeats and two deep breaths later, she recognized her surroundings.

A plush mattress, bedsheets twisted around her legs, and the fading moonlight shining through her bedroom window. Not the hard cement floor. Not the metal cuffs that had bitten into the delicate skin on her wrists. Not the dank, musty room that had smelled of urine and vomit.

Phantom twinges of fire raced along her back where the recently healed scars lay. A shiver racked her body, and she let out an unsteady exhale.

She was safe. Home.

Well, her brother's home. But holy shit, after that nightmare, Parker and Kate's home was plenty good enough for her.

With trembling hands, she slicked her damp hair off her face and twisted it into a knot at the base of her skull. Glancing at the clock, she knew she wouldn't be able to get back to sleep before her alarm went off in a couple hours. She might as well get her day started.

Rising from the bed, her legs shook—but fuck it, she had to get out of here. To move and burn off all the . . . memories. She needed the reminder that she could still run. That she was okay. That she was alive.

She pulled out a pair of black leggings and a neon pink, short-sleeved spandex top from her closet, then quickly got ready. It was still dark out and near freezing. She needed to run but didn't have a death wish. A short female out alone in the dark in icy conditions was a recipe for disaster. So, she grabbed her keys and made her way to the garage as quietly as possible.

The early hour, and the fact that it was a freezing Saturday morning, had her at the gym in under five minutes. Parking under the light post, she noted only two other cars in the parking lot as she made her way to the front door. She'd learned the hard way that situational awareness was vital.

After nodding to the lone staff member at the front desk and spotting the only other person crazy enough to be at the gym at this hour, Carmen got to work on forgetting. No, not forgetting. Processing. Recognizing the demons that continued to haunt her, compartmentalizing them, then shoving them as far down as she could.

Mile after mile, she focused. Visualized the horrors. Wrapped them up. Shoved them down. Over and over. Step after step.

Eight miles later, she slapped the treadmill's cooldown button and slowed to a walk. Sweat poured off her as she took note of the handful of early risers who'd joined her on the machines. Her mind had finally settled some, and her body was jelly. She stopped the treadmill. That would have to do for now.

With her towel around her neck, she grabbed some paper towels and began wiping down her machine. Some women glistened when they worked out. Not her. She sweated buckets and always felt bad for the poor schmuck stuck on the treadmill next to her. Because not only did she drip sweat, but her high ponytail tended to act as a sweat slingshot, whipping back and forth behind her as she ran. So gross. But what was she supposed to do? Her hair was heavy and wouldn't stay in a bun. She'd tried braiding it, but that had seemed to cause a stronger slingshot effect. Luckily, it was early enough that there was no one around her, so she could wipe down both treadmills surrounding hers in peace.

"Hey, stranger, how's it going?"

She startled and shot upright, spinning toward the voice —and toppled over as she lost her balance. Strong arms caught her, and she yelped. The man righted her, then immediately let go and took a step back, his hands out in front of him in a non-threatening gesture.

A split second later, with her own hand over her thudding heart, recognition dawned. "Holy shit, Matt." Her shoulders sagged in relief, and the breath caught in her chest released in a slow exhale. Apparently, she still needed to work on that whole situational awareness thing. "Sorry, I didn't hear you come up behind me."

"No, I'm the one who's sorry. I shouldn't have snuck up on you like that." He nodded toward the treadmill behind her, his familiar dark brown eyes assessing. "You were in the zone there."

She shifted on her feet, unsure of what to say. After her restless sleep and the physically draining run, her nerves were shot, and even though she knew this man, figuring out small talk was difficult.

Matt Alvarez. Jake's older brother. By eight or so minutes. While they were identical twins, she'd always been able to tell them apart, even at first when her brother and Blake hadn't been able to.

She couldn't explain what it was that enabled her to differentiate the two men. It wasn't because Jake was more muscular—because Matt was no slouch. At all. The man had the physique of a fitness model. Jake just took it to a whole new level. He was bulkier than Matt, but not in a meathead kind of way.

Carmen cleared her throat. Small talk, dammit. "How have you been, Matt? It's been a couple months."

"Oh, you know how it is," he shrugged. "Same shit. Different day."

She nodded. "I hear that." Did she ever. "How's Krista?"

A shadow passed over his face, and his jaw clenched, but his expression turned neutral, as if he'd realized what he'd revealed. "She's good. What brings you to the gym so early?"

Okay, then. No mentioning his wife. Got it. "Insomnia." She lifted her shoulders, hoping for casual. "You know how it is, right? The brain just doesn't stop."

"I think that's a workaholic thing, which, thankfully, I am not." He glanced at the clock on the wall. "Speaking of workaholics, Jake should be rolling in here in the next fifteen minutes or so. We lift together on Saturday mornings if you want to join us." His lips pursed as he glanced back at the treadmill. "If you're up for it, that is."

Her legs were jelly, and yet pushing her body to complete exhaustion sounded better than going home. And thinking. Then overthinking. Then stewing. But her brain was mush, and God knew what would come out of her mouth if she stayed.

"No, I don't want to intrude on your brother time. Besides, I don't know much about weightlifting and stuff." Not a lie. She always stuck to the left side of the gym where the various cardio machines lived. The other side of the gym was foreign and beyond intimidating.

"Even better, we can show you. Cardio is good for you and all, but strength training is even better."

She'd been meaning to figure out that side of the gym. The anal-retentive overachiever in her had researched the different machines and their purposes. She'd even watched videos on how to use each one. But she'd been hesitant to actually try them out in person. Not knowing how to do something—and being obvious about it—was not her favorite thing.

As tempting as the offer of hands-on instruction sounded, she was so distracted that she'd probably drop a weight on her foot or impale herself on a bar. "Nah, that's alright. I'll just wait for Jake to show up and say hi. He and I are going out later tonight, anyway."

Matt's brow lifted.

Shit. See? Mushy brain equaled word vomit.

She ran the towel that hung around her neck over her damp hair. "Nothing crazy, just dinner."

"Holy shit, you're going with him to dinner with Lara?"

Too bad she hadn't stuffed the damn towel in her mouth. She could only blink at the shock on Matt's face. Double shit. "Yes, um . . ."

"I swear," he grumbled, the shock turning into a scowl, "that dumbass's selective memory is going to be the death of him. I don't know why he puts himself through that sh—"

"Hey, guys," Jake called out as he approached.

She wasn't sure if she was thankful for the interruption or not. She didn't have time to dwell on it though, because the second Jake reached them, he pressed his lips against her sweaty forehead with a soft, "Morning, gorgeous," then man-hugged his brother with a hearty slap on the back.

Both men turned to face her, and holy shit, the two were a stunning pair.

Her breath hitched as Jake reached out and tucked a damp lock of hair behind her ear. "Good run, sweetheart?"

Matt's eyes ping-ponged between her and his brother. A smirk so similar to Jake's slowly grew on his lips. "I invited Carmen to lift with us, if you're cool with that, bro."

"Absolutely." Jake shot her a wink and flexed his impressive biceps. "I'm cool with any time I can show you up, dude. But to show you up in front of this beautiful woman? Hell yeah."

Carmen chuckled. How could she not? As much as she'd love to see the Alvarez brothers in action, she was exhausted. And said exhaustion would have her saying something stupid. Well, something *more* stupid. Something she couldn't take back.

She glanced at the wall clock and wiped her face one more time. "Rain check? I need to get home soon and touch base with one of my Brazil crews." It wasn't a lie. She really did need to check in on the Rio team. But in the next couple of hours? No. Just some time in the next day or two. However, the guys didn't need to know that.

"It's the workaholic thing, huh?" Matt asked. His uncharacteristically playful tone had her smiling. Because Detective Matt Alvarez was a lot of things, but playful wasn't often one of them.

"Afraid so. Besides"—she nodded toward the weight side of the gym—"that's all sorts of foreign to me."

"Are you sure, Carm?" Matt asked, his eyes twinkling with mischief as he eyed her up and down. "I'm more than happy to show you how to use the machines and free weights."

"Don't be a dick," Jake muttered, shoving his elbow into his twin's side.

"That's sweet of you to offer, Matt. However, like your

brother, your poker face is also shit. I'm going to head out so you can interrogate Jake like I know you're dying to do." That mock-innocent look she'd seen on Jake a million times flashed over Matt's face, and she grinned. "I can see all sorts of questions in your eyes, mister," she stage-whispered.

Matt laughed, and Jake shook his head.

"Have a good workout, boys," she said as she turned. Before she could make it two steps, Jake snagged her hand, stopping her. Then he pressed a quick kiss to her lips.

"I'll call you in a couple hours to talk about dinner tonight, okay?"

The lopsided grin he shot her melted her insides.

Holy shit. He'd just kissed her in front of his brother. She knew her eyes were wide and her mouth had fallen open. But her brain didn't seem to be working.

Fake, Carmen! This is all for show. Pull it together, girl.

With a chuckle, Jake dropped another soft kiss to her lips, then put his hands on her shoulders and turned her toward the locker rooms. "Drive safe, sweetheart, and I'll talk to you later," he murmured in her ear.

She remained rooted until he gave her a pat on her butt. She yelped. Or maybe squeaked. Either way, heat rushed over her face, and it got her moving. As she hustled to the locker room, she wanted to kick herself. Holy crap. What the hell was going on?

Grabbing her personal effects from her gym locker, she thought back on the last few days. They'd been beyond hectic, and she'd barely seen Jake since their impromptu office lunch on Wednesday.

She'd caught the briefest glimpses of the man as he'd snuck into her office—both times she'd been on calls—to drop off food with a smile and a wave. It had been a green smoothie and another trio of cookies on Thursday. *Balance,* his sticky note on the cookie bag had said. Yesterday, it had been a trio of decadent mini cheesecakes and a to-go tumbler of warm, creamy horchata. The sticky note? *And sometimes you need to indulge. Enjoy, sweetheart . . .*

She truly didn't know what to think when it came to the man. Because barely a week in, this fake relationship was better than any of her prior real relationships.

Maybe the eight-mile run had been too much, because her brain seemed to be misfiring. Or was it the lack of sleep and that god-awful nightmare that had her struggling to compute? Or maybe it was the man with the uncanny ability to muddle her thoughts?

It was probably all of the above.

***

Jake watched Carmen's tight, spandex-clad body disappear into the women's locker room. Hot damn.

Carmen was a beautiful woman. It was a plain and simple fact.

But Carmen dressed in nothing but body-hugging spandex? With a soft pink flush of exertion coloring her glistening tan skin?

Holy. Fuck. Yes, please.

It didn't matter that aside from her forearms, practically every inch of her was covered. The woman was made for spandex. The thought probably made him a creeper, but he couldn't bring himself to care. All he knew was he was sure as shit glad he'd arrived at the gym early.

"Uh, dude . . . mind telling me what the fuck that was?"

He swung his gaze to his twin. "What?"

"Nope. You don't get to play stupid with me. I know you and Carmen are friends, but you just kissed her. On the lips. Twice. At the fucking gym. *And* she said you're bringing her to dinner tonight with Lara and Dickless Douche."

Yup. All true. He smiled and nodded.

"Fine." Matt rolled his eyes. "I'll ask again. What the fuck is going on?"

"We're kind of secretly fake dating," Jake explained as they made their way to the free weights. "Carm's helping me with Lara and a couple other things, and I'm helping her with McAsshole and some other twat."

"Let me get this straight," Matt said as he started a set of bicep curls. "You're fake dating each other in secret, but you're telling me it's fake? Why?"

Checking out the weight of his brother's dumbbells, he grabbed a set that was five pounds heavier—he was mature like that—and faced Matt in the mirror. "Well," he said, ignoring his brother's eye roll as he began his own set of curls, "since, apparently, my poker face is shit, there was no point in trying to pull one over on you."

"Bullshit," Matt scoffed as he switched to overhead triceps extensions. "You guys are doing the pretend relationship thing for Lara and the tools in Carmen's life. Last I checked, bro, not only are none of those people here at the gym this fine Saturday morning, but you just admitted to me it's fake. And yet you still kissed her."

Damn. His brother had a point. A good point.

There was no need to pretend to be in a relationship with Carmen, let alone kiss her, in front of Matt. He hadn't given a second thought to revealing the truth of his and Carmen's arrangement to his brother.

It had been a pleasant surprise when Jake had walked in and seen the two of them talking. He hadn't even thought twice about greeting Carmen like he always did. A friendly kiss. Sometimes it was on the forehead, some-times the cheek or the top of her head. He had no clue how their brief exchange had ended with him kissing her on the lips. Twice. Then giving her an affectionate pat on her fine ass. In the middle of the gym. In front of his twin brother.

Yeah. His brother had a point.

"Tell me, Jake, why the fuck did you agree to go out with Lara again in the first place?"

"Because Lara and I are still friends." His brother rolled his eyes. Hard. "We are."

"That's bullshit and you know it." Jake opened his mouth to defend himself, but Matt kept talking. "You like to torture yourself. You always have."

Jake set his weights down and turned to his brother. "What the fuck is that supposed to mean?"

Matt faced him. "It means that for whatever reason, you've been carrying around this guilt for all that shit that happened with Lara. That woman is *not* your responsibility."

"It's not like that." He turned back to the mirror, grabbed his weights, and resumed his arm exercises, his movements jerky. He'd heard all this from Matt before, but it still pissed him off.

"Are you telling me that you're seriously still hung up on that woman? After all this damn time? Because, brother, if that's the case, your selective memory is having another fucking flare-up."

So what if Lara was the one who'd gotten away? Matt didn't need to know that. He scowled at his brother in the mirror. Fuck him and his perfect life.

Jake winced as self-disgust socked him in the gut. Dammit. What the hell was he doing?

His arms came to rest at his sides, and he let out a deep breath—part frustration, part disappointment, but all aimed at himself. He hated how dealing with Lara brought this out in him. The insecurity he'd thought he'd dealt with long ago, but obviously hadn't. Because every time he and Lara talked and made plans, without fail, he spiraled down this fucked-up rabbit hole.

Every. Damn. Time.

It brought up this one-sided, never-ending competition with his twin. The deep-rooted feelings of inadequacy engulfed him like a tsunami and threatened to drown him.

Every. Damn. Time.

Matt had always been the strong one, the popular one, the one Jake was supposed to be more like. He didn't resent his brother. Not at all. But there was always that tinge of jealousy, which made him feel like shit because none of it was Matt's fault.

Jake had been in and out of the hospital growing up, and Matt had been his protector, always looking out for him. By their tenth birthday, he'd undergone three open-heart surgeries, and to say he'd been scrawny and frail would be a gross understatement. When they'd become teenagers, Matt had been the one to help him at the gym so he could get bigger and stronger, better able to defend himself from the bullies at school. And at home.

Over the years, some things had changed, but a lot had remained the same.

Jake was a ridiculously successful multi-fucking-millionaire, but the why-can't-you-be-more-like-your-brother comments were still tossed his way every time he was around his parents. Matt had a wife. Matt had a *real* job, a manly job, one that served the community. Whereas Jake? Played games on his phone. Made games that dulled people's minds and rotted kids' brains.

And then there was all the shit that had gone down with Lara. All the crap that had been his fault . . .

"Christ," Matt mumbled after a few silent reps. "I love you, bro, but you're so fucked in the head sometimes." His brother returned his weights to the stand and turned to him, crossing his arms over his chest. "Why the fuck do you do this to yourself?"

Why the fuck, indeed?

Setting his own weights back onto the stand, he scrubbed his hands over his face. "I don't know, man." His brother simply stared at him. More than anything, Jake wished he could articulate how he felt—the frustration, the inadequacy . . . the fucking *guilt*—because his brother would know what to do.

"Let me ask you. When you kissed Carmen just now, were you thinking about Lara?"

He jerked back as if his brother had punched him, his jaw dropping. "What? No! What the fuck, Matt?"

"Yeah, I didn't think so." His brother chuckled. "Then why are you going to torture the both of you by going to dinner tonight? Why not instead just take that smart, beautiful woman who has agreed to play your girlfriend out to dinner —hell, maybe add in a damn movie? Just the two of you? Fuck your pride and saving face in front of Lara and Dickless Douche. They don't matter, bro. Fuck, they *shouldn't* matter. Because all this?" Matt's hand waved in his face. "This bullshit is what dealing with Lara does to you. She swirls up this misguided guilt. She makes you fucking second-guess every damn thing. Every fucking time. And it kills me to see you like this. Truly."

Well, shit. When his brother put it that way . . .

"Besides, bro, you've had a crush on Carmen since forever. Considering that woman didn't knee you in the nuts for kissing her, she obviously doesn't find you completely repulsive." The corners of Jake's lips twitched up. "Just give it a thought, okay?"

Jake nodded and held his brother's gaze for a few quiet moments.

The idea had appeal; it really did. But like clockwork, that goddamn wave of guilt settled in his belly at the thought of canceling on Lara. Damn his brother for pointing out the guilt and putting it into words. Because it made it more real. Like a living, breathing thing.

Contrary to what his brother believed, Jake held some responsibility for what had happened to Lara all those years ago. Lara's family wouldn't have been destroyed if it hadn't been for him and his selfishness.

He'd done that. *He'd* been responsible. So, as much as it fucked with his head to see her, he owed her.

CHAPTER ELEVEN

Jake got out of his Range Rover and handed the valet his keys. He rounded the hood and glanced through the windshield as the second valet assisted Carmen. He bit back a grimace as his brother's words echoed in his head.

Why the hell was he even doing this?

Jake had thought it was because of his feelings for Lara. That he still deeply cared about her, still carried a torch. But as he made his way to Carmen on the sidewalk, he had a feeling Matt had been right after all.

It was guilt.

And as his brother had eloquently pointed out—self-torture. Penance.

Carmen laughed at something the valet said, and the sound calmed the anxious rumblings inside him. His hand went to the small of her back, and he found that touching her grounded him further.

It was one thing to torture himself. But to drag Carmen with him? He needed to heed Matt's words. Was all this bull-shit really worth it?

The entire evening had *horrible idea* written all over it.

When the dinners had been just him and Lara, they'd been fine. Still a little awkward, but they had fallen into their old friendship, or some semblance of it. After her husband, Dean —or Dickless Douche, as Matt referred to him—had started joining them, their dinners had become beyond awkward. They were now downright painful.

He felt like shit for dragging Carmen into this, but as he took her dainty hand and tucked it into the crook of his elbow, the tension eased from his shoulders. Not entirely, but it was noticeable. There was something about this woman that settled him, that soothed and reset him. He wasn't going to think too hard on it. Instead, he was going to be damn grateful for it. For her.

As they made their way from the valet stand to the restaurant's entrance, his thoughts ricocheted like pinballs in his brain. He hadn't been completely honest with Carmen when he'd explained his . . . friendship . . . with Lara. He'd played it off like he and Lara were simply exes who, years later, were now good friends. And they were.

Kind of.

When he and Lara had broken up, people had assumed that the decision had been mutual. He'd never corrected anyone. Because living that lie was easier than telling the truth—that he was a selfish prick, the narcissistic asshole his father always reminded him he was.

Lara had loved him wholeheartedly, and they'd been the perfect couple. Hell, his *father* had even loved her, and the man never approved of *anything* he did.

But Jake had been selfish. As the weeks had ticked closer to his graduation date, he'd focused more on Alvarez Technologies and getting his new company off the ground than on her. So much so that he'd decided to end things with Lara —breaking her goddamn heart.

Then, as if that hadn't been enough, shortly after, he'd destroyed her family.

"Hey." Carmen's whisper broke through his bleak thoughts.

She squeezed his forearm and brought them to a halt before the restaurant's front doors. He glanced down at her as she turned and faced him, lacing her fingers with his, her dark brown gaze steady and sure.

"I don't know what's going on in that head of yours, but I've got your back." Her hands squeezed his, and just like that, some of the darkness inside him eased. "Do you trust me, Jake?"

Without question. "One thousand percent, sweetheart." He exhaled, matching his breaths with hers. "In case I forget to say it later, thank you for being here with me."

This woman would never know how much her mere presence calmed him and made him step back from the ledge of self-hate.

His brother's words echoed in his mind—words that Matt had said before. But now, looking at this beautiful woman before him, they finally resonated.

"I've got you," she repeated.

His breath caught as she rolled onto the toes of her fire-engine-red stilettos and pressed her lips softly to his.

He didn't think twice. Before she could move away, he released one of her hands and snaked an arm around her waist, pulling her flush against him. Changing the angle of his head, he deepened their kiss, briefly sweeping his tongue against her lips. When they parted and her tongue met his, warmth replaced all the remaining darkness that lingered.

Pulling away, he pressed a kiss to her forehead and met her gaze. She grinned up at him. Part shy, part sweet, and a whole lot sexy.

"What are we doing, Carm?" His voice was low and

unsteady because this woman simply stole his breath. Whatever was between them—whatever was happening—was damn near electric.

"We're going to have a delicious dinner with your old girlfriend and her husband."

He grinned and dropped a quick kiss on her lips. That wasn't what he'd meant. And he knew she knew that. But he'd give it to her. Because this wasn't the time or the place for that conversation.

"Now, we could stay out here on the sidewalk and make out like teenagers all night, but I'd hate to waste this arm-candy outfit," Carmen murmured with a wink.

He linked his fingers with hers again and took a half step back, holding their arms out wide to admire said outfit. "A-plus, by the way, on the arm candy. If I haven't already said so, you look beyond amazing, Carm."

He wasn't lying. Not one bit. His friend looked hot. Crazy hot. Delicious hot.

Carmen had left her jacket in the car. The black, long-sleeved, V-neck dress she wore hit mid-thigh and fit her like a second skin, showing off her fantastic figure: petite, toned, and curvy in all the right spots. Her long black hair flowed like a curtain of silk down her back. He didn't know much about makeup, but hers was flawless and understated. Her beauty was absolute but subtle, unlike the bright red stilettos and stunning diamond necklace she wore.

"You look pretty amazing yourself, babe." She gave him a blatant once-over, then gestured toward the restaurant with her chin. "Ready to do this?"

He nodded, but right before they reached the door, she halted them once more.

"Look, I know there's a whole lot of complicated going on in that head of yours when it comes to her." His brow arched in question, and her eyes rolled, a disbelieving grin gracing her lips. "Seriously, Jake? You sneer every time you mention Lara's husband, and you look like you're going to hurl whenever her name is spoken."

His mouth dropped open. Well, shit.

"You have no poker face with me, remember?" she teased, the corners of her lips tipping up as she moved them through the restaurant's entrance. "But my point is, please don't forget that I have your back. I've got you."

Damn, this woman was simply fantastic. "Thank you, sweet—"

"Jake," a familiar voice called out.

Glancing around the lobby, he spotted Lara and her husband, Dean. Yeah, the mere sight of the other man had his molars grinding. He'd hoped that these get-togethers would become less awkward over time. They hadn't.

"Here we go," he murmured to Carmen with his hand on her back, ushering her forward.

"We've got this, babe," she whispered, her voice steady and confident, that practiced and perfect smile gracing her face.

Matt's voice echoed in his head yet again. Why the hell did he keep agreeing to meet Lara and Dean for dinner? For so long, he'd believed he owed her that much. But did he really? Was Matt right?

Had he and Lara really been the perfect couple? Or was it simply guilt coloring the past? Why had he placed Lara on a pedestal, held her up as the standard? One glance at the stunning woman next to him—the one who held his hand—had him questioning that. Not once had he compared Carmen to Lara. Ever.

Because Carmen was Carmen. Hands down, the coolest woman he knew. There was no comparison needed.

His insides stilled.

Holy shit. Was it that simple?

It wasn't.

It couldn't be.

And this moment sure as hell wasn't the time for some fucking existential crisis. He needed all his wits about him if he wanted to get through what he knew would be a shitshow of a dinner.

The squeeze of Carmen's hand pulled him out of his thoughts. As they approached the other couple, he tried to shake off his mood. There was no point going into the evening already dreading it. Generally, he was an optimistic guy. Perhaps things would be different this time, and dinner would be pleasant. Doubtful, but fuck it.

"It's so good to see you." Lara stepped toward Jake with open arms.

He hugged her briefly, then held out his hand to the other man. "Dean," he said as they shook hands. See, he could be mature, dammit. So what if he squeezed the other man's hand a little harder than he usually would? He wanted to pat himself on the back for even acknowledging the smarmy fucker.

Jake wasn't sure what it was about Dean that made him want to put his fist through the other man's face. He couldn't pinpoint a reason, but there was something about the guy he didn't trust, didn't respect. Something that absolutely rubbed him the wrong way. Maybe it was the subtle, passive-aggressive digs the man tossed his way or how he talked down to Lara.

Shit. Jake mentally winced. *Be. Nice.*

"Carmen," he said, returning his hand to the small of her back, "you remember Lara from college? And this is her husband, Dean."

"Of course," Carmen replied, her voice smooth as honey. "It's lovely to see you again, Lara." He bit back a chuckle when Carmen thrust her hand toward Lara for a handshake.

To anyone else, it looked like a simple, polite gesture, but Jake knew she'd done it to keep Lara at bay. A hugger Carmen was not.

"I can't believe it's been almost twenty years since we've seen each other," Lara replied, accepting the handshake.

"I like to round down," Carmen said with a light laugh. "Let's go with fifteen years. A decade, even."

"Dean Gilyard. It's a pleasure," the other man said, extending his hand to Carmen. "If you don't mind me saying, you definitely don't look as though you've been out of college for more than a decade."

Yup, there was no question. Jake wanted to punch the fucker.

"You're too kind," Carmen replied, that polite fundraising smile plastered across her lips. She released Dean's hand and gestured to the waiting hostess. "Shall we?"

Once seated with Carmen to his right, Lara to his left, and Dean across from him, they placed their drink orders—which were quickly delivered—and busied themselves with the menu.

"So, Jake," Dean began, "how's your little video game thing going?" And there it was, that smirk he wanted to put his fist through.

Before Jake could answer, Carmen leaned toward Dean, her voice taking on a conspiratorial quality. "Jake would never pat himself on the back, but I'm more than happy to brag about him. His company's latest launch was ridiculously successful." She picked up her wineglass, her eyes dancing over the rim, and dropped her voice lower as she leaned closer to the man. The prick didn't even try to be sly about looking down the front of her dress. "Like *eight figures* successful." She leaned back and subtly caressed her necklace.

It was a pendant on a delicate gold chain. He wasn't a

jeweler by any stretch of the imagination, but he knew the center stone, a flawless diamond, had to be at least five carats. It was surrounded by smaller diamonds that glittered every time they caught the light. The necklace was simple but ridiculously flashy, and it hung almost perfectly above her cleavage. And though she was implying otherwise to Dickless Douche, he was pretty sure it had been a graduation gift from her grandparents.

"Jake's been so busy since the launch, but of course, I'm not one to complain." She winked at Lara.

A look flashed over Dean's face that was somewhere between annoyance and anger. Jake couldn't quite tell. But whatever it was, it had him biting down on the inside of his cheek. Hard. Damn, Carmen was good.

<hr>

Carmen glanced around the table and kept a pleasant smile on her face. Holy shit. There was awkward. Then there was *this*. To be perfectly honest, she didn't even know what the hell *this* was.

She had vague memories of Lara. Like most college kids, she'd been so wrapped up in her own life that Lara hadn't really stood out. She recalled the blonde woman being chipper and all smiles. Basically, a nice girl.

Tonight, she'd wanted to dislike the woman on sight. Whatever mind-fuck Lara had going on with Jake had put Carmen on the defensive, making her want to shield him. Because Lara brought out a side of Jake that Carmen didn't like to see. It wasn't quite sadness, and it wasn't quite anger, but whatever that dark emotion was, it was completely directed at himself. And that was unacceptable.

She probably shouldn't have kissed him earlier on the sidewalk. But in that moment, she'd seen a war waging in his head. One that had torn at her heart. He'd looked so sad, so tortured . . . so damn lost.

She hadn't thought. She'd just acted. Anything to make that hurt go away.

Since she'd been able to distract him from whatever inner war he was fighting—if only for a few moments—it had been worth it.

Glancing at Lara across the table, Carmen reevaluated her preconceptions. It was difficult to outright dislike the woman. She'd expected someone cold and calculating, but it appeared that Lara hadn't changed much since college. She was still blonde, chipper, and all smiles. However, Carmen could see the strain behind that bright smile. Not to pat herself on the back—okay, maybe just a little—but she was *much* better at the fake smile than Lara.

Something about Lara and her husband wasn't right. It had taken only a few seconds for Carmen to realize that the man was a straight-up sleazebag. She obviously wasn't an expert on successful relationships—hell, she wouldn't even qualify as entry level; she was closer to the unpaid summer intern level—but even she could feel the tension between the couple. It was that palpable. So, she'd withhold judgment on Lara.

She internally cringed. Well, no. There was the fact that the woman *was* doing some sort of mind-fuck on Jake. So, correction—she'd *mostly* withhold judgment.

"My wife mentioned you work for Clean Water Campaign," Dean said. "What is that exactly?"

The man had a deep, soothing voice, like he should be a late-night radio host. Carmen would give him that. But that's all she'd give him. He made her skin crawl.

"It's a nonprofit organization founded by my grandparents decades ago. Our mission at CWC is to build clean drinking water systems in remote areas. It started with rural communities in the US, but now we're most active in South America and Southeast Asia."

"And your role there is what?" His gaze was assessing, as if he were trying to figure out if there was a brain in her head or if she was just a pretty face. "Fundraising and donations, I assume?"

Pretty face, it was.

Dick.

Meeting his gaze, it took all her willpower not to roll her eyes. "President, actually. We currently have twenty-two teams active around the globe. I used to be based internationally, but now that I'm back in Seattle, aside from overseeing the teams and working with each local government, I'll also be doing more—as you said—fundraising and donation work, along with heading up our expansion into new areas."

He opened his mouth—no doubt to spew something passive-aggressive and likely misogynistic—but she talked over him.

"We work in conjunction with a handful of other nonprofits, so it's a bit of a logistical juggling act to get all these groups and sub-teams moving around the world together. As you can imagine, each country has different requirements, so the back-end work is quite extensive. Not to mention all the different languages and dialects. It's an exciting challenge, though. I'm fortunate that not only have I already developed such good relationships with so many leaders and government officials around the globe, but I'm also fluent in multiple languages. It makes things easier." She lifted her shoulders in a casual shrug, like it was no big deal, and took a sip of her wine.

Then, she gave him a smile that was a cross between smarmy-polite and suck-it-douchebag. It was one of her favorites. "And what was it you do again, Dean? Insurance sales, right?"

His eyes narrowed the tiniest amount, as if he couldn't tell if she was being polite or verbally flipping him off.

Timing was on her side as their waiter approached the table, ready for their orders. Once they'd made their selections, seconds ticked by in silence, and the awkward tension returned. Not that it fazed her. She simply took another sip of her wine.

"Well, that's super impressive, Carmen," Lara said, filling the silence.

"Yes, quite impressive, Carmen. Beauty and brains," Dean replied. After another blatant ogle of her cleavage, he turned his attention to Jake. "You're a lucky man. That combination is not something you find every day. Trust me, I've looked."

Though Carmen prided herself on her excellent poker face, her brows shot to her hairline. Because wow. Just wow. What an asshole.

"Oh, Dean," Lara said with a nervous giggle before engaging Carmen again. "That must have been amazing—to travel and see all those different countries. I'd love to travel one day, to backpack through some beautiful foreign country."

"Don't be ridiculous, Lara," Dean said with a shake of his head and a chuckle that could only be described as demeaning. "You'd get lost in under an hour."

Lara's strained smile dimmed, and the tension at the table ratcheted up another couple of notches. Holy shit. Why the hell was Lara married to this man?

"Dean—" Jake began, but Carmen casually placed her hand on his, giving it a squeeze. She now understood why he sneered every time Dean's name was mentioned.

"Have you traveled a lot, Dean?" she asked, moving her and Jake's clasped hands to her lap. She ran her thumb over his knuckles, hoping the small gesture would soothe some of his tension.

"Well, obviously not as much as you, but yes, I've traveled quite a bit. Some business trips up to Canada, and I've done a few vacations down in Mexico. The high-end resorts only, of course."

"Of course." Somehow, she managed not to roll her eyes. Somehow. "Did you enjoy Mexico, Lara?"

The forced smile that greeted her question had Carmen wishing she could take it back. "Oh, I've never actually joined Dean on the Mexico trips." The woman paused to take a large gulp of wine. "Jake said you returned to town a few months ago. Are you glad to be back?"

Politeness be damned, Carmen took a moment to shoot Dean her queen-to-peasant look. She then turned to Lara, dismissing the worthless fucker entirely. "I am. Though it's been an adjustment for sure."

"Where are you living?"

Before she could respond, Jake interjected, "With me."

Wait, what? Her gaze swung to Jake's, and she blinked twice. It took every ounce of control she had to school her features, to not let her eyes bug out from her head. But she managed.

———————

Silence descended on the table once again.

Jake wanted to kick himself. Shit. What the hell had possessed him to say that Carmen was living with him?

When they'd discussed their fake-relationship agreement last weekend, nowhere in the conversation had cohabitation come up. Not once. Sure, she'd later joked about needing to move after walking in on her brother and Kate—hell, who wouldn't want to move after that—but he didn't think she'd been serious.

Maybe he'd said it because of how Dean looked at Carmen—part covetous, part menacing. Not only was the guy a dick for ogling Carm like that, but to do so in front of his fucking wife? Absolutely offensive.

But was Jake being an equal douche by, in essence, staking his claim on Carmen? Like this was some sort of pissing match?

A sharp jab to his shin brought his focus back to the silent table. He glanced at Carmen. Nothing in her expression gave away how she felt about his declaration. No shock, no annoyance, nothing. But he had no doubt that the sharp shin jab had come courtesy of her pointy, mile-high heels.

"Carmen's living with you?" Lara asked.

The hair on the back of Jake's neck rose at her tone. He couldn't exactly name it, but something akin to disappointment tinged her words. And from the way Dean's scowl deepened? Jake wasn't the only one who'd heard it.

What the hell was that about?

Releasing Carmen's hand, he reached for his wineglass and cleared his throat. "Well, to clarify, Carm's technically still living with her brother, Parker, and his fiancée, Kate." He shot the woman in question what he prayed was a hopeful and endearing—rather than apologetic—smile. He could bullshit with the best of them, but dammit if Lara and Dean didn't throw him off his game. "But I'm hoping to change that."

"Even though Jake and I have known each other a long time, this is all still pretty new, so we're not rushing anything." She placed her hand atop his on the table and squeezed, giving the other couple one of her practiced grins. "However, living with my brother and his fiancée is not my idea of fun. To say that they're in the honeymoon phase of their relationship would be a gross understatement. With an emphasis on *gross*. I don't know if either of you have siblings?" She grimaced, and a slight shudder shook her body.

He couldn't have stopped his chuckle if he'd tried. Because that shudder? Completely, one hundred percent real.

"Truly," Carmen continued, "no sibling should ever witness the displays I've had the misfortune of seeing."

Dean laughed, and Jake was taken aback. In all the times they'd gotten together for these ridiculous dinners, he'd never heard the other man laugh. Not once.

"I have a brother and two sisters," Dean said, his smile going from creepy to something that looked genuine. Or as genuine as the asshole could get. "You couldn't pay me enough to live with any of them and their significant others. Especially when they were first starting out. That says a lot, too, because there isn't much I wouldn't do for the right price."

And just like that, the guy was back to being a dick. What Lara saw in the man was a complete mystery. Yet every three months or so, Jake came back to these dinners. So who was really the idiot at the table?

The waiters arrived and delivered their meals. Jake didn't bother holding back an eye roll when Dean immediately complained about the temperature of his steak and sent it back. He felt Carmen's hand squeeze his thigh, and he caught the humor in her gaze.

Yes, these dinners were painful. It wasn't just because Dean was a sack of shit. The entire thing he had with Lara was awkward. He'd known it, felt it. However, having Carmen witness it firsthand brought the complete dysfunctionality to light and showed him just how fucked up it really was.

And yes, he agreed to go to these damn dinners out of

guilt, even knowing they would never get any better. But he owed it to Lara to show up.

At least, he'd thought he did.

Now, he wasn't so sure.

What he did know was that this time around, having Carmen by his side? Having her expertly put Dean back in his place with a polite jab? Well, she made it all a little less painful. That's for damn sure.

The second the valet closed her door, Carmen exhaled loudly. "Holy shit, Jake."

He remained silent as he put his car into gear, checked his blind spot, and pulled into the street. His thoughts were all over the place. Not surprising since spending time with Lara and Dean dredged up all sorts of shit.

"When you said you wanted company at dinner because Lara's husband was an ass, I wasn't expecting *that*. I mean, seriously? There's misogynistic asshole. Then there's that guy. What was up with all the dick-swinging he was doing with you? You're a goddamn multimillionaire, Jake. He's in freaking insurance sales!"

He chuckled as he navigated the downtown Bellevue streets toward the freeway. "There is nothing incorrect about anything you just said."

He tried not to think too hard about why Carmen's anger and defense of him warmed his insides. The woman beside him had made the evening more than tolerable; she'd made it . . . better. Swirling thoughts and emotions and all.

"The jackass belittled her every chance he got. Then the fucker tried to belittle *me,* and hell the fuck no."

That brought another chuckle. Hell the fuck no, indeed. Carmen didn't let anyone mess with her. "Again, nothing incorrect about anything you said." He paused to merge onto the freeway that would bring them back to Seattle. "I must admit, sweetheart, you putting that douche in his place was worth footing the bill tonight."

Though he couldn't see it, he was pretty sure she rolled her eyes.

"I swear to God, the man literally picked out the most expensive things on the menu and then had the nerve to be all 'How's your little gaming company going?' to you. Fucker," she spat.

Jake laughed. He couldn't help it. She was so damn cute. And after that god-awful, uncomfortable dinner, it felt good to laugh.

"Who the hell sends back a well-done steak because it's 'not done enough'? The damn thing was basically charred." Disgust dripped from every word. "*Then* the little bitch couldn't even drink his whisky without wincing. And it was Yamazaki—some of the best shit out there!"

Was it wrong of him to think it was a ridiculous turn-on that she knew her whisky? Because not only was this whole conversation hilarious, but it was also fucking hot.

"I mean, come on, babe. First off, if you wince when you take a sniff of whisky, you probably shouldn't be drinking it in public. Then, you don't slam the damn drink. It's Yamazaki! You sip it like you know what the fuck you're doing. Christ."

His abs were getting a workout from all the laughing. Not to mention, he needed to find a subtle way to adjust his dick. "You have to admit, sweetheart, that watching his eyes water when he threw it all back in one big gulp was hilarious."

Her laughter filled the car, and he wasn't going to lie to himself—the sound did something to him. It was more than just a turn-on, more than a calming force . . . it was just . . . more.

Exiting the freeway, he slowed his car as they approached

a red light. He leaned his head back onto the headrest with a sigh. For the most part, it had been an uncomfortable and shit dinner. Correction—having Dean at the table had been shit; the actual food had been fantastic.

Now that it was just the two of them, he didn't want the night to end. Glancing at Carmen, he found her watching him. Some sort of mischief sparkled in her eyes, and it had him grinning, had all thoughts of Dean, Lara, and their awkward dinner evaporating. "Nightcap and debrief?"

"Yes, please." A matching grin was aimed back at him. "It's late, and God knows what I could be walking into at this hour." She shuddered.

"There is that." He laughed, then winced, not wanting to picture two of his closest friends in any sort of sexual situation. The light turned green, and he made his way home. "You know, you're more than welcome to crash at my place any time."

"There is that," she chuckled, mimicking his words.

A few minutes later, Jake pulled into his building's underground parking garage. The elevator ride up was comfortably silent. His hand remained at her lower back, his thumb tracing nonsensical patterns along her spine. Her dress was so damn soft. Probably not nearly as soft as her skin—

Whoa. *Calm your shit, Alvarez.*

Sneaking a glance at the woman beside him, a grin tugged at his lips. She was a knockout, that's for damn sure. Just because they were pretending to be a couple didn't mean he couldn't acknowledge that. Right?

He mentally grimaced. He could try to lie to himself all he wanted. It wouldn't change the fact that the more time he spent with Carmen, the more he was attracted to her. And not in a pretend kind of way.

The elevator dinged when it reached the top floor. As he ushered her into his condo, he motioned to the couch with his head. "Relax and get comfortable. I'll get us some drinks. Wine or whisky, darlin'?"

"Whisky, please. After Dean's pathetic whisky-drinking display, I feel like we need to pay our respects to the whisky gods."

Yeaaah. This gorgeous woman talking whisky? Hot.

He made quick work of pouring their drinks, then snagged the bottle of Macallan as he made his way to join her.

Lounging in the corner of the couch, she had her legs resting partially on the center cushion. Her ankles were elegantly crossed—the red soles of her mile-high heels on display. She made grabby hands at his approach. He chuckled as he handed over the glass, placed the bottle on the coffee table, and sat on the opposite end of the couch, one leg hitched up so he could face her.

"So, Ms. Cunningham." He paused to take a sip of his drink. "What are your thoughts on the first outing of 'Jake and Carmen'"—he air-quoted their names—"as a couple?"

She took her own sip, then waved a hand in front of her face. "See? No wincing. That's how it's done."

Damn, she was cute.

She sat straighter, moving her back to the side cushion and dropping her legs to the floor. When she crossed one leg over the other, he couldn't help but notice how the hem of her dress skimmed higher up on her thighs.

She cleared her throat, and when he met her gaze, her right eyebrow was arched. Her eyes danced with amusement and . . . holy shit, was that interest? Well, damn. He smirked and didn't bother hiding his blatant ogling.

She cleared her throat again, and her brow dropped. Her features schooled back into a business mode of sorts—albeit a more playful one. And *playful* was a side of Carmen he was sure many people didn't see.

"Overall, Mr. Alvarez, I feel as though the evening went well. I think we were believable and convincing as a couple without being over the top."

"I agree." His eyes roamed over her again before he met her gaze and shot her a wink. "Were you okay with the amount of PDA?" His grin grew—as did his dick—at the soft flush that stole across her face.

"I was." She sipped her drink. "I thought it was acceptable for the environment and occasion. Again, I think we were believable. Natural, even."

"I agree," he repeated. "The hand-holding was a nice touch. As were the thigh squeezes." He winked again, then waggled his brows.

She snickered. "I hate to break it to you, babe, but I'd say the thigh squeezes I gave you were more on the don't-go-all-mob-boss-and-get-us-kicked-out-of-this-restaurant spectrum rather than actual lovey-dovey squeezes."

"And the kick to the shin?"

"Oh, definitely the former." She laughed. "Sorry about that. Reflex."

He tilted his head in question.

"I'm sure it'll come as no surprise that I'm really good at controlling my reactions," she explained. "If I'm shocked, you probably won't know. Because my face?" She waved her hand in front of said example of exquisite, perfect symmetry. "Absolute control. But the rest of me?" She wiggled her fingers and pointed toward her feet. "It's my tell."

He laughed and raised his glass to her. "That's very self-aware of you to recognize that."

Her head was shaking as she brought her glass to her lips. "Not really. It's calculating of me. I've been working to shore up my weaknesses. What good is your face not reacting when the rest of your body does, right? But that me-and-you-living-together comment? *That* was a doozie, babe."

He nodded a concession to her last point, but he wasn't sure what to make of her other comment. Reactions—honest reactions—weren't a weakness. At least not in his mind. But he knew how important control was to her. He was just thankful she wasn't maintaining those facades with him. Because this version of Carmen Cunningham sitting on his couch? With a whisky in her hand and a soft, playful smile on her lips?

Sheer. Fucking. Perfection.

Speaking of honesty . . .

"Have I told you how beautiful you look tonight?"

"Why, thank you, Mr. Alvarez." She tossed her hair over her shoulder with an exaggerated wink.

"I'm serious, Carm," he said, reaching for the Macallan. "You're absolutely stunning. When I picked you up tonight, you knocked the breath out of me." That was probably too much honesty on his part. But it wasn't a lie.

He topped off his glass, then realized the room had gone silent. He swung his gaze to Carmen, who was simply staring at him. With a furrowed brow.

He held up the bottle and nodded to her near-empty glass. She shook her head, but the questioning look remained.

"What is it, sweetheart?"

Her lips pursed. "I guess I'm having a hard time telling when you're being serious or joking around." His brow raised in question, and she shrugged. "I mean, it's just us here. You don't need to lay it on so thick."

Mentally, he reared back. Because what the fuck?

Placing his drink on the coffee table, he leaned forward, snagged her glass, and placed it next to his. He resettled on the couch, but closer to her this time, one leg still hitched onto the cushion so he faced her.

"Carm, I need you to hear me right now, okay?" Her eyes

widened at his tone. He knew he sounded firm—borderline aggressive—but he needed her to listen. *Really* hear him. "You and I are pretending to be a couple for the next few months. So, yes, that technical 'couple' aspect of all of this is fake. But, sweetheart, you know what's not fake?"

He held her gaze until she gave a slight shake of her head. The doubt swirling in her dark brown eyes killed him. Absolutely slayed him.

"The fact that I have two fucking eyes." His gaze traveled from the top of her head to the tips of her toes and back again, and she remained absolutely still. She was better at shoring up her weakness than she gave herself credit for. "I respect you, Carm, you know that, right?"

He waited until she gave a slight nod.

"You're one of my closest friends."

Her gaze softened the slightest bit, and she gave another nod. "For me too," she said, her words barely a whisper.

"I think you're crazy smart, and all your accomplishments are amazing, though not surprising. At all," he added with a grin.

The slight upward tilt of her lips gave him courage. Because he was about to blow things up between them. But honest reactions, right?

"I think how your mind works is almost as sexy as you are."

Her eyes heated, and her gaze dropped to his lips before shooting back up. His dick twitched, and he leaned toward her.

"Almost," he murmured.

A smirk began to play on her lips, and the lust swirling in her eyes had all his blood rushing south.

"Because, darlin', you in that smokin' hot dress? Those fucking sexy-as-sin heels? All that luscious hair I want to wrap around my fist? That—"

His words cut off as her lips crashed against his. She tasted like whisky and a sweetness that was all Carmen. He yanked her body flush against his, and all thoughts fled his brain. All he knew was that his greedy hands were full of this woman who'd somehow gotten under his skin.

<hr>

Carmen launched herself at him. With her chest pressed flush against his, her lips ravaged his mouth. She knelt on the sofa—her knees pressed together between the cushion back and his rock-hard thigh—at an awkward half-on-his-lap and half-off angle. But she didn't care.

A part of her thought she should be embarrassed. A few compliments and some heated looks, and she'd thrown her body against his. Literally.

Up until those last moments, things had been fine. Normal, even. They'd laughed, they'd teased, they'd flirted. However, somewhere along the line, his flirty comments had no longer been said in jest. He'd meant them.

Every word he'd said had sent a wave of heat through her body. Every syllable had made her blood tingle for him. Every breath had made her resolve to keep things friendly between them crumble.

Yeah, this was a horrible idea. But again, she didn't care.

This man did something to her. Those compliments? Those heated looks? They'd lit her on fucking fire.

Parts of her she'd thought dead were sizzling with desire. For this man. For Jake.

She needed him. More than her next breath. And she needed him *now*.

Her heart raced, and she poured everything she had into their kiss. It wasn't gentle and soft. It was demanding and exploring. Every nip of her teeth and every thrust of her tongue was met with equal fervor.

But his hands were a contradiction. While their mouths devoured each other with frantic desperation, his hands soothed down her sides, as if memorizing her every curve. His fingers cruised over her thighs and played with the bottom of her short dress. He skimmed his hands down her legs to her calves, then to her ankles.

"These heels are so damn sexy," he murmured, then leaned back and shot her a mischievous grin. Her insides clenched in response. "But darlin', they're dangerous." Before she could blink, he'd removed both shoes and tossed them to the floor.

Her laugh morphed into a moan as his hands moved back up her legs to her thighs. Catching the hem of her dress, he yanked it up and over her hips. She gasped as he effortlessly lifted her and adjusted their positions so she sat astride him. Goosebumps erupted over her body when he gripped her bare ass and squeezed.

"Fuck," he hissed, biting down on her neck, his fingers tracing the tiny string that disappeared between her cheeks. He rocked her against his hard length, and she moaned. She spread her knees wider and pressed her core closer. When he fisted her hair at the base of her scalp, she groaned his name and ground down harder against his straining cock.

She needed him. Now.

Breathless, she tore her mouth from his, pulling slightly away. With one hand, she stroked him over his slacks, cupping and feeling each delicious hard inch of him. Her other hand popped the top button of his pants.

Tingles erupted over her scalp as the fist he still had buried in her hair tightened. He yanked her closer, and his mouth slammed down on hers, their tongues dueling.

Somewhere far away, a noise that wasn't their moans of passion trilled.

"Shit," Jake muttered, resting his forehead against hers.

"Your phone," she said on an exhale. The ringtone, which she recognized as his brother's, was obscenely loud in the quiet room.

"No," he murmured. "It's just Matt." Then both his hands cupped her face, and their mouths met again. Soft and gentle now, as if they had all the time in the world. His tongue swirled, and she melted into him. She couldn't help it. She was weak. But she didn't care because she wanted to feel that tongue against hers. Hell, all over her. In her.

The ringing continued, but they blocked it out.

Then it was joined by a different ring. *Her* phone. When it stopped, there was a moment of silence. Then hers rang again, this time with a different tone.

The variety of ringtones had her stilling. Chills erupted down her spine that had nothing to do with the man she still sat astride. While her heart galloped, uneasiness bloomed in her gut, and she pulled away. "Hang on." An unsteady breath left her. "It's Parker and Blake."

Jake's phone rang again, and his body tensed beneath hers. He met her gaze, and worry replaced the heat; concern replaced the desire. "Something's wrong."

She scrambled off his lap, quickly righted her dress, and reached for their phones. Jake's phone was ringing again— Matt—and she tossed it to him. She settled back onto the couch next to him, and her already quickened pulse began to race.

As Jake listened to his brother, his lips pressed in a firm line. Whatever Matt was saying made his jaw clench tighter as each second ticked by. Trepidation crawled over her skin like tiny little spiders. She pulled up her own brother's name on her phone, and it connected a second after hitting the call button.

"Holy fuck, Carm," Parker barked. "Where are you? Are you okay?"

She reared back. The panic in her brother's voice morphed the trepidation into fear. "What's going on, Park? What's—"

"Where the fuck are you, Carm?" he shouted.

Her jaw dropped, and she was shocked silent. Her heart knocked hard in her chest. She'd heard that terror in Parker's tone once before: when Kate had been kidnapped.

Before she could form a response, Jake took the phone from her hands.

"She's fine, Parker. We're at my place . . . yeah, come on over." Her eyes were glued to Jake, and she could only hear Parker's muffled responses. "Dude, just shut up and come over, okay? Matt's on his way too . . . yeah. Later, man." He tossed her phone onto the coffee table, and then, with a loud exhale, scrubbed his hands over his face.

Her heart beat wildly in the quiet room as she waited for Jake to say something. Anything.

Silence ticked by and worry churned in her belly. Resting his hands atop his head, he let out a weary sigh, his handsome face the picture of uneasiness.

"Jake?" The lone word was barely a whisper.

"Come here, sweetheart," he murmured as he scooped her up and sat her across his lap. Wrapping his arms around her, he tucked her sideways against his chest, his chin resting atop her head. "Matt's on his way over. He didn't tell me all the specifics, but there was an accident with your car."

Startled, she sat up, meeting his gaze. "My car?"

"Yeah. The gist was it was stolen earlier today and then lit on fire."

Her brows shot to her hairline, and her jaw dropped.

"Holy shit. That's awful." She frowned. That was horrible . . . but it didn't add up. "But that doesn't explain Parker. My brother was panicked, like he was truly scared."

Jake met her gaze, and the dread and worry on his face sent chills scattering down her spine. His arms tightened around her, but it did nothing to ease his next words.

"That's because when the firefighters put out the flames, they found a body in your car."

CHAPTER TWELVE

Carmen tried to scramble up from Jake's lap, but his arms tightened around her. Her heart thunked hard in her chest, and she leaned back into him, his solid body supporting her.

Holy shit.

There was a dead body in the car. *Her* car. Well, technically, it was Parker's car, but still.

Unfortunately, that was all Jake knew. Before she could fully wrap her brain around how that could've possibly happened, chaos erupted.

Matt arrived, grim-faced and solemn, letting himself in with an apparent spare key. Parker and Kate burst through the door immediately after him, with Blake hot on their heels.

Parker rushed to her the moment he spotted her. She was immediately yanked off Jake's lap and enveloped in a bone-crushing hug. "Holy fuck, Carm," he muttered into her hair. "We just got you fucking back. I thought . . ." His last words wobbled, and his arms squeezed harder.

Oh, her sweet, sweet brother. She could barely breathe, but that was okay. Because focusing on Parker instead of herself and the first inklings of fear tickling her insides? That she could do.

"Hey," she said, smoothing a hand down his back. She pulled away and framed his face in her hands. "I'm perfectly fine, little brother. I promise." She held his green gaze, and her heart squeezed as she watched him battle the fear raging on his face. "I'm fine, Park."

He gave a slight nod and let out a shaky breath. She pulled his face closer and leaned her forehead to his, like they'd done when they'd been kids and one of them had been upset. "Thank you for worrying."

"Move, fucker," Blake grumbled, elbowing Parker in the side before pulling her into a hug. "Glad you're okay." He dropped a kiss on the top of her head before letting her go. "You scared the shit out of us."

"I'm sorry for that," Carmen said, meeting the eyes of everyone gathered in Jake's great room. "But, you guys, I'm in the dark. I don't understand what's happening." She turned toward Matt. "What's going on?"

Matt nodded to the living room area. "Why don't we all sit first?"

Once everyone was seated—she, Jake, and Matt on the couch, Parker and Kate on the loveseat, and Blake on the matching recliner—Matt lifted his chin to Parker. "Why don't you start?"

Parker nodded and leaned forward, elbows on his knees. "Two cops came into The Spotted Dog tonight—"

"Wait," Carmen interrupted. A glance at her watch said it was close to eleven. On a Saturday night. Shit. "Shouldn't you guys still be at the pub?"

Her brother's eyes narrowed, annoyance clear on his face.

But she'd take his annoyance over his fear any day. "Don't be dumb, sis. Anyway, the cops came in asking if I was the owner of the Audi. I obviously said yes, and then they told me it had been found on fire just off I-5. 'Engulfed in flames' may have been their exact words."

"He then," Blake said, picking up the story, "proceeded to freak the fuck out—"

"As did you, motherfucker," Parker spat.

"As did I, brother," Blake replied, his words hollow and solemn. "As did I." A shadow darkened his blue eyes, and her heart clenched. They'd truly been scared for her. "Park said the Audi wasn't in the garage when he got home and explained to them how you were using it. We both thought you'd gotten in a wreck."

"And then," Parker continued, "the cops asked if I'd heard from you. When I hadn't, they said I needed to try to get a hold of you because there was a possible body—"

Her stomach clenched, and her eyes filled when her brother's voice cracked on the last word. Holy. Shit.

She went to her brother and gave him a hug, squeezing the crap out of him. Then she did the same with her cousin. She shot Kate a grateful smile when the woman snuggled into Parker and wrapped him in her arms.

"I'm okay, you guys. Promise," she said, sitting back on the couch next to Jake. He slipped his arm around her as she turned her attention to Matt, who was seated on the other side of him. "What else can you tell us?"

"I was at the station with Detectives Vasquez and Apone when the fire department called about the possibility of a victim being in the car. Vasquez and Apone are solid detectives. Their original assumption, since the car was parked on the freeway shoulder, was some sort of car malfunction. They were still waiting for info on the vehicle's plates when I left the station. Vasquez called me a little bit later when she found out it was Parker's car." He turned his attention to Parker. "She knew that we all know each other." He turned back to Carmen. "I let her know that you were using the Audi, but since I was almost certain you were out with Jake tonight, someone must have stolen it from your place—"

"Wait," Carmen said, her mind flashing to earlier in the evening. "After I ran my errands this afternoon, I didn't park the car back in the garage. A lawn care truck was blocking the driveway, so I ended up parking in the street in front of the house." She shrugged. "Not sure if that matters."

"It might," Matt replied. "Anyway, they were still waiting for confirmation on whether there was someone in the car when they went to talk to Parker. A guy at the station called me when it was confirmed, so I tried calling Jake a few times, but he wasn't answering."

"Park and I also tried calling you when the cops were at the pub," Blake said.

"Sorry about that," she murmured, shaking her head. All of it was so unbelievable. "We'd just gotten back from dinner and were chatting and stuff . . ." She let out a deep exhale. Holy shit. She and Jake had been making out like teenagers while everyone had been panicking about her whereabouts, about whether she was even alive.

"I know I speak for everyone," Kate began, "when I say we're just so thankful you're okay, Carm. I mean, it's tragic that someone else was in the car, but . . ."

"But we're beyond grateful it wasn't you," Blake finished.

"I'm glad it wasn't me, too." Then she winced, glancing at her brother. "Sorry about your car, Park."

"Fuck that," he scoffed. "It's a fucking car. *You* are my sister."

"I know Vasquez and Apone will want to talk with you," Matt said. "Can I give them your contact info?"

She nodded. "Of course."

He glanced down when his phone buzzed, then rose. "Excuse me for a second."

A collective sigh hit the room when Matt turned down the hallway, speaking softly into his phone.

"Holy shit," Jake said on an exhale before standing. He placed his hand on her shoulder, and she glanced up. "Can I get you anything, sweetheart?"

She shook her head. "I'm good, thanks."

He turned to the rest of the group as he walked backward. "You guys want anything to drink?"

"I'll take a beer if you've got an extra," Blake called out.

Before Jake made it to the kitchen, Matt returned from the hallway and halted him with a hand to his chest.

Dread turned her stomach when Matt's eyes locked on her. "It appears we have a bit of a problem."

"Define *problem*," she said.

"Vasquez and Apone gave me the okay to talk to you about this. They're still wrapping some stuff up with the fire department, so they most likely won't be out to see you until sometime tomorrow. But they'll definitely need to talk with you, Carm."

Drinks forgotten, Jake sat back on the couch next to her and took her hand in his. "Why do they need to talk to her? It's Parker's car."

He'd asked the question that had been on the tip of her tongue.

Matt remained silent for a moment, as if he were carefully choosing his words. When he finally spoke, Carmen wished with everything she was that he hadn't spoken at all.

"Because they told me their car malfunction theory was shot to shit. Like I said, they're still checking out a couple things, but there's a possibility the deceased has a connection to Carmen."

Her blood chilled, and her breath locked in her chest.

Jake, Parker, and Blake all surged to their feet. All three men sputtered with shock and outrage, demanding an explanation.

Carmen could barely make out their words. They were all talking at once, but that wasn't the issue. Her brain was refusing to comprehend anything, and her panicked heartbeat was deafening in her ears.

An arm wrapped around her shoulders, and she took a breath when it squeezed. "Kate," she whispered to the woman beside her, "I don't understand what's happening."

"I know, sweetie," her friend murmured. "But we've all got your back."

"You guys!" Matt yelled over the din. "Shut the fuck up already, so I can tell you what I know."

Her pulse raced, and she fought to control her breathing, to push back the budding panic. She didn't want to know. Nothing good could come from knowing.

"The deceased," Matt began, "was found in the front passenger seat. They're looking to confirm ID now, but the victim appears to be female. Between five feet and five-five and roughly between one-ten and one hundred forty pounds. Possible black hair."

Goosebumps rose on her skin, and Kate's arm tightened around her shoulders. Okay. So she and the woman in the car were similar sizes. It was just a coincidence.

Matt's brown eyes were intense when they caught hers. Her stomach rolled.

Holy shit. It better be a coincidence.

"The victim's wrists and ankles were both restrained with handcuffs."

Wrists. Ankles. Handcuffs. His words came at her like jabs.

Her vision tunneled, focusing solely on Matt. His mouth continued to move, but she couldn't hear him. The deafening pulse of her racing heart filled her head and was louder than ever. His eyes narrowed, his familiar face filling with concern.

Then all she could see was the dark and shadow-filled cement room. All she could feel were the cuffs, the metal digging into her flesh, the tight, unyielding restraints rubbing against her broken and bleeding skin. All she could hear were the lashes. The whip flying through the air and the shocking, jarring *thwack!* of contact, immediately followed by fire scorching down her back.

She couldn't catch her breath. Each shallow inhale filled her senses with moldy, dank, putrid air. The tang of urine, vomit, and sticky sweat had her stomach rolling, threatening to expel its contents.

She tried to gasp for breath, but there was nothing.

Nothing but dark and pain and fear . . .

***

Ice shot down Jake's spine as Carmen stilled, her face paling to an unnatural ashen shade. A glance at Kate, who sat next to her on the couch, showed he wasn't the only one who'd noticed.

A split second later, he was kneeling in front of Carmen. His hands cupped her face. Leaning toward her, he tilted her head slightly up until they were nose to nose. "Carmen?"

He searched her eyes, and his stomach twisted. She was looking at him. But not. "Carmen," he called again, louder this time, unease surging through him.

She blinked. That was it. Her brown eyes widened the tiniest of fractions, but nothing was there.

She swayed, and not knowing if she would pass out, he scooped her up from the couch and took her seat, setting her across his lap, one arm supporting her back, the other encircling her.

On his next breath, Parker was on the couch next to them, seated where Kate had been. His hands clasped his sister's lifeless fingers.

"Carmen?" Parker whispered. Then he shook her hands. Hard. "Carmen!"

Jake wanted to clobber him for being so rough with her, but before he could reprimand his friend or pull her away from him, she jerked in his arms. Her body stiffened, and she yanked her hands away from her brother.

"Christ, Park," she hissed, shoving him away. "Why the fuck are you shouting in my face?"

Parker reared back, his arms limp at his sides, and the already silent room stilled. Anguish and confusion were the only words for the look on his friend's face. Two emotions that were reflected by everyone in the room.

Carmen's body tensed further, and he pulled her back to his chest. Her heart hammered against him, and his arms tightened around her. "Easy, sweetheart," he murmured into her ear. "You left us there for a few moments. Gave us all a scare."

She pulled away, and her gaze swung to his. "What?"

He kept one arm across her back and brought his other to her face. Palming her cheek, he traced her clenched jaw with his thumb. "When Matt was talking about your torched car and the victim inside it, he must have said something . . . something that had you . . . zoning out."

Her eyes narrowed, and a look he couldn't read flashed over her face. Then her shoulders straightened, and she turned to her brother.

"Sorry. I didn't mean to yell at you." She glanced at

everyone around the room, then a soft, tiny smile graced her face. A smile that had his unease ramping up with a vengeance. Because that smile was fake as fuck. "Sorry, guys. It's been a long day." She turned to Matt, who stood with his arms crossed over his chest, a look of concern and . . . wariness on his face. "I know that's a shitty excuse. You and Jake were both at the gym before five this morning, too, and you guys aren't being dicks."

"Yeah, well, we'd just gotten there." His brother had schooled his expression, but Jake could still feel his twin's uncertainty. "You'd already put in a ten-miler."

"Only eight," she clarified.

Matt shook his head. "Anything over five miles—especially at the ass crack of dawn—gets rounded up to ten."

It was safe to say that he knew his twin well. This small talk Matt was doing with Carm? Yeah. His brother wasn't buying her bullshit either.

"It's late," Matt said with a sigh. He nodded toward the front door before grabbing his jacket from the metal coat stand he'd made. "I'm going to head out. Vasquez and Apone will most likely want to meet up with you tomorrow morning, Carm. Try and get some rest tonight, okay?"

She nodded, but her slight frame was still tense in his arms. "Matt?" She waited until his brother faced her. "Lots of women are my height and size. It's most likely just a coincidence."

The way his brother looked at her—as if he were biting back his words—had dread filling Jake's stomach.

"It's just a coincidence, Matt," she repeated, her voice firm, her words sharp.

"It's not, Carm."

She jolted as if she'd been struck. "You don't know that," she snapped.

Matt looked like he was debating something in his head. He ran a hand through his closely cropped hair and growled.

Actually growled.

Fuck.

The dread in his gut grew.

"There was a picture of you by the body, Carm. This wasn't a fucking coincidence."

CHAPTER THIRTEEN

Shocked silence filled the room. For five seconds. Then all hell broke loose. Her brother and cousin were both shouting at once. Jake's arms tightened around her, and though he didn't say anything, his body vibrated with . . . anger? Worry? She didn't quite know what, but it wasn't anything good.

Carmen's mind whirled. She knew she should probably be scared, but she was too confused, too shocked, to process the bomb that Matt had just dropped. There was a picture of *her* by the body? In the burned car?

What. The. Fuck.

Images flickered in her head of that dark room, the handcuffs that tore at her skin, the—

No! Focus, dammit—focus on now!

Exhaling, she pushed the twisted memories back. "How is that possible, Matt?" Though her words were barely a whisper, they silenced the room.

"Honestly, I'm not sure. All I know is that Apone said there was a photo of you next to the body. They should have more details tomorrow."

It didn't make sense. Her analytic mind latched on to the discrepancy like a lifeline. "The car was on fire. Engulfed, right? How the hell would a picture survive that?"

Matt's hands scrubbed over his face, and he let out a sigh that sounded part weary, part furious. "The photos were in some sort of fireproof envelope." He held his hands out in a helpless gesture. "I'm sorry, Carmen, but that's all I know."

Bile rose in her throat.

Photos.

Plural.

"Holy shit, Matt," Parker said. "Can we get some sort of extra security at the house?"

The words flew around her, but they weren't computing. What the hell was happening?

"Yeah," Matt replied. "I'm sure we can get extra patrols to go by. Fuck, if my captain doesn't approve it, I'll sit in front of your goddamn house myself tonight."

"No," Jake snapped.

It was only one word, but it held a world of menace in it. For some reason, it eased the fear and panic swirling within her the tiniest amount.

"Carm's staying with me," he said.

The hand he'd rested on her lower back snaked up her spine, and she couldn't hold back her flinch. But when it settled at the nape of her neck, and he gently squeezed, the fear and panic warring in her eased a little bit more.

Parker's face scrunched in obvious confusion, and his fists slammed onto his hips. "What?"

She nodded and leaned back into Jake. "I'm staying here tonight. In fact, I'm moving in with Jake."

Her brother's face turned a concerning shade of red. "What?"

"Yeah," she said, untangling herself from Jake's arms and standing. "Before all this"—she waved her hands in a circular motion—"we'd been talking about it. Now it makes even more sense."

"Dude, calm the fuck down." Blake placed one hand on Parker's shoulder while the other patted his chest. "You're gonna give yourself a goddamn heart attack." He turned his blue eyes on her. "Explain."

Everyone's concern was evident. If she were being honest, she was worried too.

No, not worried. More like completely freaked the fuck out. Matt's earlier revelation about the handcuffs had triggered her. Big time. And that had been before the photo bombshell.

But that didn't matter because there was a bigger issue. Bigger than her trembling hands that she held tightly fisted at her sides. Bigger than the bile that still lingered in her throat. Bigger than her erratic heartbeat.

Kate.

While the room had descended into chaos with Matt's revelation about the photo, Carmen's mind had whirled, desperately trying to process his words.

But she'd noticed Kate.

The woman had sat frozen on the loveseat, still as a statue. With every passing breath and tick of the clock, Kate had grown paler, her hands clasped tighter on her lap, and her knuckles whiter. Until she'd risen in silence and walked woodenly toward the hallway powder room with her arms wrapped around her middle. In the confusion and chaos of the room, the guys hadn't noticed.

But Carmen had. While her own world was getting rocked, something was happening with Kate. Something that worried her.

Was she deflecting? A little bit. She couldn't quite wrap her head around what was happening, what Matt was saying. Truthfully, the very last thing she wanted in all this mayhem was for everyone's focus to be on *her*. She was off-kilter, unable to control her reactions, and the damn flashbacks pushing against her mind left her unsteady.

So, while Carmen was deflecting, she was doing it with purpose. Something was going on with her friend. Something not right. Kate had already been through too much.

While Carmen knew her little brother loved her, she also knew his number one priority was Kate. As it should be. Whatever was going on with her friend, she needed Parker to focus on Kate and *not* her.

Carmen addressed Blake, as he seemed to be the calmer of the two. "I've been thinking about moving out for a while, and now it makes sense. Jake and I were talk—"

"The fuck you're moving out," Parker growled.

She glanced at the hallway Kate had disappeared down, then turned to her brother and snagged his hands. "Listen to me. I cannot be in the house with you and Kate right now—"

"Jesus Christ, Carm, we'll stop messing around outside our room, okay?"

"No, Park. It's not that," she whisper-yelled, shaking her head. "Whatever just happened—right now—upset her."

His head swiveled to the empty loveseat, and his eyes widened. Worry flashed over his face before he scanned the room. "Where the hell did she go?"

Carmen nodded toward the hallway, and some of the tension in his frame eased. "She's upset, and she's still getting over all that god-awful shit she went through. Park, I'm not going to subject her to detectives coming over and dredging up bad memories." She sure as hell knew all about bad memories, and that was the last thing she wanted for her friend. "I don't want *anything* to possibly trigger her and set her back—because all this shit? It will."

"Fuck, I don't want that either." Letting go of her hands, he raked his fingers through his hair. "But dammit, Carm, my car that *you've* been using for months was set on fire. Purposely. With someone in it who was not only fucking handcuffed but also the same size as you. And the fucking photo, Carm..."

Sheer anguish colored her brother's face, and goosebumps tore over her skin.

"I know," she whispered. "It's crazy."

"It's beyond fucked up," Blake interjected.

She exhaled. "Look, Jake and I were talking about moving in together anyway." Both Parker's and Blake's brows rose, and she fought a cringe. It wasn't technically a lie, dammit. "With all this new, crazy, fucked-up shit, I don't want to take the chance of you or Kate getting hurt. Park, you can't possibly want her in any danger."

"Of course I don't! But I don't want *you* in danger either!"

Neither did she.

"What about Jake, huh?" Parker asked. "You want to put *him* in danger?"

Her insides began to vibrate—fear and adrenaline begging to be released—but she somehow tamped it down. She caught Jake's steady gaze, and when he gave her a slight nod, some of the tightness in her chest eased. Her chin lifted, and she gestured with her hand to the room. "This place is like Fort Knox. We'll be fine here."

Parker's eyes narrowed, and his jaw set, but she caught the hurt that flashed in his green eyes. She stepped to him and wrapped her arms around his middle. "You need to focus on Kate. Not me." With her arms still around him, she propped her chin on his sternum and looked up at him. "Not gonna lie, Park. This shit's all sorts of crazy, but I can handle it. You know I can."

"Carm—" he muttered with a giant sigh, but she talked over him.

"All this shit could be seriously triggering for her. Focus

on Kate, okay? She needs you to be safe. She can't feel safe without you."

"You're my fucking sister." His words were like gravel. "I need *you* to be safe too."

In her peripheral vision, she saw Kate standing at the edge of the great room. Her friend was still deathly pale with red-rimmed eyes, and her hands were slightly trembling. "Thank you," the other woman mouthed.

After nodding to Kate, Carmen turned her attention back to Parker. "I will be safe, little brother. Do you think Jake would let anyone hurt me?"

His face softened, and she stepped away. Keeping their hands clasped, she squeezed.

Yes, she had a shit track record as far as relationships went. But Jake? He was her friend, first and foremost. Well, aside from all the making-out-on-the-couch business. Regardless, she knew without a doubt that Jake would do everything he could to protect her. Just as she would do the same for him.

"Besides," she continued, "this place is secure. No one can get in or out of here without basically submitting DNA. You know he's a bit obsessed with all that high-tech security shit."

"Fine," Parker said with a roll of his eyes and another giant sigh. He dropped a kiss to the top of her head before turning them both toward Jake. "You know how much I love her, right?"

Jake nodded. "I do, brother."

The two men held each other's gazes. Whatever silent conversation they were having, she wasn't privy to it.

"Alright then," Parker said with a chin lift.

Shaking her head, she scrunched her brow as they clasped hands in that man-hug-back-slap thing dudes did.

She caught Kate's eye again and was thankful some color

had returned to her friend's face. This time, Kate shrugged and mouthed, "Who knows?"

For the first time in what felt like hours, Carmen smiled. Who knew, indeed?

Twenty minutes later, Carmen let out a loud exhale as the door closed behind her brother, cousin, and Kate. After giving Parker what felt like a million reassurances about her safety and Jake showing him the penthouse unit's security features, along with some extra protections and systems Jake had installed "for fun," Parker had finally agreed to leave. While he'd given her a long, tight hug, he'd also muttered, "Don't think you're off the hook, sis. I want to know what's going on with you and Jake."

Desperate to add some sort of levity, she'd arched a brow at him and smirked. "Do you really?"

He'd shuddered and gagged, muttering, "Gross," before heading out.

With a tired sigh, she turned toward the living room area where Jake and Matt sat.

"Carmen," Matt called out, his attention focused on his phone. "Does eleven tomorrow morning work for you to meet with Apone and Vasquez?"

"I'll make it work." Grabbing a blanket off the back of the loveseat, she settled into the oversized recliner. Tucking the soft fleece blanket over her legs, she brought her knees to her chest and wrapped her arms around her shins. "Can they meet here or the coffee shop downstairs? Or do they need me to go to them?"

Matt typed on his phone. Seconds later, it dinged. "They can meet at the coffee shop. Like I said earlier, Vasquez and Apone are solid detectives. I've worked with both of them for at least a decade, but if you'd feel more comfortable with me there, just say the word."

Oh, these Alvarez men. Matt was almost as sweet as his brother.

She glanced at Jake. "Would you mind coming with me tomorrow?"

The left side of his lips tipped up. "Sweetheart, there was never a doubt."

Warmth filled her, steadied her. "Thank you," she said, then turned to Matt. "I'll be good with Jake, but I appreciate the offer."

"It's no problem at all, Car—"

"Alright, man," Jake interrupted as he rose from the couch. "You know I love you, bro, but get the fuck out of my house."

Matt blinked. Twice. Then he threw his head back and roared with laughter. Wiping a tear from his face, he rose and mock-punched Jake in the stomach. "Loud and clear, bro. Loud and fucking clear," he chuckled before turning to her.

She moved to rise, but he held up a hand, halting her. He leaned down and hugged her. For a moment, she stilled before hugging him back. Neither of them was a hugger, but after tonight . . . well, they both probably needed it.

"Hang in there, okay?" he said before straightening. "Call me anytime. Both of you." He nodded to them as he made his way to the door, with Jake following behind.

As the brothers said their goodbyes, she sank into the recliner's deep cushions. It was nearing midnight and holy shit, was she beat.

The front door clicked shut, and Jake reappeared. Her breath caught as he approached, his gaze never leaving hers. Her heart tripped as his hands framed her face and his lips met hers. Not demanding, not seeking. Just soft, sweet, and comforting.

"Don't move," he murmured against her lips. "Okay?"

At her slight nod, he straightened and stepped away. It was only then that she remembered to breathe. He quickly went about locking the front door, arming the security systems, and shutting off the lights.

The floor-to-ceiling windows illuminated the room with the city's lights, and she watched as he approached. That smile that melted her insides—part sly, part sweet—was on his face. Before she could figure out what he was up to, he swooped her into his arms, fleece blanket and all, and carried her down the hall toward his room.

Pushing the door open with his foot, he bypassed the bed and brought her into the master bathroom. Her brows rose in question. Without a word, he set her on the counter between the two sinks and rummaged through a drawer. Straightening, he produced a toothbrush, a contact lens case, and a bottle of saline, placing all the items onto the counter beside her.

He nodded toward the door. "I'll go change, and you can do your thing."

Before she could thank him, he was gone. She hopped down from the counter, folded the blanket, and placed it on the ledge of the giant, jetted, freestanding bathtub. Then, as he'd said, she did her thing.

Seconds after she'd tapped her toothbrush on the sink's edge, Jake reappeared in the bathroom.

In low-riding dark blue sweatpants.

No shirt.

Just the sweats.

She ogled him. Took him in from head to toe and then back up again. Slowly. She didn't bother pretending to hide it. By the smirk that grew on his lips, the man didn't appear to mind.

"You done making me feel like a piece of meat yet?"

"Nope," she said, popping the *P* before doing another once-over and then grinning. She opened her mouth to make another smartass remark, but he swooped her up again, carrying her back into the bedroom. "I can walk, you know."

"I know," he replied, taking a detour into the walk-in closet, grabbing something, then carrying her back to the bed. "I just need to hold you."

Butterflies took flight in her belly, and she melted. No question.

He gently placed her on his massive king-sized bed and put a T-shirt on her lap. "You change, and"—he nodded to the bathroom—"I'll do my thing."

It only took her a moment to swap into the soft T-shirt. After laying her dress and bra on the low bench at the end of the bed, she crawled under the covers. She sank into the plush mattress with a moan. The mattress in Parker's guest room—her room—was great. But this one? Next level. Either that, or her body was deliriously exhausted from the long day. Maybe both.

As she snuggled deeper, Jake came out of the bathroom, shut off the bedside light, and got into the other side of the bed. Without a word—and before she could wonder if they were going to put a polite, dividing pillow between them—he pulled her close, so they faced each other. Her arms were tucked between them, her hands clasped and resting against their chests, their legs intertwined. He had one arm tucked under his head while his other rested on her hip.

"This okay, sweetheart?"

She nodded, and her heart began to gallop. They were so close that his minty breath wafted over her lips. His heart beat steadily against her hands.

"Thank you for today, Carm. Thank you for coming with me to dinner and making it . . ."

"Less sucky?" she teased. While dinner felt like a million years ago, it had been intense. After everything else that had happened on top of that, they needed light.

"Exactly." The grin he flashed her grew somber. "I'm sorry the day ended on such an awful, fucked-up note."

She couldn't resist. She reached up and traced the crinkle between his brows. "Not your fault, babe."

"I know, but I'm sorry all the same."

This sweet man. Her thumb ran across the sharp edge of his jaw, the scratchy noise of his stubble filling the silent room. "You made it better, though. So, thank *you*."

He moved his hand from her hip to her face, his fingers caressing from her forehead down the side of her face to her cheekbone and chin. Tingles were left in the wake of his gentle touch.

The pad of his thumb ran softly over her lower lip. "I won't let anything happen to you." His voice was a rough whisper. "I promise."

Her heart clenched, and warmth pooled low in her belly. This man . . . "I promise too."

Their gazes held, and as he traced her bottom lip, before she could second-guess herself, she darted her tongue out to meet his thumb. He stilled, and she danced her tongue around the tip. His eyes heated, then darkened to a near-black.

Before she could take her next breath, his mouth was on hers. Her tongue twisted with his, and he pulled her flush against him, crushing her T-shirt-covered breasts to his solid, bare chest. Her pulse thundered in her ears, and tingles raced over her body. His hard cock was pressed to her heated sex, and his hands gripped her ass, rocking her hard against him. She groaned, and shivers erupted when his erection rubbed over her clit with the perfect amount of friction.

With a quiet growl, he nipped her lower lip, then soothed the sting with his tongue. Another growl, and he pulled away. Her chest heaved as he stared at her for a heartbeat before adjusting their positions.

"Fuckin' death of me," he grumbled.

She chuckled as he effortlessly settled her back to his front. A smile bloomed when he tucked his large body around hers and wrapped her in his arms.

"When we do this, darlin', we're not going to be exhausted." His voice was like gravel, and satisfaction surged through her. *She* did that to him. There was no doubt he wanted her. Hell, there was no doubt that they wanted each other.

He kissed the top of her head. "Sleep, sweetheart. We'll talk more in the morning, okay?"

She relaxed into him, her racing heart slowing. She wiggled her bottom against his still-hard cock until he was snug between her cheeks. Another groan met her ears, and she didn't bother biting back a chuckle.

"Okay, babe," she replied, closing her eyes. "We'll talk more tomorrow." With a sigh, she burrowed deeper into his arms, and the weight of the chaotic day lifted.

CHAPTER FOURTEEN

Carmen stifled a yawn as she moved up one space in line. The coffee shop at the base of Jake's condo was busier than she'd expected. By the look of the other patrons in their spandex and athleisure wear, most had already completed their obligatory Pacific Northwest Sunday morning outdoorsy activity. She was grateful Jake had run her back to Parker's for a quick change of clothes, as she'd have looked very walk-of-shame-ish had she still been wearing her dress and stilettos. Even the slacks and blouse combo she had on seemed a bit overkill.

Scanning the crowded café, she caught Jake's eye from across the room. He'd snagged a corner table and was on the phone—some sort of emergency with The Spotted Dog and the Food Network. Who knew? He shot her a wink, and she couldn't help but sigh.

Last night had been absolute chaos. Yet she couldn't help the smile creeping onto her face. She knew it was a sappy-as-shit smile that went against everything in their arrangement. She also was skating the thin line between fake and real. Hell, who was she kidding? There wasn't even a line anymore. It was simply one giant blur. However, at the moment, she couldn't bring herself to care.

For the first time in months—nearly five, to be exact—she'd slept through the night. No nightmares, no terrors, no restlessness. Maybe it had been the horrible sleep the night before. Maybe it had been yesterday's early rise and the punishing run. Maybe it had been the exhausting and stressful day.

Or maybe it'd been the man who'd kept her wrapped securely in his arms for the entire night.

When they'd awoken, she'd thought it would be awkward. But it hadn't been. She'd snuggled into him, and they'd lain there, wrapped around each other—him tracing circles on her hip, her tracing zigzags on his chest—in comfortable silence.

Then her phone had rung, ending their respite. The detectives had wanted to meet an hour earlier.

Finally making it to the front of the line, she placed their order, paid, then stepped to the side. One random thing she appreciated about Jake? He didn't always insist on paying for everything. Yes, paying was a gentlemanly gesture, but it was one of those things that always annoyed her. She had money. Lots of it. He probably had more, but the fact that it wasn't a big deal—sometimes he'd pay, sometimes she would—was refreshing.

While waiting for her order, she turned to the service counter to grab some napkins and bumped into the person behind her. "Oh, pardon m—"

She stilled. Holy shit, seriously? Her peaceful and happy was fading. And fast.

"Hi, Carmen. How are you?"

With a sigh and an eye roll, she stepped around Brian.

"Oh, come on, Carm," he said, reaching for her arm.

She swatted his hand away. She was done with this man.

Done. "If you touch me, I'll have Jake break every bone in your hand."

His hands rose in mock surrender, and that smarmy grin appeared on his face. "Come on, Carm, let's just grab our coffees and talk. What do you say?"

She scoffed in disgust and turned toward the pickup counter. He trailed behind her, nipping at her heels like a little dog. One she wanted to kick in the face.

Thanking the barista, she grabbed her and Jake's drinks and turned back to her ex. She had bigger issues to deal with, *real* issues. This annoying man was just that—an annoyance. One that needed to go the fuck away. "I'm done talking with you, Brian. Stop calling me. Stop texting me. You see me somewhere? You don't fucking acknowledge me. We are *nothing*. Understand?"

His eyes narrowed, and anger colored his face. "Carm, why do you—"

"I'm pretty sure the lady made herself clear," a familiar voice interrupted.

Chills inched down her spine. Her breath held as the man stepped slightly in front of her, blocking her from Brian.

"And unless you want her boyfriend beating the living shit out of you"—the brown-haired man nodded toward Jake, who was now standing, arms crossed, and glowering at Brian—"I'd suggest you take your coffee and leave, buddy."

Brian's gaze darted toward Jake, and he flinched. "We're going to talk, Carm. You can't ignore me forever," he huffed before turning and stomping away.

Her breath left in a slow exhale as the man who'd stepped in turned to face her. Her peaceful and happy that had been fading with Brian was now completely unraveling. Her worlds were colliding, and she didn't know what to do.

"Hey, Carmen," he said, his voice soft and low, his hazel eyes filled with concern. "You alright?"

She nodded and swallowed twice before she found her voice. "Thank you, Vincent."

"Carm, sweetheart, you okay?" Jake. His deep baritone soothed her nerves. The hand he placed against the small of her back steadied her.

She glanced up at him, and the turmoil roiling inside her settled. "Yes," she said on another exhale. She was. Now. "Jake, this is Vincent," she said, gesturing with her coffee cup. "Vincent, my boyfriend, Jake."

"It's nice to meet you," Vincent said, offering his hand for a shake. "We didn't get the chance to meet at the gala the other week."

Straightening to his full height, Jake shook the other man's hand and made a noncommittal murmur. He was in badass-protector mode. It probably wasn't the most PC thing to admit, but she took a whole lot of comfort in it.

"Carmen, it was nice running into you, and I apologize if I stepped on your toes with that guy."

Guilt coursed through her. "No, Vincent. Thank you for all that." She handed Jake his coffee and asked, "Could you give us a moment?"

Jake held her gaze for a heartbeat.

"Please," she added.

He nodded, then leaned down and bussed a kiss to her lips. "Nice meeting you," he said to Vincent with a chin lift.

Once Jake had stepped away, she moved them toward the window counter, where it was a little more private. "Vincent, I appreciate your help." Again.

Self-anger flashed. Why was she always the damsel in distress with this man?

Vincent shot a quick glance at Jake, who was back at their table, his focus still locked on them. "Look, I know this is awkward." His hand waved between them. "Believe me, I don't mean it to be."

Holy fuck, it was awkward, alright. But that was on her. "No, Vincent." Her shoulders bunched, and she strived to find the right words. "This is so terribly cliché, but I swear, it's not you, it's me. It's just . . ."

"I get it, Carm."

Kind eyes stared back at her. Eyes that were full of understanding.

Just like that, the buds of panic began to sprout. Those kind eyes had found her, rescued her, and helped her put her broken pieces back together. And on the heels of that kindness were the awful memories of what had happened. Memories she was having the hardest damn time stomping down.

"It's okay, Carm. I know I remind you of what happened. I wish I could say I was sorry, but I'm not. I mean," he rushed on, "I'm sorry that all happened to you, but I'd rather you look at me now with trepidation and anxiety because that means you're okay. That you were able to escape."

"So, sorry, not sorry, then?" She attempted to tease him, to lighten the mood hovering over them, but was afraid it fell flat.

He chuckled before taking a sip of his drink. "In a way. I'm sorry it all happened in the first place, and that seeing me brings up bad memories. But I'd rather bring up bad memories than not have you walking this earth."

Stop being an asshole to this man!

She attempted a smile but, again, was sure it fell flat. "I really am grateful for everything you did for me. I am. It's just seeing you here—in Seattle—it's all a little . . . surreal, I suppose."

"Small world and all that, right?"

She nodded and tried for a slight grin. "Yeah."

"Well, look, I'll let you get back to your boyfriend." He gestured with his hand for her to proceed in front of him. As they made their way closer to the front door and to Jake's table, she turned to him. "Thank you again, Vincent. For everything." She met his kind eyes. "And for understanding."

"Of course, Carmen. Ups and downs and all, we're still friends and colleagues." He nodded toward Jake. "Speaking of which, I'm sure I'll see you both next weekend at Prudence's dinner. Take care."

She sat next to Jake and placed her coffee on the table in front of her as Vincent left the café. Once the door had closed behind him, she let out the breath she'd been holding. In a massive adrenaline dump, her hands began to tremble.

"Sweetheart," Jake whispered, wrapping her shaking hands in his, "look at me."

She did, and the warmth in his gaze made her want to crawl onto his lap. Have him wrap his arms around her and make everything better. But she didn't. She couldn't. Instead, she squared her shoulders and lifted her chin. "I'm okay."

He brought her hands to his lips. His eyes never left hers as he kissed the knuckles of one hand. "Bullshit, darlin'," he muttered before kissing the knuckles on her other.

She was mesmerized. The sweetness of the gesture, the care in his eyes, his soft lips . . .

Then his words registered. "Wait, what?"

Letting go of her hands, he grabbed the seat of her chair and pulled it closer to his. The loud scrape of the legs against the tile had a couple customers glancing their way. Their chairs were now touching, and she was right beside him, their legs thigh to thigh. He draped an arm over her shoulder and leaned toward her. "I said, bullshit."

Her eyebrow arched. "Excuse me?"

"Put that away," he said, dropping a kiss to said eyebrow. "I know you're not okay. Not only was McAsshole here, but Vincent was too. You told me he made you uncomfortable—"

"Yeah," she scoffed, "but that's me not being fair to—"

"Doesn't matter, sweetheart. You're not okay, and you don't need to pretend with me. You know that." She opened her mouth to speak, but he placed a finger over her lips. "You know that."

She did. She really did. And there was no use denying it.

His finger moved from her lips to tuck a lock of hair behind her ear. "The detectives will be here any moment, but promise me we'll talk about this later?"

His dark brown eyes were so earnest, so comforting, so trusting. She couldn't *not* nod. However, as much as this man was quickly becoming her rock—hell, her best friend—she wasn't sure she could trust him with the whole truth about what had happened. And it wasn't Jake. She didn't think she could trust *anyone* with that.

"Ms. Cunningham? Mr. Alvarez?"

Broken from her thoughts, her gaze shot to the two plain-clothes detectives standing by their table. Her chest clenched, and a fresh wave of unease filled her.

Jake stood with his hand outstretched. "Just Jake and Carmen are fine." He shook both detectives' hands. "We actually met briefly a few years back at Matt's wedding. Despite the shitty circumstances, it's good to see you both. Please have a seat."

"Marisa Vasquez," the black-haired female detective said. She shook Carmen's hand and gestured to the man next to her. "My partner, Raymond Apone."

"Thank you for meeting with us a little earlier," Apone said as he settled into his seat after shaking hands with Carmen.

"Not a problem," Carmen replied.

Her voice was calm, and it reflected her composed

demeanor. It killed him to see her polite, fundraising persona in place, but he knew she needed the shield.

"If it's okay with you both, we'll cut to the chase," Vasquez said, nodding to her partner.

Apone pulled out a small notebook and then a manila folder from the messenger bag he was carrying. He set the closed folder in the middle of their four-top table.

Jake appreciated the woman's straightforward attitude. His brother had said they were solid, and seeing the two—partners who had a rhythm, a silent communication—he took some comfort knowing this team had Carmen's back.

"Alvarez—" Her gaze shot to Jake. "Your brother, that is, filled us in on what he shared with you last night. At the moment, we don't have much more than that. We still have some things to follow up on after this meeting."

"What do you know?" Carmen asked.

"The vehicle was stolen from the street between six-thirty and seven last evening," Apone said.

"The neighbors' doorbell cameras give us a pretty tight timeframe," Vasquez added. "Unfortunately, while we can see the vehicle being taken, the perp's face is hidden."

Jake nodded. They'd had a seven o'clock dinner reservation, so he'd picked up Carmen just before six-thirty. Damn. What if they'd driven right by the person who'd done this?

"Then, at roughly eight o'clock," Apone continued, "the first 911 call came in about a car fire just off the Lakeview Boulevard exit on I-5. Both Washington State Patrol and Seattle Fire Department responded within minutes. When they arrived, the car was fully engulfed, but SFD was able to put it out without issue. We're working with WSP on this, and they called us about the victim shortly after. We ran the vehicle's plates, and Alvarez—er, Matt—"

"It's okay," Jake said at Apone's frown. "My brother can be Alvarez, and I can be Jake."

"Appreciate it." The detective gave him a brief smile. "I don't think I've ever called your brother by his first name in the twenty years I've known the guy." Apone turned his attention to Carmen. "Anyway, Matt was with us at the station when everything went down, and he let us know where to find your brother, Parker."

"As we mentioned to Alvarez on the phone last night," Vasquez said, picking up the conversation and addressing Carmen, "there were photos of you in a fireproof envelope that were recovered from the vehicle."

Ice shot down his spine. His brother had mentioned it the night before, but hearing it from these two detectives? This shit had been thought out. Planned.

Anger simmered in his gut.

Apone opened the folder and slid it toward Carmen. "These are copies of the photos. Can you take a look and tell us about them? When do you believe they were taken? Where? That kind of thing."

Carmen's hand trembled as she reached for the photos, and her face paled. His arm was around her in an instant, his lips to her temple.

She silently went through the pictures. One by one, she analyzed each photo. There were six in total. All of them were of her by herself, doing everyday things. When she flipped the final photo facedown, a shiver shook her slight frame. Though he wanted to fucking howl, he squeezed her to his side as gently as he could. "I've got you, sweetheart," he murmured into her hair.

For a moment, she leaned into him, burying her face in his chest. He wanted to scoop her up, take her upstairs to his place, lock the damn door, and tuck her away from all this. Away from the detectives, away from whoever this crazy person was, away from every damn thing.

He ran a hand down her spine, and she flinched. Then he

felt her take a deep, deep breath in. On her exhale, she straightened and met his gaze.

"I've got you," he repeated.

She nodded and turned to the detectives with her spine straight and shoulders back. Pride surged through him. Damn, his woman was strong. And yes, *his* woman.

She cleared her throat before addressing the two detectives. "I don't know if Matt or Parker mentioned it, but I just moved back to Seattle recently—"

"When?" Vasquez asked as Apone scribbled in his notebook.

Her eyes narrowed in thought. "Beginning of October, so . . . what, a little over three months ago?" She turned her attention back to the photos and laid them all out faceup on the table. "It looks like all these are from the last few weeks." She gestured to the first, a picture of her in conversation with someone not in the shot. Annoyance was painted on her face in the photo. "This is from December, right after the holidays."

"Who were you arguing with?"

"My ex-husband. You actually just missed him. I'm pretty sure I had the exact same expression on my face ten minutes ago." She pointed to the second photo, which showed her carrying takeout bags from a neighborhood Thai restaurant. "Also from December, roughly around the same time. If you need, I can find the exact date. I'm sure I have the receipt in my files."

Jake pointed to the third photo. "New Year's Eve party at the pub." He'd nearly swallowed his damn tongue when he'd first spotted Carmen that night. The sparkly silver dress she'd worn was a long-sleeved number and basically a freaking turtleneck. However, it had clung to her perfectly and showed off a *lot* of leg.

His wayward thoughts quickly soured as the hairs on the

back of his neck rose. This person had been *inside* the pub. Fuck.

"We have security cameras at The Spotted Dog," he told the detectives. "All over the damn place, including the alley. Let me know if you need access to the footage from New Year's Eve." They nodded, and he pointed to the fourth photo. "Last Saturday night, her organization's annual gala at the Four Seasons."

"It's technically an invite-only event," Carmen added, then shrugged. "With all the waitstaff, hotel employees, and guests milling about . . ."

She turned her attention back to the photos, but he didn't miss the wariness in her dark brown eyes. "This person was there, Jake," she said, her voice barely above a whisper. "Watching us."

Fuck.

They shared a troubled glance. Then another inhale. Another exhale.

Carmen cleared her throat. "These last two? They're from this past week. From what I'm wearing, I think it's Monday and Thursday."

Apone looked up from his notes. "Anyone you're having problems with?"

Her lips pressed into a tight line. She gave the slightest of nods and gestured to the first photo. "My ex-husband."

"We'll need his contact information," Vasquez said.

Carmen nodded and leaned into Jake's side.

"Anyone else?" Apone asked. "Maybe someone at work?"

She shook her head. "I run a nonprofit. I work closely with a handful of people in the area, but most of the people I work directly with are overseas. There are a number of local donors I interact with, but . . . no. Our organization focuses on installing clean water systems in developing countries. We work with the local governments, so what we're doing isn't controversial. At all. We're truly very boring."

"What about personally? Issues with any prior relationships? Perhaps problems with any unwanted attention in the past?"

"Well, detectives, I've been divorced three times, so the relationship issues are many." She let out a small laugh that held no humor. "However, Brian"—she gestured to the first photo again—"is the only one still in the picture. I honestly don't know anyone who'd want to hurt . . ."

Trepidation punched him in the gut when her words trailed off. Her eyes glassed over, and her face blanched. Like last night.

"Carmen?" Vasquez's voice was firm yet soothing, as if she didn't want to startle a cornered animal.

Before he took his next breath, Carmen slapped her hands over her mouth. She shot up from her chair. It crashed to the ground as she rushed toward the restroom.

CHAPTER FIFTEEN

She should be mortified. At least, that's what the logical part of Carmen's brain said.

She'd bolted from the table and nearly taken out a toddler as she'd raced to the coffee shop's bathroom. Where she'd puked her guts out. She hadn't bothered locking the door behind her, and when Jake had come in after her, he'd simply held her hair back as her retching had turned to dry heaves.

Once she'd finished and her body had gone from full-on shaking to mild tremors, he'd simply scooped her up, tucking her against his solid chest. He'd walked them out of the café and straight into the elevator to his condo, the detectives following close behind.

He'd remained silent as he'd sat her atop the ensuite counter and placed her toothbrush and a fresh washcloth next to her. He hadn't said a word until after he'd kissed her forehead. Then it had been a simple, "Take your time, sweetheart."

She should be mortified. She'd lost it. Completely. But the terror racing through her outweighed any embarrassment.

Could *he* have found her? A shudder racked her body, and

the toothbrush dropped from her hand. Spitting the paste from her mouth, she braced her hands on the counter and desperately tried to still her racing heart.

No luck.

Anders Henriksson.

Bile churned in her belly.

The quiet man she'd befriended in Brazil six months earlier. He'd—

No. Fuck no. If she had to think about that bastard and revisit what he'd done to her, she'd only do it once, dammit.

With a renewed determination—shaky as it was—she rinsed her mouth and splashed water on her face. The reflection staring back at her in the mirror was grim and pale, eyes twitchy and frantic.

She had to do this.

Someone had been killed, and if there was even the tiniest chance that revisiting the terror that had happened to her could help, she *had* to do it.

Wiping her face, she let out a breath. She straightened her spine, prayed the bile would stay down, and left the bathroom.

She found Jake and the detectives in the living area: Vasquez in the recliner, Apone pacing behind the loveseat, and Jake on the couch. The low murmurs ceased as she took a seat next to Jake.

"I made you some tea," he said, gesturing to the steaming mug on the coffee table. "If you want something stronger, let me know."

She shuddered, her stomach rolling at the thought. "I'm good, thanks." She glanced at the man next to her. His brown eyes were filled with concern, but they were steady. Always steady. She took his hand in hers, and when he squeezed, she let out a breath. She could do this. "Thank you," she murmured before turning to the detectives, who were now both seated. "I apologize for that display earlier."

"No apology necessary," Apone said with a shake of his head.

"Are you alright?" Vasquez asked.

Her chest tightened. She wasn't quite sure she'd ever be alright again. "I'm not sure if this has anything to do with anything, but a few months ago, while I was overseas, I was involved in an . . . attack."

Jake gripped her hand, and she chanced a glance at him. Those steady eyes held hers, and he quickly switched hands, so now, instead of her holding his left hand, she held his right. Then his left arm was around her, pulling her snugly against his side.

You can do this, dammit.

"Seven months ago, I was in Brazil with CWC and met Anders Henriksson." Her stomach heaved, and she fought down the nausea. She concentrated on Apone's wiggling pen as he scribbled in his notebook. "Anders worked for a nonprofit based out of Sweden that we often partner with. He and I struck up a friendship of sorts. It wasn't romantic or anything . . . just a regular, somewhat-close friendship."

Detective Vasquez's eyes narrowed, questions obviously running through her mind, and Carmen rushed on to clarify. "Our nonprofit world is a bit of a bubble. Our groups come in—my team sets up water, another team is medical, and sometimes we have a couple other teams join to address whatever infrastructure needs there are for that particular location—and then once it's all set up and the locals have a handle on things, we're done. We move on to the next location, often together."

Her nerves calmed as she explained her work. She wasn't quite sure what that said about her, but she'd take every little bit of calm she could. "Brazil is an enormous country, and the village we were in when I met Anders was extremely remote—we were at least five hours from the nearest town, six or seven hours from a major city. So there wasn't much to do on our off-time and everyone became friendly. There was some extra work mayhem on that particular project, so our groups couldn't help but become close."

Prior to this trip, she'd been able to keep a modicum of professional distance from others. But so many things had gone wrong in Brazil, from colleague health emergencies to freak weather conditions, that the groups had become close in a trial-by-fire kind of way. She'd let her guard down. And it had cost her.

"After a couple months of moving from place to place with Anders's group, he wanted to be more than just friends. I didn't, and . . . I thought he was okay with that."

He'd acted as if he were. But she'd been naive. He'd been biding his time. When he'd tried to kiss her one evening, she'd pushed him away. His face flashed in her mind, and her heart pinched painfully in her chest.

His glacial blue eyes had been manic when she'd said no, panic and desperation flashing on his face. Then rage had contorted his features, like it had truly sunk in that she'd meant it. She'd quickly fled and thought, with some time and space, everything would be okay. That they'd go back to how things had been before.

That hadn't been the case. Not at all.

"It turned out he wasn't okay with just being friends and colleagues. A couple days after I rebuffed his advances, something happened with him and his team—I don't know what—but they let him go." The relief she'd felt when he'd left had been tremendous. The two days prior had been relentless unease. Every time she'd turned around, Anders had been there. In her face. Silently glaring at her. Even when she hadn't been able to see him, she'd felt his gaze on her, felt his anger suffocating her.

"Is that kind of thing the norm?" Apone asked. "People coming in and out of the projects?"

She hesitated. To this day, she'd never found out what had happened with him and his team. It had to have been something serious, something bad, because the second he'd left, they'd never mentioned him again. Not once. It had been as if he'd never existed. "Yes, but not like that. Turnover is normal after project completion. My team's part of that particular project was nearly done, but his team was just getting into the nitty-gritty of their part."

"That wasn't the last you saw of him," Vasquez said, her arms crossing over her chest. It wasn't a question.

Carmen shook her head, and the ever-churning bile began to rise. "About a week later"—six days, four hours, and thirty-six minutes later—"he kidnapped me."

Beside her, she felt more than heard Jake's surprised gasp. Except for his hand fisting at her hip, he'd gone completely still.

"Our part was done. The rest of my team went to the next location, but I had to go to São Paulo for some meetings. I was about to check in at my hotel when he took me." Flashes of memories assailed her. Each grisly image threatened to overwhelm her, but she pushed through. She had to.

"He held me for just over three days"—half naked and chained to a wall—"before I was rescued. A colleague found me and brought the local authorities. When they apprehended Anders, he injured one of them in the process. I was conscious when they arrested him, and he made it clear that it wasn't over, that we would still be together." She swallowed past the rock in her throat. "From there, I ended up in a nearby hospital. Then it was all a blur of getting my care sorted out and working with the US embassy to get me back home."

A couple beats of silence ticked by.

"Where is Henriksson now?" Apone asked.

Ice swept through her veins. The voice of the embassy worker echoed in her mind: *I'm sorry, Ms. Cunningham, but someone paid for Mr. Henriksson's release. The prison doesn't have a record of who paid, just that they let him go two days ago. Unfortunately, we checked with the Swedish consulate, and they have no information on his whereabouts either.*

"Right before I came home—five, six weeks after the kidnapping—I received word that he'd been released. So, I don't know where he is." She shrugged. "No one does."

Jake tried to process all the information Carmen had just dropped. But fuck. His stomach was in knots, and, truthfully, he wasn't processing shit.

Then Vasquez broke the silence. "I'm sorry that happened to you. Truly. If you could give us any information on Henriksson—physical description, who he worked for, anything—we can follow up. If we can't locate him, then at least we can hopefully get a photo of him out there as a person of interest. We'll also need your ex-husband's information so we can pay him a visit. We'll keep everyone, and all possibilities, on the table for now."

"I'd appreciate that," Carmen replied.

She squeezed his hand before standing. Vasquez rose with her. Carmen led the way to the kitchen island to, he presumed, get her phone for the requested information, seeing as that's where the detectives had dropped her purse.

His muscles ached from holding himself so tightly. But he

could deal with that. Because it was either aching muscles, or he'd go on a fucking rampage.

Kidnapped.

That magnificent woman had been fucking *kidnapped* and held for fucking days. *Days!* God knew what the hell had happened to her during that time, but from the shadows that had darkened her eyes while she'd spoken, it had been horrific.

"You gonna be okay, man?" Apone asked, his voice low.

His mouth could only gape. Fuck if he knew.

"I take it all that info was news to you?"

He gave the detective a curt nod, then turned his back to the women and scrubbed his hands over his face.

"Fuck," he hissed on an exhale.

Things were clicking into place. Carmen's abrupt return home to Seattle, the way she'd thrown herself into work, the quiet stillness and occasional sadness that would come over her when she let her guard down.

As fucked up as what she'd told the detectives was, he *knew* she was still holding back. After her reactions last night and in the coffee shop this morning, there had to be more. Much more she'd glossed over. The churning in his gut told him that what she'd experienced was more horrific than he could—or wanted to—imagine.

"We'll look into her ex and this Henriksson guy," Apone said, breaking him out of his thoughts. "Your brother isn't technically going to be on this case—conflict of interest and all that—but know that we're keeping him in the loop. Also, our captain pulled a couple other guys in to assist."

He nodded and took a little bit of comfort in knowing there were more people on Carmen's side.

"Believe me when I say that we're all taking this seriously. When we get the autopsy back from the victim in the car, hopefully, we'll know more. Until then, you have our numbers?"

"I do."

"Keep your eyes open," Apone said, his gaze intense.

"Trust me, Carm's not leaving my fucking sight."

"I have no doubts you'll keep an eye on her," Apone said with a small smile, clapping him on the shoulder. "But watch your back as well."

The detectives took their leave. Jake shut the door behind them, and once he'd turned the lock, he leaned his back against it with a heavy sigh.

Carmen stood a few feet away, her arms crossed tightly over her chest, her gaze focused on the ground.

He remained silent and waited. Seconds ticked by before she lifted her gaze to his. The worry and turmoil warring in her big brown eyes twisted his gut.

Straightening from the door, he held his arms open. "Come here, darlin'," he murmured.

She hesitated for a two-count, then launched herself at him.

He bent forward and caught her with ease. Her arms locked around his neck, and she trembled against him. He straightened with his arms tight around her, lifting her off her feet.

For a moment, he simply held her. Chest to chest, with her face buried in his neck and his in her hair. Coconut and citrus filled his senses. Her shampoo was a bright summer scent that was so at odds with the dark words that had come from her mouth.

He walked them back to the sofa. Sitting, he settled her across his lap, and she snuggled in.

"Please don't tell anyone," she said, her voice a soft whisper. "I don't want anyone to know what happened. It's too much."

Holy fuck, his heart broke for this woman. But he'd do whatever she wanted at this point. "Of course." He ran a hand down her back, and when her body jerked, he froze. "Talk to me, sweetheart."

She was quiet for a moment, then shook her head, her body relaxing back into him. "Just bad memories."

"What can I do for you right now?"

With a loud exhale, she sat up. He searched her gaze. The worry and turmoil had lessened. It was still there, but the panic was no longer lingering. "You've done more than you could ever know, Jake."

There had to be more he could do. If he could slay all her fucking dragons, he would. But right now, he couldn't. No one knew who the hell was targeting her. The helplessness had him wanting to scream, to rage, to burn down the fucking world. Whoever this piece of shit was? They would *not* touch her.

"Hey," she whispered. Her hand cradled the side of his face, her thumb tracing over the frown lines he knew were popping on his forehead. It was a seemingly innocuous gesture, but it had the tension draining from his frame. That she was trying to reassure *him*, after all she'd revealed? Damn, this woman . . .

She glanced at her watch. "It's not even noon. How about we get out of here?"

His brow arched in question. "Anywhere in particular you have in mind?"

Her face scrunched, and she nodded, untangling herself from his arms as she rose. "I'm antsy. Need to move, you know? How about we get my stuff from Parker's?" She stilled, and a flush tore over her face. "Um, that is, if the offer to move in with you is still on the table?"

"Of course it is, Carm." He stood and stepped toward her, crowding her space. Looping his arms around her waist, he pulled her flush against him. She settled her palms to his chest.

"There's so much shit going on," she said, dropping the crown of her head to his sternum. "I don't want to think about any of it right now, but my mind won't freaking stop."

He'd do anything to take the weight off her shoulders. Any. Damn. Thing.

An idea popped into his head, and his brow scrunched in thought. "Need a distraction?"

"Please." She glanced back up at him, and the hope flickering across her face slayed him.

"Want to punch the shit out of something?"

Her eyes widened the tiniest of fractions, and a small grin lifted her lips. "Not gonna lie, babe, but that sounds mighty appealing right now."

What was appealing was the thought of her sweaty and beating the shit out of a heavy bag. Badass and fucking sexy. *That* was appealing. Inappropriate? Probably. But he couldn't bring himself to care. "How about we pick up your stuff at Park's, then hit the boxing gym?" A grin grew on his face as she nodded. "However, I believe at some point today, we may have to renegotiate the terms of our arrangement, Ms. Cunningham."

She blinked twice before the corners of her lips kicked up in a smirk, the heaviness in her eyes replaced by humor. "Is that so, Mr. Alvarez?"

He leaned down and pressed a soft, quick kiss to her lips. "Not to brag or anything, but I've been told I'm quite a skilled negotiator." He straightened and stepped back. "Let's get out of here. The quicker I can get you into spandex, the better."

The laugh that left her had his insides settling, calming.

They were going to be okay.

CHAPTER SIXTEEN

It took a shockingly short time to pack up her things from Parker and Kate's place. Neither was home when she and Jake stopped by, which saved them some time. The last thing she wanted to do was accidentally spill anything about what had happened to her in Brazil. Her emotions were too unsteady—ricocheting from worry to anger to straight-out fear—and she didn't know what would spew from her mouth.

Nor did she want to rehash what the detectives had said. Or hadn't said, seeing as they hadn't determined much of anything about who could be responsible for that horrible . . . car fire? Murder?

A shiver tore through her. Holy shit. She couldn't even think about the car fire and that poor person inside. Or the pictures.

Of her.

In a fireproof envelope.

She shuddered. It was all so, *so* fucked up.

Still, she wasn't a complete asshole, so she'd sent a text to her brother letting him know she'd moved her stuff to Jake's, and he could swing by if he wanted to check in.

Two suitcases and one small banker's box later, her personal items were loaded into Jake's Range Rover. She changed into black workout leggings and another short-sleeved fitted top—this time in neon green—and they drove back to his place. They dropped her items off with his building's concierge, then made their way to the gym to "punch the shit out of something." Jake's words, not hers.

Apparently, this gym wasn't the one she was also a member at, but rather a local boxing and MMA gym that all the guys belonged to.

With each block they drove, her insides coiled tighter and tighter. The faster they got there, the better.

As they pulled into the parking lot, she prayed neither Blake nor Parker were there. She didn't want to see them, didn't want to talk to them. It wasn't because she didn't love them. She did. The issue was that they loved her right back and were ridiculously protective of her. And currently, she was teetering on an unstable ledge.

There was so much anger and terror and fucking frustration—at herself, what had happened with Anders, and what was currently happening—swirling inside her. So much shit resurfacing. Shit she'd worked so damn hard to tamp down. If she didn't hit something soon, she would lose her goddamn mind.

"You hanging in there, Carm?" Jake's deep voice was usually soothing. But not right now. She didn't even want to talk to him.

"No," she clipped out, her hands fisted in her lap.

Without another word, he parked and cut the engine. She recognized the look in his eyes. Determination. What exactly he was determined about, she wasn't quite sure. Right now, she couldn't focus, and she didn't have enough bandwidth to attempt to figure it out. Shoving her door open, she met him at the front of his SUV and followed him into the gym.

Bleach and sweat assaulted her senses. She winced as some kind of screaming, screeching music blared from the speakers. She stood behind Jake, who had a massive gym bag slung over one shoulder, when he stopped and said something to the young lady manning the front desk. What? She had no clue. It was that loud.

Moments later, he took a mesh bag from the woman and motioned to Carmen with his head. She followed him to the far side of the gym, past two boxing rings with men sparring and an empty MMA cage. The music was still loud in this area, but not eardrum-shattering.

"Sit," he said, or at least that's what she assumed, as he motioned to a long bench. She sat, and before she knew what was happening, he had her hand in his and was wrapping it in a long strip of white cloth. Before she could ask for the correct terminology—she was an anal-retentive control freak like that—he was wrapping her other hand. Opening the mesh bag, he pulled out a pair of boxing gloves that were a bright, shimmery, neon pink with yellow and orange hearts.

He gave her a sheepish grin as he fit her hands into them. "It's the only color they had in your size."

Her lips tipped up in a small smile despite the turbulent emotions ping-ponging inside her.

All business, Jake showed her a slew of basic shadow boxing movements he wanted her to practice in front of the mirror while he gloved up. She mentally paused and snickered. Gloved up. Apparently, the twelve-year-old boy in her was alive and stupidly well.

A few minutes later, Jake was beside her. Her thoughts and emotions might have been all over the place, but looking at his reflection, she could one thousand percent appreciate the man. Sweatpants and a T-shirt with its arms torn off, the sides gaping so wide she could see the cut of his abs when he moved. She wasn't complaining. Not one bit. All that raw masculinity was a delicious distraction.

"Let's do this, sweetheart," he said, leading her to a row of heavy bags. He showed her a basic combination—right, left, right, circle, left, right, left, circle—then let her have at it.

She was tentative. The first few connections of her gloved fist on the heavy bag were jarring, but she pressed on. He watched her for a bit, stopping her twice to correct her form. After a few more rounds, she loosened up, and the harder she hit, the better she felt.

"Time your breathing," he called out before slapping her on the ass and moving to his own heavy bag.

And she did. Each breath synced with each punch, and her heartbeat fell in line. Within minutes, sweat poured down her face. Right, left, right, circle. Left, right, left, circle.

A glance at Jake two bags down had her pausing. His muscles flexed and popped as he wailed on his heavy bag. With each punch, it swayed viciously.

Her eyes narrowed on her bag. She wanted *that*, dammit. Refocusing on the bag, she pictured *him*. Anders. How he'd mocked her every time she'd struggled with the restraints. How he'd laughed every time she'd cried out in pain. How he'd squealed in fucked-up glee when he'd cracked the whip down against her skin.

The scars on her back stung in phantom pain, but it didn't stop her fists. Each hit, each pop of her fist on the bag, each breath she heaved, settled the chaos inside her.

On her next exhale, Jake came up behind her heavy bag, holding it still.

"Again," he said. "But more from your core and hips, not your arms." He gave her a chin lift. "Go."

And go, she did. She wailed on the bag as he held her

target still. She lost count of how many combinations she threw, and as her muscles turned to jelly, a warmth—a confidence—bloomed in her gut.

"Break!" Jake called out, pulling the heavy bag to the side.

Her chest heaved with ragged breaths. The second her arms fell to her sides, they liquefied. She was freaking exhausted.

"Holy shit, babe," she panted, satisfaction surging through her body. "That felt better than sex."

Jake barked out a laugh.

"Damn, Carm, you've been having some shitty sex then."

Her eyes narrowed. The voice sounded like Jake's, but his lips hadn't moved. Did exhaustion create hallucinations?

Then Matt stepped into her line of vision, laughter playing on his face.

She brought her gloved hand to her chest and blew out a breath. "I thought I was losing my mind there for a second."

Matt grinned and tapped his glove to hers. "I do tend to make the ladies lose their minds."

"Fucking delusional, Alvarez," a new voice said.

Carmen turned, and her jaw dropped. She couldn't help it. The shirtless man with wrapped hands who'd stepped into their group was ridiculous. Sexy-romance-novel-cover ridiculous. He didn't stand quite as tall as the Alvarez men, but he still towered over her. Dark hair, tan skin, muscles stacked on muscles, and a shit-eating grin that said he knew the effect he had on women.

He held his fist out for a bump as his eyes took a leisurely stroll over her figure. "Hey there, gorgeous. Cade de la Rosa."

Her eyes rolled as she grinned and bumped her neon pink boxing glove-covered fist to his. "Carmen Cunningham."

Cade's brown eyes narrowed and his head tilted in question. "Parker's sister?"

She got that questioning look a lot. Being the only

Filipino in an all-white family tended to do that. But it had stopped bothering her a long time ago because, for the most part, people weren't truly being dicks; they were genuinely curious. "Yup." She nodded with a smile, popping the *P*.

"Damn, girl, it's nice to finally meet you." The man's grin grew, and his eyes sparkled with mischief. "I've heard a lot about you from your brother and Blake."

While Cade was undeniably attractive, she couldn't help but put him in the same category as Matt: stupid hot, wildly flirty, but did nothing for her.

"Shouldn't you be at your other gym?" Jake grumbled, annoyance clear on his face.

Unlike *that*. Those seven little jealousy-tinged words sent flutters through her belly.

Cade and Matt roared with laughter.

Once his guffaws were under control, Matt clarified, "Cade co-owns this place with his brother, Dante." He gestured to the men in the boxing rings. She presumed one of them was said brother. "They just opened up a fucking mammoth training facility over on Hudson Island."

"Yeah," Jake interjected. "Shouldn't your ugly mug be out there supervising and shit?"

"Awww, Jake." Cade chuckled. "You scared my ugly mug will give you some competition with this badass beauty? Good form, by the way." He shot her a playful wink, and she laughed.

Cade mock-punched Jake in the stomach, then slapped him on the shoulder. "We're meeting up with Dante and some of the guys later for drinks if you and your lovely lady want to join."

"Thanks, man," Jake said. "But I think we're going to stay in and relax tonight."

Cade slapped him on the shoulder and smirked. "Oh, I would too." He turned his attention to her. "Nice meeting you, Carmen. I wasn't lying earlier. You've got good form—" He held up his hands to Jake. "Not in a creepy way, dumbass. Besides, hitting bags is one of the best stress relievers out there. Just ask your brother and Blake. So, if you want a membership, I can add you to this fucker's." He nodded his head toward Jake with another smirk.

She did feel a lot better. When she'd walked in, she'd been a bundle of agitation, nerves, and conflicting emotions—all threatening to overwhelm her. After everything with the detectives, there'd been such a feeling of helplessness. As a Type A, it had made her want to crawl out of her skin. Not being able to do anything, not knowing where to focus her anger, fear, and hurt, was the worst feeling. But this? Beating the shit out of something? For whatever reason, it had helped. A lot.

"Thanks," she replied to Cade. "And yeah, if you could add me to this guy's membership"—her head tilted toward Jake next to her—"I'd appreciate it. This felt *really* good."

"Fuck yeah, it did." Cade smiled. "Hittin' shit is better than okay sex and cheaper than therapy, right?"

She laughed. "Absolutely." Though she really needed to consider giving that a shot as well.

The therapy. Not the okay sex.

Well . . . maybe. But *good* sex, not just okay.

She fought a cringe. *Mind out of the gutter, woman. Focus, dammit!*

After dialing her membership details in, Cade and Matt hit the boxing ring while she and Jake unwrapped their hands. Then they were back in his Range Rover, and though she was sweaty and exhausted, her mind was finally still.

Entering his parking garage, her nerves began to build, making her heart kick. Holy shit, she was moving in with Jake.

And it had nothing to do with their arrangement. At least,

not for her. Yes, it would make them look like more of a couple, but that's not why she wanted to move in with him.

He made her feel safe. Plain and simple. There was something about the man that she needed.

She wasn't a complete fool—she knew this wasn't permanent. He wasn't going to keep her, no matter how much she was starting to want him to. No one ever did. Or would. And that was okay. She could deal. She'd take every moment she could with him, even though their impending end made her more nervous than ever. Because he mattered.

She took a deep breath in when he put his vehicle in park. Before she could exhale, he was out and around, holding her door open, his hand extended to help her out. The nerves kicked up a notch. Yeah, this man mattered.

They stopped at the concierge to retrieve her two suitcases and box of miscellaneous crap, then made their way up to his floor. Once inside his condo, with a rolling suitcase trailing behind her, she turned toward the hallway that led to the bedrooms and came to an abrupt halt.

She didn't know where to go. For a moment, her heart froze, then she made a beeline to one of his guest rooms. They weren't a real couple, and she wasn't about to make any assumptions that they were more than what they'd agreed to. Make-out sessions or not.

She hoisted her luggage onto the tufted bench at the end of the bed. She began to unzip her suitcase but stilled when Jake placed her banker's box onto the dresser and lifted her second piece of luggage onto the foot of the bed.

"Take your time and get settled, sweetheart. I'll put some food together for us." With a kiss to her forehead, he was out the door.

She stood in silence for a moment, then shook her head. "Get it together," she murmured.

After hanging up her clothes and moving her empty

luggage to the side of the room, she contemplated a quick shower but lay down on the bed instead. Her weary muscles sighed in relief as she sank into the soft, plush mattress.

She must have been running on adrenaline because everything—her body, her mind, her entirety—was crashing. With another loud exhale, she closed her eyes. She'd rest for just a little bit, then unpack her box of random stuff later. Just a few minutes . . .

CHAPTER SEVENTEEN

J ake sliced the sandwiches in half, then placed the knife down. He clutched the edge of the kitchen island and hung his head.

Breathe, motherfucker. Just fucking breathe.

His mind was whirling, his need to fix things for Carmen kicking into overdrive. But he was at a loss. Despite the physical release at the gym, he still vibrated with pent-up frustration. He didn't know what to do for her. And that was unacceptable.

When they'd made it back to his condo, he'd purposely let Carmen lead the way. She'd rolled her suitcase into one of his guest rooms, and it had taken everything he had to not suggest she move her items into his room. Waking up with her snug in his arms—this morning truly seemed like a life-time ago—was something he wanted to do again. Because it had felt so damn right.

But he couldn't push it, couldn't push her. With all the shit that had gone down since last night, she was skittish. For good reason. The last thing Carm needed was him pawing at her and changing the dynamics of their friendship.

His lips pursed. He supposed having her tongue in his mouth and his hands on her ass last night had changed the dynamics before the mayhem had descended. Still . . .

Regardless, he couldn't rush this. She was too damn important.

Taking a bite of his turkey, pesto, and provolone sandwich, he added some baby carrots and sliced cucumbers onto their plates. The thumping noises of Carmen unpacking in the guest room were gone, and he strained to hear her movements. After taking another bite, he placed his sandwich down and made his way through the hallway. In the doorway of the guest bedroom she'd claimed, he stilled.

Carmen was on top of the covers, curled into a little ball in the center of the massive, king-sized bed. Well, massive in comparison to her. In sleep, she was utterly relaxed. Not something he saw very often. She was always on the go, always busy. Now, knowing a little about the horrors of what had brought her abruptly home, it began to make sense. And he understood completely. Staying busy kept you from thinking, made it easier to keep all the dark, negative thoughts at bay. Yeah . . . he got it.

He quietly took down a blanket from the top shelf of the closet and paused. Carmen's clothes now hung in the closet. A smile lifted his lips. She'd arranged her clothes by color, which wasn't at all surprising, but more than that, he loved seeing her things in his home. Hell, he loved seeing *her* in his home. Yeah, it was complicated, but he didn't want to lie to himself. He wanted this. *Her.*

The question of how was an entirely different matter. But that was jumping the gun. She was hesitant—hell, *he* was hesitant. Not because of Carmen, but because he had so much shit going on, so much damn internal baggage he'd been hauling around for what seemed like forever. This woman deserved all his attention, all his focus, and he wasn't sure he could give her that.

He took in her sleeping form, then draped the blanket over her, wishing things weren't so damn complicated. Heading back to the kitchen, he wrapped up her lunch and placed it in the fridge.

As he settled at the island to eat, his phone dinged. He glanced at the display, and dread turned his stomach.

Lara: *Thanks again for dinner last night. Do you have time to talk?*

"Fuck," he murmured. Lara and her dipshit husband were the last things he wanted to deal with. Turning his phone facedown, he took another bite of his sandwich, then reached for his ever-present laptop.

Busy. Stay busy, dammit.

Pulling up the drafts of the new code for Square Peg, he focused on the latest revisions and immersed himself in the updates of his pixilated world. He'd tackle the Food Network proposal they'd received for The Spotted Dog after. Because being busy made it easier to keep all the dark, negative thoughts at bay.

The twitch in his lower back and his grumbling stomach had him glancing up from his computer. It took a moment for his eyes to focus on his surroundings. The sun had set, the food on the plate next to him was long gone, and his gallon jug of water on the counter was nearly empty.

Stretching, he groaned as the muscles along his back protested the hours he'd just spent hunched over his laptop. As he loaded his plate into the dishwasher, he debated whether to wake up Carmen.

An unfamiliar noise had him stilling. He shut the dishwasher door and closed his eyes, focusing on the sound. When recognition hit, his eyes shot open. He was across the kitchen in a heartbeat.

He skidded to a stop in the doorway of Carmen's room, and his chest squeezed. Her legs were tangled in the blanket as she thrashed violently on the bed, moaning incoherent words.

He froze, unsure what to do.

When her mumblings turned to an escalating, "No, nooo, NO!" he moved.

"Carmen," he said, pitching his voice louder than her cries. Kneeling on the bed, he placed firm hands on her shoulders, unsure if he was doing the right thing.

With her eyes squeezed shut, she screamed. It was an ear-piercing, guttural cry that stopped his heart.

"No, please, no," she continued to murmur as she fought against his hold.

He'd never felt so fucking helpless.

"Carmen, wake up!" His hands remained on her shoulders, and he yanked her to his chest. "Carmen, please, sweetheart, wake up," he said against her ear.

Her body jerked, then stilled. Her only movements were her heaving chest.

"You're okay," he repeated over and over, wrapping his arms fully around her. "I've got you."

"Jake?"

That one trembling word tore at his heart. "I got you, darlin'," he repeated and ran a hand over her head, pushing the hair back from her damp forehead.

She sagged into his chest and let out a shaky breath. "Holy shit, Jake."

"Bad dream?" He felt her nod against him.

"It was like I was right back there," she croaked. "Back in that fucked-up basement."

His blood chilled, but he pushed his unease away. This wasn't about him, dammit. "Do you want to talk about it, sweetheart?"

"I don't know," she whispered, burying her face in his neck.

"If you do, I'm here to listen." His arms tightened around her. She was tiny against him, but while he didn't know the entire story, he knew that despite her size, this woman was so damn strong. She'd survived. He kissed the top of her head. "Anything you need, Carm. I've got you."

Their rapid heartbeats were the only sounds in the room until she broke the silence.

"I'd been traveling all day. It took about nine hours to get from the village we were at to São Paulo. I had to meet with some government people the following day, and when the driver dropped me off at my hotel, I was beyond exhausted. When I arrived, I went straight to the restroom." She shook her head, as if chiding herself. "I wasn't paying attention. The second the restroom door closed behind me, he was there. Out of fucking nowhere."

She shook her head again, then glanced up at him, disbelief clear on her face. "Before I could scream—before I could even figure out what was going on—he shoved something over my face. The next thing I knew . . . nothing."

The anger churning in his belly threatened to erupt, but he locked it down. She didn't need his rage. She needed a friend to lean on. As much as it killed him to hear what had happened to her, he'd shut the fuck up and listen.

"When I came to, it was pitch black, and I had the most horrendous headache ever. Like the worst hangover, but amplified a thousandfold." Her breath came faster, and her heart was racing against his chest. He smoothed a hand over her back. For a split second, she tensed. Then, as if catching herself, her breath evened, and she continued. "I was lying on a cement floor, but my hands were handcuffed and chained over my head to the wall. My ankles were locked together with some sort of metal restraint."

His stomach rolled. Holy. Fuck.

"It was damp and sticky, and I was too scared to scream, too scared to do anything. I just lay there in the dark for what felt like forever."

"Sweetheart, I'm so fucking sorry." His words were inadequate, but he didn't know what else to say. Beyond being furious that this had happened to her, it tore his fucking heart out that she hadn't told a soul when she'd returned home. She'd gone through this alone.

"At some point, Anders showed up."

He felt her heartbeat speed up again, and he wanted to howl. Instead, he pressed a kiss to her head, his hand continuing to run up and down her back, and he took comfort when she leaned into his touch.

"He was spouting crazy shit about how we were meant to be together. Then when he first tried to touch me, I kicked him right in the face. I knocked out two of his front teeth." A small huff escaped her, one that held the tiniest hint of satisfaction, and he squeezed her tight. His little badass. "That pissed him off, obviously, and he beat me up pretty good after . . . it was worth it, though."

They were silent for a few moments. The same question kept repeating in his head. His mouth opened twice to ask, and twice his mouth snapped shut. But he had to know how much this fucker had hurt her. "Sweetheart," he said, his gruff voice barely above a whisper. "Did he rape you?"

Her blood stilled.

"No," she said, the one word loud in the still room.

With hindsight, that single fact confused her even more. "That was the crazy thing, Jake. I mean, don't get me wrong, I'm so damn thankful he didn't, but he threatened to the entire time."

Anders's angry words echoed in her mind: *"I'm going to make you mine and you're going to fucking love it! You'll be begging me for more."*

"Every time he threatened to, the angrier he got. He'd hit me and grope me . . ." Bile rose in her throat. She could still see the black, blue, and purple bruises that had covered her breasts, her pubic area, her inner thighs—could still feel how her skin had burned and throbbed at the slightest movement. "But he didn't rape me."

"I'm so sorry this happened, sweetheart, so damn sorry." Jake's voice was like gravel, and she knew this was hurting him. "But I'm grateful that motherfucker didn't violate you like that. He violated you enough as is."

She snuggled into him and wrapped her arms around his waist with a sigh. Best to get it all out then . . .

"After the first day, when I'd kicked him in the face, he threatened to rape me. Repeatedly. But like I said, he didn't. He just beat me up. Every time, he'd get angrier and angrier. Then he broke out the whip."

Jake stilled beneath her. "What?"

"Yeah," she murmured, the sour rock in her gut turning. "It wasn't a big Indiana Jones type of whip. It was much shorter and had this cluster of metal balls at the end. Even though it was small, it was so damn effective. After he'd beat me, he'd get furious and scream about how I *made* him do this. That it was all *my* fault. Then he'd take his shirt off and flog himself until blood was streaming down his back. Then he'd do the same to me."

The sound of the lashes echoed in her ears. A shiver tore through her as the coppery scent that had tinged the damp air stormed over her senses. The hand running over her back stilled.

"My back," she whispered, nuzzling deeper into Jake's arms. "He whipped my back so badly that, afterward, the doctors were considering skin grafts."

"Holy shit, Carm," he said, his breath puffing over the damp strands of her hair. His hand resumed its comforting movement up and down her back. Warmth bloomed, fighting the chill threatening to overtake her.

"You don't wear clothes that show your back. It's why you flinch when I touch your back sometimes." His voice sounded as if he were trying to figure out a puzzle. "Did you end up getting the skin graft?"

"No. They were able to stitch it all up, though they were worried about infection for a while." The scars that remained were still a little tender. Whether it was actual physical pain or phantom, she didn't know. Either way, she was self-conscious of the scars. Before, she'd never thought twice about wearing spaghetti strap tanks, halter tops, or backless dresses. Now? No way. It wasn't so much the vanity of it all, though that played a tiny part. It was that the scars were new. Fresh. They crisscrossed her back like a fucked-up lattice. The very last thing she wanted was to have to explain where they'd come from.

"Dammit," he said, his voice steeped in sorrow. "That's why you came home so suddenly, wasn't it?"

She let out a breath and nodded against his chest. "I was in the hospital for almost two weeks. Like I said, they were worried about infection. Then it took another three weeks or so to get everything coordinated with the embassy and work."

And to heal.

She could have come back earlier, could have easily hopped on a plane and rushed home. But she hadn't wanted to show up bruised and battered. Hadn't wanted to explain the bandages around her wrists and ankles. She hadn't wanted anyone to know what had happened. So, she'd waited until the visible bruises had faded, until the scars along her back had healed enough to move without wincing.

Returning home and not saying anything had been the hardest part. She'd desperately wanted to confide in Parker. He'd forever been her greatest secret keeper. However, every time she'd opened her mouth, the words hadn't come.

Then there was the guilt.

Yes, what Anders had done to her hadn't been her fault. Logically, she knew that. But there was still a tiny seed of guilt that whispered she'd led him on, a tiny little voice that sneered she'd brought this upon herself.

She hated that voice.

Carmen knew that if what had happened to her had happened to *anyone* else, she'd be the first person saying that what they felt was misplaced guilt. That it had *not* been their fault. At all.

When it was herself though . . .

In the weeks leading up to Anders trying to kiss her, he'd never stated outright that he was interested in her, but deep down, she'd known he wanted to be more than just friends. She simply hadn't acknowledged it, just continued with their friendship, hoping he'd get the hint. The guilt was because . . . she'd enjoyed his attention. After her brief relationship with Vincent had ended the year before, she hadn't dated anyone else. Her travels had made it difficult, and she'd been told on more than one occasion, in more than one language, by more than one man, that she was too intimidating, too cold, a little bit too much.

When she'd joined the groups on that last stint in Brazil,

she'd purposely tried to relax and let her guard down. Be less intimidating. Not specifically for dating, but because after three years of hopping from location to location, she'd come to the uncomfortable conclusion that most of her friends were peripheral. More acquaintances and colleagues than actual friends.

Then, when Anders had openly flirted with her, acting as if he were interested in more than just her leadership and organizational skills, it had been surprising and . . . nice.

"Christ, Carm," Jake murmured, jarring her from her thoughts. "I'm sure dealing with the embassy on a good day is a pain in the ass, let alone when you're injured. I can't imagine how stressful that must have been."

The guilt grew, but this time for a different reason entirely. "Vincent," she said with a sigh.

"Vincent?" The surprise was clear in his voice. "What about him?" The three little words dripped with trepidation.

"Vincent and his organization were part of our team in the last couple of villages in Brazil."

"You mentioned he worked at many of the same locations as you the last couple of years."

Yes, it had been awkward after they'd broken up, constantly seeing him. However, she couldn't—didn't—want to imagine what would have happened otherwise. "I didn't tell anyone at CWC what happened to me. Outside of the hospital workers and authorities, Vincent was the only one who knew what happened." And now, whenever she thought of the man, it brought her right back to that dank, sticky basement. Actually seeing him in the flesh? It was too much. "He was the one who rescued me."

Jake pulled slightly away to look at her. "Vincent? The guy I met at the café this morning?"

"Yeah." It had been a miracle that Vincent had found her.

The basement where Anders had held her had been miles from her hotel. "After the authorities arrested Anders, I was in pretty bad shape, and Vincent helped coordinate everything—from the hospitals to my teams to the embassy. All without letting anyone at CWC—including my family—know about what had happened."

Jake was quiet for a moment. "Seeing him triggers you." It wasn't a question. She nodded and took comfort in knowing Jake could read her so well. "When we were at the gala and you told me to kiss you, it was because you saw him?"

She nodded again. "I needed a distraction."

The corner of his lips twitched. "And the first thing you thought of was kissing me?"

Heat crept over her chest, up her neck, and onto her face. She cleared her throat. "Well, yeah. Also, I knew he wouldn't approach me if we were kissing."

Jake held her gaze for a moment. Hints of amusement danced over his face, and she bit her lip to prevent a smile. Yes, she'd panicked when she'd seen Vincent. And yes, her first thought had been to get Jake's lips on hers. Because even then, there had been something about this man that had made her feel safe. "Don't let it go to your head, Mr. Alvarez," she said with a gentle nudge of her elbow into his stomach.

"Wouldn't dream of it, sweetheart."

She scoffed, then let out a breath, immediately sobering. "When Pru mentioned at the gala that Vincent had joined her Seattle team, I thought I was going to have a heart attack. I feel like such an ungrateful bitch for how I've avoided him."

"Carm, no. I'm sure he understands."

She chuckled, but it was humorless. "He does. He even said so today. But that kind of makes me feel worse, you know?"

"I do." He let out a heavy sigh. "Guilt is a bitch."

Turning in his arms, she framed his face in her hands and studied him for a moment. Her heart clenched at the turmoil swirling in his eyes, turmoil that she sensed didn't all come from the secrets she'd spilled. "Will you tell me about your guilt sometime?"

His brown eyes locked with hers, and something passed between them. What, she didn't quite know. "It's a story for a different night. We've had enough heavy for one day." He removed her hands from his face and pressed soft kisses to her palms. "What can I do for you, darlin'?"

Her heart squeezed. "Just this, Jake. Just this."

It was true. After recounting the horrors she'd endured, it felt like the weight on her shoulders had diminished. God knew it was still there, but it was a lot less heavy, a lot less painful.

"There's gotta be something I can do."

A small smile lifted her lips. If anyone understood the need to *do* something, it was her.

Her stomach grumbled, and she glanced at the bedside clock. It was coming up on seven o'clock. She'd slept through both their late lunch and dinner. Which said a lot, because she wasn't a napper—at all—and, frankly, considered them a waste of time.

She internally cringed. Yeah . . .

Her stomach rumbled again, and she peeked up at him through her lashes. "Food?"

He grinned, though it didn't quite reach his eyes. "How does a turkey pesto sandwich with provolone sound?"

Her stomach rumbled yet again, and she gestured to her belly with a sheepish smile.

His grin grew and finally sparkled in his eyes.

She framed his face in her hands—touching this man was not a hardship—and her thumbs traced his cheekbones. She tugged him closer, and her lips pressed to his, soft and gentle.

"Thank you," she murmured against his lips. "Thank you for listening."

"We're friends, first and foremost, Carmen. I am *always* here for you. Now, let's get you fed," he said, pressing a quick kiss to her lips. "And don't forget, we have an agreement to renegotiate."

CHAPTER EIGHTEEN

After a quick shower, Carmen had changed into a loose fitting top and leggings and joined Jake in the kitchen. As she was devouring the sandwich he'd made for her, his phone buzzed with an incoming call. Lara's name flashed on the home screen, and he declined it with a grimace.

"Don't not answer on my account," Carmen mumbled around a mouthful of chips—because, apparently, she *deserved* more than cucumbers and carrots after her boxing therapy session. Her words, not his. She was so fucking cute it was damn near ridiculous.

"Nah," he said with a shake of his head. "It's just Lara. I'm not sure I have the headspace right now, you know?"

Her eyes narrowed as she studied him, still chewing.

He winced and leaned back in his chair, crossing his arms over his chest. "Go ahead, sweetheart." Her head tilted, and her right brow arched. He chuckled. "Please, woman, I can see the questions churning in your gorgeous head."

Her brow arched higher. "Charming way of saying I'm nosy, Mr. Alvarez. But you know what? I'm surprisingly okay with that."

"I also said you're gorgeous, too. So that's gotta count for something, right?" He shot her his most charming grin, and she laughed.

Mission accomplished.

After polishing off her sandwich, she wiped her hands on her napkin. "It's just something your brother said when I ran into you guys at our regular gym the other morning."

It was his turn for a brow arch. "My brother's full of shit, so grain of salt and all that."

She grinned, then bit her lower lip, as if choosing her next words with care. As sexy as that looked, it didn't bode well for him. "If it's . . . difficult . . . for you to deal with Lara, then why put yourself through that?"

Well, fuck. That had been the last thing he'd expected to come out of Carmen's mouth, and it took everything he had to not let his jaw drop.

"I mean," she rushed on, "I get that you guys have a history, but if it's so damn stressful for you, then why do it?"

He let out a sigh. Why do it, indeed?

"Life is short, right?" She held his gaze, and he gave her a slight nod. "I'm sure Lara is a lovely person, but Jake, you're *my* friend. When I see something is making you unhappy, that is *not* okay—and, babe, that dinner with those two was *beyond* uncomfortable."

He didn't have a response. Nothing Carm had said was untrue.

With a slight shrug, she continued, "Something tells me that . . . awkwardness is the norm when it comes to them. So, why make yourself purposely stressed and miserable?"

There was so much to unpack there. One thing was for certain—her protectiveness over him soothed his growing unease. And shined a light on what an idiot he was.

Because he was a dumbass. He'd convinced himself long ago that Lara was the one who'd gotten away. He'd kept her on a pedestal and made her the standard against which he measured all other women. However, standing at his kitchen island with Carmen sitting in front of him, he saw the colossal flaw in that thinking.

He wasn't really comparing everyone else to Lara. He was comparing them to his idea of who Lara should have been versus who she actually was. His parents had loved her, and she'd gotten along with everyone. But they hadn't been a solid couple. Their relationship had been lacking something, something that had made him contemplate breaking up with her on numerous occasions. That missing element—as his brother had so obnoxiously pointed out—had fallen under his selective memory umbrella.

Jake had been holding on to the idealized memory of her because it had been easier to do that than put effort into meeting someone new. Because no one would or could measure up to the fake, perfect person in his head.

But Carmen? The woman had changed the game completely. She'd blown that fake, perfect person in his head completely out of the water without even trying. Not only that, but she was easily becoming his most favorite person—and that was even over his best friends and brother.

The fucking guilt, though . . .

How the hell was he going to get over the guilt?

"I thought I owed her," Jake murmured. Carmen's earlier words of concern joined Matt's in his mind. "Though I'm not so sure anymore . . ."

"Why do you think you owe her?"

How did he even begin to get into that whole can of worms? Tell her that he'd been a selfish prick, and in turn, her family had been destroyed?

Before he could formulate an explanation, his phone rang. A glance at it gave him pause. A video call from his building's secure entry system. He accepted, and Parker's face flashed on the screen. Jake let out a breath of relief. He'd never been so damn thankful to see his friend's face because he sure as hell wasn't ready to have that conversation with Carmen.

Chickenshit? Absolutely.

"Come on up, dude," Jake said, dialing the code that allowed access to his floor. "Your brother's here," he said to Carmen, turning from the kitchen island.

He stilled when her hand landed on his forearm, then glanced back at her.

"Don't think I'm going to forget this conversation, okay?" Her gaze was unflinching, yet somehow reassuring.

"I know, sweetheart. It's just a lot." More than he ever wanted to admit. Especially to her. "We've had a lot of heavy today, and I don't want to pile on more."

She nodded and rose to stand in front of him, her hand still on his forearm. "But whatever it is, Jake? It hurts you. And that's not okay with me."

Warmth bloomed in his chest. Then his heart stopped when she rolled up onto her tiptoes and brought her hand to the back of his neck, pulling him down to place a soft kiss on his lips.

"We'll talk about it later," she murmured, lowering back down. A soft smile played on her lips as she turned and headed toward the front door.

Once her back was to him, he let out a breath. He understood why Parker was here, had even been thankful for the interruption just moments ago. But damn. Now his friend was the very last person he wanted to see. Because that kiss? It was something he wanted to explore. Hell, *she* was something he wanted to explore . . .

Carmen opened the door and was immediately swallowed up in a giant hug.

"How you doing, big sis?"

"Good," she mumbled into Parker's shirt, wrapping her arms around his waist and squeezing. She took immense comfort from this lug of a guy. While they didn't always see eye to eye, he truly was the best brother.

Parker released her and slung an arm over her shoulders as they walked toward Jake, who still stood at the island. "I won't stay long. I'm sure you must be tired."

"Sort of." Her forehead scrunched. "I napped."

Parker came to an abrupt stop and faced her, disbelief coloring his features. "Seriously?"

She was sure a similar expression of disbelief was on her face. "I know, right?"

"When the hell was the last time you napped?"

Her lips pursed in thought. "Elementary school, maybe? In my defense, Jake took me to the boxing gym and showed me how to beat the shit out of a heavy bag this morning."

"What's up, man?" A grin spread on Parker's face as he gave Jake a chin lift. "I would have paid good money to see that."

"I was pretty impressive, I'll have you know. Even Cade de la Rosa and Matt said so."

"I'm sure those fuckers did," Parker scoffed with a shake of his head and an eye roll. Then his gaze grew somber. "Did it help you feel better?"

"You know, it did." Her mind drifted to her earlier conversation with the detectives. "It was a lot to process this morning."

"Remember, sis, you don't have to process everything right away. Sometimes you just need to hit shit and process later." He held her gaze. "And don't forget, we can all help."

She nodded. "I know."

His brow arched and his eyes narrowed. "Do you?"

Little punk. She narrowed her eyes right back, and he laughed. "That's what I thought."

"Punk," she grumbled.

"Yeah, but you love me."

"Sometimes I wonder," she murmured. "Can we shelve the what's-going-on chat for another night?" The last thing she wanted was to have this conversation with her brother.

"Sure, but the reason I'm here is twofold." He playfully elbowed her in the side. "You guys should come over for dinner tomorrow night."

She shook her head. "Sorry, work thing with the Downtown Seattle Association." She caught Jake's eye. "I sent you that calendar invite, right?"

He glanced at his phone, then back at her. "Yup, it's on my schedule for tomorrow."

"Jesus Christ," Parker chuckled. "You two are the biggest fucking geeks I know."

She pinched his side and twisted until he yelped and hopped away from her. "We're not geeks, idiot. We're fucking efficient."

"Nope. Gross, Carm," he groaned. "I don't want to hear the words *fucking* and *we* in relation to you two in the same sentence. Ever." He shuddered. "Tuesday then. Come to the pub for dinner?"

She mentally went through her upcoming events. "I'm good," she said, then met Jake's gaze. "You?"

He checked his calendar, then nodded. "I'm open."

"Park, can you make something good for that night's special, though?" she asked.

"Holy fuck, excuse me?" A ridiculous look of offense colored her brother's face, and she couldn't help but laugh. "Every damn thing I make is goddamn amazing, Carm."

She rolled her eyes and held her hands up in surrender.

"No need to get your panties in a twist, okay? Yes, everything you make is good." His brow arched. "I mean, it's all *great*," she clarified. "But I want something *super* great." She turned on the sister guilt. "The last day has been crazy, and I could use some good, stick-to-my-bones, comfort food, you know?"

"Fine," he huffed, yanking her into a loose headlock, "but you're still a brat. Don't think I'm not on to your sister-Jedi-mind-trick shit, because I am." She waited patiently for three heartbeats. "But I'll make one of your favorites. Beef stew?"

She shook her head, then gave him her sweetest grin. "Colcannon Shepherd's Pie?"

He groaned. "That's a pain in the ass to make for the pub." He let out a breath and rolled his eyes. "I can make some just for you. Lamb or beef?"

"Combo?" He nodded with another sigh, and she beamed up at him. "Thank you, Parker," she said in the singsong voice she knew he hated. The grimace on his face made her laugh. No matter how old they were, they still reverted to their ten-year-old selves.

"Don't push your luck, sis."

She patted his stomach, and when he didn't release his lock on her head, she elbowed him in the gut.

"For real, though," she said when her brother finally released her, "thank you for indulging my dinner request. And for stopping by."

"Don't be stupid." His arm was back over her shoulders, and he squeezed. "You knew I'd stop by to check on you. It's my brotherly duty. Like I said, my visit was twofold." He turned his gaze to Jake. "Did Kate talk to you last week?"

"Uh, yeah," Jake nodded, confusion making his brow crinkle. "About . . ."

Parker shrugged. "Something about a wireless keyboard

—or was it a mouse? I don't know, something she can hook up to her laptop, but it doesn't make noise?"

Carmen laughed the moment recognition hit Jake because his dark brown eyes lit up like fireworks.

"Both, actually," he said over his shoulder as he hustled toward his home office.

The moment Jake turned the corner, Parker spun toward her.

"Spill," he clipped out, then cringed. "Not the gross stuff. But like . . . are you really okay moving in with him? Are things okay with you guys? Is that fucker being respectful to you?"

She could only stare at her brother in fascination as the soft pink flush over his face deepened until he was scarlet.

"Do you *really* want to know, Park?" He looked as if he were debating his answer. "Look," she rushed on, saving him from deciding. "Things with Jake and I are . . . new."

His eyes narrowed. "You moved in with him, Carm. That's not the fucking definition of *new*."

Yeah. She'd give her brother that one. "I know. Regardless, things *are* still new. He and I are friends." She paused and smirked. "Who possibly do some of those 'gross' things you may have referred to earlier and—"

"Choose your next words carefully." He glared at her, crossing his arms over his chest. "I'm being one hundred percent serious here. Even though he's one of my best friends, *you* are my sister."

Her brother's serious gaze had her sobering. She wasn't sure she wanted to confess to him that what she and Jake had was an agreement. A fake arrangement. Because nothing between them felt fake. Yes, it wasn't permanent, but it was still real. At the same time, she didn't want to lie to her brother. She'd lied enough.

"Bottom line, little brother?"

"Please," he replied, his jaw clenching tight.

"Jake and I are friends, first and foremost." She did as Parker had asked and chose her words with care. "And he makes me feel safe."

For a moment, Parker held statue still. Then his shoulders relaxed, and his bottle-green eyes softened. With a slight nod, the corner of his lip tipped up in a lopsided grin. "Okay then."

What? Her brow furrowed in disbelief. "That's it?"

"Yup." He turned toward the hallway that led to Jake's office. "It's a fucking keyboard, Alvarez! How long is this gonna take?"

"Sorry," Jake said, emerging from the hallway, three different keyboards in his arms. "These two are the ones I told Kate she should try, and I pulled an extra one as well. They're all wireless, but they have different configurations for the ten-key, and I think she—"

"Nope," Parker interrupted, taking the keyboards from Jake and tucking them under his arm. "Don't care about the specifics, man. You know that shit bores me. I'll have my lovely lady call you tomorrow and you can bore her directly."

"You do that," Jake said with a chuckle. "Besides, she's much cooler to talk to than you. A lot better looking too."

Parker laughed and flipped him off with his free hand as he walked backward to the front door. "Text me tomorrow, okay, sis?"

She nodded, and her brows rose in surprise as he paused to man-hug Jake with a hearty slap on his back. "Thanks for watching over her, brother," he murmured before pulling the door closed behind him.

With the click of the door latch, they stood in silence.

Jake cleared his throat. "That went well." The surprise she felt was echoed in his voice.

"Yeah," she said as she let out a breath. "I wasn't sure what I was expecting, but it wasn't quite . . . that."

"Same," he said with a soft grin. Then he held his arms open. "Come here."

She didn't think twice. Three steps, and his arms were wrapped around her, her head resting on that perfect spot in the center of his chest.

"You okay, darlin'? It's been a crazy-ass last twenty-four."

She took a deep breath in. Was she okay? She'd been flying solo for so long—relying on herself alone, purposely keeping away from her family—that she'd forgotten what it was like to have people in her corner. People who weren't on her payroll, but actually cared for her.

He dropped a kiss on the top of her head. God, she loved how he always did that . . . the little touches, the little kisses, the little caresses.

"Tired, sweetheart?"

She should be exhausted, ready to turn in for the night, but she wasn't. She shook her head. She hadn't been lying when she'd told her brother about Jake. The man made her feel absolutely safe.

That wasn't all, though.

This man . . . he made her want things she shouldn't. Things she knew didn't work for her—had *never* worked for her. A long-lasting relationship was out of the question. Her track record spoke for itself. Aside from the emotional stuff, this man made her want. Period.

She pressed a kiss to his shirt-covered pec, then glanced up, resting her chin on his solid chest. "Weren't we going to renegotiate our arrangement?"

The grin on his face was immediate. The twinkle in his eyes decidedly naughty. "Well, Ms. Cunningham, I know what *I* had in mind, but we should probably discuss the terms in more detail."

The butterflies in her belly took flight. "Is that so, Mr. Alvarez?"

He kissed her forehead before stepping away. "Without a doubt, gorgeous." Snagging her hand, he gave her a playful yank toward the couch. Sinking into the cushion, he patted his lap.

Her pulse raced, and heat began to build within her as she settled herself across his lap. Her mind begged her to play it cool.

"Uh-uh," he said, patting her hip with a small shake of his head. "Up."

For a split second, she froze. Then scrambled to her feet, ice prickling her skin. Holy shit, had she misread things?

"First item." He took her hands in his and moved her until she stood directly in front of him, between his spread knees. "When it's just us, and you're on my lap? You're on my lap the right way." Tugging her hands toward him, a devilish grin spread on his handsome face. "On top of me and face to face, sweetheart."

It took a second for his words to register, and when they did, relief made her limbs loose. No, she hadn't misread things.

Though her knees trembled, a smirk grew on her lips and heat flooded her core. She placed a knee on each side of his lap, hovering over him. "I'm not sure I find any fault in that first item."

"I do," he murmured. His hands smoothed from her knees to her ass, then her breath left her when he yanked her tight against him. "You were too far away, Ms. Cunningham."

She couldn't hold back a moan as his hands squeezed her ass, rubbing her leggings-covered core against his hard cock. "Noted and agreed upon, Mr. Alvarez."

Her arms wrapped around his neck, and she pressed her chest harder against his. It took all her willpower to not devour him right then and there. "Second item," she said in a whisper, her breath mingling with his. "We are friends above all things. No matter our chemistry or anything else, we're friends first."

The hands molding her ass cheeks stilled, and he met her gaze, his dark brown eyes serious and steady. "Absolutely. Our friendship matters to me. Hell, you're one of my best friends, Carm." He smirked, and his eyes twinkled. His hands resumed their squeezing. "But a different kind of best friend."

"I like different." She rocked against his hips, getting almost enough friction. "Third item," she moaned as his lips found her neck. "This has nothing to do with gratitude or distraction. At least for me." Nerves warred with lust, but she needed to be clear. Transparent. Ish. "I've thought about this —about you—for . . ."

"For a long damn time, Carm," he finished, his hands moving to her hips to grind her harder against his straining erection. "Holy shit, for fucking forever."

Her nerves settled, and she melted into the heat he'd created. Every place his hands touched, everywhere his mouth kissed, turned molten.

"So, babe, if we get naked together—"

"When," he interrupted, nibbling the delicate flesh on the underside of her jaw.

Holy shit, that felt amazing. Wait. "What?"

"You said *if* we get naked together." He pulled slightly away and met her gaze. "Darlin', it's *when* we get naked. No *if* about it."

Goosebumps prickled her skin as heat soaked her panties. Holy shit, this man . . .

"Clarification then," she said on a sigh as his mouth resumed its exploration of her neck. "*When* we get naked, we only get naked with each other."

"Done," he growled, and his mouth slammed down on hers. His tongue licked at the seam of her lips, and she opened for him. She moaned as he expertly twined his tongue with hers. He pulled away, and their desperate pants filled the silent room. "Are we done with the itemized list, Ms. Cunningham? Because if so, I'd really like to lick every fucking inch of you."

Her fingers fisted in his short hair, and though only a few inches separated them, she yanked him closer. "Yes, please, Mr. Alvarez," she said against his mouth before nipping at his delicious lower lip.

They feasted on each other. Her body tingled with sensation after sensation.

She yelped when he stood and wrapped her limbs tight around him. "I've got you, darlin'," he murmured as he carried her down the hallway, his mouth never leaving hers.

Then she was being lowered onto his bed. His mouth paused its ravaging, and he straightened, standing between her spread legs. Heat flooded her core as his gaze hungrily roamed over her, then zeroed in on the apex of her thighs. One hand reached behind his neck, and then his shirt was gone, tossed to the floor.

Her breath left her as she took him in. The ravenous look on his handsome face. His sculpted chest. The ridges of his stomach muscles. The sexy V of his lower abs that pointed to the impressive length tenting his sweats.

Her mouth watered for him, and she licked her lips.

A deep rumble filled the quiet room, and her gaze shot back to his face. The man was wound tight but standing still, his body vibrating. "Can I take your clothes off, Carm? Are you comfortable with me doing that?"

Those whispered words had her heart spilling open. She'd wanted to protect herself from getting too close, from her heart breaking when this was all over. But with those tender words . . .

Holding her heart back from this sweet, sexy man was pointless. Because Jake was becoming everything to her. Comfort, safety, excitement, love. And all the damn things in between.

She held his gaze as she sat up and lifted her shirt off, tossing it over the side of the bed. Next to go was her bra. Then she held his darkening gaze as she leaned back on the bed, her thumbs hooked into the top of her leggings. "Help me with these?"

"It would be my pleasure, sweetheart." He crawled onto the bed until he hovered over her. For a moment, he simply stared at her. Then he took her mouth in a slow, deep kiss that had her toes curling.

His lips traveled over her neck and down the center of her chest. Each kiss soft. Each kiss gentle. Each kiss reverent.

He traced her belly button with his tongue, then sat up. Slowly peeling her leggings and panties down her legs, his lips kissed every bit of skin he exposed. When he pulled the last bit of her clothes off and tossed them aside, he stood at the foot of the bed and simply stared.

Excitement pooled in her belly, and her pussy throbbed. She needed him. Now.

His eyes darkened to almost black as he took her in, his gaze focusing on her most intimate spot. His body trembled, and his hands fisted at his sides, but he didn't move.

Her brow arched. Oh, hell no.

He was holding back. And that wouldn't do. Not at all.

She quickly crawled to the edge of the bed. Surprise and a hint of wariness flashed across his face as she knelt before him. He was still so much taller. She wrapped her hands around his neck and pulled until they were face to face.

"Do *not* treat me like I'm fragile, Jake." A look she couldn't read crossed his face, but she pressed on, though she gentled her tone. "I promise you I'm not going to break. I want this. I want *you*." She kissed him and poured every ounce of desire, every ounce of need, every ounce of trust into it. Breathlessly pulling away, she murmured against his lips, "I want to feel your mouth on me. I want to feel your cock deep inside me. I want to feel *all* of you."

He jerked—as if his restraint had finally snapped—and growled. Pulling her tight against him, his mouth devoured hers. Seconds later, he pulled away, his chest heaving. "I do *anything* you don't like, you tell me. Got it?"

"Yes," she whispered, nodding. "Please, Jake. I need you."

Before she could blink, she was on her back, shuddering with anticipation as he pulled her to the edge of the mattress and dropped to his knees. Tossing her thighs over his shoulders, he lowered his mouth to her dripping pussy and feasted.

"Jake," she moaned, her back arching. His strong arm pressed over her stomach, anchoring her in place. She was helpless to do anything but take it, take all the pleasure he was giving. And she wanted more.

Her hips rocked into his mouth as his lips and tongue teased her clit. Fire built within her with every sweep of his tongue, every nip of his teeth.

When his fingers pressed deep into her heat, she was lost. Tremors overtook her body, and he continued to devour her. His fingers pumped into her, his mouth and tongue never stopping until she quaked, detonated, and screamed out his name.

"You taste so fucking good," he moaned, lapping up every drop of her excitement. His fingers still worked within her, softly easing her back up. Her legs trembled, and he placed soft kisses on the delicate skin of her inner thighs.

As he stood, he pulled his fingers from her, then brought

them straight to his mouth. Keeping his gaze locked with hers, he sucked them clean of her essence. "You're so fucking delicious."

He effortlessly moved her to the center of the bed, then brought his mouth to hers as he eased between her legs. She tasted herself on his lips, and her pussy fluttered with need. Another growl. He lowered himself onto his elbows, framing her head. "Promise me you'll let me know if I do *anything* that makes you uncomfortable?"

God, this wonderful man. "I promise, Jake." She pressed a kiss to the furrow between his brows, then to his lips, and shot him a playful smirk. "But now, Mr. Alvarez, I need you inside me." She wrapped her legs around his waist and rubbed her core against his straining cock. "I want to feel every inch of you fill me."

His mouth was on hers again, and she sank into their kiss. She clutched onto his shoulders as he pulled away, and he chuckled. "Condom, darlin'," he murmured against her lips before reaching for his bedside drawer.

She took comfort in seeing it was an unopened box, not wanting to think of him with anyone else. Seconds later, he was back over her, and she couldn't think at all. His tongue tangling with hers, he slid into her in one long, deep thrust.

She cried out, and he stilled, giving her a moment to adjust.

"You're so damn perfect, Carm," he murmured. "I can't get enough of you."

"Show me," she said, rocking her hips.

And he did.

He pumped deep into her, filling her completely, and she met him thrust for thrust. Keeping a pace that drove her wild, he had her begging for release. Her second orgasm tore through her, and she shattered.

Gently riding her through it, he pulled out when she stilled. Her body was lax, every inch of her tingling.

"One more," he growled as he flipped her onto her hands and knees.

She tensed, self-conscious and unsure about this new position.

Soft kisses trailed along her back. Along the healing scars. She sighed, and her eyes filled with tears.

"Everything about you is beautiful, Carm." His gentle touch soothed her heart and calmed her soul. "You're so damn strong." Another kiss. "So damn brilliant." And another. "So damn sexy." He pushed into her from behind, and she exploded. And fell even harder for the wonderful man.

They lay in Jake's bed, limbs tangled. Her head was on his chest, and his heartbeat thumped steadily under her ear. She pressed herself tight against his side as his hand traced tiny circles on her naked hip. She'd never been so relaxed in her life.

"Sleep here with me tonight," he murmured.

She tensed, and her breath caught. She wanted to kick herself because there was no way in hell he hadn't noticed.

Breathe, Carmen. Just freaking breathe.

Taking that inhale and exhale, she forced each muscle in her body to relax. All the while, Jake continued caressing her hip.

"Don't think too hard on it, sweetheart. When we slept together last night, that was one of the best damn sleeps I've had in a long time." His hand at her hip roamed and squeezed her cheek. She smiled. He was most definitely an ass man. "You're like my own personal sexy little teddy bear."

"Fluffy and squishy, huh?" She chuckled and relaxed

further into him, tracing the tips of her fingers over the hard dips and valleys of his torso. "I'd take offense, but I'm still riding the high from that last orgasm."

"Give me a few minutes to recover, and I can keep that orgasm high going."

"Promises, promises," she teased, her fingers trailing back and forth over the faint vertical scar on his chest. "What's this from?"

Her heart squeezed when he tensed, just like she had moments earlier.

"Hey," she soothed, pressing a kiss to the solid flesh under her cheek before resting her head against him. "I showed you my scars, babe. Equality and all that, right?"

"Right," he chuckled, resuming his soft caresses. "Heart surgery. I had three before I was ten, and they did a good job cleaning up the scar on the last one. I remember seeing pictures of the earlier scars, and they were puffy and scary, like they'd taken a hacksaw to my scrawny, little kid chest."

Her head popped up to meet his gaze. "Wait. *Three* heart surgeries? How did I not know this about you?"

He shrugged. "I try not to dwell on it."

Based on the turmoil rolling in his dark brown eyes, there was a lot to unpack there. Because there was holding back, and then there was *this*. If she'd been able to come clean, then so could he.

She pinned him in her gaze, her brow arching as she silently dared him to look away. After a couple heartbeats, a grin lifted the sides of his lips. "Fine. I *try* not to dwell on it."

She kissed his chest again, not taking her eyes from his. "How's that working out for you?"

He squeezed her ass, and his chest rumbled with mirth beneath her. "Things aren't too shabby right now, to tell you the truth."

"Jake," she said, drawing out his name. "I am the master deflector, so don't bother bullshitting me. Talk to me."

He groaned and adjusted their positions until her top leg was hooked over him, his hand firmly on her backside. "Sweetheart, I don't even know where to begin. The baggage is heavy."

She traced the side of his face. "Start at the beginning."

CHAPTER NINETEEN

What was it about this woman that made him want to spill his guts? He wasn't one to cuddle after sex. His encounters over the last few years had been casual and brief.

Now? He was lying with Carmen wrapped in his arms, and he'd made damn sure there was zero space between them. He didn't want to move. Ever.

Beyond the physical, he wanted to stay like this—with her —forever. He'd never talked about his hang-ups with anyone outside of his twin. Even then, it'd been a glossed-over version. He and Matt hadn't needed the extra words because his brother had been there, had witnessed firsthand the shit-show that'd been their childhood. A childhood that, to this very day, he was ashamed to admit still fucked with his head.

But there was something about Carmen that had his mouth opening, had the words—the closely held secrets— spilling from his lips. He truly didn't want to think too hard as to why . . .

"My parents were both born in Colombia. My mom's family immigrated to the US when she was in elementary school, and my dad's family came over when he was in high school. They met in college—well, she was in college, and he was working near the university.

"Personality-wise, they're about as opposite as you can get. My mom's very proper. Her family was very well-off, both in Colombia and once they were here. My dad's family wasn't. At all. Prior to meeting my mom, he was that neighborhood tough guy who'd always get into fights. To this day, he's very much the macho type—the me-man-you-woman kind of guy." He shook his head in disgust. That toxic machismo had been the bane of his existence for most of his life. "Somehow, they ended up together."

"Are they still together?"

He nodded. How? He hadn't a clue.

"And your mom was cool with that?"

"She's still content in the defer-to-my-man role." Another long-standing point of contention. A point that ate at him no matter how old he got. Because wasn't a mother supposed to stand up for her children?

His pulse quickened with agitation, like it always did at the thought of his parents. Carmen hummed, moving her head to his shoulder to look at him. Her expression was thoughtful as she resumed running her delicate fingers over his chest. His racing pulse settled, and his gaze locked on the ceiling. While having Carmen in his arms steadied him, looking at her when he talked about this shit was another thing entirely.

"I was born with a heart defect and was in and out of the hospital. I had my first heart surgery when I was a baby. Another when I was five, and the last when I was ten." His father had never let him forget what a time-suck and financial burden he'd been. "Even after the last surgery, I was fragile and scrawny for years."

Carmen snorted as her hand smoothed over the ridges of his stomach muscles. "Really?"

"Yeah," he chuckled, the vain part of him happy she liked what she saw. "This"—he motioned to his torso—"didn't start happening until the middle of high school when Matt took me under his wing." After he'd walked in on their dad beating the shit out of Jake, screaming in his face about what a pussy he was. "Growing up, Matt was the stronger twin . . . more athletic, popular, charming . . . all of that. I excelled in academics. And *only* academics."

After another caress over his abs, he felt Carmen frown against his chest. "Sorry, babe, but I find that hard to believe."

"Sweetheart, not only was I the founding member of my high school's three-member robotics team, but I was president of both the math and science clubs. Athletic stud, I was not."

Carmen's head popped up, and the surprise and humor on her face had him laughing. "Well," she said, her eyes softening, "I bet you were still sweet and charming back then."

"Doubtful. More like awkward. Painfully awkward at that." He laughed, the sound bitter to his own ears. "Dad was extremely demanding, and Mom was . . . mostly silent. Don't get me wrong, she took care of us and was at my side every time I was sick, but Dad made it clear he didn't want her 'babying' me."

Carmen gasped. "But you were a kid. An actual, honest-to-God sick kid, at that."

"She did her best, I suppose." He shrugged, and that old bitterness rose, that anger that said his mother should have tried harder to stand up for them.

The sharp words his father had often spat rang in his ears: *Why can't you be like your brother? Why did God have to give me you?*

Jake had tried to resign himself to the fact that he'd never measure up in his father's eyes. But he'd been an idiot who'd held on to hope that maybe one day . . .

"As long as Matt and I can remember—and whether we realized it at the time or not—Dad was always pitting us against each other. Always making us compete. Matt always did great in athletics and popularity." Which was what his dad valued. "I did great with academics." Which his father didn't put much stock in because if you were the strongest man in the room, *that's* what mattered. *That's* what people would respect. "But Matt and I always stuck together."

He was silent for a moment, the bitterness and anger swirling within him. Carmen pressed a kiss to his skin, and he remembered to breathe.

"During our sophomore and junior years in high school, our parents' marriage got really rocky. Looking back, they fought a lot about us." It was the only time he could remember his mom standing up for them. It had been a brief blip in the grand scheme of things, but she'd still done it. So that was something. "My father started getting more physical with me, shoving me around. I was getting taller, but I was still a beanpole. My brother walked in on our dad hitting me once, and after that . . ."

The hand caressing his chest stilled. "That's when Matt took you under his wing."

"Yeah. I'd occasionally get picked on at school, but it wasn't too bad because Matt always stuck up for me, and everyone loved Matt. But when it started getting bad at home, Matt wanted me to be able to defend myself." Against their own father.

As much as his mother had disappointed him growing up, it had been during that brief period when she'd grown a backbone. She'd pulled them aside and said, "You're two halves of a whole. Help each other. Always. Your father is stubborn and doesn't understand either of you."

His father's angry and disgusted voice reverberated in Jake's head. He'd yell at them for being worthless. At Jake for being weak and pathetic. At Matt for daring to like art and music. And just because their father had yelled it in Spanish hadn't made it cut any less.

"Matt and I have always been close, but we got a lot closer then. It was eye-opening for us to see our father fall from the pedestal we'd unknowingly put him on. A lot of the pedestal was built on fear and not wanting to disappoint him. It took time, but we finally saw our parents as people. Deeply flawed people . . . but aren't we all?"

"Yeah, but some more than others." She pressed another kiss to his chest. "There's a difference between flawed people who belittle others to puff themselves up and the flawed ones who mostly hurt themselves. The people who hurt others just because they can are the lowest."

"Agreed. I was lucky to have Matt by my side. I'm not sure how I would have survived without him."

"Don't sell yourself short. I'm sure he would say the same for you."

"Maybe." He frowned. "Of the two of us, he's definitely the more well-adjusted."

"You're biased, babe," she said on a sigh. "Pretty sure your brother would say otherwise."

Her surety sent a wave of warmth through him. "Perhaps. He struggled a bit academically, not because he wasn't smart, but because he was involved in every damn sport. So, we became really good at multitasking. I tutored him a lot, but mostly we did it at the gym instead of the library."

"So your workaholic tendencies started young?"

He could hear the smile in her voice, and he squeezed her hip. "You're one to talk, Ms. Cunningham."

"Matt went to UW, right? I remember seeing the two of you together a lot and thinking you guys were just ridiculous."

"Ridiculous?"

She propped her chin on the hand she was resting on his chest, her eyes dancing with mischief. "You know you're hot, babe. While this"—she cruised a hand from his neck to his lower abs, leaving goosebumps across his skin—"didn't happen until a little later, you were always delicious. Then there were two of you?" She fanned herself. "Trust me, you guys were the talk of many girls. Many who would have done anything to be in the middle of a naked Alvarez sandwich."

"Right," he snorted.

She chuckled. "And this aw-shucks thing you do? Makes me want to corrupt you a little more."

"Corrupt away." His hand ran over the soft skin of her hip, squeezing a handful of her perfect ass. "But no, Matt didn't actually go to UW."

"What?"

"He was down at Oregon on a baseball scholarship, but when it wasn't baseball season, he was up at UW a lot. Even though I became tight with Parker and Blake, my brother was always around."

"Wow, I never would have guessed."

"I think it took Parker and Blake a while to realize he didn't go to school with us, too." He chuckled. "Overall, I think being away from each other on a day-to-day basis was good for us. We were able to find our footing without being in each other's shadow, if that makes sense."

"It does. When you have each other's backs for so long, it's a learning experience to branch out on your own."

"Exactly. We didn't have to compete with each other— even though ours was a friendly competition—and we found our own people. We didn't have our parents hovering over us, pointing out our flaws."

"Ahhh . . . the Alvarez twins became individual men."

A soft smile touched his lips, but then he sobered,

thinking back to that time. "Then Mom got sick our sophomore year in college." His stomach twisted as he remembered how his mom's voice had shaken and his dad's voice had cracked. "That changed things for me and Matt. We tried to support Mom as best we could, and for better or worse, that whole ordeal brought Mom and Dad closer together. They were figuring out their shit. So Matt and I tried to put our shit with our father aside. And it was good for a while . . ."

She grimaced. "Until it wasn't, right?"

He nodded. "It was like a reprieve. Then, thankfully, Mom got better. And Dad fell back into his regular asshole ways."

"Is he still?"

"Oh, fuck," he snorted. "Absolutely."

"But he has to be proud of you for all you've accomplished."

He scoffed. "You'd think, but no. He sees what I do as a joke, not a *manly* or *real* job like Matt's."

"What the hell?" Her jaw dropped, and anger swirled in her eyes. That warmth from her earlier belief in him grew. "Wait, didn't you pay off your parents' house?"

"I did. For my mom." His lip curled. "He'll shit all over me about what I do, but he has no problems taking my fucking money."

She held his gaze for a moment before laying her head back on his chest and squeezing him. "I'm sorry, babe. That sucks."

He returned her squeeze and pressed a kiss to the top of her head. Damn, this woman felt right. "So, Ms. Cunningham, with our renegotiated deal, I, unfortunately, have a lot of baggage." And they hadn't even gotten into the whole Lara bullshit. "You still cool with our new arrangement?"

He felt her smile against his skin, and when her hand traveled down his stomach, pausing at each valley of his abs, he sucked in a breath. "We all have issues, Mr. Alvarez, and as you know, I have my fair share." Her hand moved farther south, and when she took his hardening cock in her hand, stroking him with just the perfect amount of pressure, he forgot to breathe entirely. "But yeah, I'm good with our new arrangement."

228

CHAPTER TWENTY

Carmen stifled a yawn as she disconnected the video chat. Reaching for her near-empty cup, she glanced at the clock on her monitor and debated if she had enough time to run out to the café next door for a fresh coffee. Her nose wrinkled. No, because then she'd have to hunt down Jake to accompany her since she'd promised him that she wouldn't leave the office alone. Office coffee, it was.

She rose from her chair and stretched her arms above her head. Groaning, she bent at the waist and held the stretch for a five-count before straightening. Her body ached, but in the most delicious way. Her arms were sore from the boxing gym, but her hips, thighs, and abs were sore from a much more . . . enjoyable workout.

She bit back a grin. Three times they'd gone at it the night before. She'd lost count of how many times she'd flown apart in his arms. Her lips twisted in a smirk. Well, not necessarily his arms. There was something to be said about a man in ridiculous shape. Without a doubt, the man in question had stamina. He'd effortlessly moved her from position to position. Her heart fluttered, and her thighs clenched at the memory, and she knew the grin growing on her face was a satisfied one.

A loud slam jolted her from her thoughts. Before she could register the raised voices, her office door burst open. She startled, her heart knocking hard in her chest.

"Are you fucking kidding me, Carmen?" Brian shouted, slapping the door back open when it tried to close on him. He loomed in her doorway, fury turning his face scarlet. "You called the fucking cops on me?"

Keeping her desk between them, she rose and held her hands out in a placating gesture. She'd seen him upset before, angry even. This was something else. "Brian, I didn't call the cops on you. They were just following up on an incident that happened on Satur—"

"Those fucking detectives came to me at fucking work, Carmen! At *work*! How fucking dare you?"

She jerked back as if he'd struck her, and her anger began to simmer. Oh, hell no. "How dare *me*? Someone stole my car and lit it on fucking fire, Brian!" Her chest squeezed at the thought of the poor woman who'd been trapped inside. "So you had to answer some questions. Poor fucking you."

He took two angry steps into her office, and she backed away, bumping into the bookcase behind her desk. She hadn't thought his face could get any redder, but there it was. "I was in the middle of a meeting with goddamn investors, Carmen!"

This selfish asshole was fucking unbelievable. "Look, Bri—"

"Is there a problem, Mr. McAllister?" a familiar voice interrupted.

Her gaze swung to her doorway and found Matt, with Elise hovering in the main office behind him, hands wringing, face full of concern.

"This doesn't concern you, Jake," Brian spat, not looking

away from her. "Why don't you go back to your little video games?"

"Detective Mateo Alvarez." Matt stepped fully into her office, positioning himself between her and Brian.

Her ex did a double-take. He stared at Matt, and his eyes narrowed, as if trying to figure out a puzzle. "How do you know who I am?"

"You met my colleagues earlier today. Detectives Vasquez and Apone." Matt shrugged. "It's a small department." While Matt wasn't quite as broad as Jake, the man was equally ripped. Like his twin, he was a few inches taller than Brian and easily outweighed him by at least twenty pounds of muscle. "I suggest you calm down and step away from Ms. Cunningham."

With lips pinched in a tight line, Brian turned his glare to Carmen. "You're going to fucking regret this."

"Mr. McAllister," Matt said, his voice sharp, "was that a threat?"

"No." Brian sneered.

Tense silence ticked by as he continued to glare at her. God, she hated this guy.

"I suggest you leave, Mr. McAllister," Matt said.

"And I suggest, Officer, that—"

"Detective."

Brian's upper lip curled. "I suggest, *Detective*, that you stop harassing me, or I'll have to file a report with whoever is in charge of you."

Carmen's jaw dropped as Brian turned on his heel and stormed away, slamming the office's front door on his way out. Holy shit.

"Are you okay?" Elise asked, peeking into her office. "I'm sorry. I tried to stop him, but he just barged right past me."

"No, Elise, it's okay," she replied with a deep exhale, shaking her head. "I'm sorry you had to deal with that."

"Speaking of," Matt said, roughing his hand over his jaw. "You were married to *that*?"

"I know." She cringed and smoothed her hair with her hands in an attempt to pull herself together. As she straightened her blouse, she paused. "Wait, what are you doing here?"

"I'm meeting Jake for lunch." He nodded toward Elise. "She ran out of your office and thought I was Jake. I could hear that fucker shouting from the hallway. Sorry, but no one yells at my brother's girl." He shrugged.

A flush heated her cheeks, and for a moment, she was speechless. The simplicity of his words tugged at her heart. "Well, thank you—"

"I'm so sorry, Carmen," Elise interrupted, a sheepish grimace on her face, "but you need to be on Zoom with the Bolivia teams in three minutes. This is the *only* time everyone can meet."

Carmen nodded, straightening her shoulders. *Focus, dammit. You have people depending on you.* "On it. Thank you, Elise. Again, I'm sorry about what happened."

"I'll head out," Matt said, tapping her desk. "You okay?"

She nodded as she sat back down in her office chair. "Thanks for the save."

"Not a problem."

He turned to leave, and her mouth opened, then slammed shut. "Uh, Matt?" She cleared her throat when he turned around with a dark brow lifted in question. "Any chance I can have you *not* mention this to your brother?"

He flashed a smirk that was so familiar, yet not. "Not a chance in hell, baby," he said with a wink. "*And* I'm gonna mention this to Vasquez and Apone."

She leaned back in her chair with a frown. Damn Brian for making everything more freaking difficult. "I figured as much."

With a wave, Matt was out the door.

She shook out her hands and straightened her spine, then turned her attention to her monitors.

Focus, Carmen. Work first. Everything else later.

Opening the video conference app on her computer, she pasted her work smile on and clicked connect.

She glanced across the crowded Grand Lobby of Benaroya Hall and caught Jake's eye. He was deep in conversation with, if she recalled correctly, the head of another successful Seattle mobile gaming company. However, he still shot her a wink with that sexy smirk she was a sucker for.

"I assume you'll be bringing your handsome young man to dinner on Saturday," Prudence Weatherby cooed.

Carmen nearly choked on her sauv blanc. She'd been so busy daydreaming about said handsome young man that she hadn't heard the other woman approach. She internally cringed—she really needed to work on that whole situational awareness thing.

Though Prudence was the last person she wanted to make small talk with this evening, it was a relief to have an excuse to avoid the woman's matchmaking and aging-egg comments. "You know, Carmen dear, I was really hoping to introduce you to my neighbor's nephew, or that you'd rekindle your 'friendship' with that handsome Vincent, but I must admit . . ." she trailed off, blatantly ogling Jake.

Even from across the room, Carmen saw Jake's eyes widen at the woman's lecherous perusal, and she bit the inside of her cheek to keep from laughing.

"I can't blame you one bit, my dear," Prudence continued. "Not only is his bank account flush, but he is simply delectable. That face and all those muscles, I mean, he's just . . . umph!"

Carmen lost the battle and laughed, her face heating at the memory of just what those muscles could do to her. "You're not wrong." She chuckled into her wine.

"Well, ticktock, my dear," Prudence murmured, raising her champagne glass to Jake with a smile. "If you plan on making babies with that specimen, God knows you're not getting any younger."

Annnd there it was. Carmen's molars ground together, but she managed to keep a pleasant expression on her face. Somehow.

Prudence nodded to another person across the room, then turned back to Carmen and air-kissed her. "Don't forget to bring him on Saturday. It's a casual dinner event, so please encourage him to wear something more . . . fitted. I may be a few decades older, but I'm not dead, my dear."

"I'll see what I can do."

Prudence waved at Jake as he approached, and Carmen grinned.

"So," she began as Jake moved to stand next to her, his hand resting at the small of her back. "Do you feel like a piece of meat?"

"Not gonna lie, darlin', but I'm feeling a little violated," he replied with a slight shudder. "You know how you have a great poker face?"

She nodded with a smile.

"Well, *that* woman doesn't, and let me tell you." He wrapped an arm around her waist and pulled her closer to his side—business-appropriate closer, of course. However, when he leaned down and spoke softly in her ear, goose-bumps erupted over her skin. "That woman was thinking some dirty thoughts about me."

Carmen bit back a laugh. "Was she now?"

"Afraid so." His lips nuzzled the tiniest bit closer to her

ear. "I'm a little traumatized, and I think you need to make it better."

She pulled slightly away and looked up at him, finding humor and heat in his gaze. "Is that so, Mr. Alvarez?"

That sly grin lifted the side of his mouth. "Let's get out of here."

Her forehead scrunched. As tempting as the offer was—and it was beyond tempting—they were at a networking event where she not only needed to actually network but also touch base with some of CWC's donors. Hopefully, she'd also meet some possible new contributors.

Jake laughed, the sound warm and soothing, and his arm around her waist squeezed. "I can see the war in your eyes, sweetheart."

She cringed. "Sorry, but I really do need to make more connections in the community—outside of my bubble, that is. I've been gone a long time."

Putting a bit of space between them, he leaned down to speak into her ear again. "Have I told you that your drive is ridiculously sexy?" He dropped a quick kiss to her forehead, and for a heartbeat, she froze.

Public displays of affection were *not* something she did.

Her mind flashed to the kiss she'd shared with Jake at the gala, and she internally grimaced. Okay, public displays of affection were something she *tried* not to do. That particular occasion had been desperate times and all that.

This was different. As brief as Jake's kiss just now had been, she didn't know how to react. At all.

"Relax, darlin'," he murmured, humor dancing in his eyes. "No one's looking. You trust me, right?" She nodded and remembered to breathe. "Good," he said, straightening to his full height. He popped his elbow out for her to take. "Madam?"

She smiled. How could she not? Her shoulders relaxed as she hooked her arm in his.

"Care to meet some tech geeks outside of your nonprofit bubble?"

"I happen to *love* tech geeks." Her smile froze on her face. Shit. Had she said that out loud? She bit the inside of her cheek and prayed her face wasn't as flushed as it felt.

"Darlin', that's good to know." The deep rumble of his chuckle had her face heating more. "This particular bunch of tech geeks have questionable social skills, but they're good guys. They also have too much money, and I'd be more than happy to help you divest them of some of it."

"By all means, lead the way," she said, laughter easing the final remnants of her tension.

The remainder of the evening was a success. With Jake at her side, she was introduced to an entire group of new possible investors. The "tech geeks" were exactly as he'd described, and they were enthusiastic about giving back. Was it most likely a tax write-off for their companies? Sure. But tax write-off money spent the same as altruistically donated money; the dollars would fund CWC's programs regardless of what tax breaks the donor received.

For once, the matriarchs in her nonprofit bubble didn't hound her with blatant matchmaking attempts or comments about her relationship status. When she did speak with them, they discussed their upcoming projects and some of their recent successes.

Carmen wasn't going to lie—it disappointed her immensely that it had taken a man on her arm for these women to take her seriously. But it was what it was, and there was nothing she could do to change it anytime soon.

As the networking event came to a close, she realized it had been eye-opening. Outside of the old guard—the women who'd known her since she'd been in elementary school—

Carmen had been taken seriously and treated as a consummate professional. At past events, no one had ever approached her unless they'd wanted to discuss CWC or needed something. And no one had *ever* casually joked with her.

But people had tonight.

She hated to admit that she'd enjoyed herself this evening. Hell, she'd laughed more at this event than she had in . . . well . . . ever. Laughing and work events did not go hand in hand.

At least, they hadn't. Tonight had been different. And it was all because of the man next to her.

She glanced at Jake as their Uber driver maneuvered the downtown Seattle streets. Had they actually defined what their new arrangement was before they'd torn each other's clothes off last night? If so, she couldn't remember. Whatever it was, this non-relationship relationship felt . . . right.

Whether they were networking or working out or simply having coffee, being with Jake was easy. Natural. She'd never had a relationship like this.

Then there was the inferno between them.

And not only was Jake funny and smart and crazy hot, but he was so damn thoughtful.

After the craziness with Brian earlier in the day, she'd been slammed with back-to-back-to-back video and conference calls. What had Jake done? He'd snuck into her office while she'd been on a conference call and placed two cookies —one oatmeal raisin and one snickerdoodle—and her favorite boba tea on her desk. Then he'd shot her a wink with that sexy smirk and left.

When her calls had finally wrapped up, Elise had informed her that he'd purposely waited until she was on the conference call before dropping off her goodies because he hadn't wanted to disturb her during her video calls.

Sweet. The man was so damn sweet.

However, it was bittersweet. She knew a long-term relationship wasn't in the cards for her, and she needed to constantly remind herself to enjoy the now.

If only she could squash that fluttering whenever he looked at her. That fluttering that wanted *this*—with *him* —forever.

But no. Three strikes and you're out. Long-term was not a match for her. Her three divorces were undeniable proof. As was the truth that she'd held back from everyone. Outside of her lawyers' offices, she'd never discussed the specifics of her divorces. Nor had she ever commented on the general assumption that she'd left all three of her faithless, gold-digging husbands.

Because that hadn't been the case.

Thanks to her strong and poised facade and the NDAs the men had signed, no one knew that each one of her husbands had filed for divorce from her. She prayed no one ever would. Hell, they'd all left her long before the papers had been served.

She'd never admit it out loud, but each divorce decree had put a permanent crack in her heart, in her confidence, and in her self-worth. Even all these years later, they still hurt, still had her chest clenching painfully tight.

The fact that she let them continue to hurt her made her weak.

But the pain was more than dented pride. It was humiliation. Because while she had countless professional and educational accolades, the men who had vowed to love her forever—who she'd truly believed each and every fucking time—had all found her lacking in the most basic way. Not only as a woman, but as a human.

Boring. Cold. Deficient. Not worth the hassle.

And those men didn't hold a candle to Jake. Not even

close. He'd come to mean more to her than any of her exes. He mattered more than she'd let herself admit.

The knowledge that their relationship had an end date stung. If she allowed herself to give in to the idea of more, when he eventually left, she wasn't sure she'd survive. So no matter what the fluttering in her stomach said or that tiny voice in her soul whispered and hoped for, she needed to remember that everyone always left her.

She winced at the lie she was feeding herself.

But maybe if she repeated it to herself enough—that she hadn't already completely fallen for the man—maybe she'd eventually believe it.

The day flew by. Before Jake knew it, the alarm on his phone buzzed, letting him know it was six o'clock. He and Carmen were due at the pub in thirty minutes for dinner with the crew.

His busy day had started out perfectly: with his face buried between Carmen's soft thighs and then her riding his dick like it was her job. The damn woman was a perfectionist and workaholic, so that said *a lot*. He couldn't stop his grin from exploding.

When they'd arrived at work, he'd admittedly had a spring in his step. They'd parted ways, and he'd spent most of his day with his designers and coders, brainstorming additional possibilities for the next update to their Square Peg world. For the first time in what seemed like forever, he'd enjoyed every second of his workday.

He glanced at the short stack of papers on his desk and frowned. A large part of his day's enjoyment had been because he'd avoided these fucking papers. Resumes for a CFO.

He ran a barebones ship at Alvarez Tech. It was just him

and a handful of graphic designers and coders. He occasionally had an office admin, but they tended to not last very long. He wasn't quite sure why. Though he'd been accused of being a micro-manager on more than one occasion.

Bullshit was what that was.

So that left the big-picture work, along with the day-to-day details and the company's financials, to him. Not to mention the advertising and promotion work he did for The Spotted Dog.

He wasn't complaining. At all. He loved what he did for both Alvarez Tech and the pub. But he was fucking exhausted.

As much as he didn't want to admit it, he needed to delegate, and the most logical place to start was Alvarez Tech's financials. No, it wasn't that he didn't *want* to admit it. It was that he *loathed* admitting it. Because it was something he should have done a while ago, but he'd been too damn stubborn to listen to advice.

He'd recruited Kate, who ran her own bookkeeping company, of which The Spotted Dog was a client, a few times to help him with his company's books. Each and every time, she'd reamed his ass—politely, of course—and put him in his place about his lack of bookkeeping abilities. Something his accountants also liked to remind him about every quarter.

Looking at the handful of resumes on his desk, he had to admit that Kate and his accountants might have all had a point. It stung his pride, sure. But spending the day with his designers and coders had reminded him why he'd started his mobile gaming company in the first place. All that work didn't tire him out. It didn't even feel like work.

It was the day-to-day shit and the financials that left him exhausted. Shit that had to get done, but that he always put off until the last possible moment because it was boring as fuck. Not the most mature way of handling things, but there were only so many hours in the day.

He eyed the resumes again and vowed they would be a top priority tomorrow. If he could get the financials off his plate, he could spend more time doing what he loved—creating fun worlds people could get lost in. And spending more time with Carmen.

Earlier, while she'd been on a conference call, he'd dropped off lunch for her—a chicken and roasted beet salad. He wondered if she'd enjoyed the cookies he'd added. Her favorites were oatmeal raisin and snickerdoodle, but today he'd mixed it up with a mint chocolate chip, an iced oatmeal, and a sugar cookie topped with Fruity Pebbles and a milky glaze. He'd had one of each, and they'd been phenomenal.

He wasn't quite sure where his obsession with feeding the woman had come from. He knew she was just as busy, if not busier, than he was. He also knew Carmen prioritized her meetings and schedule above her own needs, resulting in the bad habit of forgetting to eat. She was already tiny, and the last thing he wanted was her wasting away. So he'd taken it upon himself to help, to make things a little easier for her.

Yes, he brought her heathy-ish meals, but considering how hard she also worked out—five-mile runs were a cakewalk for his badass woman—he also brought her some treats. Because who didn't deserve a treat?

The alarm on his phone buzzed again, and he quickly organized his desk before shutting down his computer. As the last one in the office, he locked up before heading down the hall to CWC.

Jake glanced around the full table, and a sense of happiness—of rightness—filled him. The Spotted Dog had been Blake's dream, and it had been no surprise to anyone when he'd recruited Parker to run the pub's kitchen. But Jake had been surprised when Blake had asked him to be their third partner.

Yes, they were best friends. And yes, he and Blake had started their own small tech company in college, which they'd quickly sold to Microsoft for a heinous amount of money. But still.

While they were all close, Blake and Parker were more like brothers than cousins. The two reminded Jake of him and Matt, so he'd been beyond honored to have been invited to join them.

When The Spotted Dog had first opened, Alvarez Tech had already been established but hadn't yet blown up, and his friends' willingness to be flexible with his hectic schedule meant the world to him. No matter how busy he was, he always did everything he could to help the guys. They handled the day-to-day operations, so he dealt with marketing, advertising, and whatever promotional help they needed.

Glancing around the table—from Parker and Kate, to Blake and Raven, to Carmen next to him—he couldn't help but smile. For the longest time, the guys had held the reins of the pub in a tight grip, doing everything themselves, never taking days off. They'd been the epitome of owner-operators. Lately, though, they'd started delegating to the rest of the pub's more than capable crew. This evening, Adam was in charge of the kitchen in Parker's place, and Melody was behind the bar.

"Balance," Parker had said to him not so long ago. "I didn't have that before, but all the craziness with Kate made me see what I was missing. You should give this balance thing a shot sometime, man."

Jake glanced at the woman seated next to him. He doubted Parker had intended what he'd said to apply to his sister. Regardless, balance sounded nice. Balance with Carmen sounded even better. He really should give it a shot.

"So, Carm," Parker said, bringing him back to the conversation, "I made an extra Colcannon Shepard's Pie, so make sure you take it home with you tonight, okay?"

"Thank you, little brother." She beamed at Parker, and Jake's heart squeezed. Damn, she really was the prettiest thing.

A sharp kick to his shin had him jerking. He glanced across the table and met Parker's glare.

"Dude. Please keep in mind that's my sister you're looking at all"—Parker waved his hand in the general direction of Jake's face—"like that."

The table broke out in laughter as Kate elbowed Parker in the side with a murmured, "Oh, knock it off."

Jake peeked over at Carmen, and aside from her cheeks being slightly more pink than usual, she didn't seem upset by her brother's jab. Which was reassuring because he wanted—no, needed—to renegotiate the terms of their arrangement again. He wanted to chuck the entire thing and just continue what they were doing. Together. Exclusively. And possibly—his chest clenched—forever.

He knew that he was jumping the gun, but the thought of being with Carmen like this—comfortable, surrounded by their friends, sneaking lecherous looks at one another—for a long, long time had his insides tightening. The more time he spent with her, the more of her he wanted. He'd truly never wanted anything, any*one* as much.

He could be honest, though, and say the thought of forever with her scared the fuck out of him.

She was skittish. No one came out of three divorces unscathed. He also knew she hung on to their arrangement like a shield to protect herself from him, just like she used her poise, impeccable business clothes, and fake smile as armor against others. And he wasn't sure he was enough to get past all her defenses, enough to convince her to give them a chance. A real chance.

Even if she did, when Carmen found out what he'd done, how his selfish actions had destroyed Lara's family, he doubted she'd remain with him. A sour ball rolled in his stomach. What he'd done was unforgivable, and he wouldn't blame her when she walked away from him.

"Any new updates, Carm?" Blake asked, interrupting Jake's thoughts.

She tensed, the tightening of her shoulders minute, the clench of her jaw almost unnoticeable. Almost.

He leaned back in his seat and placed his hand on her thigh, gently squeezing.

Sitting taller, she brought her napkin to her lips. She cleared her throat and rested the fist clutching her napkin next to her near-empty plate. Her free hand drifted to her lap, and she clutched his hand. Hard.

His gaze locked on her profile. Her beautiful face remained composed and relaxed, never letting on that she held his hand in a death grip. He intertwined his fingers with hers and, without thought, brought her hand to his lips, then placed their connected hands back onto her lap.

Her face swung to his. Surprise flashed in her big brown eyes before they softened. She held his gaze as she took a deep breath in, then slowly exhaled.

I've got you, he silently told her.

The corners of her lips twitched up, and she gave him the tiniest nod before turning to their table. "I talked to Detective Vasquez earlier today. Unfortunately, she didn't have much of an update. They still don't know who's behind this, and they're following up on some possible leads."

"Did they mention what those leads were?" Parker interjected.

Carmen shook her head. "They got the autopsy results back, but they're still waiting on the lab results. Apparently, you can tell age and ethnicity from the blood test. They couldn't identify the woman, but she was my height and roughly my size. Thankfully, I guess, she didn't die because of the fire or smoke. She'd been shot three times." She paused and cleared her throat again. "She also had a broken shoulder and forearm. Somehow, they determined all her injuries, including the gunshot wounds, were before . . . that she'd already been dead before the car fire."

Jake released her hand, yanked her chair closer, then wrapped his arm around her shoulders. She melted into his side, and his lips found her forehead. She'd shared all this information with him earlier, but hearing her say it again? Heartbreaking.

Silence descended on their table; the only noise came from the surrounding pub activity.

"Holy shit, Carm," Raven murmured.

"What can we do to help?" Kate asked.

Carmen gave a small shrug. "I don't know. It's basically a waiting game right now. Besides, this guy"—she leaned her head on his shoulder, and he wanted to pound his chest like a fucking caveman—"has been my shadow when I'm not in the office."

"You're damn right I'm your shadow, sweetheart," he muttered as their friends chuckled.

"However, you guys should also know something . . ." Carmen straightened and shot him a nervous glance as their table quieted.

From his lunch yesterday with his brother and his earlier conversations with Carmen, he knew what she was going to say. He removed his arm from around her shoulders, retook her hand, and gave her an encouraging nod.

"So, Brian has been causing some problems—"

"What?" Parker interrupted.

"That motherfucker," Blake growled.

Carmen held up her free hand in a pointless attempt to calm her brother and cousin.

"Listen," she continued, talking over them. Her voice was strong and steady. She was back in business mode. "Matt was at my office yesterday when Brian caused a scene."

It took everything Jake had to not scoff. *Scene*, his ass. Instead, he bit his tongue and silently held her hand.

"We talked with Matt yesterday, and again this morning, and he encouraged me to file a restraining order."

We.

That one word had warmth easing the budding anger that McAsshole had evoked.

"You'll do it, right?" Parker asked, his voice holding a hint of panic.

"It's done, Park," Carmen replied, her expression softening.

"Matt's handling the paperwork personally," Jake added.

"Good," Blake spat, while Parker simply nodded. "I'll let the pub crew know if that motherfucker shows up here, his ass gets kicked out."

"I appreciate that," Carmen said. "I have a hard time believing he has anything to do with the car and the . . . dead woman, but like Matt said, with everything going on, the last thing I need is Brian harassing me."

Matt had also said that Vasquez and Apone were keeping McAsshole on their person of interest list. The bastard didn't have an alibi for Saturday night. But Jake kept his mouth shut because it wasn't his information to disclose.

"Going back to what you guys can do," Carmen said, turning her attention to Kate. "Everyone needs to stay alert. The detectives don't know much right now, so we need to keep our eyes and ears open."

"No one goes anywhere alone," Kate said with a firm nod. "Sadly, this isn't our gang's first rodeo with awful people. Make sure you call one of us if Jake's unavailable."

Carmen nodded. "Thanks."

"I hate to break this up, but I need to give Melody her break," Raven said, rising. She rounded the table and stood behind Carmen. "I know you're not a hugger." Leaning down, she wrapped her arms around Carmen's shoulders from behind. "But I don't fucking care," she murmured, hugging her tight. "We may not know each other all that well, but you matter to every person I love, so you matter to me."

Carmen chuckled and squeezed Raven's arms, her dark brown eyes growing misty. "Thanks, Raven."

After a few moments, their group disbanded. Raven to relieve Melody behind the bar, Parker to relieve Adam in the kitchen, Kate to the pub office, and Blake to bus tables and greet some of their guests. Jake and Carmen swung into the kitchen to pick up their extra shepherd's pie before heading to the elevator that led to the building's private garage.

Carmen sighed when the elevator doors closed, leaning back against the wall.

"You okay, sweetheart?"

"You know what?" She straightened and took his free hand, weaving her fingers with his. "I hadn't realized how much I needed that. Part of me is still scared shitless, but knowing everyone's staying vigilant helps."

He brought her hand to his lips. "We've all got your back, Carm. You're not alone in this."

"I think I'm finally realizing that." She glanced up, her dark brown eyes shimmering with emotion. "And it means so damn much."

The elevator dinged their arrival at the underground parking garage.

"Good," he replied as he shot her a wink, tugging on her

hand when the doors opened. With his attention on Carmen, they stepped into the garage.

She came to an abrupt halt and gasped, the color draining from her face. "Jake?"

Chills shot down his spine, and he swung his gaze in the direction she was looking. It took a heartbeat for his brain to register what he was seeing.

The parking space where his Range Rover should have sat was . . . empty. What the fuck?

His eyes narrowed, focusing on the "Reserved for J. Alvarez" sign, and his heart kicked. His name was crossed out in sloppy black marker. Beneath the sign, four photos were taped to the cement wall. Even though he was too far away to see what the pictures were, dread clawed at his insides.

"Stay here," he murmured, handing over the casserole dish. He made his way toward the wall, and Carmen went with him, keeping her body pressed tight to his side. "Carm," he hissed, glancing at her.

"I'm not standing there by myself," she hissed back, her voice trembling.

Fuck. Right. "Stay close," he muttered, pulling his phone from his pocket.

When they reached the photos, his blood turned to ice. He wrapped one arm around Carmen's shoulders and yanked her closer, dialing his brother with his free hand. The call failed.

He groaned as his eyes darted around the garage. The underground cement parking garage. No fucking cell phone reception. Shit.

After quickly taking a picture of his parking sign and the photos taped to the wall, he turned them back toward the way they'd come. "We need to get the fuck out of here," he said, hustling them to the elevator.

CHAPTER TWENTY-TWO

They spilled into the building's lobby the second the elevator doors opened. Carmen would have fallen on her face if not for Jake's firm grip on her arm.

Bile rose in her throat. Holy shit. Those photos . . .

She was vaguely aware of Jake barking into his phone as he led her back into The Spotted Dog and pulled her through the crowded pub. She was in a daze. Everything sounded muffled, as if she were floating underwater.

Jake didn't let her arm go until they were in the office. Before she knew what was happening, she was seated on the couch with Kate in front of her. Her thoughts were cloudy, unfocused, but she recognized the worry that pinched her friend's face. She felt a slight yank and realized Kate was tugging on the casserole dish she hadn't even known she'd been clutching tightly in her arms.

Holy fuck. What was going on?

Her stomach rolled. The photos had been duct-taped to the wall. She'd only seen them for a few seconds, but that had been enough. They were seared into her brain, playing in slow-motion like a fucked-up slideshow.

The first was a shot of her at the gym on Saturday morning, running on the treadmill. It was clear and crisp; you could see the sweat pouring off her and the mask of focus on her face.

The second showed her, Jake, and Detectives Apone and Vasquez at the coffee shop, sitting around their table with the first set of pictures laid out before them. The fine hairs on her arms lifted. It wasn't a still from a security feed. No, it looked like a photo taken from somewhere *inside* the café.

The third photo was also from last Sunday. At the boxing gym. A wave of nausea swept through her as she recalled the image. It showed her laughing with Jake, Matt, and Cade. Laughing. Like the stress from earlier that day had been momentarily lifted. Like some crazy person wasn't watching her every damn move.

And the fourth . . .

Holy fuck.

The fourth photo had bile tickling her throat again. It was of a burned body on a stainless-steel table. The surrounding area was drab and clinical, but bright under fluorescent lights. She didn't know for sure, but Carmen was almost certain it was the woman who'd been shot and then burned in her car.

Carmen blinked, and the woman's blackened, peeling skin came into sharper focus in her mind. Saliva pooled in her mouth, and her stomach heaved. She shot off the couch and stumbled toward the garbage can next to the desk. Her stomach emptied.

Painful heaves racked her body as she clutched the edge of the bin. When she finally caught her breath, a hand settled on her shoulder.

Her head hung with exhaustion as she sat back on her heels. The hand on her shoulder moved to her elbow and squeezed.

"Let me help you up, sweetie."

Raven.

Someone else grasped her other elbow. "We've got you, Carm."

Kate.

Glancing at the women flanking her, she nodded weakly and leaned into them as they helped her rise on shaky legs to her feet.

Carmen's eyes darted around the room. It was just the three of them. "Where's Jake?" Her voice was raspy, and her throat burned. The lingering acid in her mouth had her stomach churning anew.

"In the hallway with the guys," Raven answered.

"He knew we had you and didn't want to upset you further," Kate added.

Her brows scrunched in confusion. "Upset me further?"

"Sweetie," Raven began, "the man's on a fucking warpath. He's on the phone with Matt and pissed beyond belief. I don't think he wanted you to see him like that."

The office door banged open, and Carmen flinched. Jake stormed into the office, then came to a halt as his fiery gaze met hers.

"Fuck," he growled. As he crossed the short distance between them, a look she couldn't decipher flashed on his face.

Before she could take her next breath, he wrapped his arms tight around her and pressed her face into the center of his chest. His heart beat wildly beneath her cheek, and his chest heaved in time with his unsteady breaths. Then he pulled away, his gaze was laser-fixed on hers. "I need you to go upstairs with the girls." Turmoil clouded his dark brown eyes. "Please."

She nodded. "What about you?"

"We'll all be up soon. I have to pull our security feed first."

His lips dropped to her forehead and held. "I'm so fucking sorry, Carm."

She pulled away to look at him, and the distress and guilt swirling in his eyes killed her. Straightening her spine, she framed his face in her hands. As scared as she was, he needed to hear her. "This isn't your fault, Jake. None of this is. The fault lies with whoever this sick asshole is."

She held his gaze until some of the turbulence in his eyes eased. Her thumbs caressed his cheekbones, and she attempted a smile. "I'd kiss you right now, babe, but I just puked my guts out, so there's no way in hell that's happening."

As she'd intended, the corners of his lips twitched up. He pressed another kiss against her forehead. "We'll be upstairs soon, sweetheart."

The second she walked through the doors of Blake and Raven's top-floor apartment, Raven steered her directly into the master bedroom. Or rather, into the master bedroom's massive walk-in closet.

"It's gonna be a long night," Raven said, opening drawers, then holding up two pieces of clothing. "Yoga pants or shorts?"

"Don't bother arguing," Kate called out from the bedroom. "Raven's a steamroller when she's got a bug up her butt."

Carmen smiled. Something she hadn't been sure she'd do again tonight. She nodded toward Raven's right hand. "Yoga pants, please."

Raven tossed the black leggings at her, then turned her attention to another drawer. "Baggy shirt or fitted?"

No-brainer on that one. "Baggy." Another piece of clothing flew at her head.

"And here . . ."

Two balled-up somethings came at Carmen. Both bounced off her chest and silently landed on the carpet.

"As amazing as those Stuart Weitzmans are, sweetie, I'm pretty sure it's gonna be a fuzzy-socks-and-no-underwire kind of night."

After retrieving the fuzzy polka dot socks, Carmen picked up what turned out to be a soft, lacy, burgundy bralette. Straightening, she met the other woman's violet gaze. "Thank you, Raven."

"No problem. What I said earlier holds true. You matter. And not just because you're Parker's sister. The way you calmed down Jake? Even though the man was losing his shit, you had every right to focus on yourself. But you didn't. You took care of him instead. That makes you badass." Raven shot her a wink as she headed toward the open closet door. "And your choice of stilettos doesn't hurt either. I'll put a toothbrush on the bathroom counter for you. Come on out when you're changed, okay? I have a bottle of Macallan with your name on it." Raven's nose scrunched for a moment, then she shrugged. "It may taste like shit after the toothpaste, but I'm sure you'll get over it."

Then the woman was gone.

A second later, Kate was in the doorway. "See what I mean?" She grabbed the doorknob and began pulling the door closed. "Raven's a steamroller. It's easiest to just give in. We'll be in the living room if you need us. Take your time." With a sweet smile that was typical Kate, she closed the closet door quietly, leaving Carmen in silence.

Carmen let out a loud, rickety exhale.

Holy shit, pull yourself together . . .

This was usually when she'd shore up her armor and reinforce her walls. When she'd push down all her erratic emotions—fear, anxiety, uncertainty—and wrap herself in the poised persona that had gotten her through her three divorces and a brutal attack. When she'd don her tailored clothes and make sure her appearance was impeccable.

Sharp. Shrewd. Confident.

Glancing down at the clothes in her arms, her chest tightened.

Soft, comfortable, cozy clothes lent to her by her cousin's fiancée. Warmth filled her and somehow pushed down that fear, anxiety, and uncertainty.

Fuck that poised persona. Where the hell had it gotten her?

Alone. Hiding behind a cracked facade.

But no more.

For the first time in forever, she had people in her corner. People who weren't merely business associates and colleagues.

They were family.

All she had to do was take that first baby step, dammit.

With a newfound resolve, she kicked off her heels, and her toes sank into the closet's plush carpet.

She could still keep her secrets. After all, no one needed to know about what had happened in Brazil or the nature of her divorces. But she didn't have to insist on going at this alone. Not anymore.

She was done hiding.

Jake followed his two best friends into Blake's apartment. His gaze swung across the room until he found Carmen.

With Raven next to her, Carmen sat in the corner of the couch, her knees pulled up to her chest and a glass of scotch in her hands. Aside from the obvious change of clothes, she looked relaxed. Comfortable.

He released the breath that had been lodged deep in his throat. Thank God. He'd been so fucking worried. Seeing Carm like this—relaxed with Raven and Kate—eased some of the tension bunching the muscles in his shoulders.

Still, he immediately crossed the room to her. Comfortable or not, he needed her in his arms.

"I'm booting you out," he murmured to Raven. While his gaze never left Carmen's, he saw his friend's brow arch in his periphery.

Raven chuckled as she rose, patting him on the arm, and he took her seat.

Before Carmen could say a word, he hauled her onto his lap, careful not to spill her drink. It was only once his arms wrapped around her, once she settled against his chest, that he could breathe again.

"You okay, babe?"

His eyes closed for a moment. Was *he* okay? Damn, this woman was something else. His lips fell to the top of her head, and his arms tightened. "I'm much better now," he murmured with a sigh. "Brace, sweetheart. Things are about to get crazy. Matt's on his way up, and Apone and Vasquez will be here once they're finished in the garage."

She tensed. "They're here?"

"They got here as soon as they could. Brought a full crime scene crew with them too. To say the SPD is concerned is a gross understatement." And *that* was also an understatement. Not only had their captain accompanied Detectives Vasquez and Apone tonight, but so had SPD's chief of police.

"I suppose the photo of us with the detectives was a bit . . . unsettling." She paused and swallowed. Loudly. "Not to mention the autopsy photo from the morgue."

All one thousand percent true. Every person he'd seen in the parking garage had been pissed.

A knock at the door had him looking up as it opened.

Matt strode in, his face pinched, his posture coiled tight as he took in the room: Jake and Carmen on one couch, Kate and Raven on the other, and Parker and Blake at the island, Jake's laptop fired up in front of them.

Jake met his brother's gaze, and the back of his neck tingled. Call it a twin sense, but he knew he wouldn't like what Matt was about to say.

"Apone and Vasquez are finishing up in the garage, but before they get here, what do you know?"

Jake shook his head, frustration simmering anew. "Not much." He nodded toward Parker and Blake. "We pulled the security feed, and it looks like it was tampered with. It was either cut or paused or . . . something. We haven't been able to figure out how. One second, my Rover's in its parking spot, and the next second, it's fucking gone."

"What?" Carmen whispered, sitting up to meet his gaze.

His jaw clenched, but he kept his arms around her gentle. "There's nothing in the back end that indicates the system was breached, but it obviously was."

"Come take a look," Parker called out, and Matt joined the two men at the island.

"The video from when the car was stolen and the pictures were put up was wiped, but there wasn't a disturbance in the time stamp," Blake explained to Matt, pointing to something on the screen. "Unless there's some sort of magic time warp in the garage downstairs, someone hacked in and fucked with things. And this someone is really fucking good."

Jake's molars ground together. That was the part that pissed him off. Both he and Blake knew computers and coding. They'd both made fucking millions of dollars off that knowledge. They could do simple hacks. But this shit? Next fucking level.

Matt let out a low whistle. "I'm going to be honest with

you. Our tech guys are good, but"—he gestured to the laptop —"figuring this out may be above their pay grade."

"Shiiit, it's above *our* fucking pay grade," Blake grumbled, gesturing to Jake. "And we got paid fucking well for all the computer shit we know."

Matt's lips pursed for a moment. "Do you want me to put a call out to the Hudson Security guys?"

Jake stilled, and the frustration tearing at him eased slightly. Now there was an idea. A damn good one.

"Who are the Hudson Security guys?" Carmen asked.

"They're friends of the de la Rosa brothers and run a high-end security company based on Hudson Island," Kate answered.

His friend's matter-of-fact tone had Jake's brows lifting. "How do *you* know them?"

"Through Cade and Dante. I do the gym's bookkeeping, and they introduced me to the Hudson guys since they're all doing a side thing together." Kate turned her attention to Carmen. "They're a good group. Like Dante, they're all former military guys."

"They do all sorts of security shit, including cybersecurity," Matt added, nodding to the laptop. "You have the money, and they can figure this out a whole hell of a lot faster than our group can with all our hoops and bureaucratic bullshit." His brother frowned, then met his gaze. "That's coming from your brother and *not* an SPD detective." He shrugged, mock innocence on his face. "In fact, none of you heard any of that shit from me."

"Of course not, man," Blake said with a chuckle, slapping Matt on the back.

"If you could set up a call," Carmen chimed in, "we'd appreciate it. We can go to them if it makes it easier."

Jake stilled. There was that *we* again. And just like last

time, it eased something in him. He didn't know what, and frankly, he didn't fucking care. His arms tightened around her as he pulled her back against his chest, resting his chin on top of her head.

So long as Carmen was safe, that's all that mattered.

CHAPTER TWENTY-THREE

The second Carmen cleared the doorway, she toed off her borrowed Converse, thankful she and Raven were the same shoe size. Dropping her work clothes, heels, and purse into a heap on the floor, she let out a groan. She was wiped out. Completely. Freaking. Exhausted.

It had taken another forty-five minutes for Detectives Apone and Vasquez to join them in Blake's apartment. Then they'd asked a slew of mind-numbing questions.

Yes, Blake owned the building. Yes, the garage was supposedly secure. Yes, the only ones who had access were the guys and the pub staff. Yes, they'd permitted additional garage use for her, Kate, and her and Parker's parents whenever they were in town. No, their folks weren't currently in town. Yes, those were the only people with garage access. Yes, they could match up the video security footage with each garage card access swipe. Over and over and over again.

The guys had shared the altered security feed from this evening with the police. They'd also given them the last thirty days of the entire building's video surveillance and garage access logs. It had been eye-opening to see how many cameras they had around the building, but to her, it all looked like a dead end.

Jake had also let the detectives know he'd retained the Hudson Island crew to look into the security hack. He and Matt had spoken with Gavin Frazier, the head of Hudson Security, before the detectives had arrived, and Carmen hoped like hell they'd be able to find something to point the detectives in the right direction. Because she wasn't sure her nerves could handle much more.

The evening had continued for yet another hour, and dread had filled her when she'd figured the detectives were about to go over everything again. But Jake had called an immediate halt, then bundled her up, borrowed Blake's extra car, and driven her home.

Now, she trailed a few steps behind the man and wondered why she'd insisted on walking when he'd tried to carry her from the car. Each step was a chore. She followed him as he made his way to the kitchen, dumping his phone and wallet onto the corner of the island.

"Want something to drink?"

The idea of anything alcoholic had her queasy stomach protesting. "Just water, please."

She glanced down when Jake's phone lit up. The ringer and vibration were obviously turned off. "Lara's calling," she said, holding out his phone to him. Her eyebrow arched at the impressive string of curse words that immediately spewed from his mouth.

He reached over, jabbed the decline button, and then spun back toward the refrigerator.

Okaaayyy.

His phone display dimmed, then, seconds later, flashed with a voicemail notification. Knowing his password, she unlocked his phone. Her jaw dropped. He had seven phone notifications and thirty-eight unread texts.

What the hell?

Jake wasn't one to leave messages—text or phone—unread. They were anally similar like that. The little red notification numbers on their phones drove them both batshit crazy.

She cleared her throat. "Everything okay, babe?"

He turned back to her and handed her a glass of water. "Sorry," he grumbled, his jaw tense. "Lara's been blowing up my phone tonight. Shitty timing."

"What's going on?"

He shrugged, the simple movement jerky. Annoyance radiated from him. As he strode by, he snagged her hand and tugged her along with him. "I don't know. I haven't checked any of her messages." Flopping down onto the couch, he took the glass of water from her hand and placed it on the coffee table. Then he pulled her across his lap. "Don't really give a shit right now, either."

Exhausted as she was, she couldn't help the smile that spread on her lips. She draped her arms around his neck, her fingers raking into his hair. The sound he made was somewhere between a groan and a growl. Whichever it was, his eyes closed, and he pressed his head into her hands.

This sweet, sweet man. While she'd been answering the detectives' questions, he'd been doing the same. As well as talking with the Hudson Security team, looking over the security footage, pulling whatever files the detectives had needed to be pulled, and God knew what else. He had to be just as tired—if not more—as she was. And she was fucking beat.

She pulled her hands away and quickly rose. His eyes flew open, and she chuckled at the pouty look on his face. "Babe," she snickered, "do you think I'd leave you hanging?" She patted his shoulder as she stepped up onto the couch. "Scooch," she murmured, wedging herself between the corner of the couch and his back. Positioning him between her legs, she wiggled until she could get into prime back-rubbing position. Her hands settled on his shoulders, and she squeezed, digging her thumbs into the tense muscles below his neck.

"Fuuuck, Carm," he groaned out.

For a few minutes, she silently worked the knotted muscles of his neck and shoulders. His moans of approval and thanks had her smiling.

"There's a lot going on right now, for sure," she murmured. "But I feel like there's something else. What's going on with Lara?" The muscles beneath her hands tensed anew, and she redoubled her efforts. "Talk to me, babe."

Leaning into her touch, he blew out a breath. "It's all of it, Carm. The garage, the photos . . . none of that shit should have happened." He was quiet for a moment, the silence charged with his frustration and anger. She waited patiently as he worked through whatever was going on in his head, continuing to knead the muscles that were becoming tighter beneath her hands. "I fucking promised you, Carm." His words were a harsh whisper. "I fucking promised nothing was going to happen to you."

His words, and the anguish hiding in them, broke her heart. Oh, this man . . .

Without a word, she rose from behind him, then repositioned herself so she sat astride his lap. The way she was supposed to sit on him when they were alone. Wrapping her legs around his waist, she tucked her body against his much larger frame, cupped his handsome face in her hands, and waited for him to meet her gaze.

When his eyes remained locked on the wall behind her head, she cleared her throat—loudly—and gently squeezed his jaw, forcing his attention to her.

The guilt rioting in his brown eyes slayed her. Absolutely

slayed her. What she wouldn't give to take this man's pain away. "Jake, babe, none of what happened is your fault. You didn't do any of that."

"But I didn't prevent it either, Carm."

Anguish. Pure anguish crossed his face, and she wanted to shake him, love him, do *anything* to take that anguish away. "*You* didn't take those pictures. *You* didn't tape them to the wall. *You* didn't fuck with the security feed."

"I should have double-checked the security cameras in the first place. I knew someone was out there fucking with you, but I slacked. And before you say anything," he rushed on, "I should have protected you better. Instead, I was selfish. I didn't recheck the feed because . . ."

"Because why?"

He let out a sigh. "Because I just wanted to go home, turn all the shit off, and spend time with you."

"Jake," she said, drawing out his name. God, this man was too much, and she absolutely loved him for it.

She stilled at the thought. Worry and self-doubt prickled her gut, but she pushed them away. She needed to focus on this sweet man.

"See?" He leaned away from her, scrubbing his hands over his face. "It's just like fucking before. Me being fucking selfish put you in danger. If I hadn't been so selfish, we might have caught whoever this is. And you could have gotten hurt, dammit. You could—"

"I *didn't* get hurt, and you don't know if you would have caught the person. That's a guessing game at best." Something he'd said tugged at her. "What did you mean when you said, 'Just like before'?"

He tensed. Nothing.

Her hands went to his jaw again. "Jake." She pressed a soft kiss to his lips. "Babe. Please talk to me. Please."

He closed his eyes and shook his head.

She bit back a grumble and gently kissed his eyelids. Stubborn, stubborn man. "Does this have to do with Lara?"

His body went rigid, and she wasn't sure if he was even breathing. Then he gave the tiniest of nods.

"I destroyed Lara's family. I destroy things, Carm." His voice broke on her name. "I don't mean to, but I do."

Her brow furrowed, and a chill crawled down her spine. Not for one second did she believe that. But she knew *he* believed it because, holy shit, the amount of guilt this man carried was atrocious. If she had to be strong for both of them, then so be it.

Schooling her features, she caressed the side of his face. "I'm going to need you to expand on that, babe."

He was silent for so long she didn't think he was going to reply. Then he did.

"I killed Lara's father."

———◆———

Jake's breath seized in his lungs. Holy shit. He'd never said those words out loud.

His mouth opened to gasp for air, but nothing came. Everything was stuck, like there was a giant boulder in his lungs threatening to burn a hole right through his goddamn chest. For the life of him, he couldn't breathe.

Fuck. Was he having a heart attack?

"Breathe, Jake."

His gaze swung to Carmen's, and before he could blink, her soft hands were cradling his face. Her beautiful brown eyes focused solely on him. "Breathe, babe." Her soothing voice was strong and steady, and, at last, he could take a deep breath.

His eyes closed—part in relief, part in embarrassment— and he rested his forehead against hers. A shiver tore through him as his thoughts drifted back to the day he'd fucked up.

"Talk to me, babe," she repeated, her hand caressing the stubble along his jaw. "I'm going to be honest with you, okay? I'm having a hard time believing you killed Lara's father."

Opening his eyes, he met Carmen's gaze. Trust and certainty stared back at him. Neither of which he deserved.

He desperately wanted to continue whatever this was with Carmen, desperately wanted to be worthy of her. He cared about her so fucking much. But hiding this wasn't fair to her. She'd find out about what he'd done sooner or later. As much as he didn't want to, it was best to tell her the truth —rip the Band-Aid off and all that bullshit. Let her walk away now, before their lives were even more intertwined.

With his arms still wrapped around her, he leaned back on the couch, taking her with him. He sighed, resigned to the fact that this could very well be the last time he got to hold this amazing woman in his arms. But he had to come clean.

"Lara and I had been dating for a couple years, but a month before I graduated college, we broke up."

"Mutual thing?" Her head was resting on his chest, tucked perfectly under his chin, as her hand traced circles over his heart.

He opened his mouth to say yes but paused. That's what he'd always let people think—that it had been a mutual decision—but that hadn't been the case. "I'd bought her an engagement ring the month before, and it had been burning a hole in my damn pocket. I'd convinced myself that I was just waiting for the perfect time to propose. But that wasn't it."

It had been his brother who'd made him see the truth. A truth that he'd conveniently forgotten until this very fucking moment. Selective memory. Wasn't that what Matt always accused him of? Shit.

His brother had flat-out asked him what the hell he was doing. Why he was going to ask a woman he wasn't in love with to be his wife. He'd obviously taken exception to his twin's comments, and their subsequent fight had turned to blows.

Afterward, while they'd both sat on his couch with bloody lips, Matt had turned to him and asked, "Do you remember what you told me when you were thinking about breaking up with her a few months ago?" As he'd started to shake his head no, his brother had kept talking. The little fucker. "You said, and I quote, 'I can't breathe when I'm with her.'"

A wise little fucker was what his brother was.

"Things between Lara and I hadn't been working for a while, but I was in denial about it all. Matt made me pull my head out of my ass."

Carmen chuckled. "Of course he did."

"Turns out, I hadn't been waiting for the perfect time to propose. I was just putting it off. So I broke up with her instead, graduated, and focused on getting Alvarez Tech off the ground. That was that."

Or so he'd thought.

Carmen remained silent, her fingers continuing to draw circles over his chest. He committed that little touch to his memory. He was about to blow up all this perfection.

"Lara's birthday was a few weeks after my graduation. She called me up and invited me to dinner, saying her parents were in town." Carmen's fingers stilled for a moment, and his breath caught. He exhaled when she resumed her circling. "Turned out she hadn't told her parents we'd broken up. She was crying and asking if I could do her this one last favor. I agreed, and she promised that after dinner she'd tell them we weren't together anymore. None of that happened. Dinner was a fucking disaster. It started out fine—I'd always gotten along with her folks—but then Lara told them we were talking about getting married."

"Holy crap, Jake."

He cringed. "I know, but I kept my shit together." He'd been so damn mad and so tempted to walk the fuck out. Her father had beamed with pride, and her mother's eyes had shimmered with tears of fucking joy. But he'd bitten his tongue. "Until she announced that we were also talking about having babies."

Shame filled every pore of his body.

"I fucking lost it. I yelled at her and demanded she tell her parents the fucking truth about us. She sat there frozen, so I broke it to them that we *weren't* getting married. That there were sure as fuck no babies in our future. That we'd broken up a couple months earlier. That that had been the first time I'd seen her since, and the only reason I'd agreed to dinner was because she was supposed to tell them the truth afterward."

Guilt flowed through his veins.

"I apologized to her parents for the farce and threw some cash on the table. Since I'd driven everyone to the restaurant, I told them to catch a cab. And they did." His voice caught on the last word.

Regret hollowed out his gut.

"Her dad was in the front seat." His throat tightened, and before he could continue, he had to clear it. "Lara and her mom were in the back. On the way to her parents' hotel, their taxi was T-boned by a drunk driver." His nose tingled, and he swallowed past the lump in his throat. "Her dad died on impact."

"Oh, Jake," Carmen said on an exhale. Her arms wrapped around him, and she squeezed.

He didn't deserve her sympathy. Not one fucking bit.

"Turned out that earlier that week, her dad had been

diagnosed with pancreatic cancer. It was extremely aggressive, and the doctors had given him three months. Tops." Heat scorched his face. "Lara wanted to make him feel better, to give him a little bit of comfort. She wanted him to believe she was happy and would be taken care of." Shame festered and spread. "Not only did I rob her father of knowing she'd be taken care of after he was gone, but I also robbed both Lara and her mom of those last three fucking months. It was all my fault."

"No, babe. It's not—"

"Carm, if I hadn't been so selfish, if I had just shut the fuck up and trusted Lara, she and her mom would have had those last few months with him. Her dad wouldn't have died that night. And he sure as fuck wouldn't have died knowing that Lara was *not* getting married or having kids or even in a relationship anymore. I stole that from all of them."

Trepidation soured his belly as Carmen sat up and stared at him for a moment, a contemplative look he couldn't read on her face. The room was silent outside of his erratic heartbeat.

This was it. The moment he'd dreaded. He could hear the words now: *How could you do that to Lara? How can you live with yourself knowing you took those last few months away from all of them?*

He desperately wanted to break eye contact. The last thing he needed to witness was the moment this amazing woman started looking at him with disgust, with that practiced and polite smile. But for the life of him, he couldn't look away.

Her poker face was impeccable, and he couldn't tell if she was about to end their physical relationship, end their friendship, or tell him straight-up to fuck off forever.

Carm's eyes narrowed, and her mouth opened slightly, as

if she were considering her words. Shit. His chest tightened, and that burning weight squeezed his lungs again.

"You know I care about you, right, Jake?"

Oh fuck, here we go. But . . .

He couldn't get his throat to work, so he nodded.

"Does Lara blame you for her dad dying?"

He shook his head. Where was she going with this?

"Was she mad at you for telling her parents the truth?"

His mind flashed to the memory of Lara's face after he'd revealed the truth. Hell, all their faces. Hurt. Disappointment. Defeat. "Lara was devastated. They all were. And *I* caused that."

***

She knew Jake well, yet so many things clicked into place as he finished his story.

"Jake," she said on a sigh. She wanted to cuddle this man, to wrap his big, muscular body in her arms and whisper reassurances that *none* of it had been his fault. That it had all been shitty timing and a horrible, tragic fucking accident.

But she knew that wasn't going to work. Not with him. Because the amount of guilt and self-hatred this man carried —*years* of it—was too much. Too ingrained in how he thought about himself. Too debilitating. And it tore at her freaking heart.

He would continue to cling to the guilt like armor. Because the way he was looking at her? Like he was waiting for her to lay into him? Like he expected her to be disgusted by him and his "selfish" actions? That said it all. He wouldn't believe her, no matter what she spouted about his innocence.

So, there'd be no cuddling or whispered reassurances for him. But that didn't mean she was giving up on the man, dammit. If she had to beat it over his head, then so be it.

Keeping her tone light and conversational, she asked, "Were you the drunk driver that hit their cab?"

Surprise flashed in his gaze. "No."

"Do you blame the cab driver for her dad's death?"

His brow scrunched, like he couldn't figure out where she was going. "No. It was *my* fault they were in the cab in the first place."

"Well, you probably *should* blame the cab driver," she said with a shrug. Brown eyes stared back at her in disbelief. "Maybe if that person were a better cab driver, they could have avoided the whole accident in the first place." His eyes narrowed, annoyance flaring over his face. "Or better yet, babe, how about we blame the drunk driver who actually fucking hit them?"

His eyes closed, and he huffed out a breath. His body remained strung tight under hers.

She reached out and stroked the side of his face. She couldn't help it; she had to touch him. "You know where I'm going with this, right?"

His eyes opened, and he nodded. "Logically, I know. But here?" He made a fist and held it over his heart. "Here, it's still my fault."

Her chest squeezed, and before she could tell herself otherwise, she wrapped her arms around his torso and gathered him in a hug.

"Jake, I'm not making light of what happened. It was awful and tragic and horrible. But if it's anyone's fault, it's the drunk driver's. You know that. Your misplaced guilt? It's just that. Misplaced." He opened his mouth, but she kept on talking. "Is it heartbreaking and devastating that her dad died knowing those things were in limbo for her? Yes. But how about this? What if Lara had actually talked to you beforehand about all of it? About her dad's diagnosis and how she wanted to make it better for him. Would you have gone along with it if she'd asked?"

"Of course."

Of course he would have. Just like he'd gone along with their relationship. Because he was a sweet, wonderful man. "So why blame yourself?"

He remained silent, that crease between his brows out in full force.

The stubborn, stubborn man was clinging harder than ever to the guilt, so she pivoted. "Here's another way to look at it. Would you say that *I'm* at fault—at least partially—for what happened to me in Brazil?"

He jerked backward, and his eyes blazed. "The fuck you are. *None* of that was your fault."

"I know Anders is to blame for what happened. But . . ." She shrugged, her own guilt simmering in her gut. "One could argue that if I hadn't misled him or rebuffed his kiss, then—"

"That's bullshit, Carm. Blame-the-victim bullshit."

It was. But those thoughts had pinballed in her head for so damn long. "Well, I should have checked in at the hotel immediately. I should have been more aware of my surroundings. I should—"

"For fuck's sake, sweetheart, no. That's bullshit, and you know it."

She opened her mouth to agree, but then snapped it shut. She could be honest with him. They both carried so much damn guilt. If she could fight for him, she could also fight for herself. Right? "I don't know it, Jake. But I think I'm getting there."

And she was. Somehow, seeing this wonderful man beat himself up for something that he'd had no control over put everything in perspective and made her situation a little clearer. "It's all the same stupid guilt logic, babe. Shouldas, couldas, and wouldas. They don't change anything. They only make us feel like shit."

"That . . . is all fucking true, sweetheart." The corners of his lips tilted as his hands framed her face. "We're quite the pair, huh?" He brought her lips to his for a gentle kiss that warmed her heart.

"I want you to know that how you reacted back then wasn't selfish. You were hurt. You thought she'd lied to you. Just like how it wasn't selfish that you didn't triple-check the security feed in the garage because we wanted to spend time together." He opened his mouth to, she assumed, argue, so she kept on talking. "Because if you tell me *that* was all selfish, then me coming home and not telling anyone what happened to me in Brazil was selfish too."

He was quiet for a long moment before he nodded. "Thank you, Carm."

"Nothing to thank me for."

"We'll agree to disagree on that." His lips brushed hers again. "Nothing's going to change overnight, but how about we come to a new arrangement, Ms. Cunningham?"

Her chest kicked and nerves twisted in her belly, but she kept her expression neutral.

"How about we toss out the whole 'arrangement' aspect of our relationship and see what happens?" He shrugged. "You kick me in the ass when I do the selective guilt thing—"

"*Misplaced* guilt thing."

"Right," he chuckled. "Ass-kicking for me for the *misplaced* guilt thing. And when I see you doing the same over what happened to you in Brazil or what's happening now, I get to—"

"Kick my ass?"

"Mmm, no. I was thinking along the lines of finding you a suitable distraction with a more intimate kind of . . . physical outlet."

Her eyes rolled, then her breath caught when he snaked a hand into her hair.

"I want to know where this goes with us, Carm."

She swallowed. It couldn't go anywhere. She knew that. As much as she loved him—because she absolutely did—and as much as she wished otherwise, she knew that. "How about we take it all one day at a time?"

"That, I can do," he murmured against her lips. "And, sweetheart, if we have to take it minute by minute, we'll do that too, okay?"

"Okay," she said, her heart squeezing.

"So long as we're together, right?"

What she wouldn't give to be with this man forever. As much as it would hurt in the end, she'd take everything she could. "Right."

CHAPTER TWENTY-FOUR

"Jake!" Carmen cried out, her nails digging into the muscles of his forearm. The sharp sting sent a bolt of pleasure through him.

They were both lying on their sides, her back to his front. Jake hiked her top leg higher and continued to thrust inside her from behind. For the last three days, she'd woken him with sex. He'd happily returned the favor when he'd awoken before her this morning.

Her tight pussy fluttered around his cock, and he moaned. She was close. "Come for me, darlin'," he growled into her ear. His hand moved to rub tight circles over her clit, and the fluttering turned to squeezing. Seconds later, she tensed, her thighs trembling, and she moaned out his name.

"That's it, Carm. Get it." He pumped harder, riding her through her orgasm. Nothing felt better than this. The way her body milked his cock was pure fucking ecstasy. Tingles skated up his back, and four deep thrusts later, he emptied inside her.

He held her close, their heartbeats racing, their breaths

ragged. Despite the stressful week, this—waking up with her in his arms each morning, getting to be deep inside her—made it all better.

Letting out a groan, he pulled out, immediately missing her heat, and rolled onto his back. After he moved her so she lay atop him, not caring one bit how messy that got him, his arms fell limply to his sides. They'd agreed to scrap the condoms since she was on birth control, and he was grateful. Because being bare inside her was the most wonderful feeling in the world, and he'd take messy over condoms any day. "Holy shit, sweetheart. For the record, if this is part of our one-day-at-a-time thing, then count me in."

She chuckled, her head on his chest. He was all-in no matter what but was trying to keep things between them light. Despite agreeing to give them a real shot, he knew she was still skittish, still holding back.

He didn't mind. Not one bit. Something about this woman made him want to push all his insecurities down and show her how good they could be together. Despite the guilt issues he had, he wanted to fight for her, fight for *them*. And he had no doubt it would be a fight.

Carmen was a master at holding herself apart, keeping herself behind a protective wall. He wasn't the most patient man, but with her, it didn't matter how long it would take; he'd tear down that wall brick by damn brick.

With all the shit with the stolen cars, the dead woman, and the photos of Carmen, their group had closed ranks. It was the buddy system at all times. The only time Carm wasn't with him was when she was at work. Her office manager, Elise, was usually there with her, but at Parker's request, Kate had been working from the CWC conference room this week as well. Neither woman had complained. They knew being together would keep Parker's worry at bay.

It was no secret to anyone that Kate and Carmen meant the world to him.

Outside of work, Jake had been her shadow. Between commuting to and from work, boxing at the gym, dinners at the pub, and their nights—and mornings—in his bed, they'd spent basically every moment together.

Two days after the parking garage incident, they'd received a call from Gavin Frazier at Hudson Security. His team had uncovered a partially deleted image—a blip in the video—from the surveillance camera positioned outside the parking garage entrance. An unknown man—someone who definitely should not have had access to the garage—had exited an hour before he and Carm had discovered the photos and his missing Rover.

The man's face had been turned away from the camera, and he'd worn a stocking cap on his head, but they'd been able to narrow down that it'd been a white male, roughly five-ten and between one-seventy and one hundred ninety pounds.

How fucking frustrating was that? Because that basically described every other guy in Seattle.

Frazier had cautioned that the image could've been planted. Whoever was responsible for hacking into the security feed was damn good, and Frazier had doubts that this person would have been sloppy enough to leave a partially deleted image for them to find.

So, they were no closer to knowing who was behind all this shit.

The SPD was hitting dead end after dead end as well. They still hadn't identified the deceased woman from the car fire, and there were no leads on Jake's missing vehicle, either.

"What's on your mind, babe?" Carmen asked, tracing her thumb over the wrinkle he hadn't realized had popped on his forehead. "The frown on your face makes me want to find a way to distract you."

His fingers traced over the scars on her back, and his heart soared when she didn't flinch. "I wouldn't be opposed to your brand of distraction, sweetheart."

She chuckled, kissed his pec, then clasped her hands on his chest and propped her chin on them. "What's going on in that handsome head of yours?"

"Just thinking about how we're no closer to knowing what's going on. And the fucking waiting . . ."

"Oh, I hear you," she said, crinkling her nose. "Patience isn't either of our strong suits."

That was an understatement. "The fact that there's been—"

Her phone rang, startling them both.

With her still sprawled over him, he reached an arm out to his bedside table and snagged her phone.

Dread filled every cell of his body when he glanced at the display.

Detective Apone.

She settled next to him on the bed before taking the phone and answering. Pulling the sheet to her chest to cover herself, she placed her phone on her lap.

"Detective, good morning. I have you on speaker with Jake."

"Good morning to you both," he replied, his deep baritone filling the silent room. "I'll cut right to the chase. First off, we've been in touch with the Hudson Security team. They shared the image they retrieved from the security footage. We'll keep you updated if we're able to make a match. Second, we just received a call from the Bellingham Police Department that there's an abandoned vehicle matching the description of Jake's Range Rover. They didn't tell us much, but they requested we head up there, so once we get off the phone, Vasquez and I will be on our way. I just wanted to let you know."

"We appreciate it," Carmen replied. Her voice was calm and steady, but her knuckles were turning white from how tight she was clasping the sheet covering her. His arm went around her immediately, and the unease brewing in his gut lessened when she leaned into him.

"Look, you guys," Apone continued, "I know this has been difficult for you, but please know we're following every lead we have."

She blew out a breath, her frustration evident. "I know, Detective. Jake and I were just discussing how patience isn't either of our strong suits. But the 'wheels of justice turn slowly' and all that, right?"

Apone chuckled. "Exactly. Vasquez or I will be in touch with you later today with what we find in Bellingham. Either way."

"Thank you for calling. Drive safe," she said before disconnecting.

His hand stroked up and down her back as she took a moment, inhaling and exhaling deeply. When she turned to him, the frustration and worry written all over her face mirrored his own emotions. What he wouldn't give to make all this shit go away.

He dropped a kiss to her temple, then gathered her close. "What do you say we go punch something, sweetheart?"

She nodded, the anxiety dissipating from her eyes. "Yes, please. Then after, I think we should have some shower time before the dinner at Pru's tonight. You know, to ease the stress."

He grinned. Apparently, he wasn't the only one who was insatiable and using the excuse of stress relief. "I like your thinking, Ms. Cunningham." Then he wrinkled his nose. "But do we really have to go to Pru's?"

"Please." She laughed. "Like you don't love how those ladies ogle you." With a playful pat to his cheek, she rose. "Oh, and Pru specifically told me it's a less formal affair. So do the lady a solid and give her a thrill—wear a shirt that's a little more fitted to show off your guns, okay?"

"Oh my God," he groaned, taking the pillow next to him and softly whacking her with it.

She yelped, grabbed another pillow, and smacked him right back, laughing.

They both froze when his phone rang.

Grabbing it off the nightstand, she glanced at the display and held it out to him. The playfulness in her eyes from moments ago was gone. In its place was a soft, gentle look that he couldn't quite read.

"It's Lara," she said. "You should talk to her."

He hesitated.

Then, before he could blink, she pressed the accept button, and his phone was to her ear. "Hi, Lara. It's Carmen. Hang on just a second while I get Jake."

She held out his phone, challenge shining bright in her eyes. "Talk to her," she mouthed.

He'd been avoiding Lara's calls all week. He knew he should talk to her, but he wasn't sure what the hell to say.

After taking the phone from Carmen, she pressed a kiss to his jaw. "I'll get the coffee going," she whispered before grabbing his T-shirt off the floor, slipping it on, and disappearing out the door.

He cleared his throat, bringing his phone to his ear. "Hey, Lara. Sorry for not calling you back sooner. Things are a little crazy right now."

"Not a problem. I hope everything's okay?"

It wasn't. But Lara didn't need to know that. He cleared his throat again. "What's up?"

"Oh." She was silent for a moment, as if startled by his

question. He frowned. "Well, at first, I wanted to thank you for dinner. Then, the more I thought about dinner, the more I realized I owed you and Carmen an apology."

Shit. He really didn't want to talk about Dickless Douche. But being the dumbass he was, he asked, "Apology about what?"

"Dean. He was awful." Jake wasn't going to argue that one. "Even more so than usual. And the way he was with Carmen . . ." She sighed. "Do you know if she took offense to him? I mean, she probably did and—"

The moment his woman's name came out of Lara's mouth, he jerked. "I have to be honest—I'm not comfortable discussing anything about Carmen with you."

"No, no," she sputtered. "Of course not. But Jake . . ."

She was quiet for so long that he pulled his phone away to make sure the call hadn't dropped. He opened his mouth to say her name but froze at her next words.

"Seeing you with Carmen was hard."

Oh shit. The back of his neck tingled. "Uh . . . Lara . . ."

"You're happy with her—like, *truly* happy and comfortable." He didn't know what to say, so he remained silent. "When we were together, it was always so on and off. Hot and cold. Like how it is with Dean and me."

He couldn't hold back a groan. "Jesus, please don't tell me I was like *that*?"

"No." She chuckled, though it was humorless. "Dean's an ass. Seeing you with Carmen was eye-opening. It showed me how it could be. You know?"

"Lara," he said on an exhale. They didn't have these types of conversations. It had been *years* since they'd talked beyond anything surface-level. He was floundering, so he decided on the truth. "I don't know what you want me to say."

"Nothing, I guess." She was quiet for a few moments, then her words came in a rush. "I left Dean."

His eyes widened in surprise. The words *good for you* were on the tip of his tongue, but he bit them back. "Are you okay?"

"I don't know," she whispered, her voice shaking. "This is the first time I've been alone since you and I broke up. Since my dad died."

His gut soured. "Lara, you have to know I'm so sorry about what happened that night. How I ditched all of you at the restaurant and then your dad—"

"No, Jake. That . . . that wasn't . . . no," she stammered. "*I'm* sorry. I should have talked to you earlier. I never should have lied to my parents in the first place. It wasn't your fault. It wasn't my fault. The drunk driver was to blame for that terrible accident." She let out a weary sigh that he felt down to his soul. "That's the thing, right? One day, it could be all over, just like that." He heard her fingers snap over the phone. "And I don't want to waste my life on someone like Dean."

"You shouldn't, Lara." She was too good for that asshole. "Are you okay? Do you have a place to stay?"

"Yeah, I'm staying at a friend's until I can find something more permanent."

He opened his mouth to offer her the use of his cabin on Hudson Island, but he held back. "Well, let me know if you need help, alright?"

"Thank you," she said, then cleared her throat again. "Are we okay, Jake?"

"I think so, Lara." And they were. Though he was pretty sure they both knew they weren't going back to those awkward dinners any time soon. He wanted the best for her, but for his own sake, he needed to put distance between them. Give himself space.

"Well, thank you for answering my call, Jake. Please know that I really am happy for you. Carmen seems great."

"She is." A small smile lifted his lips. "You'll land on your feet, Lara. I know you will. You don't need Dean in your life, and again, if you need anything, let me know, okay?"

"Thanks. Take care, Jake."

She ended their call, but he kept his phone to his ear. "Take care," he murmured into the silent room.

A weight lifted off his shoulders.

CHAPTER TWENTY-FIVE

Prudence Weatherby's home was beyond lovely. As a member of one of Seattle's founding families, she held claim to the rarest of the rare—ten undeveloped acres along Lake Washington's waterfront. The enormous backyard gazebo was strung with fairy lights, decorative gauze, and the perfect amount of greenery. Discreet, built-in heat lamps kept the open space warm despite the January chill. A string quartet played in the corner while the waitstaff passed hors d'oeuvres, champagne, and wine.

Carmen chuckled to herself. *This* was Pru's version of a casual dinner event.

"Holy fuck," Jake whispered. "No wonder you said I couldn't wear jeans tonight."

Hooking her arm in his, she pulled them deeper into the room to where their hostess was holding court.

"Brace yourself," she murmured at the same time he groaned, "Oh, shit," under his breath.

Pru spotted them, and Carmen had to bite the inside of her cheek to not laugh. The other woman's eyes sparkled with excitement as she beckoned them over, ogling Jake in his gray slacks and fitted black button-down that showcased his broad shoulders.

"Carmen dear, go make your rounds. You can leave this one with me. Now, Jake," Pru began, effectively dismissing her, "have you met Vincent Kapler?"

Carmen chuckled as Jake stole a quick kiss. She waved a greeting to Vincent, then did as she'd been told and made her rounds, greeting colleagues, business acquaintances, and old family friends. She enjoyed the exquisite appetizers and wine while keeping an eye on Jake, who stood next to Pru like a royal attendant. He seemed to be enjoying himself, as he was having an animated conversation with Pru, Vincent, and another of Pru's friends.

She caught Jake's eye and pointed toward the exit leading to the guest house, where the nearest restrooms were located. He nodded with a smile, and then, when Pru patted his bicep, he shot her a wink before turning his attention back to his group.

God, he was so damn cute. She didn't blame the older woman one bit for falling all over the man.

As she stepped out of the gazebo, a hand gripped her upper arm, jarring her from her thoughts. She gasped and yanked her arm away, her hands fisting. She spun and came face to face with Brian. He took two steps back, his hands raised in a non-threatening gesture.

"What the hell, Brian?"

"I'm sorry, Carm—"

"What part of *restraining order* do you not understand?"

"I just want to talk, I swear. Ten minutes. That's it."

Her head had been shaking since the moment he'd opened his mouth. "No."

"I'm sorry I lost my temper. I never should have gone to your office like that. I'm sorry."

Her arms crossed over her chest. What the hell was going

on? Brian never apologized. Ever. She looked closer at him, and the frown on her face deepened. His cheeks were ruddy, which she could attribute to the cold temperature, but he was sweating and twitchy, his eyes darting around behind her. He was up to something. "Just tell me what you want and then go." She was so damn tired of this man.

"I want *you*, Carmen."

Oh, fuck no. Her eyebrow arched, and she pinned him with her gaze. "Try again."

"I know we talked before about an alliance—"

"*You* talked about that. Not me."

"You were right, though. An alliance would be stupid. I want more than that. I swear, Carmen. I miss you so much."

She shook her head. "No, you don't, but I know you want something."

"I want us to be together again."

She couldn't stop her eyes from rolling. Right. "For what reason?"

"Because we were good together."

She scoffed. Why was she still standing here? "You and I both know that's bullshit. We don't even like each other."

"That's not true—"

"Well, I sure as hell don't like you." She sneered. "And I know for a fact you don't like me. You didn't even like me when we were married."

"How can you say that? Carmen, I *loved* you."

She barked out a humorless laugh. "You loved my money. You loved my connections. You sure as hell didn't love *me*, let alone *like* me, seeing as you were fucking multiple women the entire time we were married. So again. What. Do. You. Want?"

He was silent for so long, she didn't think he'd answer. When he finally did, disgust and disappointment washed over her. But there was no surprise. None at all.

"The alimony you were paying me . . . it's all gone."

"It's been three years, Brian. My required alimony payments are over. Get a better paying fucking job." Revulsion had her lip curling. "I'm going back to the party. If you're not gone in the next minute, I *will* call the police. Then money will be the least of your problems."

"But Carmen, I owe too much. I bet—"

"You again," a deep voice interrupted from behind her.

Brian's eyes widened, then he spun and rushed away toward the main house.

She glanced at the man now standing next to her.

"You okay?" Vincent asked.

"Yeah," she said on a sigh, the tension leaving her shoulders. "Thanks."

"That the same guy from the coffee shop?" She nodded, and he frowned, turning to stare at where Brian had run off. "Is he hassling you?"

She shook her head, at a loss for words. "I don't know what the hell his deal is."

"Well, I'm not sorry I interrupted then." He shifted on his feet and stuffed his hands into his pockets. "Um, the reason I'm here is because I think your boyfriend needs some extraction help."

The corners of her lips twitched. "Extraction help?"

He grinned. "Yeah, you could say that." With a chuckle, he nodded toward the opposite side of the room, where Jake still stood next to Pru. But now, they were surrounded by a gaggle of heavily jeweled women. "Pru called in her ladies . . . and they're all very, very handsy."

Carmen laughed. The look on Jake's face was pleasant enough, but she could see the hint of panic from here.

Vincent nodded to the group, then popped his arm out for her. "Shall we?"

She placed her hand in the crook of his elbow, and they

started across the room. "How did *you* manage to escape Pru's attention?"

"Oh, just a somewhat friendly—and highly awkward—reminder that I work for her."

Carmen laughed again. "Ahhh, the good old sexual-harassment-lawsuit reminder. Nice."

"Exactly." He leaned toward her, his voice turning into a conspiratorial whisper. "Be forewarned, Carmen, I do plan on dropping you off *near* Jake, but no closer. I plan to make a hasty retreat to the opposite side of the room ASAP."

"Noted," she replied, smiling as they neared the group. "Thank you for the escort, Vincent." It took her a split second to realize she actually meant it. The panic she usually felt with him was absent. And she was pretty sure she had Jake to thank for that. Progress.

"You're welcome, and not to overstep, but I'm glad we were able to do this." He gestured between the two of them. "Despite everything, I do consider us friends."

"Me too, Vincent." For the first time since Brazil, she was comfortable around him. Vincent had been a friend, one she'd known for years, and she wouldn't let what had happened in Brazil take that from her. "Me too."

He smiled and nodded toward Jake with his eyebrows waggling. "Good luck getting him away from those ladies."

Turning toward the group, she bit back a laugh as all five women surrounding Jake roared with laughter at whatever he'd just said. The guy beamed, obviously over the hint of panic and eating up their attention. Whether she'd be rescuing him or dragging him away from his doting fans was a toss-up.

"Ladies," Jake said, nodding to her as she approached, "as much as I've enjoyed myself this evening, I think it's time I take my gorgeous, better half home."

"Oh, but it's early!"

"Aren't you so sweet!"

"You two must come over for dinner soon!"

"Sorry, ladies, but thank you for having us," Carmen said while Jake extracted himself from Pru.

As he wrapped an arm around Carmen's waist, his phone rang. He checked his display with his free hand. "If you'll excuse us, ladies," he said with a frown, all the earlier playfulness gone. Concern inched up her spine as he steered her away from the group and brought the phone to his ear. "This is Jake."

His steps faltered, and the hand at her hip squeezed. Worry turned her stomach as his jaw clenched tight.

"We'll be right there," he said curtly.

He remained silent as he pocketed his phone and laced his fingers with hers, hastily walking them toward the coat check.

"Jake?"

"That was Detective Vasquez. They need us at the police station."

Her stomach dropped. She'd been frustrated all week with the lack of information. Now they were about to get some answers. Whether they liked them or not.

The harsh glare of the conference room's fluorescent lighting, the drab cement walls, and the faded industrial carpet were a stark contrast to the softly lit waterfront gazebo they'd been at just thirty minutes earlier. The scents of stale coffee and damp carpet were an insult after being surrounded by Pru's fragrant winter blooms.

Though Carmen wore her heavy dress coat, she couldn't stop the shiver that tore through her. Before she could wrap her coat tighter around her, Jake draped his wool jacket over her shoulders. Despite their surroundings and circumstances, a soft smile lifted her lips. That sweet, tiny gesture did more to warm her than his jacket ever could.

Jake had driven them to the SPD's West Precinct in record time. Once they'd arrived, they'd been immediately escorted to the no-nonsense conference room. It was just past eight in the evening, and aside from the three officers at the entrance, the place was deserted. Now they were waiting. And waiting.

After fifteen more very long minutes, there was a rap on the door, and Detectives Vasquez and Apone hustled in.

"Sorry for the delay," Vasquez said, placing two manila folders on the table as she took a seat.

Apone remained standing, his arms crossed over his chest, as he addressed Jake. "Your vehicle was recovered by the Bellingham PD this morning. It was found parked at the end of the street in a residential neighborhood."

"Was it set on fire like mine?" she asked, her mind flashing to Parker's burned-out Audi.

Apone shook his head. "No fire. No obvious damage. However, there was another body. And more photos."

Time stood still. Holy fuck.

She reached for Jake's hand. Only when he squeezed did she remember to breathe.

"Look at me, sweetheart," Jake murmured.

As she did, she tried to school her features, but it was no use. Dread, confusion, and fear. She knew all were written on her face.

"We take this one minute at a time, Carm. Together. Got it?"

She nodded but knew he didn't believe her. Hell, *she* didn't believe her.

He cupped her face, forcing her gaze back to his. "I've got you." The fierce determination and tenderness staring back at her eased some of the tension knotting her shoulders. "One minute at a time. Are you with me?"

This time, when she nodded, she believed it. The quick kiss he pressed to her forehead soothed her anxiety further.

"Sorry," Carmen said, then cleared her throat. She turned her attention back to the detectives. "Please continue."

Apone shook his head. "No need to apologize. I know this has been one giant roller coaster of shit."

The corners of her lips ticked up in a tired smile. Understatement of the decade. "That it has."

"The chief of police has gotten involved—"

"Really?" Jake asked, his brows rising.

That didn't bode well. On the one hand, it was reassuring that the SPD was taking their case seriously. However, it also meant shit had gotten extremely critical.

"Yeah," Apone continued with a sigh. "He's working on getting the body transferred to us, and asked the ME to put a rush on it. We're hoping for autopsy results by end of day tomorrow. Monday at the latest."

"ID?" Carmen asked.

"There was no ID on the victim," Vasquez said. "What we do know without the autopsy is that the victim is male and was killed before being placed in the vehicle. He was shot multiple times. Once in each thigh and once in each shoulder. Then three in the face, point-blank." When the longtime detective cringed, ice shot down Carmen's spine. "With the extensive damage to the victim's face, we've been unable to identify him."

"Holy shit," Jake murmured. He took her hand in his and squeezed.

Her chest clenched, and her stomach twisted painfully. Holy shit was right.

Vasquez patted one of the folders in front of her. "We sent

the info we have on the victim to your guys at Hudson Security."

Carmen's brows shot up. "Really?" She was by no means an expert in police procedures, but she assumed that sharing information, particularly with a private group, was highly unusual.

Apone shrugged as he took a seat. "The chief wants this handled ASAP." He tapped a second manila folder. "More photos. There were three this time."

He pulled two photos from the folder and placed them on the table. Both were from The Spotted Dog's parking garage, showing various uniformed officers and crime scene techs milling about. In one photo were Apone, Jake, and Parker. In the other, Vasquez and Blake.

Carmen frowned. No wonder the chief was involved. Again, she was no expert on these kinds of things, but the photos didn't look like they'd been pulled from the security cameras. Either someone internal was leaking photos, or whoever was responsible had set up their own cameras in the garage. Cameras everyone had missed.

A wave of apprehension washed over her, and she blew out a breath, clutching Jake's hand like a lifeline.

"Carmen," Apone said, again tapping the folder. "We need to discuss the third photo." The amount of caution he'd injected into those words made her roiling apprehension morph into something beyond worry. Beyond mere uneasiness. Into something terrifying.

"The photo is of you," Vasquez said. The woman's usually brusque tone was tempered and soothing, which had the fine hairs on her arms rising. "We believe it's a photo from Brazil from when you were held captive."

A violent surge of nausea slammed into her, and her lungs seized.

Jake's strong arm was around her in an instant, squeezing.

"I've got you," he murmured, his forehead resting against her temple. "Breathe, sweetheart."

It took two tries before she could let out a shaky exhale. Then she focused on the arm around her, the man holding her up. "One minute at a time," she said softly, battling the bile that was threatening. "Together."

"That's right." His whisper was fierce. "I've got you."

She nodded and took another cleansing breath. Turning into him, she pressed a quick kiss to his lips, then brought her focus back to Vasquez. "Can I see the photo?"

The other woman hesitated. "Are you sure?"

Carmen's spine straightened, and Jake's arm dropped from around her. Taking one of his hands in hers, she met his steady gaze. "Please don't look at the photo until I say it's okay."

Surprise flared in his eyes, but it was quickly replaced with understanding. After he nodded, she turned back to the detective. "I'm sure."

Opening the folder, Vasquez revealed the last photo.

The blood drained from Carmen's face and left her light-headed. She couldn't hold back a gasp of horror and clutched Jake's hand in a death grip.

Holy. Fuck.

It only took a couple seconds for the photo to be seared into her brain.

She was lying on the ground, huddled next to a cement wall, her wrists handcuffed together. The cuffs were attached to a chain bolted high on the wall, extending her arms above her prone body. Her ankles were locked together in metal restraints, and her clothes were half-ripped from her body, revealing skin that was nothing but black and blue. Her face was a myriad of bruises, her eyes nearly swollen shut. Her tangled hair was plastered to her blood-soaked and sweaty skin.

Her heart hammered in her chest as she closed the file folder with a trembling hand.

Vivid memories battered her mind. For a moment, she was back in that dark, humid room. The hard, unforgiving cement floor beneath her. The blood trickling from her wrists ever so slowly down her arms. The stench of sweat, blood, vomit, and waste filling her nose. The fire scoring her skin with each lash.

As fast as the memories had flashed in her mind, they faded. She refocused on the firm hand rubbing circles along her spine and the soft lips gently pressed to her temple. She took another unsteady breath and leaned fully into the man beside her.

She was alive.

She'd survived.

And she could get through this.

Taking a moment to bury her face in Jake's chest, she inhaled his calming, woodsy cologne. She looked up at him, and he caressed the side of her cheek. "Hanging in there?"

She pressed a kiss to the palm of his hand. "Yeah."

He glanced at the closed folder, then back at her.

She softly shook her head. She'd do anything to not have him see that photo. Not because she was ashamed or embarrassed, but because once that image burned into his brain, it would haunt him forever. It was no secret he wanted to protect her. And she loved him for that. Seeing the photo would tear something in his soul, and she refused to let that happen. "You don't need that in your brain. Trust me, babe."

He stared at her for a moment, then brought their clasped hands to his lips. "I do."

Turning back to the detectives, she gestured to the closed folder. "From the lack of marks on my back, the photo is from the beginning of my captivity. Anders beat me up the first day, but it was on the second day that he started whipping me." Her back zinged with phantom pains. "By the end, there were dozens of open lashes on my back."

Apone nodded, anger simmering in his eyes. "We've put a BOLO out for Henriksson. As far as Homeland Security can tell, he hasn't entered the country—under his legal name, anyway—but we've notified all counties in Washington and northern Oregon."

"Until we locate Henriksson," Vasquez said, "it's imperative you both exercise caution." She nodded to Jake. "That extends to your business partners as well, seeing as they're also in the photos. We're still keeping all options open as to who's behind this, but the photo from Brazil . . ."

"He gave himself away with the photo," Carmen murmured.

Vasquez nodded. "We believe so too."

CHAPTER TWENTY-SIX

The next few days were a blur. Their group had been in lockdown before, but now it was ridiculous. Even though it was admittedly stifling and smothering, Carmen wasn't going to complain. Not one bit.

After the revelations from Saturday evening, they'd gone on the super-duper buddy system. Basically, it was only home, work, and dinners at the pub. Jake was her constant shadow, and if he was too busy to come with her somewhere, like her doctor's appointment the day before, Matt took his place. Armed, of course. She'd asked if he was sure he had time to babysit her, and he'd simply met the question with an eye roll. Yes, she thought it was a bit overkill, but again, she wasn't going to complain.

So now it was Wednesday, and she, Elise, and Kate were sitting in CWC's conference room, where Kate was still working each day. They were sorting through the lunch haul that Jake and Matt had just delivered—the super-duper buddy system extended to not just the women of their group, but the men as well.

Various wraps, green smoothies, and mini cheesecakes filled the conference room table.

"There's so much food," Elise said with a chuckle. "Jake, you should probably call over some of your crew to assist."

"Hell no," Matt scoffed. "You ladies pick what you want, then Jake and I will take down the rest."

Kate turned to Jake. "What? No cookies? And I've heard so much about your expert cookie selections," she teased.

"Oh, shit, we forgot to pick them up." Jake grimaced. "I did order some. I promise."

Carmen chuckled. "Of course you ordered some. Because *clearly*"—she waved at the table full of food—"we're lacking in food."

"You ordered the good ones, too, right?" Matt asked.

"Of course," Jake answered, then shot a wink at Carmen. "*And* a few extra oatmeal raisins to get you through the afternoon, sweetheart."

After shoving a mini cheesecake into his mouth, Matt rose and grabbed a green smoothie. "I'll go pick them up."

"Wait," Carmen said. "Should you be going by yourself?"

"You do remember that I'm a detective, right?" Matt asked with a smirk.

"Yeah, but still. You shouldn't go by yourself." She rose and caught Jake's eye as she reached for a smoothie. "I trust your cookie selection and all, babe, but I want to see for myself what other flavors they have. Besides, I could use a break from these damn walls." She paused after taking a sip of her drink. "Are you okay if I go with him?"

Jake glanced at his brother for a moment, then back at her before nodding. "He does carry a gun for a living." He crooked his finger at her, then tapped his lips.

She chuckled and made her way to him, dropping a kiss on his mouth as Matt made gagging noises behind them.

"Christ, Alvarez, are you twelve?" she asked Matt once

they were in the elevator. The elbow she jabbed into his side let him know she was joking.

"What can I say?" He shrugged. "I never miss a chance to give my brother shit. I know you guys are taking things slow." His brow scrunched. "Well, aside from the whole living-together thing. But you know what I mean."

She chuckled as they exited the elevator. "I do."

"Anyway, I think you're really good for him." Stepping out of the building, he glanced around as he moved her to his left side. "You and I are still getting to know each other, but I think he could be really good for you too."

"Thanks," she said as they made their way to the cookie shop three buildings down. "I think so too. Jake has made all of this . . . craziness . . . better. I'd be a basket case without him."

"Basket case?" Matt snorted. "Doubtful, Carmen. Doubtful."

"Fine. How about closed off and priming for a stroke due to repressed emotions?"

He barked out a laugh. "Better. That's more in line than *basket case.*"

A loud pop startled her, and she flinched.

She quickly glanced around, and when her gaze landed on Matt, she gasped.

Shocked and surprised eyes stared back at her.

She cried out, and her heart stopped. Her mind refused to believe what she saw.

A red patch bloomed on Matt's chest. As he tried to turn, he staggered, then fell backward to the ground.

"Matt!" Her heart raced as she knelt over his prone body. Her hands shook violently as she covered the bloody wound on his chest and applied pressure.

She frantically whipped her head around. Spotting wide-eyed bystanders huddled behind a metal garbage can, she screamed, "Help! Call 911!"

Tears filled her eyes as she turned back to Matt. His pallor was gray and his lips were turning blue. "Matt, hang on," she begged. "Please hang on."

His eyes were glassy, and as his focus moved over her shoulder, his body tensed beneath her hands. "Go, Carm," he wheezed. "Run."

Before his words could register, there was a thud, and fire burst through her skull. Then everything went dark.

CHAPTER TWENTY-SEVEN

A sharp pinch at her ankles had Carmen stirring. She tried to kick whatever it was away, and fire shot up her legs. She groaned, then cringed as the sound set off a vicious pounding in her head.

She opened her eyes a tiny bit at a time, but flashes of light blurred her vision. After a few deep breaths, the flashes eased, but the pounding in her head continued. Nausea washed over her.

Tamping it down, she tried to focus on . . . anything. But everything was wobbly. She knew she was lying down, but her equilibrium was shot. Even though the cement under her hands was solid, her body felt like she was floating in water.

Her vision swayed, so she locked onto the crack in the ceiling above her. Only once the crack in the drywall had steadied did she let her eyes roam. The pounding in her head was painful and constant, matching each of her heartbeats.

She was in a basement of some sort, lying on the cold cement floor. From the fire shooting over her ankles, she could tell her legs were bound together. Her wrists were handcuffed, and her arms were stretched above her; the cuffs were attached to a chain bolted to the wall.

Just like Brazil.

Her heart kicked, and the pounding in her head intensified.

Moving her gaze around the room, she gasped at the man sitting silently in the corner.

Brian.

"I'm so fucking sorry, Carm." Tears made his glassy blue eyes glow in the dim room. "I had to do it."

She stared at him in disbelief, her own eyes filling with tears. Her mind was muddled, but only one thing was clear. "You shot him."

"I'm so sorry."

When he rose and stepped toward her, she flinched. His arms came out in a pleading gesture. "Please. I had no choice. You wouldn't listen, and then you slapped that restraining order on me." His breaths were coming in pants, his Adam's apple bobbing. "He said he was your friend. That he could help me."

Nothing Brian was saying made sense. "What are you talking about?"

"I kept messing up," he continued, as if he hadn't heard her. His gaze ping-ponged around the room. "I knew my luck had to turn. It fucking had to." He moaned and scrubbed his hands over his face, sounding like an animal trapped in a snare. A tremor of fear shook her body. "It didn't and I owed more and more money. He said he'd wipe it clean. All I had to do was this . . ."

For a moment, she had no words. Then she recalled their brief talk at Pru's party. Money. Was he talking about a gambling debt?

Her mind scrambled, blocking out the sharp pain building in her shoulders. "Brian, if this is about money, I can get it for you. If you let me go, I'll give you whatever money you need. Just please let me go."

He shook his head. "It's a lot, Carm."

"I have a lot. How much do you owe?"

"A million."

Her eyes widened. She didn't know anything about gambling debts, but that seemed exorbitant.

"It just kept adding up . . ." His voice was full of awful wonder, as if he couldn't believe the figure either. "You have to understand. I had no choice." His gaze returned to hers, and resignation and dejection stared back at her. "I've seen what he can do. So I did it. I had no choice, Carmen. It was either you or me. I had to."

"And you couldn't even do that one thing right."

She jerked at the deep voice, her attention shooting to the darkened doorway.

Goosebumps tore over her skin. The voice was familiar, but she couldn't quite place it.

Her jaw dropped as the man stepped into the room, his attention on Brian.

Vincent was immaculately dressed. Khakis and a crisp, white button-down shirt. Brown loafers, brown belt, and a gun in his right hand.

She froze when he turned to her.

"Carmen, my sweet, are you okay?"

Her heart stopped. Ice skated down her spine at the adoring gleam in his eyes. What was going on?

CHAPTER TWENTY-EIGHT

The last two hours had been pandemonium. Sheer, god-awful pandemonium.

Sitting in an uncomfortable chair in a cramped Harborview Medical Center waiting room, surrounded by his two best friends and a sea of blue, Jake's heart was still lodged in his throat.

He'd been joking with Kate and Elise about something when he'd heard the gunshot. He'd raced down the stairwell, and when he'd burst onto the street, it had been pure chaos. People had been everywhere. Some shouting, some pointing down the street, some crying. Sirens had wailed in the distance, and his brother—

Jake's breath locked painfully in his chest, and tears spilled down his cheeks. He didn't bother wiping them away. A hand landed on his shoulder and squeezed. Fuck.

Blake had been kneeling over his brother with his hands pressed down on his chest. Parker had been standing over them, fury and anguish on his face as he'd shouted at someone on his phone.

When he'd reached his brother, his heart had nearly

stopped. His twin had been an unnatural shade of gray, his lips purple. "Her ex," he'd wheezed out, his glassy eyes blazing with rage. "The one with the restraining order."

Then the ambulance had arrived, and there'd been a flurry of medical and law enforcement personnel. Jake had desperately tried to get into the ambulance with his brother, but he'd been held back.

As the ambulance had pulled away, he'd fucking roared until his throat had gone hoarse.

Carmen was gone. And that motherfucking piece of shit had shot his twin brother to get to her.

In all the mayhem with the photos, stolen cars, and dead bodies, they'd overlooked the fact that McAsshole had still been harassing her. She'd filed a restraining order against him, and they'd all mistakenly dismissed him. Like a fucking piece of paper could prevent him from doing what he'd done today. Fuck!

"Hang in there, man," Blake said from beside him—his hands and shirt still covered in Matt's blood. His voice pulled Jake back to the present. To the waiting room filled with Matt's fellow detectives and officers.

Jake glanced to his right, and his chest clenched painfully. Parker.

He slung an arm around his friend's shoulder and squeezed. When tears slipped down Parker's face, he simply squeezed tighter. There were no words he could say. No platitudes to give. Carmen was missing. She had been taken by her fucking ex-husband in broad daylight.

Leaning back in his chair, Jake closed his eyes, replaying his brother's words in his mind. Replaying the playful moments in the conference room before Carmen and Matt had left. And his fucking heart broke.

Matt and Carmen.

The two people he loved above all others. One was his literal other half. The other was, hands down, his better half.

They *had* to be okay. They had to.

Someone cleared their throat, and Jake opened his eyes.

Detective Vasquez stood before them, determination and ferocity blazing over her face. "We're going to get this motherfucker. Mark my words—Brian McAllister is going fucking down."

"Every officer is on alert. Here and in all the surrounding counties," Apone added, his arms crossing over his chest. "Alvarez will pull through, and we *will* find Carmen."

It wasn't a question. Jake appreciated the man's confidence.

He took in the cramped waiting room and found comfort in the fact that they weren't alone. Matt's brothers in blue had descended en masse. They were gathered in small groups around the room, some talking while others paced.

In his row of chairs, Parker and Blake flanked him. Kate and Raven had been at their men's sides earlier but were currently with Jake's parents down in the cafeteria.

They were in the second hour of Matt's surgery, and so far, they hadn't learned much more about what had happened. Multiple witnesses had reported that Carmen and Matt had been walking down the sidewalk, and McAsshole had simply walked up behind them. He'd been about six feet away when, without warning, he'd shot Matt in the back. His brother had fallen and Carmen had tried to help him. Her ex-husband had cold-cocked her with the butt of his gun, picked her up, and rushed her into a nearby car. Then sped off. It all had happened in under a minute.

Bile rose in his throat. He refused to think about the possibility of life without either of them. Life without Matt and Carmen was *not* a fucking option.

"If you or your parents need anything, let any one of us know," Vasquez said.

"Appreciate it," Jake said, his voice like gravel.

Apone's phone rang, and the detective stepped away. "Vasquez," he barked seconds later, waving his partner over.

The detectives tensed as they listened to whoever was on the phone, and Jake's anxiety skyrocketed. Something was wrong.

"What the fuck's going on?" Parker murmured.

After what felt like forever, both detectives were back in front of them. He, Blake, and Parker rose to their feet.

"That was Hudson Security," Apone said, his expression grim. "They were able to ID the body from the Bellingham incident. It's Anders Henriksson."

Shock furrowed Jake's brow. "Carm's attacker from Brazil?"

Parker jolted next to him. "What attacker from Brazil?"

Jake ignored his friend, his mind whirling. "That doesn't make sense. The picture from Brazil. We all thought *he* was the one who had to be responsible for the pictures, the stolen cars, the dead body . . ."

What the fuck was going on?

"Back to basics. What do we know?" Vasquez asked, then continued, the question rhetorical. "Henriksson attacked her in Brazil—"

"What fucking attack?" Parker shouted.

"I love you, brother," he hissed at Parker, "but shut the fuck up right now." He turned his attention back to Vasquez. "Go."

"Henriksson was arrested. Someone bought his way out of jail, then he disappeared."

"Then he shows up here months later," Apone continued. "Dead. Fucking tortured, with his face demolished, so it takes time to ID him. However, he was left in *your* car to be found."

"Whoever this fucker is," Vasquez muttered, "he's smart and wants to rub it in your face."

Jake scrubbed his hands over his face. Frustration clawed at him as his brain tried to connect the dots. "It doesn't make sense. Henriksson is the *only* one who knew about what happened in Brazil. Outside of the US embassy workers and hospital staff, Carm said *no one* knew—"

His heart stopped. Dead. In his fucking chest.

"Fuuuck," he growled.

Vincent.

At the questioning look from Apone and Vasquez, he continued.

"*Vincent* knew. He's the one who rescued her from Henriksson in Brazil. They'd been colleagues for a while, and they worked together a lot overseas. He'd been showing up in the same locations as her for the last couple of years, but Carm had attributed it to their line of work."

Dammit! How the fuck had he missed this?

"She'd mentioned offhand how she thought it was odd that he'd taken a job here in Seattle after she returned home. Ever since she's been back, she'd been avoiding him because he reminded her of what happened in Brazil." Things were clicking into place like a really fucked-up puzzle. "But their organizations work closely together, so she runs into him a lot. They're friendly. We even saw him last Saturday at a dinner party."

"What else do you know about him?" Apone asked, notebook at the ready.

Jake racked his brain, his heart kicking hard in his chest. "Fuck! Nothing. He works for Prudence Weatherby's nonprofit. Vincent . . . Kaner? Kader?"

"Kapler," Parker spat. "Vincent Kapler."

"Wait, this can't be a coincidence," Vasquez said, her jaw

clenched tight as she turned to Apone. "Remember Carmen's call on Sunday about McAllister?"

Jake froze. Carm's call on Sunday? "What about McAsshole?"

"Carmen called me and told me that with everything going on Saturday night, she'd forgotten to mention that McAllister had broken the restraining order. That he'd talked to her briefly at that party you were at but had run away when her colleague, *Vincent*, approached."

"No, not a fucking coincidence," Apone muttered.

"Hold tight," Vasquez said as she and Apone stepped away.

They huddled with another group of detectives, and Jake desperately wanted to know what was going on. But his mind was in a whirl. He could see where Vincent and Henriksson intersected, but he couldn't make the connection between Vincent and McAsshole.

Resigned to let the detectives do their thing, he turned to Parker. His friend looked ready to crawl out of his skin, but thankfully, Blake had a supportive hand on his cousin's shoulder. With lead in his gut, Jake motioned to their seats. He pushed down the worry that he was crossing a line and told his friends about what had happened to Carmen in Brazil.

All that mattered was getting her back safe. She could be pissed at him for telling her brother. Hell, at this point, he'd be grateful if she was. Because that would mean she was there with him. Pissed or not, Jake just needed her by his side.

After his overview—he was already breaching her trust and didn't want to give too many details without her permission—both his friends remained silent.

"Why didn't she say anything?" Blake asked, his voice rough.

"I fucking *knew* something was wrong," Parker said, guilt lacing each word. "I should have pressed, but I was so wrapped up in my shit I let it slide. Fuck!"

"That," Jake said, pointing his finger at Parker. "That right there is exactly why she didn't say anything. She didn't want you worrying about her. So much was going on with Kate. The *last* thing Carm wanted was you worried about her too." He paused for a heartbeat. "And I think she didn't want you guys to look at her differently."

"Fuck that noise," Parker growled. "She's my goddamn sister and I'll look at her however the fuck I want!" Then he blew out a breath, and his shoulders fell, deflating like a balloon as the fight left him. "But I get what you mean. God knows I hovered over Kate like a damn mother hen after all that shit went down." He scrubbed his hands over his face, frustration emanating from his every pore, before he met Jake's gaze. "She okay?"

Jake gave a slight nod. "She's getting there." Or at least, she had been before all this. But now?

No. She'd get there, dammit. She would. "I'll make damn sure to get her the rest of the way there if need be."

Blake slapped a hand on his back. "We'll all get her there, brother. We'll rally behind that stubborn woman until she tells us all to fuck off."

Parker smirked. "Which she will. And then we'll rally some more."

"Damn right," Jake said, a soft smile lifting his lips. They were in Carmen's corner. They just needed to get her the fuck back first.

Jake startled when police radios squawked and multiple phones rang at once. Glancing across the room, he met Apone's gaze as the other man listened to whoever was on the other end of his phone. Suddenly, all the officers and detectives in the small room were in motion.

Jake's stomach dropped when the words *shots fired* came through one of the radios. At Apone's clipped approach, he braced.

"Stay here," the detective said. "There's activity at Kapler's address."

Before Jake could reply, Apone, Vasquez, Matt's partner Tran, and all but two of the police officers were gone.

"Holy fuck," Jake murmured.

Blake's hand returned to his shoulder. A glance at his friend showed that his other hand was on Parker's back.

"Carm's gonna be fine," Blake said, a steely determination behind those four words. "Our girl's been tough as nails her entire fucking life. She's not stopping now."

CHAPTER TWENTY-NINE

"Were my directions unclear?" Vincent said, his attention on Brian. His voice, his expression—everything about him—was calm and indifferent, borderline uninterested. "Or are you just incompetent?"

Her heart pounded at the abject fear on her ex-husband's face. He'd gone ghostly white in seconds and sweat dotted his brow in the frigid room. She held completely still, not wanting to make a sound, not wanting to do anything to bring Vincent's attention to her.

He shook his head at Brian, disgust and pity playing over his face. "You shot the wrong brother."

Her heart kicked.

Without warning, Vincent fired twice. A bullet into each of Brian's thighs.

Carmen pressed her mouth against her shoulder to muffle her scream.

Then Vincent fired twice more, once into each of Brian's shoulders.

The sound was deafening in the small room, and Brian writhed and moaned on the cement floor. The acrid scents of urine and gunpowder assaulted her senses, and she bit back a whimper. Blood and pee darkened Brian's pants, and her heart ached. There was no love lost between them, but he didn't deserve this. *No one* deserved this.

"Not only did you shoot the wrong brother," Vincent continued, his calm tone filling her with a terror unlike any she'd experienced, "but you didn't even get a kill shot. And you were *right there*." He shook his head and tsk-tsked. "Not quite sure how the hell you missed."

Vincent raised his gun again. Three shots in quick succession.

Carmen screamed, her heart stopping as Brian's face exploded and gore sprayed on the wall behind him. Terror blanketed her mind. She tried to scramble away from the horror, but the restraints kept her in place. Her breath was stuck in her chest. Tears streamed down her face.

Vincent turned toward her, and bile surged up her throat. Fear kept it down.

"He was useless. But you knew that."

"Please," she begged. "What are you doing?"

"You always go for the useless ones, and I just don't understand." He paced the small room as if casually strolling down the street. "After we stopped dating, the few men you went out with were plebeian at best. Dull and lifeless and not worthy of you. Then Anders showed up and sparked something in you. For a moment, you were actually interested in that idiot. However, fool that he was, he came on too strong, didn't play the long game."

He pinned her with his gaze, and she froze. She couldn't even swallow. "It worked to my advantage. I got to play the hero in the end, rescuing you from him. But like this one," he kicked Brian's lifeless body, "Anders was useless. He wasn't supposed to touch you. He wasn't supposed to mar an inch of your perfect body. But he did." A darkness passed over his face, and her stomach twisted.

"Please, Vincent," she pleaded between sobs.

"Oh, my sweet Carmen, don't worry. Anders tried to make up for it. Tried to get back into my good graces. Who knew the man was such a whiz with computers? But he was sloppy. Said it was because he was afraid." He shrugged. "Rightfully so, I suppose. Rest assured, my sweet, I made him pay for touching you. See, I know how to play the long game."

Her stomach turned, and saliva pooled in her mouth. "What do you want from me?"

"Wasn't the other night nice?" he asked, dismissing her question. "You and me chatting at Pru's dinner party like we used to. Old friends. It was lovely, comfortable even. Like it should be." He crouched next to her, and it took everything she had not to recoil when he ran a finger down the side of her face. "I've done everything for you, my sweet. Yet you choose everyone but me."

He stood abruptly and continued to walk the room. "You must have told Jake what I did for you, because instead of looking at me like he wanted to beat me to a pulp, he was much less hostile on Saturday. Cordial, even. He seems like a nice enough guy, but he's not good enough for you, my sweet. He doesn't deserve you."

Vincent shrugged again. The movement was so casual, so carefree, so contradictory to the words spewing from his mouth. How had she not seen this side of him? How had she misread this man?

"And this one?" Again, he kicked Brian's lifeless body as he walked past. "Not quite sure what you ever saw in him. He's weak. This imbecile owed so much money to the wrong people. I knew I could get him to do what I needed."

Dread and fear warred within her. "And what was that?" Her voice was barely above a whisper.

"Get rid of your boyfriend and take you. Two birds and all that. But this time, when I played your hero and savior, we'd make it work. Sure, you'd be sad at first, but I'd be there for you. Like I've always been there for you."

She trembled, her vision wavering as he crouched beside her again, his fingers trailing over the bloody restraints on her wrists. "He wasn't supposed to do this," Vincent murmured. "He wasn't supposed to hurt you."

"But he did," she whimpered, hoping to gain some sort, *any* sort of sympathy. She needed to stay alive. And she'd say whatever needed to be said to make that happen.

Vincent's left hand rose, and she flinched—with both fear and pain—as he caressed the side of her head. When he pulled his hand away, it was covered in blood. His expression hardened.

He jerked up and moved to where Brian lay. For a moment, he just stood there. Then rage filled his face, and he fired over and over and over into Brian's chest until the only sound in the room was the click, click, click of the empty gun.

"Please stop," she sobbed. Her ears rang, and there was a loud buzzing in her head. She could barely see through her tears.

"We are meant to be, Carmen. I will do anything for you. I've followed you around the world, but you didn't get it. Do you understand the extent of my devotion to you now?"

Her breaths came in raspy hiccups, but she nodded. "Please, Vincent. I'll do anything you want."

"I know you will, my sweet. You'll learn to love me. I promise." He caressed the side of her face. Vomit rose in her throat, and she swallowed it back down. "We'll take it all one day at a time. You'll see."

One day at a time.

Her mind flashed to Jake. *He* was who she wanted to spend one day at a time with. Not Vincent. But she'd do whatever she could—say whatever she had to—to get back to him.

Vincent rose and rummaged through Brian's pockets before returning with a small silver key. He removed her bindings. "Let's get these off you. I'll bandage you up, and we'll get out of here. How does that sound?"

He sat her up, and a wave of nausea rolled over her. Turning her head to the side, she puked.

"I've got you, my sweet Carmen," he cooed, rubbing her back. "I'll take care of you."

Her stomach heaved again.

He helped her to her feet, whispering words of encouragement and everlasting love that made the tiny hairs on her skin rise. With his hand on her back, he guided her through the door to a dark staircase. She took a step up, then stilled as the pounding in her head intensified.

Move, Carmen! You have to move!

The steps swayed, and she whimpered, clutching onto the handrail with her right hand.

Vincent was next to her on the narrow staircase in an instant. "I'll take care of you, my sweet," he whispered, wrapping an arm around her waist and taking her weight.

Bile rushed up her throat and splattered on the stairs.

"I'm sorry for having you down there. It was selfish of me," he said as he helped her slowly up each step. "I wanted it to be like Brazil, where I could be your hero."

They reached the top of the stairs, and he opened the door, one arm still wrapped around her. He turned her down a short hallway, and she wobbled. She braced her right hand against the wall as another wave of nausea surged through her.

The daylight coming in from the windows was too much. It blinded her, and she winced, the throb in her head escalating with a vengeance.

"I'm afraid you may have a concussion, my sweet Carmen. But one foot in front of the other," he encouraged, taking more of her weight. "That's it. You've got this. Just a few more steps to the kitchen, my sweet."

His arm tightened around her waist as he helped her take the final steps. Then he jerked to a halt.

Her eyes flew open, and her chest clenched.

"Freeze! Put your hands up!"

Police officers surrounded them in a semicircle. Countless guns pointed at them.

Before she could blink or form any sort of thought, she fisted her hand and swung. She made contact with Vincent's jaw. His grip at her waist loosened, and she flung herself to the ground.

Chaos erupted.

Heart racing, she scurried across the floor to the nearest wall. She cradled her hands over her head and curled into a tight ball. She slammed her eyes shut.

Please, please, please let this nightmare be over.

Shouts surrounded her, then two booming gunshots silenced the room.

Her blood chilled. She focused on her breathing, praying that it would keep the nausea at bay. As activity picked up around her, she zeroed in on the steady throb at her temple. Her eyes stayed shut while people spoke in murmurs.

A hand touched her shoulder, and she flinched away, whimpering.

"Carmen," a familiar voice said. "It's over."

Peeking up, she winced at the light, then met Detective Vasquez's steady, dark brown gaze.

At the sight of the detective, her body relaxed. The nausea

eased and the throbbing in her head morphed to a dull, manageable pounding. She took her first steadying breath in what felt like hours.

"Go slowly," Vasquez said, easing her up to sit.

Once upright, Carmen glanced around. She'd been curled up on the kitchen floor. Her chest squeezed. Because Vincent had been going to bandage her wounds . . .

"Holy shit," she said on a long exhale.

"'Holy shit' is right," Vasquez replied. "How's your head? Feel like it's gonna fall off?"

She nodded, then cringed, immediately stopping the motion. "Yeah. It sure does." She took in another cleansing breath, and her chin trembled. Her limbs began to shake. She gasped, her gaze darting to the detective in panic.

"You're okay. Just keep breathing. Follow me." Vasquez took both of her hands and squeezed while demonstrating deep breaths. "Keep breathing, Carmen. Nothing to worry about at all. This is just the world's most massive fucking adrenaline dump."

Carmen choked out a laugh, and tears ran down her face, but she followed Vasquez's breaths. "Oh my God," she wheezed as her heart threatened to beat out of her chest. "I feel like I'm gonna die."

"Yup," Vasquez said. "That sounds about right."

After a few more breaths, the shaking eased, though she still felt jittery. It took two tries to ask the question she feared most. "Is Matt okay?"

A shadow passed over Vasquez's face. "He was still in surgery last we heard. But he should be out soon."

"Jake?"

Vasquez's smile was a weary one. "We made him wait at the hospital." She glanced up as the EMTs wheeled a gurney into the kitchen. "We'll make sure you get to the same hospital."

· · ·

Forty-five minutes later, the door to her ER room burst open, and Jake and Parker poured in, a nurse hot on their heels.

Her brother made it to her first.

"Concussion," she squeaked as he hauled her into his arms and squeezed.

"Shit, sorry," he murmured, easing his grip. After a softer squeeze, he pulled away enough to meet her gaze. "You promise you're okay?"

She nodded, then grinned as Jake slapped him on the shoulder, elbowing him aside.

"Move it, Park," he growled. "She's mine."

Her stomach fluttered, and her heart took flight.

Yes. Yes, she was.

"Cool your jets, fucker," her brother grumbled, stepping aside.

Then nothing else mattered. Jake's arms were around her, easing the last lingering bits of tension. Everything outside of this, outside of *them*, melted away.

He buried his face in her hair, his breaths warming her neck. She couldn't have stopped the tears from falling even if she'd tried.

This.

This was what she wanted. This was what she was done running from.

She didn't know what the future held. But she knew she wanted it to include Jake for as long as she could have him. One day at a time. Minute by minute.

His arms around her tightened. "I love you, Carm," he murmured into her hair. "So damn much, sweetheart." He pulled away, and their lips met, soft and gentle. Then he rested his forehead on hers. "I didn't want to jump the gun with you. I wanted to give you time to get used to us. But after everything"—he pulled away and held her gaze—"I need you to know that I love every fucking thing about you, and I am *not* letting you go. I've got you. Forever."

Her heart kicked hard in her chest. Hope bloomed deep in her gut. And the remaining nerves and whispers of worry faded. Framing his face in her hands, she pressed her lips to his. "I love you, Jake. Forever."

EPILOGUE

Jake glanced around the Four Seasons ballroom and smiled. It had been three and a half weeks since the worst day of his life. But they were all getting back on their feet, falling into their new routine.

The shimmering ballroom was decorated in all things Valentine's Day. Carm's parents had embraced the holiday theme for their forty-fifth wedding anniversary. Was it a little cheesy? Sure. But who cared? Because they all had so much to be thankful for.

It was love and happiness all around.

Next month was Blake and Raven's wedding. The week after that, they were heading down to Mexico for the Alvarez family reunion—maybe that event wouldn't be love and happiness, but they'd be in Mexico, so it was bound to be a good time.

And they were going to Mexico with Matt.

His chest tightened whenever he thought of his twin brother; he constantly had to remind himself that Matt was okay, that he was still with them.

His brother had been in the hospital for a full week.

Much to Matt's frustration, his recovery was going slower than he wanted. While the gunshot had missed anything vital —thank God—there had been a lot of nerve damage, and he still didn't have full use of his right arm.

Then, to make a shitty situation worse, while Matt had been in the hospital—and for reasons his twin refused to disclose—he'd left his wife. Or rather, he'd told her he was filing for divorce, and that if she didn't move out by the time he was discharged, he'd "kick her ass out."

Matt's words, not Jake's.

Unfortunately for Matt, Krista had refused to leave the house. So when he'd been discharged, his brother had moved in with him and Carmen. Not that they minded. Not at all.

Matt had been with them for over two weeks and still refused to say why he'd left his wife. *Grumpy bastard* didn't even begin to describe his brother. To top it off, Apone and Vasquez still hadn't been able to identify the woman from the car fire, and Matt was itching to get back to work and help. But the doctors wouldn't clear him, not even for desk work. That took the man from being a grumpy bastard to a miserable bastard. But he was an alive, miserable, grumpy bastard, so Jake would take it. He could wait his brother out.

Looking around, he took a deep breath and let the happiness in the room settle over him. It was fitting that they were in this ballroom. The last time he'd been here, he and Carmen had started their arrangement. And now? Well, now he couldn't imagine his life without her. He caught her gaze as she spoke with Pru two tables over.

She smiled at him, and his heart kicked. It was one of Carm's real smiles, not that painful everything-is-okay smile she'd donned the week after Vincent had been killed by the police—the week Matt had been in the hospital. It wasn't her phony, professional business smile either, the one that she always had at the ready, the top dog in her arsenal. Yes, that smile was still beautiful, but not like *this* smile. This one lit her eyes and made her glow. And when she smiled at him like that, he needed to be near her. To touch her. Feel her. Remind himself that she was safe, and that she was all his.

He sauntered over and interrupted their conversation.

"I'm sorry to break in, Pru." He wasn't. Not one bit. And by the twinkle in the other woman's eyes, she knew it. "But I need to steal this gorgeous woman from you." He held his hand out to Carmen. "Dance with me, Ms. Cunningham?"

She placed her hand in his and rose. Her smile was magnificent. "Of course, Mr. Alvarez."

He led her to the middle of the dance floor, and they greeted various couples they knew along the way. Taking her in his arms, he tucked her close. They swayed comfortably for a few beats before he asked, "What would you say about making a new arrangement?"

She tensed in his arms, and wariness flickered over her face.

He quickly dropped a kiss on her lips. "It's a good arrangement, I promise."

Her eyes narrowed for a moment, and then the corner of her lips tipped up in a smirk. "How good are we talking?"

"Well, Ms. Cunningham." He leaned down to whisper in her ear, dropping his voice low. "I was thinking along the lines of daily orgasms."

"Hmmm, interesting. But, Mr. Alvarez"—she shot him an exaggerated grimace—"I already get that."

"True," he chuckled. They both did, and it was damn near perfection. "But you get that as my girlfriend." He swallowed past the sudden nerves that popped up and pressed on. "What if I told you these proposed orgasms would be even *better* than what you're getting now?"

"Hard to imagine." She grinned, and her brown eyes danced. "But color me intrigued. Do tell."

"Well, you'd still get them daily—as many as you wanted, in fact—but they'd be better than now because you'd be getting them as my wife."

She went still in his arms, and her gaze shot to his. Surprise, excitement, and tenderness warred on her gorgeous face. "What?" she whispered.

He squeezed her hip and continued swaying to the song. "We agreed a while ago that we'd take our relationship one day at a time. One minute at a time if necessary. Right?"

She nodded, a soft smile on her lips.

"It still holds true, Carm. Because there is no one I'd rather do all that with—minute by minute, day by day—than you."

A tear slipped down her cheek, and her mouth fell slightly open, as if she couldn't believe his words. He gently wiped the tear away with his thumb. Then his hand was buried in her hair, his thumb caressing the delicate skin along her jaw. "Let's do this together. What do you say?"

After a moment, her mouth snapped shut. Her eyes narrowed playfully and her brow arched. "Is that your final question, Mr. Alvarez?"

"Of course not, Ms. Cunningham," he replied with a grin. Then he laughed as her jaw fell open again when he dropped to a knee. He snagged her left hand and brought it to his lips. "I love every damn thing about you, and I promise to do this one day at a time. With you. Together. Will you please, *please* be my wife?"

She clasped her right hand in a tight fist in front of her mouth, and tears spilled down her face as she nodded. Then she was in his arms.

"Yes," she whispered in his ear. "I would love to be your wife."

Standing, he lifted her off her feet and brought his lips to hers.

Cheers and whistles rang out around them.

"The ring, bro!" Parker called out, and the crowd laughed.

"Oh damn," Jake chuckled, setting her back on her mile-high heels. He wiped another tear from her cheek before laying a kiss on her lips. After all, how could he not?

He dug the ring out of his pocket, snagged his woman around the waist, and hauled her to him. He held the ring between them, showing it to her.

He'd chosen a band-style ring with patterned marquise diamonds edged by rows of delicate, round diamonds. Simple, beautiful, and classy. Just like this magnificent woman in his arms.

"Holy crap, Jake," she gasped. "Are you kidding me?"

He wanted to pound his chest like a caveman at her obvious approval.

Her eyes misted as she held out her left hand. He slipped the ring on her finger and ignored the cheers around them. Because when she gazed up at him with that combination of happiness, love, and a little bit of awe shimmering in her big brown eyes, all that mattered was her.

"Spend forever with me, Ms. Cunningham?"

She grinned up at him. "You've got yourself a deal, Mr. Alvarez."

ENJOY THIS BOOK?

Reviews encourage other readers to try out a book. They're so important to getting the word out about a book and mean the world to every author.

I'd love your help in spreading the word. If you could take a quick moment to leave a review on your favorite book site, I would be forever grateful! You can do that on Amazon, Goodreads and/or Bookbub. Thank you! :)

ALSO BY CHRISTINA SOL

THE SPOTTED DOG SERIES

Redemption

Reclaiming

Returning

THE HUDSON ISLAND SERIES

Summer 2023

ABOUT THE AUTHOR

Christina Sol is an award-winning author who writes what she loves to read — romance filled with heart, heat, and suspense.

When Christina's not writing , reading, or knitting, she's watching football or fueling her planner, sticker, and washi obsession.

Christina lives in the Pacific Northwest with her husband and two children.

CONNECT WITH CHRISTINA ONLINE
www.christinasol.com

instagram.com/christinasol.author
facebook.com/christinasol.author
bookbub.com/authors/christina-sol
tiktok.com/@thechristinasol

ACKNOWLEDGMENTS

My wonderful readers: thank you for choosing to spend your precious time reading Jake & Carmen's story. I know there are a million other options out there to choose from, so thank you *so* much for choosing Returning.

Heather G, Jen C, Danielle R, Lynne P & Megan S: thank you all for making this story shine—your feedback and honesty mean so much!

LJ at Mayhem Cover Creations: your covers are amazing & I *so* appreciate your patience with me. Thank you!

Todd, Lucy & Jackson: you three are the best. There's no way I could do any of this without you all.

My family & friends: thank you *so* much for all your support! It truly means the world to me.